The Professor's Daughter

My Gratitude

Goes to many of you readers and followers who requested phase two of the award-winning novel "The English Professor." Your encouragement motivated me to sit down and put words on paper for this highly desired novel.

Here is the preview for you readers who enjoyed the suspense of Andrew's longing and burning infatuation for another man's wife. Francesca's dilemmas and tribulations with their many twists and tragedies threaten her from escaping the deadly reach of her husband. Their heightened physical longing results in a daughter, the fruit of their love. Here it is in continuation,
"The Professor's Daughter."

The Characters

Gracy Robertson	The Main Character
Leonello Dante	The Student
Alvaro Fernandez	CEO
Fabiana Taverna	The Godmother and Cousin
Diego Frarano	Older Stepbrother the Attorney
Daniele Frarano	Younger Stepbrother The architect
Romero Placido	The Student
Gianni Cecco	The Student
Rosella Balladic	Diego's Friend
Ingrid Klein	Daniele's Live-in Mate.
Francesca Fernandez	Mr. and Mrs. Fernandez's Daughter
Andrew Fernandez	Their Son
Sabrina Fernandez	The Third Daughter.
Morris Robertson	Gracy's Estranged Cousin
Walter Robertson	Gracy's Cousin
Roy Gagnon	The Mobster
Marc Diez	The Investigator
Carmela Dante	Leonello's Mom
Matteo Dario	The Principal
Giacomo Rondelli	The Professor, Math Teacher

The Professor's Daughter

Gina Iafrate

Chapter One

The burning desire in her soul was strong. "I need to save him." she kept saying as she held on to him, leaning over rubbing his hand, caressing his forehead. Andrew was struggling deliriously. "No!" She kept screaming. "I cannot bear to lose you Daddy!" Gracy continued, imploring that he hold on to life. A nurse tried to alleviate her despair. Gracy's deep sorrow would not relent. Although the grip on him was tight, Andrew's body was letting go. "Please God! Help me! Transmit my energy into his lifeless body". Regardless of her pleading prayers and strong efforts, her dad passed on to his other dimension, leaving her grief stricken and heart broken.

A year had passed. Today was his anniversary. The melancholy that had taken over her existence since his loss had been difficult to overcome. Andrew Robertson was regarded with great respect by everyone. The English Professor they had called him. It had been only three short years since he and his beloved daughter had settled in Agrigento, relocating from Australia. They had been well accepted by the locals. Andrew and Gracy, in retrospect, had soon responded with their own kindness and numerous good deeds. They volunteered at the hospital, nurturing and feeding the sick, visiting the lonely, and reading to the visually impaired. They were both English teachers. Andrew had retired; he didn't hesitate to offer free tutoring to the students having to repeat courses over the summer months for fall exams. The teaching was hard and rigid in Sicily. The studies were taken seriously. One only passed if he or she deserved top marks. Most students would be remanded to continue on to the fall exams to make the year.

Andrew, together with his daughter, had finally found contentment here. After losing Francesca and surpassing all the tragedies, he had continued to live on only for his precious daughter Gracy. Oh! How he adored his Gracy and she, in return, existed to apotheosize him. She was the perfect picture of her mother Francesca. Her long black hair adorned her oval face; the big brown eyes gleamed in beauty; the docile smile from her lips portrayed her kindness. She moved swiftly with her slim medium stature, demonstrating the mannerism of a Sicilian native but she was English born.

***

Gracy, with Dad gone, was now totally alone. Often, she would lose herself in deep thoughts reminiscing about her childhood with the person closest to her, her beloved daddy. Her mom had been taken away from her at birth; therefore, she never had the pleasure of indulging in her embraces, love and affection. Her daddy had played the double role of parent and, together with her maternal family, they had kept her mom's vision alive. Later, she was given the gift of having found her two stepbrothers whom she considered a priceless legacy.

This Sunday morning March 6, 1961, she was reliving the pain. She got out of bed, pensive as usual; rubbing her temples, she stared out her bedroom window. She looked up at the cloudless blue sky. It was splendid, serene, promising a bright day. *I need to get my head in gear and force my mind out of this sadness.* Slowly forcing her body, she made her way down the stairs to the lower floor.

She had awakened to the chirping of the birds out there. They were harmoniously in accordance with themselves. *If only my mood would change to be a little like those birds. My existence would be easier to tolerate.* She slowly stepped out on the balcony of her living room. There she stood mesmerized. The vast extension of almond trees down the valley were spectacular, all hers to admire. *Without Dad this year isn't the same.* Tears freely spilled down her cheeks involuntarily. The birds were having a feast among themselves, flying in the mist of the earthly creation from one tree to another. They added to the beauty. The climate in February and March was amiable as the sun's rays omitted warmth from early morning. The almond trees were glorified in their mantels of pink and white, each at different stages in bloom.

Gracy just stood there. She took a deep breath while her memories were rushing back. *Here I am overlooking the deep valley in Agrigento. Where is my Daddy? How I miss him.* She cried out loud in despair as she couldn't stop the flashback.

They used to sit on that balcony every morning and every night sipping their coffee to begin the day and to watch the sunset with an aperitif and, later, tea. Here they would relate to each other their daily events and here, Daddy would profess his support and affection of Gracy's dreams and hopes. They both regarded the Valley of the Temples, which extended all the way down to the river, a piece of heaven. Andrew used to say often, "This is the best legacy left to both of us lovey, from the love of your mom, Francesca."

She remained there entranced. Nature transformed its beauty each season. It was spectacular at this time of year, although she battled these days to continue living in harmony. The loneliness was adamant in surfacing and flooding her mind to disturb her existence. Godmother Fabiana's voice resonated often in her thoughts. "Gracy, you are too sensitive and emotional. Don't forget my girl, you have your mother Francesca's blood flowing through your veins. It is her legacy of love and affection that has been gifted to you. This is why you adore our family and most of all your dad." *How right she was. I need to be more carefree,* she thought. Now her much loved aunt, Fabiana's mother had gone to heaven - another loss. Here she was with all this graceful beauty but with hardly anyone left to share it with. She took another look up at the bright, blue sky and down to the river. It was flowing like nothing had changed. She shook her head asking herself. "Why has so much changed in my life to mar my existence?"

"Yes!" she exclaimed asserting herself. "Dad never ceased talking about mom; her memory kept him alive." Trying to convince herself, she murmured. "Now he is there in heaven with her." She had gotten into the habit of talking to herself lately as she wandered around the house. The place had become like a museum. Everything was in proper order, but the quietness in the lifeless rooms was suppressive. She chided herself out loud. "Gracy stop living in the past, I know Dad didn't like it when I was sad."

The balcony door squeaked open behind her; before she had a chance to turn, a gentle arm touched her shoulder. Gracy's body shuddered and she should have been frightened, but a familiar voice whispered "Gracy" She turned. There he was, standing beside her with his head tilted and a loving smile. "I have been here a while, quietly watching you. What are you doing and thinking, Missy?" She jumped joyfully as her body jolted with a sudden burst of energy. She threw her arms around his neck. "Oh! Diego! What a surprise! I am so happy you are here. You couldn't have come at a better time." She was crying from happiness and relief from her lonely misery. "When did you arrive from New York?" she asked, wiping her tears.

"Lovey! Let me look at you. What is the matter? I don't like it when you cry or are sad. I know you by now dear sister. After there was no response from the doorbell, I let myself in with my key. You had me worried for a while there. I stood back watching you totally in another world."

"I am sorry, Diego. You are right. I was engaged in my own thoughts out here, feeling sorry for myself." She gave him another big hug, not wanting to let go. "My God! Diego, I am so glad to see you."

"I came here to pick you up. It's going to be a beautiful day. We made plans for you." her stepbrother Diego announced.

Diego was now in his mid-forties. He was tall, a touch of grey on his sideburns starting to show. His facial expression was pleasant, but serious. His forehead showed aging lines. He felt, being the eldest, it was his role to assume family responsibilities after he had graduated university. He had graduated with honors from Harvard in Business Law. His honesty and care manifested well.

"Diego, I am delighted you just appeared" Her eyes kept searching around.

"Where is Daniele?" she asked.

"Daniele, my dear sister, had to remain behind in New York against his will. He sends his regrets. You know how much he wants to be with us." He responded in his teasing English accent to bug her, as he reached pulling her close to him.

"We had to hire new people in the different departments, plus a new CEO to oversee the new hotel. One of us had to be there."

"I understand. I know you guys are dedicated. Otherwise, you wouldn't be so successful."

"Don't you worry; business wise we are doing great. I am more concerned about you and Daniele's wellbeing lately?"

Her forehead creased with worry. "What do you mean?"

"It's his relationship with Ingrid. I have seen him disturbed these past couple of months. I am sure she is giving him a hard time."

"Really! I am sorry to hear that. Daniele is kind. He doesn't deserve to be mistreated."

She turned away from Diego and thought to herself. *Funny he should say that. The last time I visited my brothers in New York, Ingrid seemed to put Daniele down continually. She was arrogant toward him and cold toward me also.* However, she wouldn't dare say anything to her brothers.

"Gracy, forget about Daniele and his relationship with Ingrid. I have come for the weekend to Sicily especially to be with you my dear sister" He knew Gracy would be reminiscing at this time of year. They had not forgotten that her dad had passed away a year ago this day; she would be in a dire state.

"It's so thoughtful of you Diego. What would I do without you and Daniele and our relatives in Palermo? You give me reason to live." She stepped over to hug him. She had no trouble showering her brothers with affection. She released her embrace and smiled at him, "Come Diego, let's take another look out here. Soon nature's transformation will turn to its next phase. You know how much dad and I loved this time of the year. We enjoyed watching it all. The miracle of nature in this part of the world is something to be grateful for. No wonder my mom loved this place and was the happiest here."

"Why do you think it was gifted to you Missy? And, of course, your dad to enjoyed it also. Our mom was the kindest soul. Too bad you never got to know her. You can rest assured she loved you immensely." Diego wanted to pacify his sister, but his own emotions were raw about his mother, especially after the revelation of how she died. The tyranny of his own father had shocked the hell out of them. *Please don't let me go there. This is why we love Gracy so much. Thanks to Andrew, Mom might have had some moments of joy.*

He shook himself and continued. "She has been looking after you from up above and us too."

Looking at her sternly he said, "Let's be grateful." He placed his arm around her shoulder and guided her inside. "Gracy, enough with the scenery. I need my strong espresso to boost my energy in the morning."

"At your service, Sir! I am ecstatic that you are here; let's go into the kitchen."

Diego was all smiles and guided her affectionately. Gracy loved being on the subject of her mom. She continued her gabbing.

"Yes, Godmother Fabiana always reminds me that Mom is looking after me from up above."

"You have been well taken care of and you are a lucky girl to have had your loving dad and brothers to protect you, wouldn't you say so?"

"I am grateful to have you and Daniele. I am a lucky girl. But I can't help missing my dearest dad."

"We know how sentimental you are; otherwise, we would scold you. This is why Fabiana insisted I come for the weekend."

"Oh! I thought was your idea?"

"Of course! I already had my flight booked! You know Fabiana always likes to play mother hen in reminding us of our duties." He responded with a little sarcasm.

The aroma of Illy coffee soon infused the air. She promptly served the espresso for both. *Pronto,* ready! Diego." They sat down on the swivel stools by the open concept kitchen counter. Diego turned around, jokingly swinging his stepsister's chair. "Gracy let's face the outdoors. I don't want to miss a moment of the beauty you have from everywhere in this house. Daniele sure did an excellent job in his artistic creation of this place. He is our brilliant architect wouldn't you say?" The opposite wall was open to a large, glass triple sliding door allowing an infinite view of the magnificent outdoors.

"Yes, he did. He is brilliant, I must agree."

"It's all part of our Italian heritage. In New York, our buildings are distinguished. Wait until you see our new Las Vegas hotel in its finishing touches."

"I don't doubt it."

"Sis, I must say, I love law and what I am doing. I am fortunately enjoying both worlds with my brother. We had no choice. Our father dictated our careers to suit his needs and our future, I guess. But what a mess! I had to clean up after him. He was corrupt. He made his own rules and that meant he made his own problems. Now business is thriving."

Gracy had heard some of the stories from Fabiana and Aunt Lora. They were unpleasant so she tried to change the subject. She stood up caressing Diego's arm. "I am glad. You both deserve it. Okay brother of mine. No more sad stories. Since the espresso cups are now empty, let's move on."

Diego took a deep breath reminding himself he was on a mission. He reached for his sister's hand, saying, "Yes! Go get ready and let me take you for a sumptuous breakfast in the city. Afterwards, we will stop at that famous bakery in Agrigento, Trombley. Remember? Your dad's favorite bakery. We will pick up some cannoli and other baked goods. Then we'll leave for Palermo. The baked goods will be our treats for our nieces and nephews. Fabiana and the rest of them will be anxiously waiting for our Sunday brunch. You are going with me. Fabiana insisted that I not return without you. A change of scenery would do you a world of good." He frowned and continued "It is not good for you to be here alone these days or any other as a matter of fact. We will discuss that another time. Now, get going. You know how delighted everyone will be to see you."

Gracy looked up at him sorrowfully but affectionately. Without responding she thought about how right he was.

Chapter Two

Gracy and Andrew, had settled together in their new built home. Daniele, her stepbrother, with his gifted skills in architecture had created a masterpiece for their residence. The admirable home, sat on the hilltop of Agrigento's east side and had an enormous acreage of land surrounding the three-story mansion. The interior and exterior with its spectacular, marble inlays sparkled at the reflection of the sun rays. It's winding garden paths were meticulous, and professionally landscaped. Gracy and Andrew had great pleasure decorating. Andrew jokingly sat Gracy down, saying, "Lovey, my precious, what do you say, if I will take care of the outdoor and you concentrate on the interior? Of course, my dear, we will consult one another for approval."

"Dad, I know you can turn those bare grounds into marvelous flower beds and paths. This place will be an enviable Italian villa for us and for our families and friends to enjoy."

Together their dream home had taken shape; a work of love that took them two years. Gracy had decorated the interior with the finest custom-made furnishings. The large rooms welcomed you in their lustrous ambiance. The three colours' schemes picked for the interior, blue, white, and deep turquois, intermarried perfectly. The sun filtered in well until sunset as the sky in pinkish yellow extended to the far horizon. Every night before sunset Andrew used to pour an aperitif in champagne glasses for the two of them and would stand there on the terrace calling out to his Gracy "Come, come lovey and let us enjoy and admire the sunset."

This was all marvelous. Gracy considered herself lucky at this stage in her life. The decision had been fulfilling once they had returned to this part of the world which was her mother's ancestral home. Her two stepbrothers, her Godmother Fabiana and her lovely Aunt Lora, Uncle Anthony, and Cousin Joseph, the Taverna clan, had showered her and her dad with love and affection from her childhood. Often, she had questioned her dad about his side of the family. "Dad don't you think we should contact your long-lost brother and his family? I feel sorry for you. Family is important. Maybe we should plan a trip to America and look them up."

Andrew's eyes always changed when Gracy mentioned his family. He would evade the subject totally.

"Dad! Please, don't do that? I need an answer. I am entitled to know what my paternal relatives are all about. It's not fair! You owe it to me Dad." She would insist.

"Gracy, believe me we are not missing anything. My brother never showed any affection or care for me or our parents. I hate to tell you this. He was a selfish individual, a user, and a sponger. Your grandparents died broken hearted. They were sick and incapacitated. He never came to see them. Don't remind me or get me started. Please Gracy, lets us be happy with what we have. I bet his wife and children are the same." When she noticed how upset he was getting, she wouldn't insist further.

Apologizing she would say "Oh Dad I'm sorry I brought it up. I won't mention them again. You cannot blame me for desiring to seek them out. It's more for you, although I must admit curiosity also. Dad, I confess, I feel guilty, I have Diego and Daniele. They are so kind to me and the rest of my relatives. You have no one from your family."

He would give her a hug and look her straight in the eyes, "Gracy! You know you are my life; my universe revolves around you. Don't you worry about me. I am doing fine. Don't waste your time seeking the Robertsons. You are blessed with your brothers and the family you have here darling; leave it at that!"

"Dad! Of course, I know how fortunate I am."

"Promise me one thing lovey" He looked at her seriously. "You will marry someday and have children. Make sure you will teach them love, affection, and respect, family first."

"Dad!" She was smiling bent her head with loving eyes. "I have had a good teacher."

"We have been both fortunate. We have been blessed with your mother's loving people."

"Don't forget yours and Mom's blood runs through my veins. How can I be different?"

For the past year, she often walked around reminiscing about the discussions she and her dad would have, especially once home alone. The sorrow in her heart was relentless and she missed him so. *Oh Dad, why do I feel so empty? Am I ungrateful and selfish?* She often would ask herself that when she questioned life.

She had accepted a position at the University of Agrigento teaching what she knew best, English. The Italian literature resonated music in her ears. She loved it. Dad had insisted on being fluent in three languages. French wasn't spoken much here. She felt embarrassed at the outdoor market where they spoke the Sicilian dialect which was too hard for her to comprehend.

She was now twenty-five years old and immensely dedicated to her work. The days would slip by as she kept herself occupied teaching her classes. Most of her students were eager to learn and showed great love and respect for her. As always there were three or four students that challenged her at times. She was determined to win them over. Her dad used to say "Lovey, your class has to be the best. Your students are the result of your teaching. You must create a stimulating atmosphere. That is your number one priority. Make your teaching fun and captivating. You must instill in them the desire to learn and keep them always motivated. Encourage them; choose to praise with diplomacy and delicately point out corrections." Andrew leaning forward and almost scolding used to say "Lovey, one thing you must remember, give of yourself fully. You will see. The rewards will be gratifying." His words resonated whenever she encountered some difficulty, especially with those characters that sometimes chose to dispute her ideas and were defiantly challenging her. Her love and dedication for her students had gained respect and admiration of the university staff and the president and of most of her students.

Unfortunately, once she returned home, the silence with the loneliness would hover over her like a black cloud burrowing deep into her heart and soul. Often, she would let herself fall into crying spells. It was all due to the emptiness of her surroundings. Her father was no longer there as her cherished confidante.

***

This morning unexpectedly, dear Diego had appeared. He had come to cheer her up. Although she was much younger than her brothers, she had much respect for both and especially Diego being the oldest; she considered him her protector. Now he had come for her; she wasn't going to disappoint him.

She thought. *For my precious brother, I better change my mood. I must get myself together, physically and mentally. After all he came all the way from New York and drove from Palermo, for me.* She shook herself to snap out of her unpleasant thoughts and cheerfully put her arms around him smiling "Diego My dearest it's your call; whatever you say. I will be ready in no time. I will dress up for you. Yes! I would love to go to Palermo to see the rest of the family. Thank you! It's a great idea." She stood on her tip toes to reach his height and kissed him on his forehead and ran energized to get herself together.

In the meantime, Diego's mind was filling with his own concern. Pensively he rubbed his forehead. *I don't like the situation of my sister living here alone. I must convince her to either move to Palermo or New York, where Diego and I are within reach should she need us.*

12

Gracy, bounced in to interrupt his thoughts. She was beautiful, ready for him.

"Here I am! What do you say brother of mine? Do I pass with your approval?" She posed like she was ready for the runways of Milan, like Francesca, their mother, used to do.

"You are so vain! No different than mom used to be. She always had to look her best."

"You blame her? After all she was a fashion designer!"

"I know. Her fussiness would drive us boys crazy sometime. It would have been fine with you being a girl. Boys liked to be ragged sometimes. We always had to look our best. I know she meant well."

"Let's not get carried away in sentiments, my dear. You must be getting hungry.

Let's go!"

She peeked at the mirror jokingly. She grabbed a hat and popped it on her head to compliment her outfit, playfully trying to lift her spirits.

"I am surprised you haven't captured someone's heart here. These available Sicilian guys, you would sure break their heart with your beauty."

"What do you mean? No, I am not interested in anyone, why would I be?"

"Why may I ask? Don't tell me the available bachelors don't find you attractive?"

"After the recounting of mom's suffering from her first marriage and Godmother Fabiana's and Aunt Lora's stories, I have no desire to get involved with any one here."

"Good! As you know anyone interested in you has to pass our approval first." He looked at her with mock sinister eyes.

"Yes! I have been told! Don't I know that. God help me, with you and Daniele. My two Sicilian protectors"

"Eh! Sis, it's for your own good. Your father's last request from me was to look after you." She smiled at him, pleasantly, feeling reassured to have someone that really cared.

Diego protectively placed an arm around her shoulders. Gracy's mood escalated. The affection from her brother was like stumbling upon an oasis in the middle of a desert. It gratified her thirsty for security. Now, she was comfortably looking forward to seeing Fabiana's family in Palermo. *Let me have a fun day, enjoy my brother and relatives to the fullest.*

She promised herself to suppress any worries that would surface in her mind to jeopardize her happiness. Her dear older brother had come across the ocean for her. *No! I cannot worry Diego. I will not mention anything of my concerns about my classes although I must admit those characters in my class do give me the chills. I feel they are up to no good.*

Chapter Three

Here they were Sunday afternoon, in Palermo as they had been over the past few years with Daddy, just in time for lunch. As soon as they pulled in by the gate all their cheerful and smiling family was waiting Fabiana with her two daughters, and Fausto Gagliano her husband, Joseph with his wife and the two boys, and Anthony Taverna, now widower. It was Sunday morning and as usual after the mass service at St. Rosalia's Church, up on the mountain, the family gathered for their Sunday brunch. Since Fabiana's mother had passed away, Fabiana had taken over the role of keeping the tradition going. "I must keep the family together." Fabiana insisted "It's my duty."

The cheerful greetings would always be gregarious and affectionate, especially the young girls. As for Fabiana, she had always adored her Gracy since birth. Uncle Anthony had aged immensely after losing his wife Lora. But being the patriarch, regardless of his aching body, he never refused the get together. He also loved his niece as she reminded him of his beloved sister Francesca.

"How are you my dear? I knew you wouldn't let Diego down. Your admirable brother wouldn't come back by himself."

"Oh! Uncle Anthony!" Gracy gave him a big hug. "You know I love to see all of you, and I miss you terribly if I stay away too long."

"We must take care of that" interjected Fabiana and Joseph.

They all fussed over her, and she enjoyed feeling spoiled by them all.

The table was set and together they consumed the traditional Sicilian meal that had been passed on from her grandmother to her mother Francesca, and to Aunt Lora, Fabiana's mom.

Once the meal was over, they moved outdoors for bocce game. They loved to compete in partners against one another. Gracy was right in there to compete. Dad, her cousin Joseph and Uncle Anthony had made sure she had learned the game well to excel and honor her partners. The day was glorious in company of her family; before they realized it was time to head back to Agrigento. Fabiana, in her motherly role, truly cared for Gracy. Ever since Andrew had died, she never relented trying to convince Gracy to abandon Agrigento and move closer to them In Palermo. "Gracy, my lovey" she would start and as she had learned from Andrew "We don't like you being there alone. I worry about you. You must decide and put my mind at ease. We want you nearby. We can see each other often; God forbid if something was to… I would never forgive myself. I don't want to sound pessimistic or negative. I don't like you being alone."

"Oh! Godmother, please don't torment yourself. I am fine. I love my students, and the classes I teach. The university is great, and I have met some nice people there. Please don't make me feel guilty. I must stay on; I owe it to my alumni. I am their teacher. I won't even mention the people I look after at the hospital."

She didn't dare want to admit to Fabiana that her life at home, since she lost her dad, was lonely and miserable. She didn't mention the imperfect class at the university. *I must be brave. After all, Dad and I chose to build there, Mom's favorite place. Francesca had gone to school there. I cannot be a Nene and run away. Grow up Gracy.* She would scold herself to strengthen herself.

***

Diego extended his stay one extra day, but he would leave the following morning. Like Fabiana, he was troubled also about his sister being alone in this opulent home. Besides, hadn't he promised Andrew on his death bed to look after Gracy. They had plans for her, him, and Daniele. Often, they sat down to discuss their sister. They felt it was their duty to look after her wellbeing. The grandfather clock struck the time. It reminded him to place a call to Daniele in New York. On the first ring Daniele was on the line, teasing him.

"Pronto! Ready." Italian style.

"Heh! Bro! How are you? How are things going? Miss me yet?"

Daniele kept talking relentlessly "Everything is fine! I am doing double duty. No problem. We got everything under control. Your new manager is on the ball. I tell you this Spanish fellow doesn't miss much. You will be pleased once you see for yourself. Don't be concerned about what's happening here. How is Lovey?"

"This is why I stayed an extra day; externally, she pretends to look fine. Bro, believe me I read her well. She can't fool me. I am sure she isn't that happy when she's alone. When I first got here, her eyes were red, swollen, consumed by tears. I think she is falling apart internally."

"What do you think? Of course, she lost her dad, is all alone in that place, and it is the anniversary of his death; how do you expect her to be happy? I am glad you took the time to be there."

"Don't worry. I will handle it. Tonight, I will delicately present our intention to our sweet Gracy in such a way that she will feel that the decision spontaneously came from her. I know how to be diplomatic."

"You are the lawyer. Give her a hug for me and see you at the airport tomorrow night. Safe flight."

"What! Are you coming to pick me up? I can take the hotel limo!"

"Diego, you been gone for few days. I missed you. Can I have dinner with my brother? Besides. I need to talk to you."

"Great, as you wish. See you then."

Diego, being the older brother, felt obligated to be available for any member of his family.

Daniele's life lately had also been a nightmare because of his girlfriend Ingrid. He couldn't wait to see his brother also. He could read between the lines. The pressure she was putting him under . . . she had been pressing to set a date for the wedding or else she would walk out on him. Their supposed love relationship had turned into a warzone. Daniele, deep down, wasn't ready for commitment but she was relentless.

Diego figured his brother was still troubled. The night before he left for Sicily, Daniele had related to him the scope and regularity of Ingrid's tantrums. More than once, she had walked out on him, slamming the door, giving him an ultimatum. So, here they were on both sides of the ocean- two brothers with a dilemma to solve. Diego was preoccupied with convincing Gracy. Daniele was afraid his girlfriend would go through with her threats.

Gracy had left in the morning for work. Diego had the day to himself at the villa, working on debit and credit projections for their new hotel. Before he realized it, it was time for him to pick up Gracy at the university. He liked to do that when he was in town. Besides caring for her, he wanted to present himself around her for protection. He was more accustomed to the Sicilian mentality of protecting their women. She bounced down the steps of the building waving to him. Gracy, smiling joyfully once she saw him, asked "How is my favorite brother?" She stretched to kiss him on his cheek.

"How was your day? Those students must adore you since you are so dedicated to them."

"Diego to be honest, most of them are attentive, intelligent, motivated. Then, of course, the world is not perfect. I hate to tell you there are about three or four students that have no business being in my class."

"Really! Why is that?"

"They are distracting, don't participate. Their assignments are never done. Some days when my morale is low, I feel I am wasting my time with them. Then, other days, I tolerate them patiently. Diego, you know me. My dad would say to be determined to win them over. I have to win them over."

"I am sure you will, Sis. Maybe you should introduce me to them next time I am in town.

Maybe, a pep talk will do them good."

"Not a bad idea; not to worry about them. There is always the odd one. Should it get really bad, I will relay it to my superior."

Diego had made reservations alla Trattoria dei Templi renowned for their specialties.

"Gracy I thought you would like it here. Fish is their specialty but whatever you like is available."

"Diego! I must please you my dear, I am fine with anything. The restaurants here are superb, regardless of where you go."

They ordered a mixture of fish for appetizer, followed by fettuccine in red salsa and a fabulous dessert-the green sponge cake filled with fruit soaked in liquor. Diego was eager to get Gracy in a relaxed atmosphere so he could fully get her attention to get his message across. He thought, one step at the time to reach the plan we have for her.

He gently reached out to take both Gracy's hands, looking her straight in the eyes, "Gracy, my dear sister, I am speaking for myself and Daniele. You are part of our lives. From both of us, I am requesting that you be with us on August the 15th. We will be opening our new hotel in Vegas; the mayor and all the dignitaries will be there. We would like you to stand between myself and Daniele to inaugurate our new place. Without you it won't be the same. You must come and we will not take no for an answer. This is why I am giving you plenty of notice. My secretary will book your flight. What do you say?"

She smiled sorrowfully "Diego, the sincerity with which you say it makes me think I must try my best as to not disappoint you and Daniele. Let me check with the university and get back to you."

"Sis! Can you please take a leave of absence? We would like you to spend some time with us. Can you do that for your old brothers?"

She took a deep breath to calm her uncertainty "Diego, I understand. This is where my mom wanted me to be. I believe, this is where my dad and I have been the happiest. Let me be for now. I am confused, I must admit to you that at times I feel sad, but my heart is here in this beautiful island of Sicily where my roots took hold." As much as she wanted to pretend all was fine, she knew that, once Diego left, her solitude would torment her soul. She was torn between duty and desire.

Little did she know that fate would intervene, and circumstances would change? The heavenly world that she and her dad had created would crumble into nothingness.

Chapter Four

Diego left and Gracy's somber mood resumed. She was missing him immensely already. She put her heart and soul in teaching, vowing to herself to win over her troublesome students. Most of her class, regardless of the disinterested few, were cooperative and respectful toward her. Their willingness motivated Gracy to get up in the morning and to get to the university. The time for the final exams was approaching. She was determined to prepare them well so that they would excel without difficulty. A new supply teacher had recently been hired due to another teacher's sick leave. His name was Giacomo Rondelli. A brilliant fellow she had been told. He would teach Math after her English class.

This morning, once she got to the classroom, she saw that most of the students seemed restless and distracted- more than usual. The three troublemakers, Gianni, Romeo and Leonello, were really misbehaving. They were out of control, goofing among themselves and instigating others. "God help me this morning!" she muttered quietly to herself. But they got noisier and more out of control. Her nerves got the best of her. She banged a ruler on her desktop. In a loud voice she called out "Leonello! Stop your nonsense or I will have you expelled. You are disturbing my class." He made a serious face and pretended to straighten up. Gracy, turned to continue writing on the blackboard. Once finished, she addressed the class. "What I am writing down on the black board is important information. Please pay attention! It's all for your benefit." Leonello's gaze was on his two friends. He smirked at her attentively-a false pretense. Soon after, he resumed his goofy actions influencing the others to ignore her. "Give her the salute Gianni boy." The rest started to laugh outload. They were throwing papers around, misbehaving. They were in an uproar again. She tried hard to control her irritation, but their disrespect continued. Once more the discouraged teacher called for their attention. They chose to ignore her. She slowly walked over to the three of them and just stood there silently. They were so totally absorbed in their antics that they didn't even notice her standing there.

"Why are you challenging me today? Since I have walked in this morning you three have been challenging me." Of course, it was no surprise to her. The ringleader, Leonello, was the worst one. As she retreated, pieces of papers were everywhere. She picked one up that was not far from her desk. The scribbling message on the note was unpleasant and immensely disturbing. She chose to ignore it.

The next morning, they had arrived earlier than usual. They had settled at the far back of the classroom. From the corner of her eye Gracy watched and suspected they were plotting something. She stood a certain distance pretending to be occupied, while listening to Leonello' talking smart. He was instructing the other two. "Eh! Guys, if this guy doesn't mark generously. We can always break his arm and, if he is really a hard marker, an arm and a leg."

Gianni asked, "What makes you say that Leon?" They had shortened his name, calling him Leon- lion like the wild ferocious animal.

"Do you know him?" Romero interrupted.

"My brother's friend was in one of his classes when he was here before. Rondelli seemed to have a resentment against him, so he didn't pass him. He had to repeat the year. Some other fellows told me to watch him. He is a hard marker."

"Why does he resent Sicilians?" retorted Gianni.

"Who knows? Maybe he thinks he is superior to us. After all he comes from the mainland."

"We will fix him up; don't you worry Leon" remarked his friend, Romero.

"Not only him- what about Miss Queeny, with her special walk, twisting her teasing ass?" Leonello's crude remarks encouraged their laughter.

"What about her Aussie accent?" Gianni whispered.

The guys were murmuring to each other. Gracy couldn't quite hear everything but she knew it wasn't good.

"Gianni you kill me with your stupid notions. Never mind her accent. What about that piece of ass? You guys don't tell me you don't feel anything watching her, when she twists her rounded ass in those tight skirts she wears. Those legs of hers in her high heels, drive me crazy."

"You devil Lion," laughed Romero out loud. Gianni followed.

Gracy stood there perplexed, watching them slap each other, goofing around, as they were totally in a world of their own. *They must be drugged!* Her skin broke out in goose bumps. *These guys scare me.* The disturbing statements that she had half overheard, it was alarming. *Jesus! These young fellows are truly crazy. Leonello is definitely on something. He looks spaced out. The other two fools seem to be under his spell. They listen attentively, approvingly. I wonder what they meant about this Queeny. Who is Queeny?*

Dragging her feet, she made her way back to her desk. She decided to ignore any bad thoughts. The rest of the students were arriving. Gracy took a deep breath in resolution and called the class to attention. Her eyes fixed at the back of the class. Her looks were focused sternly on the culprits. "All of you, pay attention to what I am warning you. As you know exams are soon approaching. You have been given several assignments. We have been engaged in many discussions on the subject. You have been assigned research to be done. All our hard work has taken place together in class. The purpose of it all has been to prepare you for exams that will be presented to you. Please take your time. Do it well. I expect you to submit your papers to me, precisely and correctly. I can assure you; you will be marked according to your true merits. I would be doing you great injustice by shortchanging you, by grading your work with what you don't truly deserve. I will be fair and reward you exactly by the evaluation of your correct answers. Let me make it clear. Low marks will hurt me more than you. My biggest goal is to empower my students with knowledge and excellence. Am I clear? Do you understand?"

They all clapped hands, standing up in agreement. But the spaced-out jokers didn't respond. Gracy, took another deep breath hoping to calm herself. She wondered if the message had gotten through to them. No sooner had she finished her spiel when a knock on the door startled her. "Yes, come in."

The principal peeked through as the door opened and proceeded to walk in with an older gentleman. "Miss Robertson, I want you to meet our new Math teacher here, Mr. Giacomo Rondelli. He will be taking over your class, afterwards."

She tried her utmost to smile. Cordially she nodded, extending her hand to welcome them. "My pleasure to meet you Mr. Rondelli."

"The pleasure is mine, Miss Robertson."

After their introduction and exchange of pleasantries, they turned to address the class. Miss Robertson, called her class to greet Professor Rondelli. After her brief introduction the principal, Matteo Dario, presented Mr. Rondelli in a fuller introduction to the students.

"Students! I am honored to present to you Professor Giacomo Rondelli." They had remained standing to welcome him; most of her diligent students with manners were respectful. When Gracy's eyes darted toward the troubled ones, sure enough, Leonello was sitting down, his legs sprawled wide, his facial expression aloof and removed.

The other two were also sitting with their legs sprawled, nonchalantly, imitating him. Mr. Dario's voice broke her spell, as he continued. "He comes to us highly recommended. After much convincing, he decided to join our staff. He brings us a wealth of knowledge to pass on to you. I must say, he is definitely an asset for our university. We are extremely fortunate to have him as part of our family. I admit it took some convincing for him to leave *la Basilicata citta' di Bari* and to relocate to our beautiful city here in Agrigento."

Gracy recalled the earlier statements made by her troublemakers. She couldn't help visualizing the fate of the poor gentleman- a broken arm or a broken leg that those mischievous students had threatened. *Yes, they were planning to harm this poor man even before meeting him.* She took another inquisitive look at him. He came across as a mild man with and aura of placidity. *God forbid,* she thought, *what would they be capable of? Or who knows what other craziness they had planned. They mentioned Queeny. Who could be Queeny? They must know my father and I had relocated from down under. I don't trust them. That Leonello guy spells trouble. He acts so strangely at times. I must find out more about him.*

26

Chapter Five

In New York, Diego and Daniele were busy getting themselves updated from the few days they were apart. "Tell me Diego, how is our sister doing? You had me worried."

Diego bent his head down as if to replay his time with her. "I hate to tell you; I didn't find her at her best when I surprised her. I must say, her face immediately lightened as soon as she saw me and even more so once we joined the family clan in Palermo. I honestly believe, Daniele, we must work on removing her from that house. I know she is attached to that place. She wants to be loyal to mom's memories, your design of it, her father's cherished time there. No, she must move on." Diego's concern grew deeper as he assessed his time with her in Sicily.

"I agree that she is solitary there on the outskirts of the city. The gardener goes two half days a week, a cleaning lady every second week, because no one messes up. At night she is alone; there is no one there. The crime and break ins in that area, leaves much to fear."

"Daniele, you tell me! I wake up at night sweating from nightmares, worrying, about her."

"We don't want to resort to the actions of our crazy father, having mom followed."

"Let's not go there Diego. He had other motives. The honour and he was protecting himself mainly. He didn't care about her! We were young and had no choice other than to abide by his rules but we don't have to follow them now."

"We will take care of our Gracy soon. I promise Bro. Tell me what's been happening here these past few days."

"The interviews are complete. Every department has been well assigned with the best interests in mind. The employees are great, not to mention, the right person in charge of every section. The best CEO is this Alvaro Fernandez, as I mentioned to you on the phone. Wait until you meet him and judge for yourself."

"Good! Encouraging, business wise. Tell me, what else? If I am guessing right, your relationship with Ingrid, is upsetting lately."

"Yes, you guessed right- very much so," He nodded in agreement.

"Why? You don't have to tell me if you don't want to."

"Diego! Come on, you are my older brother."

"I am listening"

"As you know, she insisted on moving in with me. Which at first didn't suit me right. I must admit, I didn't mind after a while. Now every day she is pressuring me to set a date for the wedding and she wants to have children. I am not ready for that. She threatens me in every which way. We are constantly fighting. You remember Dad's warning? Well, it's happening. She is after position, security and money."

"Do you really love her?"

"I think so and I think we are fine the way we are."

"Diego, women have their own desires and dreams. Either you choose to abide by them or you must change route."

"I have to think about it. But right now, we have to concentrate on the new Las Vegas hotel and get that going. I cannot be sidetracked by wedding plans! I must confess, she is great in bed, but her greediness turns me off. She wants me to buy a six-million-dollar home."

"Daniele, your concern makes sense. I admire your strengths business wise. Ingrid doesn't want to hear about that. She is after self-gratification, the good life. The route to evil is money. You and I have a lot to offer. Gracy too for that matter."

"Let's drop the subject. You must be tired. You need a good night sleep. Let's call it a night." They parted with a brotherly hug.

Diego had been in many relationships, making it clear to the women he dated or kept company with that he would make no promises or demands. Angelo Frarano, their father, constantly warned them, *"You guys hold a high position. I must say, thanks to my bloody sweat. You are worth un patrimonio. A fortune. I warn you! Open your eyes! Be careful who you get involved with." Dad's sinister mentality was atrocious. We resented it so much. We used to fire back at him when we got older arguing, especially when I was studying law. "Dad, please, do you believe in falling in love? Besides there are prenuptial agreements. Have you ever heard of that? " Angelo would not listen to them. "Sure, sure, you fools! Believe that! There are smart lawyers in this country, especially in New York. I know lawyers that can create arguments to turn your reasoning upside down. Women clean you out, especially if there are children involved. God help us!" Then he would walk away.*

They both knew their father wanted them to be involved with someone their equal, or at the very least someone compliant. After his death, they both felt free to see and keep company with whoever they wished. Diego had become an attorney, a dedicated one at that and a workaholic -more than his father was. His exposure to the law in the large firm was an eye opener. He confessed to Daniele and himself that their warped father's statements weren't that wrong after all. The divorce rate was escalating, not to mention the battles in custody lawsuits. Prenuptial agreements were shredded to invalidity. Some of his own friends had ended up in the poor house, derelict. Diego wasn't eager to get involved long term with anyone. He had a lot of female friends. He was seeing Judge Rosella Balladic, occasionally, when he needed a companion for business functions. She was dedicated to her work; they were good friends. He was glad his heart wasn't stolen by anyone as of yet.

Daniele often asked him. "Diego, what is wrong with you? You are getting old. Don't you want to get serious with someone and have a family?"

"Daniele, I am perfectly fine. I have you, I have my precious Gracy to protect and look after. I have my family."

Diego was bothered at times once he had learned the shocking revelation of his mother's murder; it had left him numb. The resentment, the hatred toward his father was immeasurable. It was a good thing he was dead. His parent's marriage had had an impact on his life. No wonder he had no desire to commit himself with anyone. The observations and unforgiving behaviour of his father with other women. Those madams being paid well, flashing his hundred dollar bills. . . the memories were repulsive. Diego often told his family and friends "My life is full. I have my practice, our father's inheritance and our growing hotel chains to look after. No time to spare. We have had opportunities presented to us which we couldn't refuse. Here we are expanding further in Las Vegas."

This morning, although jet legged, he made his way to the office ready to resume his duties. His secretary Giorgina had walked in, wasting no time reminding him of meetings she had booked him into for the day. She also carried a pile of files in her hands for him to go over. "Mr. Frarano, these are all the documents you need to oversee regarding the transaction of the new hotel. Afterwards I will pass them on to the other firm with your approval. " Diego took a deep breath, asking. "When is this new fellow taking over some of this work?" He was somewhat annoyed, being tired from lack of sleep.

"Yes, Mr. Fernandez! I think you will be pleased. He was recruited from Washington. Smart fellow! By the way, Daniele called earlier before you came in. He asked me to make reservations at that popular restaurant, Il Giardino for the three of you, should you be able to join them. You will meet our new fellow."

"What time? Will I be able to make it? You are handing me a lot of work here."

"1:00 pm! You should be able to? Your next appointment is at 3:00 pm. Sorry Mr.Frarano, I hate to overload you. There is also one more pressing request. I would appreciate if you could possibly make the rounds checking out the refurbished departments on the third floor. I am holding payment until your approval. They have called a couple of times."

"Miss Giorgina, I appreciate, the way you safeguard our affairs, especially our finances.

You could always send partial payment holding back security. We don't want to risk the service of good people, and our company labelled for slow payments."

"I understand. But I feel better once I know everything has been properly completed and passed your inspection."

Diego was a workaholic, but the demands on him were overwhelming. The stress lately had been affecting his wellbeing. Daniele had been noticing his brother struggling with so much to handle. He himself couldn't help him, especially when it came to the demands at his law firm. Lately, he taken upon himself to get more help for his much-loved brother.

It was getting late. Diego looked at his watch and dropped everything to meet Daniele and Alvaro, both waiting at Il Giardino restaurant.

When Daniele spotted him coming in, he exclaimed. "Here is my brother, I knew he would be here regardless of his schedule."

They both got up to greet him. Daniele was all smiles and was quick to introduce Alvaro Fernandez.

"Diego! I want you to meet our new assistant Mr. Alvaro Fernandez,

Diego promptly extended his hand with a welcoming smile. "Nice meeting you Mr. Fernandez."

"Likewise, my pleasure meeting you Mr. Frarano!"

They sat down as the waiter arrived with the light champagne that Daniele had previously ordered. "Well cheers and welcome to our company, Mr. Fernandez." Diego saluted.

"I am honored to be part of your chain. I must say, I am looking forward working with both of you. I must add that I heard nothing but good things about you brothers."

Diego thought. *I am glad. If you only knew the cleanup I had to do to clear our business, our name, and or personal lives mucked up by our father's way of operating.*

Many years had passed since his death. *Thank God. We mustn't speak ill of the dead.*

Their reputation had been restored. "Thank you, Mr. Fernandez, my brother has given me excellent feedback with regards to you. I am pleased to hear that. I trust my brother fully. We are looking forward to your expertise and contribution to our company."

Alvaro Fernandez was a handsome young man in his mid-thirties. He was a fairly tall gentleman with a pleasant demeanour. A docile smile governed his face, big brown eyes, dark black hair and bronzed skin. Diego noticed his effectiveness in communicating supported by his pleasant expressions. The slight Spanish accent suited him well. He had to agree with Daniele. Fernandez was vastly personable indeed.

Diego glanced at the time, again. It was getting late. He rushed back to his office to find Ingrid waiting and unexpected. "Ingrid! Nice to see you. Sorry I am late. Giorgina neglected to tell me who my next client was."

"She couldn't. I insisted on seeing you." She was walking back and forth irritated.

"Please sit down, Ingrid. Calm down. What can I do for you?"

"Diego! Your brother is totally insensitive toward me lately. My biological clock is running out. I want us to get married; he doesn't want to commit. I am ready to walk out on him.

Believe me, I will not walk out empty handed. I will sue him. We have lived together for ten years now. I have jumped at his demands. I am entitled to severance for working with him and living with him. You know. You are the smart lawyer."

Diego scratched his head; he was tired and his timing was off. "Ingrid, please. I need a good night sleep. Can we discuss this further in a couple of days? Give me a chance to digest this from every direction. You are upset today; give it a rest. Do it for both of us, please."

He offered her a hand and guided her out the door. Shaking his head, he was more than ready to call it a day. "Thank God she left." He took a deep breath.

***

Gracy in Agrigento was placing the key in the front door of her villa. It was dark. She had finished a long day's work later than usual. After teaching her class, she had gone to volunteer at the Civic Hospital. The kitchen had been short staffed today. Some of the extremely ill patients needed to be fed. She had offered to feed them. Some others enjoyed her reading. She couldn't deny it to them. Gracy and her dad were surprised to find how many elderly people couldn't read or write. Many of them were also vision impaired. They loved to listen to the sound of her voice reading. She would read to them with perfect expressions of the characters in the stories. Some patients commented. "You should have been an actress, Miss Robertson!"

Gracy, was pleased but also humble at the same time. She simply got so much pleasure out of bringing joy to these sick and lonely people. She looked forward to spending time with them. Gracy's heart pained when one of them passed away. Diego had left strict orders not to return home late at night. He would call her or make sure she called him once she returned home. Peace of mind he used to say. Gracy thought *He was totally ridiculous. Dad wasn't as overprotective as my brother. He puts worry in my head.*

When she related Diego's overprotectiveness to Fabiana, her godmother would side with her brothers. "Gracy they have good reasons to worry. You are an attractive girl. I hate to remind you. Your mother has left you well off. Your brothers, I won't mention. You could be a target. There are a lot of good people here, mind you. I won't mention the criminal ones."

"I will definitely not live in fear, Godmother" she responded.

"Good for you! We don't want you to. Your brothers and your family are overprotective. As you know, we would all feel better if you moved closer to family."

Andrew used to tell his daughter when she got restless about seeing the relatives, "Someday you will meet someone and fall in love. You will have a family of your own beside your brothers and the Tavernas." He hoped she would surprise him, sometime by introducing him to someone she cared for. His daughter, like him, seemed to glory in her work with no romance in sight.

Tonight, she had gotten back later than usual and tired. *It would be 2:00 am in New York. Too late to call Diego.* She had picked up the phone but before she could replace it, suddenly, a big blasting noise made her turn. A huge rock rolled to her feet. A pile of shredded glass rained around her body. The floor was covered, and blood was spilling from parts of her legs. Gracy froze. The phone dropped out of her hand dangling from the wall.

Chapter Six

Pieces of glass had pierced parts of her flesh. Her legs were hurting badly; the bleeding continuing. She needed to do something. Her powerless body wasn't responding. She stood there breathless and afraid to move. Only quietness echoed in her ears. She waited anxiously waiting to see if anybody appeared and listening for any additional noise out there. She didn't know how much time had lapsed since her brain wasn't focused on what to do next. Suddenly screeching car tires reached her hearing. They were speeding away. *God help me. Who could have been out there and who wanted to harm me intentionally?* The huge rock stood there, not far from her feet, as evidence. The shattered glass was all over, even on the furniture. The large window was broken. *No neighbours close by. I must report this to the police.* She realized the phone was off the hook. The call to Diego had never materialized. The timing was still off. *No, I cannot call Diego now. He will be so alarmed.*

She dialed the emergency number 112. The trail of blood followed as she moved. One foot was deeply slashed. She needed a doctor because of all the blood loss. Her legs gave up, she fainted. Luckily, in no time, a rescue squad, fire trucks and an ambulance, was at her door. They found Gracy unconscious on the floor with all the debris. The paramedics immediately attended to her wound to stop the bleeding. The police arrived on the scene looking around, trying to figure out what had taken place. The paramedics were rushing to get her to the emergency. "She has lost too much blood. You will have to ask questions later." The paramedic added shaking his head. "Ma Sicuro, certainly it's best you attend to her wellbeing right now." Answered the carabiniere, officer. They took off, the sirens blaring away. Gracy ended up at the same hospital where she had volunteered earlier. The injuries from the cuts were severe but her emotional state worse. After the doctor checked her, he ordered the nurse to give her a needle. The morphine would help her relax and fall asleep which she badly needed.

Gracy drifted away, in a world of peacefulness for the duration of her medication.

Much later, she woke up frantic, looking around and realizing she wasn't in her home. The recollection immediately replayed in her brain. She immediately wanted out of there. *I need to get back home. I need to call my brother, Diego!* She was concerned. She forced herself to get up; her feet and legs were extremely sore. The wound had required many stiches. It needed to heal. A nurse walked in, accompanied by a *carabiniere.* "Miss Robertson, I am officer Emilio Gambare assigned to your case. How are you doing this morning?"

"The best I can, Officer. Anxious to get out of here. I need to get back home. My class, my students are waiting for me."

"Miss Robertson, we are more concerned about your wellbeing for now. You were quite shaken last night. My superior ordered me to ask you some questions this morning. If you are able to help me."

"Mr. Gambare, I'm sorry but I really need to get in touch with my brothers, my family in Palermo. They will be worried sick if they get wind of this incident."

"Not to worry. Everything has been taken care. Your brother called while we were still at the house investigating. Yes, I must say he was extremely alarmed. We reassured him of your wellbeing. You will be glad to know that some family members from Palermo are on their way here."

"Oh my God! I will never hear the end of this. The way they are."

"I need to ask you some questions in order to proceed with the investigation."

"Would you have any idea who might be wanting to hurt you? Did you see anyone following you home last night? Did you hear anything out there before that big rock reached you?"

Gracy's thoughts went to the three troublemakers in her class straightaway. *How can I accuse them if I am not sure?* "Officer, I don't know." They had a million questions for their investigation. Gracy was tired. "Please, can we resume this later?" she turned to the nurse. "I want to talk to the doctor. I need to go home. I have to look after the repairs, the condition my place was left in!"

"Miss Robertson it's up to the doctor. You need to heal. He will decide."

Soon after Dr. Spence walked in "Miss. Robertson, I suggest you take some time off work.

You been through a trauma and few of your wounds were pretty deep. We want to make sure you're healing properly."

No sooner had the doctor left when Fabiana, Uncle Anthony and Joseph appeared at the door, obviously alarmed. "Gracy, my darling, how are you? My God! When the police called, we had such a scare. We couldn't get here fast enough." They took turns hugging and kissing her.

Gracy knew how emotional they were. She put on a good face. "I am fine Godmother. Don't worry. I will be back on my feet in no time." Her protestations did not put an end to hovering. Their caring and concern continued. Uncle Anthony Taverna had immediately called his connection at the police department. "You must find out who wanted to harm my niece. No slacking on the investigation. Please report to me as soon as you find any information." Not to mention that when the news was passed on to Diego and Daniele, they called day and night to be brought up to date on her wellbeing.

Uncle Anthony and Joseph informed her, "Gracy, don't worry about the house. Your brother has already ordered the glass work to be replaced. The place will be in perfect condition for your return home." She didn't doubt that and she also knew they wouldn't relent with their pleas for her to move or to let them care for her. "You cannot live alone Gracy." They were all after her to change her mind about her life and where she was headed.

The officer in charge of her investigation paid her another visit. "We have received a phone call from Mr. Diego Frarano, and Anthony Taverna's lawyer. They, again, left strict orders not to slack on this investigation. We must do our job. This is serious. You could have gotten killed last night. Miss Robertson, we have reason to believe there was more than one individual wanting to harm you. We traced several footsteps of different sizes. Whoever these individuals are, they are extremely dangerous? We found a gallon of gasoline and matches thrown about. I don't want to alarm you. You need to help us. Something or someone aborted their action."

She listened pensively. In the meantime, she didn't trust herself to mention people. "Officer, I need to talk to my brother first and my Uncle Anthony's lawyer. In the meantime, I will remain vigilant."

"Look Miss Robertson, we think something happened to abort their plan. We suspect they had intended to put your place on fire. God knows what other plans they had other than arson. Could be some youngsters on drugs. You have nothing to add or tell us at the moment?"

"No, not really." She was pensive trying to make sense of all she had experienced and all that she had heard from the *caribinieri*. She didn't know yet that her fate had been planned even if the plans of her assailants had been, as the police had said, aborted.

Chapter Seven

The fear she was experiencing now that a day had passed was minor in comparison to what she felt the night before. If the attackers' plan hadn't been aborted, maybe she wouldn't be here. Who could assure her the sordid ordeal wouldn't happen again?

Gracy, after much insistence, was able to convince the doctor to discharge her. She wasn't surprised to find Godmother Fabiana, Uncle Anthony and Joseph waiting. After all the hugs and affectionate manifestations were exchanged, Fabiana couldn't wait to check her out to make sure she was healing well. "Gracy, are you sure you are okay? Lovey! We couldn't wait to get you home." They were all ready for her to be picked up and by the time she got home her phone was ringing off the hook with Diego and Daniele both on the line.

"Oh my! You guys, I am so sorry to have alarmed you. I am fine, nothing to be concerned about." Deep down, she was shaken to the core

Joseph, her cousin, and Uncle Anthony interjected, "Nothing to worry about! We saw the size of the rock. All that shattered glass. I hate to think of it. God almighty must have saved you. I saw that piece of solid stone could have killed you. We are not finished until we talk to the officer in charge."

Fabiana was walking around, murmuring "Thank you Santa Rosalia, our protector."

Since living in Sicily and being near her family, Gracy had gotten used to them turning to Santa Rosalia, the patron Saint of Palermo. They were such devoted Catholics; she had to respect their beliefs. She tried to act cheerfully and make light of the situation. In the meantime, she had to admit her soul was troubled, but her heart was rejoicing at having family there. They were her security blanket.

Fabiana, put an arm around her. "We are here now; don't you worry about a thing.

Joseph has inspected everything properly. Dad already called his lawyer in Palermo. He requested someone from La questura, over and above the police force, to protect you."

"Godmother, it could have been some pranksters motivated by boredom or jealousy to disrupt my place. I notice lots of people driving by and slowing down to admire our home."

"Never mind. What they did is unforgivable."

Gracy's mind couldn't help going toward those hoodlums in her class. Over the past few weeks she had never seen Leonello so spaced out. *He must have been on drugs of some sort.* The other two also. She didn't dare mention them to anybody. The university was informed about her situation. She had taken the doctor's, and also the officer's, advice to take some time off. In the meantime, her hunch felt right but she refused to admit it to herself.

A supply teacher took her place announcing to the class that Miss Robertson was on a leave of absence. In the classroom, Leonello was sitting at the center in the back, Gianni on his right and Romero on his left. The rest of the class was in front of him. Leonello could see everyone, and this position gave him a sense of control. The ability to delegate rendered him powerful. He stretched his leg to kick Gianni on the shin, and afterwards turned to Romero. He got their attention. "It's going to be a boring day guys. Do you like looking and listening to that old bag up there? I feel like excusing myself and getting out of here. What do you say?"

"Leonello are you nuts! All three of us! It's too obvious!" Responded Gianni.

"Don't you miss Queeny?"

"Eh! It was your idea to order Romero to do what you wanted."

"She triggered my patience by making us wait there in hiding for so long. Why did she have to come home so late?"

"Leonello, you need to calm down." Gianni warned his friend.

"I would have been extremely calm if she had come home as usual, and we could have crawled in and surprised her in bed as we had planned. I could have taken my pleasure but no, she buggered everything up. She made me mad."

"Leon, suffer today, instead of looking at Queeny's swinging ass at the front we're stuck with the old hag up there." added Romero.

"You guys better do as I say; we will give her a few days of grace. I am determined to have my way with her-the ultimate pleasure I have promised myself."

"You better count me out Leon. Take Romero with you. I prefer not to." retorted Gianni.

"What! You *strunz*, idiot, you have no choice. You will be our bodyguard. The last one to indulge, should you care to."

"I am with you Leon. Gianni boy has always been a chicken shit. You know that. I don't know why we let him hang around us. We should replace him." Romero stated.

Gianni didn't like the way they were talking. His thoughts were spinning in his head. *What am I going to do? Stay under my mother's skirts all night? Yeah! Count the rosary beads with her; that will be fun.* Gianni was the son of the widowed Maria Salva. He was the youngest in the family with two older sisters. His father had been killed in a robbery attempt when Gianni was very young, therefore he never known him. His mother was a good woman who worked hard in the fields to support the family. Gianni had met Leonello and Romero back in high school. He was glad to be accepted as their friend. Leonello, came from a large family. His father had a bad reputation as a ruthless criminal- abusive and unforgiving. Romero was the son of a Mafioso that had been in and out of jail. Gianni was a bit younger and, having been surrounded by only females at his house, he looked up to his buddies, but he didn't like Leonello's actions and edicts. Oh, Leonello always made sure he ruled liked a king.

***

A couple of months passed, Gracy's fear seemed to dissipate. She was aware of her surroundings. She resented the limited late outings. She refused to make changes, promising the family to spend the weekends together. At the same time Diego's and Anthony's lawyer reported all was clear and not to worry. The surveillance was successfully implemented and the investigation ongoing. Gracy had just terminated her class for the day. She sidetracked, walking into the cafeteria for a bite to eat. There, she spotted the Math teacher sitting alone. He waved her over and got up to greet her. "Miss Robertson, please join me." Gracy gladly sat down, happy to exchange few words with the new teacher.

"How have you been, Mr. Rondelli?"

"Good, all good. I love Agrigento, the university as well. I am giving myself a few more months. Then I will plan to move my family here."

"I am glad. That sounds great. We were told you would be an asset for this place."

"Thank you for your kind words. It all depends on my family's approval. Then I will decide "

"Mr. Rondelli, if I can be of any help, please, I will be glad to assist in any way."

"Miss Robertson, sorry about your problems a short while back. Everything is fine I hope."

"Yes, all is well, I am not sure what brought that incident on, but I am fine."

"I apologize for asking." He hesitated.

"Please, Mr. Rondelli, feel free; after all we are all friends here at the university."

"Most of my classes are great. I noticed that in your class and mine also, there are a few individuals that can be distractive, troublesome. I hate to point out anybody; do you have the same problem or is it my teaching."

"Mr. Rondelli, I hate to say anything unpleasant about our students, or to engage in malicious gossip. I must confess, yes, there are three or four individuals in my English class that try my patience."

"If you don't mind I will name them to you. Leonello Dante, Romero Placido, Gianni Cecco. Occasionally a female joins them. I hope she stays away from them for her sake."

"You are right on, Mr. Rondelli; they spell trouble."

"I have had them checked out. I must say my findings were disturbing."

Gracy brought her hands to her temples. She didn't dare mention broken arm and broken legs.

Her gut feeling was not good about those three, now the female? She would keep her eyes open. *They sure spell trouble.*

44

Chapter Eight

The year's end had soon approached. Gracy had been careful in handling the exams.

To her surprise Gianni had done fairly well. Romero, and Leonello's papers needed a lot of polish. *I will be doing great injustice moving them on. My students have to be fully knowledgeable in their subject matter.* She would read and re-read their papers. The decision was to help them regardless of their behaviour and discuss the matter with her superior, Matteo Dario. She walked into his office with their papers in hand. "Mr. Dario. I need your advice here. I could overlook these papers presented to me. Romero and Gianni could move on to the next class. The same applies to Leonello, which is much worse." She handed him the papers to take a look for himself. "Please, I want to be fair Mr. Dario. English literature is my forte'. It's engrained in me by my dad; his reputation was perfection."

"Miss Robertson, please leave the papers with me. I want to scrutinize every line in fairness. Can you check back with me tomorrow?"

Gracy, went home concerned about Mr. Dario's final decision regarding the boys' academic future. Her phone rang early the next morning. "*Pronto!*"

"Miss Robertson, sorry to call you at home. Would you please come in earlier? Say my office at 8:00 am. I have been called unexpectedly to attend a conference later. I sensed you want to get this matter resolved."

"Yes, you are right. I will be there,"

In no time Gracy entered Mr. Dario's office, holding her breath. "Good morning, Miss Robertson, sit down please." He picked up the papers and slammed them on his desk. "Miss Robertson, my apologies. I am well aware of your credentials. These papers are an offence to our university, our teaching, and your intelligence."

She listened, wide eyed. "What do you suggest I do?"

"What I suggest- no question- is to remand the students to repeat. Fall exams won't do. Total repetition of the class."

Gracy, knew the same, but she was afraid of the boys' response. "Mr. Dario, what would you say, if I take it upon myself to teach both of them, over these summer months, privately at my place? They will only concentrate on English with no classroom distraction."

"Their families will not be able to pay the tutoring. Leonello, and Romero both come from troubled families struggling to survive. I met Leonello's mother, a good woman." He shook his head.

"Mr. Dario, they don't have to pay me! If I can get through to them and teach them that will be my reward."

"Miss Robertson, I admire your generosity. Are you sure you want to take these two troublesome students in your house?"

"Yes! If I can help them, why not? It will mean so much to me. My dad and I have survived our lonely lives due to the kindness of the people placed on our path in the course of our lives."

"Miss Robertson. I admire your good intentions. Good luck, go ahead; give them a second chance. We will see them in October exams."

Gracy chose her words carefully when marking their papers. Gianni was promoted, barely making the mark. Leonello and Romero were deemed to repeat in the fall semester.

She walked to Leonello's desk at the end of the day and asked the two of them to please remain after class. "I would like to talk to you both. After you receive your papers."

Gianni, curious, "Eh, guys, what's going on? Why do you have to see Queeny?"

"Who knows maybe she wants …" Romero quickly cut off his words. "He is too young. Don't you know his mother is a half saint?"

Gianni, didn't like when they made fun of his mother. *If I want to be accepted, I have to ignore their comments.*

Romero, grabbed Leonello's ear. "Listen to me schmuck, what will we do with her?"

"Nothing! Let go of my ear. Before I give you a twist of you know what."

"We don't have the results of our papers. Let's wait and see."

Gianni, listened aside. He hoped all was good. *I hate to act on Leonello's plans.*

If I deny his wishes or back out I know he will do me in. Oh man, I am doomed.

That night Gianni went to sleep interrupted by nightmares. Screaming, he woke up in a full of sweat, disoriented and walking in his room. His mother heard him and ran over to calm him down. These episodes had been happening often lately. Maria Salva was worried about what was going on with her son. Gianni's thoughts returned back to Leonello's plans. *God, help me. I must get away from those two, before I destroy my soul.* Since that horrible night, anxiety had overtaken him.

When Miss Robertson handed him his report, he quickly glanced at it up and down.

He couldn't believe his eyes. He looked up "Thank heaven I passed." He joyfully called out to his two friends. "Eh! Leonello, Romero." He placed an arm on each of their shoulders, while they were absorbing the results of their papers. "This calls for a celebration! Where to tonight? I am ready!"

Leonello slowly raised his eyebrows, a scary look on his face. "You scum bag!" he said, slapping him with full force with his back hand. The unexpected blow sent Gianni flying and he lost his balance.

"Leon, what's gotten into you?"

"What's gotten into me? The bitch sent me to repeat! My all summer is fucked up.

Look for yourself." He shoved the papers, rubbing it on his face and screeching like a lion.

"What about you Romero?" He remained silent.

"Show us. Don't tell me I am the only one." Screamed Leon.

"Here look for yourselves."

"Never mind tell us!"

"The same"

"What you mean the same. The same as who? There are three of us here?" Leon demanded.

"Both of us, Leon."

"Romero, I barely made it, but I passed." responded Gianni apologetically.

"Well good for you. That leaves me and Leon repeating, should we want to continue."

"I am so sorry, you guys."

"Don't be sorry, Gianni boy. From now on you will be the one to take the lead. We, buddy and I, plan and you execute." Leon looked at Gianni severely.

50

Chapter Nine

Gracy, went home emotionally disturbed. Her stomach churned at the idea of remanding her student. Dad had always preached about giving the students what they deserved. He had said that in the long run everyone would come out ahead. She knew deep down he was right. She thought of Diego and Daniele and had heard accounts of how their father was hard on them. They were both sent to the best school in Boston. He would threaten them should they not graduate with top honors. Andrew, her father, used to say to her, "Gracy, I never condoned their father's behaviour. Your stepbrothers are both brilliant. Diego, highly sought for his knowledge and Daniele's for his unique work." Gracy, was trying hard to convince herself about what had to be done with her students. *I am willing to give of myself in order for those fellows to gain full knowledge. I can't wait to talk to them. Leonello and Romero, will thank me in the long run.* Her reasoning was sound and reflected the way she had been brought up, and what she believed. Yes, knowledge is power.

Leonello, and Romero, didn't even go home that afternoon. They proceeded to go to the bar, drinking away until late evening. Gianni had gone home to bring the news to his mother. "Mom, you will be happy to know I have passed." He wasn't too proud to show his marks. His conscience was bothered by his barely making it. He had a plan for his future.

His mom used to preach to him. "Gianni, you need to learn more languages, especially French and English; move up to the North, mainland, France or England. There you might find work and have a future." People emigrated often for financial security, and he wanted too as well. He knew she was right. He could feel the poverty was crippling them. Growing up was hard in this era and on the island.

At the bar Leonello, consumed by alcohol asked "Romero! Where is that Gianni boy?"

"We are running a tab here; we better put it under his name. After all wasn't he bragging that he passed?" responded Romero also under the influence. Gianni didn't show up. He saw his mother's blistered hands and decided to give her a hand with feeding the few animals in the stall. Helping her with those chores gave him a chance to reflect on those guys. He didn't like their criminal behaviour. What they had done to Queeny that night bothered him. Leonello ruled, forcing him and Romero to do his bidding. *Eh,* he thought, *she was lucky Leonello changed his mind from what he originally had in store for her. She might not be alive today.* Reflecting on that, scared him. "I must stay away from both of them. Leonello is the worst one. As for Romero, Leonello's ideas don't bother him; he laughs about it."

When he mentioned how it bothered him-how he felt sorry for Queeny, Romero responded with "Grow up bud. It's all in good fun. You haven't seen nothing yet."

The next day, after the alcohol wore off, Leonello, went over to call Romero. He remembered; they were to talk to Queeny. They would listen to what she had in mind for now.

"Romero, that shmuck, fooled us last night. He never showed up. After the meeting with Queeny, we will go grab him from under his mother's skirt."

"I would say so. It's time we teach him to keep his word. He stood us up. Tonight, he must pay double. No tricks from or for him."

"Of course not. He is such a pup! He wouldn't know where to begin."

"Gianni doesn't know his ass from his whatever... he will have to watch us!"

"We need to find an old bag to teach him a few tricks."

***

They walked into the classroom where Gracy, was graciously waiting for them. She greeted them cordially, giving encouragement as she started on the subject matter.

First, she addressed Leonello because he had the worst mark. "I am so sorry for the final annual results of your class performance Leonello. It hurts me more than both of you probably. My greatest hope is to help my students thrive in the knowledge of what I am teaching. I thought I made myself clear before the exams papers were distributed."

She turned to Romero, "This goes for you too and Gianni also. I noticed your distraction in class. I blamed myself sometimes. As hard as I tried I didn't seem to succeed. My good intentions were to pass on to you the best knowledge. That is my teaching motto as you know. Apparently, it didn't work with you two, and some others as well." They were listening. She had captured their attention.

"I want you to know, Mr. Dario and myself, discussed your marks, your situation. We, together, tried to come to the best solution for both of you. Listen up. Teaching, for me, is a serious matter. It is a major concern for me that you have to repeat a year. Therefore, I will offer you my time to re-prepare you for your fall exam. I hope to tutor the both of you, three times a week, in my home. I promise, you will have my undivided attention. You, Leonello, need to apply your gifted intelligence that you are currently taking for granted. You, Romero, focus on what is assigned to you instead of looking for entertainment. That is how you shortchanged yourself. I am all yours- pick my brain. One rule will be implemented once you step in my house. The only language we speak is English."

They listened hard. They were both there in the moment. There was no goofing around, no distraction. Gracy felt good. *If I can save these two, mission accomplished. Thank you, God, Dad up there.*

They got up and shook hands. Leonello and Romero looked at her, hypnotized. "Thank you Miss Robertson. When do we start?" asked Leonello. He had no doubt Romero would follow suit.

"Next week, Tuesday, Thursday, Saturday. Two to four."

Romero said, "I will be there." They cordially left.

Romero couldn't wait to quiz Leonello. "Eh! What are we doing? Are we mellowing under her spell or are we going ahead with our original plan?"

"Leave it with me. Let's get a hold of that Gianni boy. I would like to twist his ears, for his absenteeism. We will go from there."

***

Gracy, couldn't wait to resume her role as teacher. She picked up the phone to inform Fabiana of her plan. Fabiana, didn't want to alarm her so she kept her opinion to herself.

"Gracy, you should inform Diego. Both your brothers, as you know, expect you to go to New York this summer. Once you are tutoring you will be committed. How are you going to manage that part?"

"Diego wants me in August. I will have to take one week off. They will understand."

Fabiana wasn't convinced but she decided not to insist and to let Diego handle the situation.

Gracy, checked the time difference, proceeded to call Diego. His secretary promptly connected her. "Gracy! I was just about to call you. How are you doing? School is out. Are you bored yet?"

"Diego I am never bored- lonely, yes. This is why I am calling. I decided to tutor a couple of students this summer for fall admission."

"Gracy, who are these students? Have you had them checked out? I admire your dedication, but you need to be careful. Daniele and I can't wait for you to get here.

We need you with us. With the inauguration of the new hotel, plus everything else going on, please don't shortchange us."

"Diego, I understand. I have decided I will come for a week in August. These two students need me badly, otherwise they will lose the year."

"Lovey! Please, can you get someone else to teach them? We are counting on you to be here beforehand to oversee some of the activity. The inauguration wouldn't be the same without you."

"I am sure the top decorators you guys have in the U.S. will do a fabulous job."

"Gracy, I am serious, Daniele was counting on your supervision in that department."

"What about Ingrid? She is the decorator for the company."

"Lovey, don't mention Ingrid right now. She is causing Daniele a lot of grief lately.

I wouldn't be surprised if they part soon. "

"You had mentioned the war zone. I thought it had passed."

"Apparently not. Our Daniele needs both of us. He is struggling under strain. Sis, Giorgina will book your flight. *Va Bene?* All good."

"No, Diego I cannot back out from this commitment. Sorry, I will be there in August, I promise."

Diego wasn't happy. He had to oblige to her wishes, knowing how dedicated she was.

The following week, at two o'clock, Leonello and Romero, were promptly at her door.

She noticed, Leonello was shaven and sported a neat army haircut. He could pass for a decent young man. Romero was not as groomed, but he was half decent. She wondered about Gianni Cecco, thinking: *If these guys are going to benefit from my teaching, I should have remanded him also. He would have improved his knowledge and marks.*

A week went by and they were responding well. The aloofness in Leonello's face had changed to interest. Gracy, couldn't wait for the next class. She challenged them more and deeper every day. From grammar to past tense, to the comparison of shorter sentences from Italian to English, both students were learning.

This Saturday night, the boys were going to la Gondola for a fun evening. There they met the Fleece, the girl of last month, looking for tricks. Gianni boy, walked in, moving slowly toward them. Romero, nudged Leonello, "Look who is walking in from the dead. He has been hiding, ignoring us for the past month."

Leonello ignored him. The minute, Gianni got near, He grabbed his lapels and shook him up.

"You are not part of us anymore. You stood us up, remember? You thought you were better than us that night because you passed, and we didn't. Get out of our sight, before I smash your face."

"Sorry, Leon, it wasn't that. I was scared."

"Scared to come and celebrate your promotion?" He shoved him away.

"No, not that at all! I panicked for what you were going to do to Miss Robertson. You wanted me to buy the gasoline, remain outside. Once you and Romero had finished having your way with her, you wanted me to ignite her place on fire."

The local call girl, usually eyeing for costumers, spotted them. She quickly bounced her way toward them, "Leon, introduce me to your friend?" Leon ignored her; his grin was not friendly.

"Calm down what's going on? I have no problem performing three tricks. Introduce me to your new buddy."

"You don't want to meet him. He still has wax under his ears." responded Leon.

They all broke into a big laugh. Romero added. "Go back and hide where you came from,

Gianni. We are doing just fine without you. We don't need you anymore."

Gianni shoulders drooped. He put his head down and walked away before they could see him in tears. His staggering footsteps took him home like a beaten puppy dog. Maria Salva called out. "Is that you Gianni? I am in bed. My body ached so much tonight. If you want something to eat, you will have to help yourself, dear."

"No mom, I am not hungry." He went straight to his bedroom and threw himself on the bed, his sorrowful emotions tearing his heart to pieces. After hours of tossing and turning his body finally gave into sleep. The replay with his friends soon followed with nightmares. Screaming he pulled the covers off, rolled on the floor, trying to orientate himself. Nothing seemed clear. The sweat was dripping off his body as he looked around lost in the darkness. His mother was banging on the door, calling out frantically. "Gianni! Gianni! What's going on? Please open the door." He was stunned. *Where am I?* Slowly he realized, *I am dreaming.* He finally managed to open the door at his mom's pleading. The terrifying event was still vivid in his eyes, but he found refuge in his mother's arms, blurting out in tears.

"Mom, Mom, I am scared, I am really scared and hurt."

Maria Salva became more alarmed. *Dear God, what has happened to my son?* "Gianni, please, come here, dear." She hugged him affectionately "Let's put the light on and talk to me. Tell me what's bothering you, lately. I have noticed you haven't been yourself, dear."

"Mom, my so-called friends have rejected me. But what has been troubling me the most is the plan Leonello has dictated for Miss Robertson. 'Who can I talk to?' Should I go confess to the *carabinieri* or the priest? But I will be arrested also, as an accomplice. The stunt Leonello made us pull to amuse himself was against my will. But I had to, otherwise he was going to have Romero beat me. Now I heard that they go there for their afternoon classes; it is absurd! They will hurt her Mom! I cannot repeat what he has planned. I must intervene. I don't know where to start."

"Dear, dear, I am here to listen. We will find a way. With God's will, whatever it is, we will solve it together Gianni. You cannot live in fear like that. If Miss Robertson is in danger, we have to find a way to stop them."

"Mom that is what I had planned to do; talk to them and stop them. Last night they made fun of me and told me to get lost. They had this girl with them, and you don't want to know what kind of a girl. Mom they are up to no good."

She held him tenderly "Gianni, my dear son, don't you worry. Mom will pray for them, "

"Mom, always with your prayers. They make fun of you, and it's humiliating."

She kept rubbing his head, "Gianni, I believe in my prayers. Son of mine, you should be glad they don't want you in their company. Bad deeds, corrupted behaviour, they belong to Satan. You are spared."

"Mom, I had planned to talk them out of it. Now I can't. How can I report their intentions to the authorities?"

Chapter Ten

Leonello and Romero, had been faithfully attending their afternoon sessions of English classes. Gracy's enthusiastic teaching was extremely effective with them. They seemed to follow her well. She would challenge them, in remarkable conversations, using refined words. The assignments given to them were delivered back completely and appropriately as she had requested. Gracy was puzzled. *Leonello's demeanour seems to have changed. Romero will follow suit. Does the change of atmosphere, not being in a classroom with thirty some students, or the seriousness of losing a year credit make a difference? It was time to buckle up with no goofing around.* Beside the teaching results, she couldn't help noticing that their personal grooming had also improved. Both of them had re-claimed a personal polish that had been missing in class. They had been in the habit of dressing and clowning in a slovenly way. Gracy felt a pang of remorse for their friend Gianni who had been promoted without a comprehensive understanding of English. It was best to leave well enough alone since Diego didn't agree fully with having these students in her home. They hadn't received any information in resolving the incident that had taken place few months prior, so he was still concerned, as was she.

Gracy, on this Saturday morning, decided to treat herself with a trip to the open mercato, the market, for fresh local fruit. There, while paying for the big green grapes, she felt a hand on her shoulder. Someone was leaning to speak to her. She turned to find Mr. Rondelli beside her. "Mr. Rondelli! How are you? You like this place also I see!" She looked at his purchases.

"Miss Robertson, how are you? Enjoying the holidays?"

"Yes! The days, fly by fast keeping me busy. What about you? Is your family here yet?"

"No! Not yet. We will settle before the fall, I am sure. We are still looking for a suitable place, preferably not far from the university."

"You will find it! Are you busy teaching summer courses?"

"Yes I am. As matter of fact, I have several classes. My students keep me busy."

"I am also." She smiled.

"I haven't seen you around at the university." He asked puzzled, "What classes are you teaching? Mornings or afternoon?"

"You haven't seen me because I have only two students- Leonello and Romero.

I decided to teach them privately in my home. Three times a week from two to four."

He was totally taken aback. "Miss. Robertson, are you serious? Those guys we doubted?" he asked, holding back further comments. Gracy sensing his hesitation, commented, "They are learning, and I am enjoying teaching them." He didn't respond; his eyebrows narrowed. She continued: "Yes, I am taking a chance hoping to mold them. I must say my brother is not in agreement with me. He thinks I am crazy. Believe it or not, I had my doubts." Smiling, she continued trying to convince him, but more herself. "So far so good! Both of them are participating in my sessions well. Leonello, especially, has turned into a sponge absorbing all the knowledge he can."

"I am glad, Miss Robertson. It's been nice seeing you. *Buona giornata.* Good day" He extended his hand to say goodbye. Much disturbed, he scratched his head, while his stomach churned. *I should have warned her.* The flashback replayed in his mind. The night after the exams terminated, he was walking home. A girl approached him when he had almost reached his place. She quietly started talking to him, put an arm under his, and pulled him around the corner. He was confused but didn't want to be rude, thinking that she could have been a student from the university needing help of sort. Before he had a chance to figure anything out, suddenly two, hoodlums jumped on him. They were wearing hoods and masks. One put an arm around his neck pressing his Adam's apple, practically stopping his breathing. The other held a knife to his belly. The girl spoke gently. "Professor Rondelli, you have two students in your class Leonello Dante, and Romero Placido. If you know what is good for you," the arm tightened around his throat and the knife jammed piercing his skin. "You will do as you are told. You will give them a good passing mark. Do you understand?" Another squeeze, the girl continued ordering. "Now, should you reveal tonight's episode to anyone you will find yourself at the bottom of the Mediterranean Sea." They let go and disappeared, leaving him struggling to catch his breath and shaking like a leaf. He made it back to his room at his *pensiona.*

The university had requested a contract for one year, with two more consecutive. The island of Sicily was considered by the people of the mainland to be a piece of heaven dropped in the Mediterranean Sea. The people he had met were kind, cordial, and respectful. He had always desired to relocate to this spectacular place. The climate was mild, and Agrigento, famous for its history and the Valley of the Temples, was a touristic paradise. Not to mention, there was Taormina, Messina, and Cefalu'. This episode had shocked the hell out of him that night and it had left him fearful and doubtful about the contract. For a couple of weeks his shaken body had remained in a traumatic state. He wasn't sure if the two attackers were his students or hired killers. The girl, he had never seen before. She had uttered the orders. *Maybe the girl was forced into her actions,* he thought. *She looked sweet and innocent when first approaching him.* He wouldn't dare reveal the attack to anyone. He had been in denial. Now this day, it had all replayed back. A new fear zipped through his brain down to his spine. Gracy Robertson! *Would those two delinquents pull something on her? She is certainly vulnerable.*

Chapter Eleven

While Professor Rondelli tormented himself, Gracy was happily conducting her teaching with the two individuals challenging them to the fullest. "Today we will study our verbs. Pay attention to our discussions. Our next lesson will be essay writing. One will be in first and another in second person, in present and past tense, singular and plural. Then I want to hear translations from Italian to English in shorter form, polished. The classes she conducted were like a game at play. The guys were enthusiastic, enjoying the teaching and learning at the same time. Gracy, talked to them and taught them in the style of learning they needed.

A month had gone by, and everything was proceeding well at the Valley of the Temples on the outskirts of Agrigento. Diego, was faithfully checking on his sister, calling often. The surveillance officer had no disturbances to report. The people who were troubled were Gianni and Mr. Rondelli. Each of them had their own secret debate at the core of their soul. Maria Salva had promised her son to pray for those two. However, Gianni didn't believe in his mother's prayers, so, he felt lonely and abandoned in his misery. He stayed away from those individuals. He knew Leonello, would have fun cracking his jokes. Romero would be going along, following orders and laughing.

Professor Rondelli was busy with his repeating students. It was serious now because October exams would be their crucial chance for the year. When he got back to his pensiona at night, he walked the floor, talking to himself. 'I am not so sure if I should move my family to Agrigento yet.'

While Gracy' felt gratified, she had no more doubt in her mind. Her decision had been right. Teaching Leonello and Romero was rewarding. They were responding well, eagerly learning.

They had lost the aloofness they displayed in class with the other students. With the next assignment, she was going to test their understanding and mindset with a selected subject.

"Ok! Fellows, for next week, let's write an assay of five hundred words or more.

The subject will be titled Revelations of My Inner Feelings. I will give you some inspirational ideas. Describe your earnings, your goals, your desires, the positivity in your life, obstacles and how you overcome them with courage, fear, determination. Happiness."

They looked at each other, then both turned toward her. Leonello spoke, ''Miss Robertson, are you serious?"

"Yes, do you find something wrong with that title?"

"Does it have to be truthful, or can it be fictional or dishonest?"

Gracy looked at both of them seriously: "I prefer you search deep in your soul. Then, write down what you feel, what you seek or wish life would offer you."

Leonello jokingly shook his head, stretched his legs like he used to do in the classroom and stated. "Miss Robertson, you don't want to know what my inner soul desires."

"Write it down; we shall hear it. By the way, I prefer that each of you recite it. We will pretend that you will be the actor on the stage and me the audience. I am getting excited already and looking forward to it."

Romero asked, "Will the mark count for our exam?"

"It will be taken in consideration. As you know, it's the exam itself that counts. Not to worry though. Try your best."

The two fellows left somewhat confused. Gracy thought. *I am glad I have given them something to think about that pushes them to search deep into their inner soul.* She had no doubt in her mind they would deliver the best. The squeal of the telephone resonated in the room diverting her attention. It was none other than Diego. "Gracy, how are you doing sis? Just checking on you."

"Great! How are you? Tell me what's going on there. How is Daniele?"

"All is well with me. As for Daniele, I am not sure. One day he is fine; another, his morale is down. You know Ingrid has been threatening to leave and sue."

"Diego, I don't understand. I thought she loved him."

"I guess her love had hidden motives. I didn't call to talk about Ingrid. My secretary has you booked for the 14th of August. You will arrive here; the next day we will fly together to Vegas. Giorgina will send you the details."

"I will have to make some arrangement for my two students. You know I must get back as soon as I can. They have exams I am committed to them."

"Gracy, why you choose to make life hard for yourself? You didn't have to tie yourself up. Daniele and I prefer to have you here with us. You promised the summer months."

"Okay, fine. This will be over soon. Okay!"

"Take care of yourself. Love you sis. Call you tomorrow night."

She knew they were right. For some strange reason, a power stronger than her forced the need to tutor those guys. So far, she felt rewarded and likewise they seemed happier. *They don't know all my teaching methods come from my dad. Yes, that's how he taught me, tutoring one on one. Maybe Leonello didn't like being in a classroom. He was restless...*

instigating others, disturbing my class. Gracy tried to justify the young guy's behaviour.

***

Leonello, that night at home, alone was doing his own soul searching. He had refused to go to the bar tonight when Romero called. That was unusual for him. There after few beers, his dulled brain was spontaneously irrational. Tonight, surprising himself, he seriously chose to be alone, muttering to himself 'I need to compose that assignment'. The house was quiet for change. There was some feast in town and all the family had gone to the piazza. He rejoiced in the privacy. *A luxury I don't have too often.* He slammed the door to his so-called bedroom shut after he climbed the wooden ladder stairs to the attic. As dingy as it was here, he found refuge from the relentless bickering of the household. He grabbed the folder with lined paper, pencil and eraser. He preferred to write in pencil with the anticipation of lot of erasing. The wobbly table with an old beat-up chair was his working station. A grimy window opened up to the roof. The moon was glowing favorably adding to the dim lighting. This place had been fine as a young boy. At eighteen, his body had surpassed the height of the ceiling. It wasn't pleasant to crawl around with the ceiling bearing down on him, but hell would break loose should he complain. His father would slap and kick him around, barking out of control. "It's time you guys get out into the world and earn a living with your own sweat."

"Dad, where can we go to earn some money? There are no jobs available."

There was no reasoning with him. In his violent rage, he would take it out on all the family. His mother often had to cover her face, a scarf pulled over her forehead and eyes, to hide her bruises. The emotional aversion he felt for his father worsened especially when he watched him drown himself in alcohol. Leonello knew the aftermath well. When he was younger, his body shivered in fear. As he got older, in retaliation, he had bashed his father a few times.

He begged his mother to leave. "Mom, why are you staying with him? He needs to be locked up and the keys thrown away. You need to press charges." No one listened. They continued living in terror. His father was in and out jail. The violence continued unpredictably.

His mother loved the family. She was concerned about her sons. Often, she would take Leonello aside to advise, "Leonello, you are young. Seek immigration. You must go north to the mainland or abroad; plan your future. There is no hope here. We are dirt poor"

"Mom where can I go without a trade or an education? No one wants me or my brother."

Leonello, hated his household; the inferno was relentless. The frustration was such that he saw himself turning out like his father. He was now in his teens, starting to admire the girls. His broken soul needed help. As much as he detested his father's behaviour, it also scared him. He realized its effect was hindering him and his relationships.

"Miss Robertson, and her father the professor, what a difference!" he muttered to himself holding his head in his hands. *All the students talked about them. They were unique in every respect. She has been grieving badly for his loss. Would I be grieving for my father? He is a terror?* "Someone help me." he cried in despair. He put his head down and let the tears spill freely. *I planned to destroy her because of my feelings of resentment and yes, jealousy. Now she has taken us into her home, tutored us from the kindness of her heart. My father has nicknamed me guastic, stinking trash. I don't think she considers me stinking trash.* A boost of energy spurred him to action. Much animated, he grabbed a pen and his thoughts started to flow on the paper. "I don't have to search deep into my heart to know my thoughts because they are right in front of me. I want to make Miss. Robertson proud."

68

Chapter Twelve

Leonello, began his assignment by simply putting down exactly how he felt.

Revelations of My Inner Feelings

I live in a chaotic household. At night when my body finally reaches my cot, stretched on a mattress filled with corn stock pressing on my skin, I toss and turn trying to find comfort. I plead to the universe to turn this miserable life of mine into calmness with some stellar serenity. I also murmur quietly to some God, if He exists, to turn this anger accumulating in my soul into kindness. This individual needs help, I plead. I know I would have gotten a good beating from my father had he known I would lose the year. My mother wouldn't stop crying. My older siblings would ridicule me, putting me down. *Guasticci,* stinking trash, suits you well they said. I want to bash them all in my misery. No way my parents would or could pay for this tuition. Maybe, I am beginning to think, some source up there cares for me and also my friend Romero. He isn't much better off than I am. Here we have Miss. Robertson, offering her home, free tutoring. The pleasure of her well-mannered teaching and company privately- all to ourselves. I can't wait to get there. I miss our sessions on the off days.

I feel good when I am there and can't wait for Miss Robertson to start speaking. She is dedicated, trying all avenues to open our minds to observe and retain. I say to myself. "I must learn. I want to learn." Shame on me for my distorted mind playing tricks on me in and out of that classroom. I know I resented everyone around because they looked down at me. The guilt has been agonizing my being since I started this class. I lay awake at night tossing, in remorse. I say to myself 'Yes, guasticci, the absurd nick name my father and siblings call me, you well deserve the affliction.' My feelings are changing, with Miss Robertson's influence. I will try in earnest to be a better person. '

***

He woke up the next morning with Romero whistling outside his home. The bickering and fighting among his siblings were deepening. He stepped in the kitchen ignoring them all and rushed out to talk to his friend. The paper was well tucked in his folder like a treasure under his arm. He slapped his friend on his shoulder with a smiling grin on his face. "Romero, have you done your assignment?"

"Assignment! It doesn't have to be presented until tomorrow afternoon; what's the rush?"

He looked at him, raising his eyebrows. "Leonello, am I imagining things or is the Lion turning into a lamb?"

"What do you mean?"

"I see you mellowing, turning into a scholar, paying attention, to Miss Robertson."

He grabbed him by the shoulders, turned to face him, and looked straig*ht into his eyes* "Eh! I am no fool! Have you still got the hots for our *professoressa?* Tell me the truth?"

Leonello didn't respond. *I mustn't lose face.*

"Have you forgotten who the one who was ordering us around. What you had planned for her? Did you change your mind? You kicked Gianni Boy out because he didn't follow suit?"

Leonello brought a hand on his forehead. "Yes, you are right. We can be in deep trouble for the mischief we created a while back if the authorities get wind of it. I have been asking myself how I ever could

70

have ordered others to hurt her. Her benevolence for us and for our future is truly coming from her heart."

"Then I am not wrong. You have had a change of heart?"

"I would say so. This essay she has given us, it's a real clever one. She is digging in our souls. The clever *professoressa* is working on her students without us realizing it. Last night writing my essay I discovered what triggers my horrendous behaviour."

Romero listened attentively thinking: *Is this the Lion, talking?* "Then it's all good you're turning into an intellect on the merits of full participation."

"Romero, go, work on your essay, seriously, and see what you come up with. I am ashamed of some the goings on in my household and family. Maybe this is why I want to destroy the world around me most of the time."

"My friend, my household isn't much better. Miss Robertson has the world at her feet.

She's rich, educated; she has panache and is beautiful with her provoking sex appeal to top it all."

"I will not contest that for sure. She has it all."

While the friends were having their early morning discussion, with good intentions Gianni and Professor Rondelli, were troubled in their decision of what to do. Gianni feared immensely for Miss Robertson and the possibility of her being hurt. The professor feared that the goons who had attacked him wouldn't relent on taking the next action for their amusement.

By mid-afternoon, Leonello and Romero, to Miss Robertson's delight, were proudly reading their essays to their benevolent teacher who was giving them all the attention they needed.

"Leonello, great writing. If it all came from the depth of your soul, it's all good."

She smiled at him, understanding him more and more. Romero's assignment wasn't as insightful as Leonello's, but it was interesting as well. There is good in everyone, she thought, and she praised and encouraged them. She was so elated with joy that she went over to Leonello. She placed her hand on his head and ruffled up his hair. "I told you, you could do it. This mark will be taken in consideration for your fall exams." She turned to Romero, and said "Yours too, Romero. Well written and I am proud, both of you."

When Gracy, went to bed that night she lay awake planning the next assignment. She searched back to some of her difficult past lessons. *Of course, Dad was always there with his clever quizzing to turn me around.* The classes continued and before Gracy realized it, August had soon approached. It was time to fly to New York. She was duty bound to the two dear people in her life- Diego and Daniele.

Diego had called her intermittently filling her in on their plans and what to expect with her role in the family business that they wanted to share with her. Gracy had planned to leave her students enough work during her absence to keep them learning and out of mischief. In First Class, the flight from Rome to New York was a breeze. When she arrived at JFK Airport the two of them were waiting for their precious Gracy. "Sis, you have one day rest and then on we go to Vegas," announced Diego, in his fatherly protectiveness. She was all smiles between the two. Daniele put an arm around her in the limo whispering in her ear. "Would you consider staying one night at my place instead of the penthouse Diego has reserved for you at the hotel?"

"Daniele, we will work on it. I want to be fair and spend some time with you and Ingrid also. Don't worry."

"You can go shopping in Manhattan. Ingrid knows the best boutiques. Eh! Maybe you can buy a new wardrobe you might want to take back to Sicily."

"Can't wait; I would love too."

The glorious time with her loving brothers was just beginning.

The next morning the phone rang and Gracy playfully answered expecting Diego to check on her, but, to her surprise the female voice greeting her was Ingrid's. "Hello, Gracy, welcome to NY. How are you? Daniele tells me you and I are going on a shopping spree."

"Oh! That brother of mine won't let me rest. Thanks Ingrid, I would prefer this afternoon, if we could. The time change has thrown my body clock off."

"I guess; call me when you are ready to be picked up" she answered curtly.

The annoyance in her voice, resonated in Gracy's ears, *Maybe Daniele has made her feel obligated which he shouldn't have done, but I am not going to dwell on it.* She pulled the covers over her shoulders, grabbed the soft pillow beside her and cuddled to comfort her body for a badly needed rest.

The shopping spree had no restrictions. There was an open account ready for her at the most exclusive boutiques in Manhattan with only one-of-a-kind designs offered to the special sister of the Frarano brothers. Diego, and Daniele, had both made recommendations, in order to offer their precious sister only the top of the line. After all, she was to be their trophy of admiration at the grand opening of the new hotel in Vegas. They admired her and were ever so proud of their half-sister. Although Gracy was humble and modest, she went along to please them; however, the aura surrounding Ingrid didn't feel comfortable. The underlying resentment and curtness was manifested in Ingrid's annoyed voice. She told Gracy "Yes, this shopping spree is a job ordered to me for your service."

"Oh! Ingrid I was considering our shopping a fun thing for two girls to do as loving friends."

"Sorry, Gracy. You should talk to your brother. I am not just an employee anymore. I live with him. I have my rights. He chooses to have me play which ever role suits him, whenever he wants."

Ingrid had moved to New York from Washington with the qualifications that the company required. She was to oversee the decorating of the suites. As time passed, she was promoted to be Daniele's assistant also. Their relationship had gone beyond business to personal. Now she had demands that he wished to ignore. Ingrid was causing him grief which he wished would go away.

"The chaperoning and company was ordered to you by those two?" asked Gracy.

"Yes! Daniele said that I must do this and I must do that because his sister is coming. He is the boss and I am the slave. You are to be the star for the opening beside them. I have work to complete the work at the Marquis, but I am not invited. He sure looks for me when I have to serve his other needs, especially in bed."

Gracy, scratched her head. Ingrid sounded beyond irritated. *I don't like it. No, I don't understand their relationship because I have not been in any relationship. Dad always warned me not to give myself away. Respect yourself Gracy! He used to say. Too bad Ingrid is angry. It shows her hatred not her love.*

Chapter Thirteen

The preparations were all in order when they arrived at the Grand Hotel in Vegas. Indeed, the imposing structure was an eye opener for everyone to admire. All the dignitaries were there. The news media were enthusiastically praising Diego and Daniele, especially Daniele, for his extraordinary creativity. The brothers proudly introduced their sister from Italy to everyone they could. She was overjoyed to be with the two best people in her life. Ribbons were cut and the mingling crowd moved indoors to the fabulous reception room of the grandiose hotel. Alvaro Fernandez stood a short distance from them while the ceremony carried on. He had been hired by Daniele to run the new place. He was reserved in his demeanour, not wanting to infringe on the three main people who deserved the recognition. His eyes had been fixated on the stunning girl between them, whom he had heard to be their half-sister. He would wait his turn to be introduced. As he stood waiting, Diego waved him over with a big smile. The new CEO, politely approached, extending his hand in congratulations to both brothers. Gracy, smiling, stood aside. Daniele, put an arm around her shoulders, "Gracy, I want you to meet our CEO, Alvaro Fernandez, from Washington. He came highly recommended to us to make this place a great success."

"Nice to meet you Mr. Fernandez. Congratulations."

"The pleasure is mine, Miss. Robertson and thank-you." His heart drubbed at the touch of her hand. It was attraction and desire at first sight. *Am I dreaming? A poor hombre like me, an immigrant from Spain, she will never...* Diego broke the spell and invited him to join them at the table where a late breakfast was ready to be served.

"Let's go my friend, please. Our reserved table is waiting for us."

The sound of Alvaro's voice resonated in Gracy's ears. His expressions were profound and loving in the kindness and respect he showed toward her brothers and herself. Little did Alvaro know the same spark that had ignited in his heart had done the same in Gracy's heart. Gracy didn't dare let anyone know. She was shocked at her awakening interest. She couldn't wait to be alone to concentrate on her feelings. Later, she envisioned his gentle smile, his big dark eyes that were darting in admiration. *Alvaro's demeanour expressed kindness with deep emotions from his soul. I am impressed.*

After the big inaugural day, they decided to fly back to New York the next afternoon.

Gracy, wanted to ask about Alvaro's plan, cautious in not wanting to give herself away. Diego astutely detected that his sister was in no rush to be leaving. He asked. "Eh! Sis, you like Vegas don't you?"

"It's seems like a fun city. There is a lot to see, a lot to do. Yes, it's interesting. I wouldn't mind spending some more time here."

"What's your impression of our new CEO? A Spanish fellow, single, great credentials, hard worker I am told. He sure needs to bring this place to success.

We have lot of money tied into this project. Failure is unacceptable, my father used to say. He was a dictator but he was right"

She walked close to him, smiling "Diego! You and Daniele are gentlemen, not dictators. You both surround yourselves with the right people."

"I don't know about that; sometimes I have my doubts. I don't believe in implementing harsh treatments. You have to treat people with respect. Remember there is good in everyone. Once you concentrate on their special qualities, you will be rewarded with such."

"Diego, you are so right. This is why I look up to you. You sound like my father. He used to say that also!"

"Aunt Fabiana told me that your dad couldn't understand why it was so difficult for my mom, the martyr, to leave my dad. A Sicilian girl, doesn't not walk away from her marriage, no matter how bad the situation."

"I see, old school belief and religious indoctrination. My dad was brought up in London so he didn't practise Catholicism until I was born. You can't really blame him for not understanding."

"Gracy, let's forget the horrible past between our fathers. The best result, we have you. Daniele and I feel blessed." He kissed her on her forehead.

"Diego, you mentioned Daniele," She let out a deep breath to continue. "Tell me, why is Ingrid so angry at him. It bothers me that Daniele needs to appease her constantly."

"Gracy, that's another matter. From my understanding there is more to the situation that meets the eye. I need to take it up with my brother before it gets out of hand." he responded. His creased forehead showed his concern.

78

Chapter Fourteen

While Gracy's glorious journey in New York was pleasurable, these days her mind had been totally taken with the fast life of the city and her two loved ones. The place across the ocean- her home, Agrigento, her students, the patients at the hospital had been placed in a far corner in her mind. Once she was with her brothers, she lived to fulfill their wants and needs, never minding or complaining on her part.

****

Little could Gracy imagine what was taking place in Agrigento. Gianni Cecco had become a nervous wreck. He was totally unaware of her absence. The tormented young fellow couldn't sleep at night worrying about his two mischievous friends and of what he knew they had planned for Miss. Robertson. In his despair he had confided to his mother. She had become even more fearfully stressed than her son. Relentlessly, she insisted that he go to the caserma, the police station, to report them and confess. "Mom, they will kill me."

He repeatedly voiced, "I am in deep trouble." In her honest belief, she kept begging him to do as she asked. As a next step, she called Father Alfonso the priest of their church for help and to talk to her son. "Dear Lord" the priest exclaimed looking up to heaven. "You must, son! Report this as soon as possible. We are talking about a good soul's life to save here; something disastrous could take place. Do you realize that?" His hand continued to make the sign of the cross. Gianni was panicking even more; his body shook as if a live wire had zipped through him. He had stayed away from both of his friends, avoiding them at all cost because Leonello would order Romero to beat him up and he would execute it without mercy. Lately, due the priest's urgent advice, his panic had escalated; therefore, he had resorted to discreetly spying on them. Late at night he had spotted them with the floozies in town. Leonello's voice replayed in his ears, "She likes to turn tricks at *ore B* in the late hours". Since the night of the beating he had stayed away from them. Now that he was convinced to save Miss Robertson, over the last few nights he was taking a big chance stepping out. He walked crouched down like a scared rabbit. *God! Please, don't let me be seen by those two. That girl is just as bad. No, I cannot continue living in fear.* The acidity was churning in his stomach.

After much convincing, Gianni accompanied by his mother and the priest walked to the police station. Romulo Giordano was assigned to the report. He invited them to sit in a small private room. "Please sit down," he gestured to them. He had a pen and paper, ready to take down notes. The priest politely spoke. "We have this young man here; he has suffered silently under the influence and actions of a couple of bullies. Gianni Cecco here, and his mom sought my help. I am here on their behalf to see if we can ratify things and stop further incidents that might take place by these individuals."

"Thanks, Father; we are always grateful for any help in criminal activity. I must stress, the cooperation of our citizens, makes our job easier to solve and stop crime."

"Signor Carabiniere, in this situation I must ask you. Will our young man here be pardoned or given some grace in recognition for his report and confession? He will tell you that he was forced to participate. Plus, I can assure you that the situation and the actions of these individuals have caused him much pain and suffering." They all looked at each other, Gianni and his mother especially, hoping for relief and not more trouble. The officer saw Maria Salva holding her beads, a plea for mercy in her eyes. He looked at Gianni who had fear and agony manifested in his

eyes. He felt sympathy for the mother and the young man. He gently spoke, addressing Father first.

"I am sure my superior will admire your decision to come here. I will take down the information; it will be presented to him and his committee. The final decision will be up to them, in accordance with the law."

The priest turned to Gianni with an encouraging smile. "Gianni, go ahead relate to the officer your episode and the future plans that were put in place."

"Please go ahead. I am ready." The police officer, Romulo Giordano, methodically took down all the information. Sure enough, here was the light needed to shine on the Miss Robertson's incident and its resolution. The police investigation and private surveillance assigned to la questura by Diego Frarano from New York and Anthony Taverna from Palermo was still on going. It was a big advantage for the police to have such information. Romulo Giordano couldn't wait to present what he had learned to his senior *Marescialle*, the chief of police.

Gianni and his mom, with the blessing of the priest and police, returned home. But his heart, was beating hard not knowing what would take place next. His mother kept a watch on him now even more, fearing those thugs would get to him and hurt her son.

Gianni didn't know his two friends were now indulging in their new pastime. Marmellata the jam, was teaching them the pleasure of their sexuality. Yes, that's what they called the floozy, *Marmellata...* the jam. She was older than them, not Sicilian. She had settled in Agrigento, after visiting the island several times and falling in love with the area. Leonello and Romero surprisingly were influenced by her. The two vagabonds, late evening, would experiment with their sexual kicks. *Marmellata,* much experienced in her art, would manipulate them and they obliged. Romero, was simply taking it all in as teenaged hormonal satisfaction. Leonello instead, had other fantasies in his mind. Deep down in his heart an attraction for Miss Robertson had worked its way more and more lately. He had found himself daydreaming about her. The desire to have his way with her would make his body shiver in cold sweat. When he categorized the obstacles from every direction, it made him both sad and nasty. The false pretense of macho bravado was what it was- a cover up of failure and insecurities. Since afternoon classes had started with the English *professoressa*, it had awakened both happiness and sadness in him. He couldn't admit to Romero his weakness or the suffering. *Oh! How I miss the beautiful English girl.* His soul was tormented; his eyes shed cold tears when he was alone. His thoughts were disheartening. *Not even in your wildest dreams, buddy, do you have a chance. I can't wait for her return. If nothing else, at least I get to see her instead of just longing for her only in my fantasies.* Leonello's secret couldn't not be unveiled. He would be ridiculed by his family to no end. Romero also, should never know. Leonello was eighteen and had a mad crush on his first true love one sided.

Chapter Fifteen

In New York, Gracy's departure had approached faster than they all wanted. Diego had made a special request. It was their last evening. He felt it was his duty to organize a private dinner for the three of them. He called Daniele in the afternoon,

"Bro, we have run out of time with so much going on. Tomorrow night Gracy is leaving. We need to have a good talk with her, just the two of us." What he meant was please don't bring Ingrid along. He didn't say it, hoping his brother would understand. "We will meet at seven tonight at the penthouse of the Riverside Hotel."

"Why at the hotel and not a restaurant."

"Daniele, we want total privacy. This is why I prefer the penthouse. We will order room service. If you agree with me, you and I have some serious convincing to do without interruptions."

"I see what you mean. Ingrid won't like me leaving her out."

"Daniele, this is a private family affair. Anyone other than you and me is not part of our decisions. *Capisci?*"

"I understand. You are the attorney and know about the ins and outs of legality. Ingrid won't like it! She is going to throw another tantrum."

"Daniele, as much as I want to sympathize with you, that is your problem and we can discuss it later. However, as you know, certain family affairs have to be kept private."

Daniele knew that his brother was right. He swallowed hard. "Diego, I can't wait for us to be together."

The penthouse with VIP service had been assigned for Gracy's stay while in New York. She loved the accommodations. Diego only wanted to provide the best for her. The champagne was chilling; a sumptuous meal had been delivered. Here it was their last evening. Gracy had dressed for her brothers and cheerfully embraced them as they arrived. She tried hard to hide the sorrow layering her heart. The time had flown by so fast. Diego opened the champagne bottle and handed them the stem glasses.

He addressed Gracy. "Gracy, our dear sister, we shall drink to your health and happiness.

I am speaking for myself and Daniele. Our wish for you is that you will return to us, for a permanent stay. We want you with us. I cannot stress enough, the joy and fulfillment in our hearts will only be complete when our beloved sister lives close to us."

"Diego, you bring tears to my eyes. I feel so loved by both of you. Do I really deserve this depth of affection?"

"Eh! I am getting on, Sis, don't kid yourself. We need you. You are the only real blood we have. Although you have a different father, you are the spitting image of Mom. The blood flowing in your veins is Sicilian. It is no matter you were born in England."

"Now, Daniele it is your turn." he hinted to his brother. Daniele was less of a speaker and more on the shy side, but, he adored his family. "Yes, Daniele, let me hear your voice. By the way where is Ingrid tonight?" asked Gracy. Before he could answer Diego cut in, "It's our last night together. I preferred that it would be just the three of us."

"Oh! Diego she won't like that. She will resent me for stealing Daniele away from her."

"No. She has no right. Certain family matters are private, Daniele, has something serious to tell you that concerns only the three of us." He addressed her making a clear gesture like he was speaking in court to a judge or jury, making his point in a court case. Rolling her eyes, she walked over to Daniele and kissed him on the cheek. She smiled, darting her eyes between both of them. "We are having fun," she whispered into Daniele's ear.

"Diego likes the role of father figure…our protector. Aren't we lucky?"

"He knows all the rules of the law." answered Daniele.

The lavish dinner was consumed. Relaxed and satisfied, Daniele was ready to present their intentions and revelations to Gracy. Diego's goal, more than anything, was convincing her to stay. Daniele, spoke first. "Sis, the new hotel in Vegas, it's titled under your name. We took the liberty to do that because we want you to have ownership of some of the assets here in the USA. Diego and I own six major hotels in New York. They are doing well with the exception of one. We have consulted with a major analyst from Washington; our plans are to resolve the problem soon." He looked at Diego. "OK. Now, Diego you continue."

"Gracy, listen hard. We cannot keep worrying about you being in Agrigento alone, Daniele has a girlfriend tormenting him and who knows when he will give in and marry her and have a family of his own? This fellow here," he pointed to himself placing a hand on his heart, "I refuse to get married. So, my dear sister, we have so much invested here besides my law firm. I cannot sleep at night knowing you are in danger in that house, teaching some those fellows that come from corrupted families. Who knows- druggies or worse? The volunteer work at the hospital, I understand. If you care about us as much as you say you do, you must join us here. We can protect you, care for you and look after your well-being. Please consider what we would like for you." He walked over to her, placed an arm around her shoulders. "You need our protection."

"Diego, I know you are right, and I appreciate your devotion. Both of you have been God sent. How can I get rid of the home that my mom left me as my legacy? Dad loved it also. I am torn. I want to be with you guys but I love my place also."

"Gracy, no one is telling you to get rid of what you have there. You can work it out so that you have the best of both worlds here and there. Maybe in the winter months, when New York weather is unbearable and Sicily's climate is milder, we can all go to Agrigento. Rent the place out and leave only a wing of the house for your availability. Let us stay together in peace here. Gracy should you care to get involved, there is a lot to do here."

Daniele took over. "Gracy, what about dating? Do you date at all? You are attractive. Don't tell me no one has eyes on you."

"I must be like Diego. No interest so far and no one has struck me." The Spanish CEO surfaced in her mind. She had been introduced to him and he seemed interesting. She dismissed the thought with a blink of an eye.

The shrill ring of the telephone interrupted their conversation. Daniele, held his breath. He expected Ingrid to be calling him, hunting him down. To his surprise it was Diego's answering service asking for his brother.

"It must be important for them to call me." Diego excused himself.

"Hello, Diego Frarano here."

"*Pronto*, Mr. Frarano, Emilio Gambare here, *il carabiniere*, the officer in charge of your investigation. We have made progress. I wanted to let you know."

"Really! Thank-you. Please hold on for a minute." He excused himself and walked in the next room for privacy. He quickly grabbed a pen from his pocket and paper from the desk to jot down what he could. Besides, he needed to protect Gracy should anything potentially unpleasant occur.

"I will send you a written report, Mr. Frarano, with the specific information. Of course, it's up to Miss Robertson and yourself to press charges. We have the two offenders and a signed witness report with documentation."

"Would you mind telling me who the offenders are? I am an attorney, licenced in New York. We will hire someone from a law firm in Sicily."

"You will receive a paper copy with all the information. We must consult Miss Gracy Robertson first."

Diego walked out to join the two who were anxiously waiting. He waved his hands up. "All I know is that they got the culprit and made progress on the investigation. They will talk to you Gracy, when you return. No revelation of who they are. I will eventually find out."

"Gracy, I wish you wouldn't leave tomorrow." interjected Daniele.

"My two students need me. I have an obligation toward them. I mustn't let them down."

"Gracy, I want for you to seriously consider what we discussed before. Consider our suggestions so we can all have peace of mind."

Gracy, pensive, lowered her eyes transitioning in a world of her own. *Maybe they are right. But I feel that I am needed in Agrigento also. What is it that chains me there, my mom's grave? Her wishes? Those students' futures? Yes, they are eager to better themselves by learning English, so necessary for them to move on. How can I take it away from them?* The principal had claimed no one could teach English like she and her father had done. They had all the knowledge and skills to encourage success in students. She had no way of knowing that the very people she feverishly wanted to help had orchestrated to destroy her entirely.

88

Chapter Sixteen

Emilio Gambare, accompanied by another officer, was the first to contact Gracy on her arrival home. He felt proud to report their progress on her case. When he related to her the report about her students, she was shocked at what they had planned to execute. Hugging herself, she tried hard to calm her fright. Her inner intuition had been correct, but she never imagined to that extent.

Officer Gambare said, "Miss Robertson, you need some protection here. We will keep surveillance on you and the offenders as much as we can. Unfortunately, we need to be extremely cautious. We need you to press charges against the two students. We are ready to take them in. As for the young man that helped us out, unfortunately, he falls into a category of having been victimized by these two individuals. But he still participated. He helped us out at the same time."

"Mr. Gambare, I am tutoring these two students right now. I know they were trouble in the classroom. They caused me a lot of anxiety, stress and even grief at times. I can assure you, there seems to be a change in both of them. They are behaving respectfully and they are eager to learn. I couldn't be more pleased with them at this point and time. I am preparing them for fall exams. I hate to disrupt what we, together, are accomplishing." She was being sincere. The officer questioned himself if those two scoundrels deserved her generosity.

"Miss Robertson, we have to go according to the law. It is our duty to remove these criminals that harm our society to protect our citizens."

"Please Signor Carabiniere, let's not rush into anything punitive. Allow me to consult with my brother and talk to our family lawyer here. I can assure you, the last thing I want to do is cause harm to these students."

"Miss Robertson, I am doing my job." He couldn't believe her hesitation. He thought: *If the crime had been committed to one of the Sicilian locals, they wouldn't be so forgiving.* He brought his hand to his impressive hat, saluting her as he left. "I will check with you tomorrow. *Signorina,*"

Once the officer left and Gracy remained alone, she stepped out on the balcony trying to breathe fresh air. "Oh no! I cannot believe what the officer revealed to me. I need to clear this bad energy around me." It was pitch black out there. The moon was hiding behind the clouds; a rain storm was brewing. *It looks spooky out there tonight.* The past week, she had admired the panoramic view of New York with its skyscrapers from her VIP penthouse. *What a difference!* She inhaled a deep breath to fill her lungs and retreated inside. The still quietness of the emptiness reigned all around her. The fear vibrating through her body wouldn't leave her. "Am I going insane?" she asked herself. In an emotionally debilitated state she shuffled, her feet moving her body forward. "I need to function." She forced herself to check all the doors and windows, balconies, to make sure all entries were locked. Once back in her living room, she dropped her exhausted body on her dad's reclining chair, seeking comfort. Her brain was foggy playing tricks on her. Her teeth wouldn't stop chattering, panic had engulfed her entirely. She couldn't believe what the officer had revealed to her. *Why would Leonello and his accomplices want to hurt me?* The sadness deepened into her heart and soul, her head pounding out of control. She slumped her body in total abandon as cold tears ran freely down her cheeks. There she remained until the next morning when the sun's rays filtered through the balcony glass, caressing her tear smeared face.

***

In contrast, Leonello, this night, was sleeping on his cot and indulging in pleasant dreams. He couldn't wait for the next day to arrive. The evening before he had happily enticed Romero to drink on. Their new friend *Marmellata* had offered her tricks. He refused. After toasting and cheering to the tutor's return, he happily left them and went home.

Romero, winked at *Marmellata* saying "He is *mezzo pazzo*, half crazy." Shaking his head, "Poor Leon."

"Am I getting this right? Is he dreaming? He has a crush on that snob- the English teacher who pretends to be a good Samaritan at the hospital, at the university, and everywhere." She made a face. "If you ask me, I bet she only goes there to latch on to some doctor or to make out with some of the intern. Yeah! You guys are naive! My friend does janitorial work at the hospital and told me she is a pain in the butt. Your Miss English girl is forever leaving written notes of complaint at the nurses' stations. The rooms aren't clean enough. Mr. or Mrs. So and So's hygiene isn't what it should be. The nurses' aides should be supervised. She quizzes the patients whom she visits looking for trouble. I will tell you that she sure knows how to sweet talk to the doctors in her Aussie accent. Have you ever seen her on dates? Why? Because the ordinary Sicilians aren't good enough for her." added *Marmellata*.

"*Marmellata,* that's malicious gossip. Miss Robertson does good deeds. Don't believe what they tell you. Does it occur to you, she looks out for those sick people? She cares. Some of them are from the surrounding towns. Their families cannot be there daily. Miss Robertson has a generous heart and isn't charging us anything for tutoring. It is totally from kindness and care for us students."

"Oh! Oh! I wonder . . . let me know. What is her real motive?"

"*Marmellata,* sincerely we goofed around all year. No way that we could pass. I know it bothered her. Please don't let Leon hear you talk badly about her; he will break your neck."

"Why? He has a crush on her! Poor stupid Leon. He is in for a rude awakening."

"Forget it. Pretend you don't know anything. I don't want any trouble with Leon. When he gets mad . . . I hate to tell you what he is capable of."

"Don't tell me; I have seen him. Lately he isn't under the influence. His brother is in jail. No more supply I guess until he gets out or finds a replacement."

"Let's drop the subject. It's been all good lately, thanks to Miss Robertson's inspiration and encouragement."

"Okay. I wonder how long it will last knowing Leon's bad moods."

"*Marmellata,* you don't like Leon much, do you?"

"It's not that I don't like him. I resent his ordering us around. Good thing the burning of the house failed. You and I wouldn't be here talking. That Gianni Boy sure got a good beating.

I thought Leon wouldn't give up until he was totally breathless."

"He does get out of control at times. I must admit. It's hard to take for me too sometime. But I have also seen him break down and cry. Who knows? His mood sure shifts from good to bad or vice versa quickly."

Chapter Seventeen

The undercover officer hired by Mr. Anthony Taverna and Diego Frarano had been following and watching them. Leonello was the prime suspect who seemed to be giving the orders. The officer had carried out his investigation, totally undetected since the incident had occurred. The officer was surprised that, lately, nothing malicious had taken place. When he had conducted earlier investigations, one of his colleagues referred to them as drug heads. God only knew what they would be capable of committing under the influence of whatever substance they were taking.

***

The two vagabonds arrived back to their tutoring class smiling, pleasantly welcoming back Gracy home for her return. She had been trying hard all morning to calm her emotions and her crying spells. When they arrived behaving normally, she thought: The bad news has been a nightmare through a bad dream. *Shame on me for believing it all and driving myself insane.* Leonello walked in smiling, wide eyed and admiring her. Stretching his hand. "Welcome back Miss Robertson. Did you have a good trip?" He turned shyly to address Romero. "My buddy and I missed our English classes and you, of course, Miss Robertson." A flash of joy overcame her and her fears. *Has the devil I knew turned into a saint?* Romero followed also with praises. "Yes, Miss Robertson, we missed the classes and you too. We counted the days for your return."

"Oh my! Thank-you" Smiling and encouraged she continued, "Well I am glad to be back, and see you both also. Let's get down to some serious work then and resume our learning."

The class was pleasantly conducted, the assignments well presented. After class they were curious to hear more about her trip. Both young men expressed their strong desire to someday see the Big Apple. "Of course, you will. This is why you are learning English. Languages will open doors for you and great opportunities for your future. Once you master English, I encourage you to take up Spanish. Eh! Fellows, you have a lifetime of learning ahead of you."

"Easier said than done Miss Robertson," answered Romero.

Gracy frowned "What do you mean Romero? Don't ever underestimate yourself; learning is a lifetime effort." She glanced at Leonello who was listening wide eyed "You want to be empowered both of you? Don't you? It's your call, fellows." They were both paying attention intensively. She was their teacher, but from her core deep down she felt like she was their mother. They didn't know that Miss Robertson was following the teaching of her father who was driven by the love in his soul. He had fulfilled both parenting roles and done such a good job at that.

The classes continued harmoniously. Fall arrived. Leonello and Romero passed with honors. It gave Gracy such pleasure. Yes, she had taken the right approach to turn those two around. Otherwise, at eighteen they would have remained a year behind. Time was precious. When sinister thoughts came to her mind about them, she immediately denied them. She continued teaching diligently at the university. When praises were expressed by the principal, the parents, and the pupil themselves, euphoric bursts of encouragement would zip through her body. Each time she would look up to heaven she would whisper to herself. "Thank you, God and Dad, up there." Her dedication to her students paid off.

As for Leonello and Romero, they were continuing their studies conscientiously, often seeking the help of their admirable teacher.

Leonello, would seek opportunities to talk to his Miss Robertson. He was now nineteen. The girls in town were ready and available for him; unfortunately, his heart only desired what he couldn't have- the fulfillment of his secret love for Miss Robertson. Lately his feverish desire had been tormenting his soul day and night. He hated himself. *Why has my anger and resentment toward her turned to mush? I cannot reveal it to anyone. Why has powerful Leon turned into a lamb? Especially Romero, he looks up to me... forget about Marmellata. She won't get anywhere in life playing her tricks. Gianni has been excluded but maybe we should get him back as part of our trio.*

It was close to the end of class first term. Gracy had a pile of papers to mark for her pupils. She excused herself from the hospital volunteer program and went home early. It was November. The evenings were getting darker earlier these days. She was just getting settled to start her work when the doorbell rang. *I am not expecting anyone.* Reluctantly, she took the stairs to go down, opening the door. "Oh! What a surprise!" Her body remained frozen still for a minute, hesitating. *Should I let him in or close the door shut.* There stood Leonello well-groomed and dressed, holding a bouquet of yellow roses. "Miss Robertson, sorry I came unannounced. May I come in?" Gracy, breathless and speechless, suppressed a hint of rising fear. Then, miraculously, some sense of peace kicked in.

"Of course, Leonello. Please, do come in."

Once they reached the spacious living room, Leonello, blushing, extended his hands.

"Miss Robertson, these yellow roses are for you."

Gracy didn't know what to make of it. She brought a hand on her chest "For me! Leonello thanks. Why the roses? I don't understand."

"Miss Robertson, please accept and enjoy these roses. My humble offering of admiration is a thanks for all you have done for me. Your friendship means a lot to me. I care for you."

Gracy, was confused. *Is this good or bad for me to accept flowers from one of my students alone in my house?* "Leonello! Thank-you. You shouldn't have."

Leonello felt her reluctance but then, he himself too felt some. Gibbering away he said, "Miss, Miss Robertson." He continued nodding his head from side to side. "If you allow me I will explain." He noticed Gracy had remained confused as she held the roses. "It's okay! Let's place them aside for now. You can rearrange them at your leisure after I am gone."

He is not going to harm me is he? I can arrange them after he is gone. She put her hand on her forehead trying to push her bad thoughts away. The flowers were placed aside. When she turned to face Leonello she bumped right into him as he was so close to her. Immediately discomfort invaded her and she stepped backwards, distancing herself. She was pinned to the edge of the island. She felt threatened. A cold shiver went through her. Not knowing Gracy's state of mind, Leonello looked at her admiringly and then spoke.

"Miss Robertson, I think you are so beautiful. I like you a lot. As matter of fact, I am in love with you. Please don't resent me. I cannot control my heart for what I feel for you."

Gracy, shocked, wanted to disappear in the thin air. Her eyes were wide open but she did not want to see her student or hear what he was saying. She was ready to scream and order him to get out. She noticed Leonello's eyes fighting tears. Quietly, he lamented "Miss Robertson, if you allow me, all I want to do is to reciprocate your kindness. We belong to two different worlds you and me. I come from a corrupted, broken family. You are the daughter of the admirable Professor Andrew Robertson, a noble man. So, I know you are out of reach for me. I can only dream the impossible dream. I am willing to accept that. Please let me be your servant. I would like to assist you in any way I can. Please reach out to me, if I can help you in any way. I promise you I will place a lid on my heart and soul to stifle my feelings for you."

"Leonello, I am sorry and shocked. I had no idea you felt that way about me. You caused me a lot of anxiety with your behaviour, especially with the terrifying attempt to really harm me. How did you manage to turn yourself around?"

He knelt down, "Please, please forgive me. It wasn't me. I was under the influence- drugs, alcohol, you name it. My brother is in jail right now, so any substance is not available to me. My dad is also locked up for his involvement in drug and alcohol dealing. It's sad for me to say this. I hope they keep them both there for a long time to come, until I can escape from this rotten world of mine." He looked sad as he continued. "You see Miss Robertson, I was jealous of you! You seemed to have it all. A rich girl from a foreign country, educated and admirable. You are praised and admired by everyone. You are so pretty and sexy. I would drown myself in whatever I could get my hands on, stealing from my brother or his friends. It wasn't me. When I came down from the highs, the rotten moods would return. They gave me the power to cause trouble, especially when those fellows looked up to me." He was speaking and avoiding eye contact. Gracy, was patiently listening; his confession, he sounded so sincere.

He brought his face up to stare at her. "I knew I couldn't ever have you. I wanted to destroy you somehow. But, deep down, I felt miserable."

"Leonello, your distorted actions were grave, not only regarding me. You ruled Romero. Gianni, poor Gianni, he barely made the class and there were more who you bullied. How many more did you influence Leonello? I was concerned about all of you. I would lay awake at night questioning. Some days I felt too discouraged to come to class."

"I am so sorry! As I said, I have been clean since they took my brother and my father away. Attending your classes here, your advice, your lectures, your encouragement, they made me look at life completely differently. Your offer to tutor us has been an eye opener for me. It showed me how you dedicated yourself to performing a good deed for your worst student- me who had been so rotten. This is why I am here."

"Leonello! You are a smart young man; listen to yourself. Did I hear you right? No more drugs, remorse, and a change of mind and heart. . . plus, plus. That is my reward Leonello.

I feel in my heart that you will go far in life with your new attitude. My wish for you is to stay away from drugs at all costs. Abuse, alcohol and drugs will ruin a life as you have seen. Just promise me that you will stay determined. I am here as your friend to help you along."

"Thanks, Thank -you Miss Robertson."

He grabbed her hands brought them to his lips smothering them with spontaneous kisses as tears ran down freely. Gracy's eyes followed him, touched by emotions and relieved from pain at the same time. *I have experienced no motherly love in my life. At times I have been miserable, resentful, selfish, questioning why God had taken my mom away before even giving birth. This poor soul has only been exposed to cruelty- so much pain and suffering hindering his present, past and future.*

She embraced him in motherly love and held him in her arms. Afterwards, she put her hands gently on his shoulders, shook him and looked straight in his eyes. "Leonello, listen to me. I think deep down you are a good young man. You are so young. You only think you are in love with me because you are in desperate need of affection. You are confused; believe me. I feel for you. Be thankful that you have a family; try to make the best of what you have. Your mom- concentrate on your mom. I am sure she loves you and aches for you. You must show her support in a good way, not by drowning yourself in substances that fog your brain. I am an educator, a teacher, trying to direct you in a good way. She hugged him encouragingly and asked him to sit down. Afterwards she continued. "You were jealous of me because according to you I had everything." She turned her face away from him to hide her rising emotions "Did you know, I was raised without a mother? Did you know how many days and nights I cried wanting the love of a mother like other children had? There was only my dad and myself in hiding. I was taken from her womb, because my mom was murdered- murdered Leonello and now I have lost the most important person in my life-my Dad. You want to feel sorry for yourself Leon? We could all feel sorry for ourselves. We need to make the best of what we have. I was taught by my Godmother that it is a sin to feel sorry for oneself." She gave Leonello a big smile as he listened attentively. The message had gotten across. Leonello humbly smiled, kissing Gracy on the cheek.

"Thank you, Miss Robertson. You are a great teacher." He walked away sorrowfully. On his way home, slowly shuffling, he was deep in thoughts. *Gracy is not only admirable, but she is also a great human being. God help me get over her. I love her so! His soul felt somewhat relieved, but remorse was still carving his core. Miss Gracy Robertson can you ever forgive me? Her kindness is immeasurable. In my pain I wanted to destroy her out of jealousy. Thank God Gianni refused to torch her home.*

At the same time, the vigilant eyes of Emilio Gambare had discretely followed him, watching his arrival and departure. Leonello, in a world of his own, never noticed the undercover policeman hired by the Fraranos or was aware of the situation at hand. He was their number one suspect because of his and his family's reputation. Romero was also being watched for any wrong moves. The informant Gianni had made it clear that they were forced to act upon Leonello's orders. Lately he had to be confined indoors, shaking in his own seclusion. Whenever he was forced to step out, his eyes darted everywhere to watch his back continuously. He knew Leonello hated his weakness for not carrying out orders. The fear, now, was more intensified since he had squealed on them.

The newest addition to their group, *Marmellata,* would do anything to please those boys, all for getting stolen money out of them or referrals for her tricks. The stealing going on at the outdoor market had escalated. She would distract the male vendors with her flirting, while the boys did their job snatching cash or items to sell later for their own gain. *Marmellata* was the perfect match for Leonello. Gianni, in his innocence, didn't know how much Leon hated himself. He also did not know that Leonello's heart had been stolen by the only woman he cherished and desired- Miss Robertson who was totally out of reach.

Chapter Eighteen

While things were looking up for Gracy in Agrigento, in New York, Diego and Daniele were diligently making plans to relocate her. Daniele had instructed Ingrid to redecorate the VIP suite at their newest hotel right in Manhattan with the most comfortable and up to date furnishings. He had also instructed her to check flight availability. The brothers were going to surprise her for her twenty-seventh birthday- a celebration with the Tavernas from Palermo, to be celebrated together in New York. She couldn't refuse. Since Diego was totally committed to so many projects these days, Daniele was totally in charge. He knew Diego wouldn't object to any of his extravagances because he cared so much for Gracy. Despite being a successful attorney, businessman and a highly admired bachelor, Diego's interests were mainly in playing the older brother. Providing for his family gave him much pleasure. The demands on him these days were immeasurable, especially from the law firm.

The new CEO they had hired, Mr. Alvaro Fernandez, was presently handling Las Vegas and the new hotel in New York. However, this hadn't brought much relief as he too was swamped. They were in the midst of full season. The elite tourists arriving from Europe needed to be taken care in the most all-inclusive way to which they were accustomed. Fernandez had grown up in Madrid, therefore he carried out his responsibilities with a European charm enhanced by a Spanish flair. He liked to open the evenings with the dancers. The kitchen was given strict orders to serve exquisite delicacies. The bar had an abundance flowing champagne for his new guests. He possessed a wealth of knowledge in his field; but still, approval from his superiors, Diego and Daniele, made him feel better. In his sincere manner he would say. "Diego, Daniele, pardon my intrusion for taking your time. I need to relate to you both what I intend to do, fully aware of the expense. A full account of activities and their costs in advance is necessary; although I believe my methods will bring in a lot of profit. Your pardon if I am wrong. The secret is to instilling the holiday spirit in our guests from their arrival. I like to lift their hearts and bring serenity to their souls right from the minute they set foot on our domain. That said, I need cooperation all around me and help from other employees. Together, those efforts can be fruitful with your blessings."

Diego and Daniele both listened attentively noting Mr. Fernandez's enthusiasm. He promised effective results. They looked at each other understanding clearly. Diego spoke first. "Alvaro, I am sure you are a man of integrity. My brother and I agree to give you carte blanche on your leadership. I don't need to remind you that there are sharp accountants on our team, weighing the debts and credits weekly plus at month's end. I am definitely not worried as long as you are aware of your requirements. I am sure Daniele likewise feels the same." Saying that he slapped Daniele on his shoulder for verification of his statement.

"My brother is right Alvaro. We put a lot of trust in you. I am sure you will be honorable. As you know I am working to put together a birthday celebration for our sister. Your touch with the Spanish music and entertainment will impress her. As for the meal, the kitchen chefs know what to do."

"Yes, Alvaro, we want your input. Daniele and I want her to fall in love with New York and our intention here is to have her join us and reside here, close to us. She is alone in Agrigento and she is my biggest worry."

"Why is that? It is unusual for her to choose to stay apart from her family." he answered, creasing his eyebrows.

"It's a long and complicated story Alvaro. We cannot go into that now. I will say one thing. She feels an obligation to a legacy left to her by our mother and a duty to her father's memories."

"We must show her a good time. In time, she might change her mind." Alvaro responded smiling as he envisioned their sister, the lovely girl he had been briefly introduced to at the opening ceremony. Time was ticking so he extended his hand to move on. "Well fellows, thanks for your time. I wish you good luck with your family. I must go and get my act together. I promise you I will do my best for your sister's party."

The three of them shook hands and Alvaro Fernandez happily parted. Daniele, lately, hadn't had the opportunity to talk to his beloved brother as much as he cared to because of the demands at hand. "Diego, please, give me a few minutes of your time." At the same time, Daniele's beeper was buzzing in his pocket. He looked at it and shook his head in annoyance. It was Ingrid. He ignored it so as to not lose the opportunity with his brother. "Diego, I need to talk. Can we meet for dinner as soon as you can, sometime this week please?"

"Daniele, your need sounds urgent. I will call Rosella to cancel whatever we had planned tonight for heaven sakes. You know my family comes first." Rosella, his lady judge friend, was used to having their shared dinners cancelled.

"Thanks bro, tell me when and where"

Without responding, he dialed Rosella's number to cancel.

"Daniele, tonight at seven pm. You pick the place."

"Great. I will call you later."

In the meantime, Daniele's guilt kicked in and he figured: *Better call that bug before I lose my nerve to tell her off.* The minute she answered, she was ready to attack him.

"It's about time you picked up. I have been trying to get a hold of you for the past hour. Where are you?" She was talking as loud as she could.

"Ingrid, please talk to me calmly; stop screaming. I cannot make out anything you are saying."

The next thing he knew, she was sobbing hysterically like a spoiled child. Daniele took a deep breath: *God help me with her. I have no option but to calm her down.* "Ingrid what is the matter now? What has happened to you? Please calm down. I cannot have you call me every minute hysterically like this." Finally, she started to talk. "I need to see you! I need to be with you! Your secretary was rude to me. She wouldn't tell me where you were. I had to resort to a beeper from one of the employees. My mother called. My dad had a stroke. He is in intensive care. I need to get home. You must come with me."

Daniele was stopped in his tracks. He needed to clear the cloud forming in his head. He changed his tone. "Ingrid, yes, we must go. I will cancel dinner with my bother tonight and inform my secretary. As soon as you want to leave, I will be ready for you. Meet you at home darling."

On the other end of the line, Ingrid smiled, while calm flowed through her veins. That is what she needed- his attention, his total devotion. *Why do I have to go to the extreme to get him on my side? He is obsessed with his hotels, his brother, and his family making demands on him, especially that spoiled stepsister of his. I hate that bitch. Those two think she is bigger than life. I hate her. I have to do all this work to accommodate her. Who in hell does she thinks she is to deserve all that? She is the product of an illicit affair from their mother so she is not even legitimate family. She sure has both of them wrapped around her finger.*

Daniele rushed home feeling remorseful for his adverse feelings toward her lately. He had left the house this morning extremely resentful. Now he promised himself to be more sympathetic and consider her needs. His thoughts of unloading to Diego were totally erased. Yes, his intentions had been to seek his advice on how to gently part from Ingrid. His mixed-up feelings were playing tricks on his weakness. He would be all ready for Ingrid instead. He felt sorry for her now. Her dad's stroke was serious matter. He knew she needed his support above all. How could he even consider of abandoning her at this time? Besides, she was one of the best interior designers. Her professional qualities were immeasurably important for their hotels. She had been placed in charge of renovating for their princess Gracy and this meant so much to him and his brother.

The dinner with Diego was promptly cancelled. To Ingrid's delight, the two left for Washington where her family lived. Holding Daniele's hand and having him beside her showing her full support, gave Ingrid a sense of security.

Shortly after their arrival, Ingrid's dad passed and her pain intensified. Daniele's support made the cruel world around her bearable. The funeral was well attended, including her neighbours and the entire Robertson family. Old man Robertson had died a couple of years back. Their four children had grown up with the Klein family, so they all came to pay their respects with their widowed mother that still lived in the area.

Ingrid proudly introduced the family- Walter, Morris, Sara, and Elise and Mrs. Robertson to Daniele. "They were our good neighbours next door. I went to school with Walter. We grew up with them. Mrs. Robertson is a nice lady." She added no more but shook her head. At the celebration of life moods were lightened as guests were relating episodes in their past relationships with Mr. Klein. Walter and Morris had their mischievous stories to share and to chuckle over with the people. Daniele came to a realization. *They have the same last name as our Gracy. I know the Professor always avoided talking about his family. He never encouraged Gracy to look for them. He even forbid her to do so. They were originally from London, England. They lived in the US who knows where? I am just wondering if by chance there could be a connection with the professor and Gracy. Wouldn't that be something?*

Gracy finally would have some family on her paternal side. She often had bemoaned not knowing them.

"My dear brothers I love you immensely. But it would be nice to know some family of my English heritage."

"Oh, we are not enough for you? My dear sister, I see! Let me tell you something. Did you ever inquire about the Meridional folks? They are affectionate, loving, always supportive, and ready to help."

She would give them both a big hug. "I know, I know. Dad and I have been so grateful. We would have never survived without the Tavernas. Not to mention my biggest gifts- Diego and Daniele who I adore."

He shook off the memory but Daniele made a note to enquire further about the Robertson connection. *Why not ask Ingrid?* He stood there analyzing them, watching for clues. The widow, Mrs. Robertson, spoke with an English twang that was not so polished. The girls spoke a perfect American English. Morris and Walter had a certain New Yorker slur which he questioned. While he was doing all this, he was nurturing a drink and leaning over with one arm on the bar. He was wondering what his relationship with Ingrid would entail from now on. Her mom lived alone in Washington. He was sure she would have to make frequent trips to look after her well-being. Maybe, just maybe, her demands on him would be less. At the moment Ingrid seemed to be right at home with her neighbours, chatting away with the fellows like old friends. He preferred to give them their privacy by keeping his distance. The older fellow, Morris Robertson, had made some inappropriate remarks to Ingrid and her brother. Daniele shook it off thinking it was his upbringing that caused his sensitive reaction. Shamefully he muttered to himself, "Who am I to judge? I don't know these people." He finished his drink and proceeded to join them but his smile was more forced than genuine.

Chapter Nineteen

On the other side of the ocean back in Agrigento, Gracy had totally been carried away reading to one of her favorite patients. Her eyes were tiring. She lifted her head and saw it was getting dark out there. She jumped up realizing that her time had been long overspent. She better get home. A nurse walked in, startling her. "Miss Robertson, you are still here? You are spoiling these patients of ours. Your volunteer time lapsed hours ago."

"Oh, Yes, I know. Mrs.Rosali wanted to hear the end of the story. I just carried on and lost track of time."

"You are such a good soul. No wonder they love you here."

"Thank you. I must get out of here now." She grabbed her belongings, tossed her reading books in her bag, kissed Mrs. Rosali on her forehead and rushed out to her car. Diego had made her promise no more late evening shifts at the hospital. They wanted her home at a decent time for her own safety and for their peace of mind. Gracy, ready with the keys in her hand, looked up. To her disbelief there was another surprise; standing by the driver's door with a hand on the handle stood a well-groomed young man with a big smile on his face welcoming her. She was taken aback. "Leonello, what a surprise! What are you doing here?"

"Nothing other than wanting to see my beautiful ex-teacher. I want to keep an eye on her for her safety."

"Leonello, please, you know you shouldn't. I am serious. You could get into a lot of trouble pursuing your old teacher."

"Not unless you complain or if my intentions are malicious." His eyes gleamed in admiration like a puppy madly in love with his patron.

"Look here Leonello, this is not funny. You must stay away from me, regardless of your intentions. Do you understand?" She was talking now in an irritated tone, hoping to get through to him.

"Miss Robertson, all I wanted was to see you. I have no intentions of getting you in trouble."

"Your intentions might be admirable. I cannot take the risk of being seen around with my student!"

"Former student, if I might add." He corrected her.

"Leonello, I am serious, former or not former. I don't approve and don't like it. Please go away or I will report you."

He looked at her with his pitiful brown eyes and a sorrowful face ready to break down in tears.

"Oh! God help me." She felt sorry for him; however, she knew her reputation was at stake.

"Leonello please. You mean well. I admire your concern and kindness. I am well aware you need someone to reciprocate your caring. But not with me!"

"Look here Leonello, from the bottom of my heart, believe me, I cannot, or will not get involved with a former student."

"You mean intimately?"

"Not intimately or otherwise. I have only tried to do my job-what has been required of me to help my students with their benefit in mind only."

"Miss Robertson, you are amazing! This is why I admire you and love you so much."

"Thank you Leonello. You are an amazing young man also. You deserve only the best in life. I believe in you. Now, if you will excuse me; it has been a long day. I must go home before my older brother contacts his bodyguard if he doesn't find me at home for our evening check in."

Leonello put his head down and walked dejected. The rejection was disheartening.

He was nineteen. How could he stop his heart from feeling for the beautiful English girl? He suspected his friend Romero also had the hots for Miss Robertson. Romero knew he couldn't dare cross him because Leonello would smash his head in. Leonello had caught him few times staring at Gracy. "Eh! Don't try anything funny. Get your frustration out with Marmellata. Miss Robertson is mine."

Gracy went home disturbed; her troubled brain churned in deep thought. *I never expected to feel troubled in life by someone's caring emotions. Leonello is so young. It's just an infatuation. He will get over it.* Dad had wanted her to date but since they had moved here dating had become different. It was serious and strict and she was getting to be an old maid at twenty-six, going on twenty-seven. In any case, no one had struck her attention so far. She had no interest in anyone let alone a student.

Maybe Diego and I came from the same mould. We choose to dedicate ourselves to the good of others. Daniele is not that happy in his relationship. I know Ingrid badgers him continuously. If love is supposed to be so wonderful, I certainly haven't found it. Dad used to tell me about mom, how she had stolen his heart. It must have been wonderful to find a soul mate.

The shrill of telephone distracted her from her thoughts.

"Pronto! Hello!"

"Hello, Sis, you are late. I called twice already. I was getting concerned. Where were you until now?"

"Okay Detective Frarano, at the hospital where else. I got carried away reading to Mrs. Rosali. It simply got later than I intended." She didn't dare mention Leonello's surprise otherwise he would probably fly home or report him immediately to his connections at the *carabinieri, la caserma.*

"Gracy, Gracy. You know I will relax more when I know you are within reach. Daniele, is in Washington; he should be back tomorrow night. I think Ingrid will stay on with her family for a few extra days. As you know her dad passed."

"Yes I was told. I feel badly for her."

"She has siblings and her mom to help her so it shouldn't be too bad, unlike yourself all alone."

"I know. My dad is in my heart at all time. I miss him so."

"Don't I know that? Sorry to say I don't miss mine. I sure miss our mom though! Not a day goes by that she isn't in my mind. Let's change the subject so we don't get sentimentally carried away."

"Yes, Diego. Tell me how your day was? Daniele tells me you're working harder than ever these days. You seem tired and stressed. Diego we need you, so take care of yourself. What are you doing?"

"We are hiring new people; it takes time. The new staff needs to be trained. Our new fellow is doing a great job. We are still interviewing more people. You met our new Spanish fellow; he was supposed to relieve me from the hotels' demands. It hasn't happened because of the new place in Vegas."

"I am sure you and Daniele will work it out."

"Look Sis, I will be less stressed when you join us. It has to be soon. You love to teach and you can do it here, although there is so much to do in the hotels. You could choose which ever department you prefer. Promise me?"

To pacify him she answered "Okay! I will think about it."

"Promise me. Think about your new life here so that I can relax more, if you should care."

"I promise. Let's call it a night. We are both tired. Tomorrow we will turn a new page."

"Ciao, good night."

"Good night, love you Diego."

"Love you too."

As always, conversing with her brother and listening to his voice on the speaker phone helped her fill the ghostly empty room. Once the line went dead, the heavy quietness resumed her discomfort.

Every night Gracy would carry out her routine dutifully, checking, doors windows and balconies to make sure everything was locked up to protect herself from the cruel world out there. Fear sometimes invaded her mind as she replayed the past incident that instilled disturbing thoughts in her head. Could she trust Leonello, Romero, Gianni and whoever they plotted with? After all under the influence of drugs and alcohol, who knew what they were capable of? Her mind played tricks on her and her brain wouldn't shut down some nights. She went to bed overtired, but sleep would not take over to calm her body. Her mind was circling, wondering what she should do.

She wanted to be faithful to her obligation here in Agrigento. Diego and Daniele wanted her there with them. *My dad isn't here anymore. Maybe I should go.* She was tossing and turning, tormenting herself with questions. A storm had been brewing earlier in the evening. It had now erupted into thunder and lightning. The sky had opened up releasing a relentless downpour. The wind had picked up violently causing havoc in the valley. The violent force from the north of the Mediterranean seemed to be competing with the fury of the mare Ionio. Gracy half paralyzed had rolled her body into a ball. She lay there frozen while the storm had its way. The fury of the water and wind was more that her balcony doors could bear. A blast of thunder and lightning cracked right into middle of her bedroom, barely missing her. She screamed but no one could hear her. The worst she could ever imagined happened. The balcony doors sprang open and water was pouring in like the river flowing down below the valley. The storm was relentless and menacing. Cracked branches, debris and broken glass rattled about. Terrified she cried and curled up on the bed afraid to move. She didn't know what to do. The room was flooded. God only knew what had happened to the rest of the house.

The first to arrive was Leonello, banging on the door, followed by two officers- one of them, Emilio Gambera, was the surveillance hired by Diego. They found Gracy trembling and out of her senses. "Miss Robertson we are here to help." They offered to call for an ambulance. She refused. Since they had relocated to Sicily she wasn't aware that such storms could take place here. The carabinieri were kind and sympathetic. Leonello stood right there, truly feeling for his ex-teacher. He sincerely wanted to help alleviate her pain. The officer started to ask him questions. "Officer, I just want to help?" He felt ashamed and guilty, deeply remorseful for his first dealings with Miss Robertson. To think that he had resented her for having it all. He had influenced other students to harm her, all due to his foolish comparison of his life and hers. He had not understood Gracy's pain and suffering- the nightmare of being taken from the womb of her dying mom, hiding from the reach of the mobsters, living alone without her dad and his own bad behaviour. However, a transformation in his mind had taken place because of her good deeds and generous heart. *She is a lonely kind soul. Shame on me.* He scolded himself. They had come to her rescue, and he would take care of her. She needed his help.

Chapter Twenty

Six months later

Gracy had awoken in good spirits. This morning the sun rays were luminously filtering throughout her balcony. She jumped out of bed resolved to start a fruitful new day. She stepped out on her balcony to fill her lungs with the air flowing from refreshing gentle breeze. On the horizon, the blue sky had tied itself to the sea. Only serenity reigned out there today. One could never imagine that this peaceful air surrounding this jewel of an island could turn into such a devastating storm causing trauma as it had the past months. The experience had helped her make up her mind to move forward. This time she wasn't going to deter her decision. At eight o' clock, Gracy walked into Mr. Dario's office to carry out her dutiful promise to Diego. She had promised herself today that she would knock on the door of Mr. Matteo Dario and hand in her resignation. In the past she had changed the dates so many times because of her indecision. Today she was determined to bring her unrest to an end. The house, at Leonello's insistence, had been perfectly restored.

Gracy walked into Mr. Dario's office. "Mr. Dario, regretfully, I must hand in my resignation. I want to thank you for the opportunity you have given me. It's been a wonderful experience to teach and work here. I have come across some wonderful people- you, your staff, and some brilliant students. Yes, there were also some troublesome students, but I can happily report they have been reformed. Thank you for your help, guidance and good advice. It's been my pleasure to teach here and be part of this university."

"Miss Robertson, it's been a privilege to have you on our team. You came here with much to offer and immeasurable knowledge. You and your dad have been assets for our university and your dedication to your students is commendable. You will be much missed.

Should you one day change your mind, there will always be a place for you here. You are highly recommended. I cannot thank you enough. I wish you luck on your new endeavour. I am sure you will prosper wherever life takes you."

"Thank you for your encouragement and kind words Mr. Dario."

They shook hands and Gracy, with mixed feelings, walked away without turning back. She got home, dialed Diego's number and there he was on the other side of the world, responding *"Pronto,* Hello"

"Diego, I have handed in my resignation. I will be ready to leave the first of next month."

She heard Diego exhale a deep breath. Thank you, Mom or whatever heavenly being is up there.

"You made my day. Daniele and I will be counting the days."

"Diego, my dear brother, you and Daniele are the most precious legacy my mom left me."

"You, as well, are our dearest."

"Have a good night and a big hug to you and Daniele."

Immediately, after hanging up. Diego placed a call to his younger brother.

"Daniele, are you standing up? Maybe you should take a seat."

"What's up Bro? Have you purchased another hotel?" responded Daniele.

"No! Much better. Who cares about more assets? Our sister Gracy, will be here the first of next month."

"Finally! For sure now?"

"That is what she told me! Make sure Ingrid has everything in order for her."

"I will. She keeps running to Washington to her family. I will check things out myself or get someone else to continue."

"Daniele, I don't have to tell you that having Gracy here with us will be like having mom around once more. We don't have to worry about her safety or her being alone in Sicily."

"This is the best news I have had lately, Bro. You are right. She talks like Mom. She looks like Mom and she has a heart like Mom." They parted, both delighted. Daniele couldn't wait to pass the news on to Ingrid. When she walked in loaded with shopping bags he said "Ingrid, I am glad you came home. I have good news to tell you."

"Oh! I could use some good news, after what's been happening here and at home lately.

I will say something has to give. What is it darling? I am listening." She placed the bags on the counter and gave him a big hug and a lingering kiss.

"Gracy is coming for good the first of next month. Finally, we convinced her." He was all smiles and his eyes gleamed.

Ingrid didn't react at all. She was cool as a cucumber. She turned her back and returned to her bags.

"Ingrid! Don't you have anything to say? Aren't you glad my sister is coming? By the way, Diego wants you to make sure everything is in order for her." Disturbed, she turned around. "Diego and you Daniele are both insensitive. I just lost my father." She answered indignantly. "You want me to concentrate on your sister when I need to go check on my family. Who is more important?"

"Ingrid I didn't mean to insult you or suggest neglecting your family. Gracy relocating means a lot to us and we cannot disappoint her. She is the only family we have. As you know we love her dearly. It is a big move for her; besides she is doing it more for us. Our poor sister has gone through hell in her life. We are all she has got. The Tavernas have young families of their own. They have been good to her, but she is Diego's and my responsibility. If anything happened to Gracy, Mom would turn in her grave. Besides her dad's last request as he was holding Diego's hand and mine was "You guys look after Gracy. Will you?"

"Daniele, I didn't come home to listen to tales about your sister and her father.

I have enough to contend with of my own. I just lost my own father. I will only do what I can." She grabbed her full shopping bags and walked away, leaving Daniele puzzled. He brushed a hand through his hair while unpleasant thoughts rushed through his brain. *I have a feeling Ingrid doesn't want my sister in New York. Our poor Gracy.* Daniele wasn't wrong with his thinking. He should have figured it out long ago.

He heard the bedroom door slam and Ingrid didn't come out the rest of the evening. She remained there brooding by herself. *All I need is that spoiled bitch here, as if his brother Diego isn't enough. Now I will have to contend with their sister also. I bet she will have them both wrapped around her fingers. She better not try anything with me. I'll tell her where to go so fast that her head will spin. They want me to fix things just so for the queen. That bitch has already overburdened me because her brothers want only the best items imported from Italy for her. I'm sick of Diego and Daniele making me jump to their commands. It's time to look after number one.*

Chapter Twenty One

Daniele was agitated when Ingrid behaved in that petulant manner. Her strange outburst worried him immensely. This was why he hesitated in making a matrimonial commitment with her. There were a few other reasons including her nasty outbursts and unfavorable remarks about his siblings. He loved his family; no one should come between them to alienate them or tear them apart. She was one of the top interior design graduates from Washington State University. She was well versed in her field. Their hotels had been highly regarded since she had put her expertise at work. The illustrations in magazines had spread world-wide, bringing them a high volume of clientele. Their profits had been soaring thanks to Ingrid's artwork and talent. She kept reminding him that their corporate bank account had turned from red ink to black. Ingrid was indeed a master in her work, highly sought and much in demand. The Frarano boys were lucky to have such skilled employee on their team.

Daniele had fallen in love with her. At the beginning of their relationship, Ingrid was sweet, charming and had demonstrated many good qualities. When it came to men, she knew how to attract them. They would fall under her spell. Ingrid dressed the part, in every which way she needed it. Her impeccable appearance complimented her plan for the day. She made no secret of it, saying to Daniele. "I need to meet this client today. I know it will go in my favor." Daniele knew she was flirting to entice her clients. It bothered him. He tried to ignore it. He wasn't sure if he was fortunate or unfortunate to have fallen in love with her. Every now and then, she would complain. The rewarding life they were sharing didn't seem enough. Her demands were unjust. When he detected outbursts of jealousy against his loved ones that troubled him immensely, especially lately. The peace in Daniele's household in New York was disrupted and unpredictable. He didn't like it, especially if his dear sister was joining them. Daniele thought to discuss the matter with his brother or to lay everything in the open with Ingrid hoping they would come to a compromise.

***

While Daniele was trying to iron out his personal problems in New York, Gracy was excitedly planning her move. Although she was sorrowful to leave her beautiful surroundings, it was time to make her brothers happy. "A change abroad might be good for you Gracy." God mother Fabiana had encouraged her on. "She has finally made the decision. She must stick to it." she told her family.

It had been decided that her home, her mother's legacy, would never be sold. It would be passed to the next generation should she someday have a family of her own but so far no one had stolen Gracy's heart. As for the house, Diego had suggested they could return here sometime in winter to escape the cold winter of New York but only if she missed it so much.

Luck seemed to be on her path. She was carrying out her plan in good humor these days. The Math teacher at the university, Giacomo Rondelli, approached her. "Miss Robertson, I have decided to relocate my family from Bari. The visits of my wife and children have made them fall in love with Agrigento. We need a place to live."

"I am happy for you Professor Rondelli."

"Miss Robertson, would you be willing to rent part of your home."

Gracy hadn't thought about it. Her interest was raised. "Mr. Rondelli, let me think about it. I think I would. That would give me peace of mind." She preferred the place to be occupied. Once the agreement was reached, she also suggested.

"Mr. Rondelli, Leonello could help you and your family get settled, and guide your family with any needs."

At first Professor Rondelli was startled at her suggestion of Leonello helping them. He remembered his terrifying incident but kept it to himself. Gracy sensed his reluctance. She quickly added how Leonello had changed under her influence.

Leonello had kindly offered his hand in helping her with chores or whatever her needs were. She was hesitant at first but after scolding herself into positive thinking, she accepted his help as she could feel his sincerity without maliciousness.

On the first of October Gracy landed in New York to the delight of Diego and Daniele. She was so happy to see her beloved brothers. Now, more than ever, she felt her decision had been the right one. They accompanied her into her quarters at the penthouse. "This is your place, Lovey. Its VIP should you need anything." said Diego. Tears of joy freely ran down her cheeks. While hugging Diego and then Daniele she exclaimed "What did I do to deserve all this?"

"Sis! We are so glad you finally fulfilled our wish. We want you to have only the best." Daniele put an arm around her shoulders and spoke. "Come, come on the terrace. This is New York all lit up. This is where we want you so that the three of us can see each other often and share our lives."

Gracy was breathless. The illuminated skyscrapers of the city were breathtaking. Life below was vibrant, alive and on the move. The place assigned for her to live was fit for royals. A double door, opened in a spacious living area which was furnished to perfection. The soothing colors of blue and white awoke her soul. There was a soft Italian leather sectional, plush cushions and a custom furniture brought in from Italy. There was also an open concept kitchenette and bar with drop lighting in Murano crystals. The master bedroom was on the right and the guest bedroom, totally private, was on the left. The bathrooms were just as luxurious. The amenities were unbelievable. Diego spoke for both brothers.

"Sis, this is a special card for the VIP and is at your service all day and night should you need anything. The tables are freshly replenished with specialty snacks at all times for our distinguished guests. All is at your disposal my sweet sister."

Gracy was so touched. The smile on her face radiated with pleasure; her heart beamed joyfully. "You guys are too much. All I really need is your love and affection."

Diego extended his arm and pulled her toward him to kiss her on her forehead.

"Gracy! That, you have for sure; don't ever doubt us. You mustn't forget we have mom's blood in common."

Daniele, always standing beside his brother in support, moved closer and gently grabbed her hand announcing. "Gracy, we know you need rest for a couple of days- jet leg, loss of sleep and all that. Please, Saturday night I instructed Ingrid to prepare a welcoming party for you at the Rainbow Ballroom on the 25th floor. She has invited many people who are anxious to meet you. The festivity is in your honor. We are looking forward to the celebration."

"Oh my God! Here we go; more fuss just for me." She shook her head. A quiet evening just the three of them would have been her preference; how could she disappoint them. Gracefully, she moved between them; put an arm over their shoulders and pulled them over to her. "Whatever you say, my masters. I cannot disappoint you. By the way Daniele, can I help Ingrid in any way?"

"Ingrid has everything under control. You just rest and look after yourself. We will come and get you and proudly escort you." They gently hugged her and parted for the night.

***

Gracy walked around, once more admiring her new domain and thanking God for her blessings over and over. She slipped into her deluxe bed overwhelmed with joy. The change of time was playing havoc on her body. Tossing and turning, she waited for sleep to overtake her. Her brain wouldn't shut down. Her thoughts were racing everywhere. This new life had just begun. One thought was convincing. *My brothers were right. Since Dad died my loneliness was overbearing. I am so glad I came. My brothers mean to me more than any earthly possession. Being with them is so much better than being alone in the mansion in Agrigento.* Deep down she promised herself to adapt to the fast-paced life of New York, embracing what the future would hold for her. She would not disappoint her dear brothers.

The next day she had totally lost track of time when a knock on the door jolted her from her sleep. She glanced at the clock on the wall. It was 1:00 pm. in the afternoon. "Oh my." She threw off the covers, grabbed a house coat and reluctantly made her way to the door, still confused by her surroundings. Whoever was at the door was persistent with the doorbell. She slowly opened the door, peeking out. "Gracy, sorry! I must have awakened you. I was told to check on you and take you to the shops in Manhattan if you are up to it."

"Sorry, Ingrid. Please come in. I had a hard time falling asleep last night. I was sound asleep when the doorbell rang. I can't believe I slept until now. I guess with the time change, my body is confused."

"I am sorry to disturb and I understand Gracy. Welcome to New York anyway. I am only following orders. What can I say? Diego and Daniele, both ordered me to make sure I looked in on you today should you need anything for the party, or for whatever your needs would be."

"Ingrid, thanks. It's so kind of you. Those brothers of mine mean well. You have enough to deal with already. I appreciate your offer and thanks again. I am fine."

Ingrid was relieved. She did have more than she could handle these days. God forbid if she hadn't pursued their orders, especially Diego's. He would be very perturbed. Daniele had made sure to remind her this morning before he left for the office in Vegas with Mr. Fernandez.

"Gracy, if I were you, I would go back to sleep and continue resting. There is still tomorrow. Diego will be in court all day. Daniele is out in Vegas until tonight. So, it's your time to rest fully. I am sure they will want to have dinner with you tonight." she enthusiastically encouraged.

"Thanks, Ingrid. I won't go to sleep again. I have phone calls to make. It will be good for me to just organize my things around here. Of course, I would love to see my brothers tonight."

Yeah! La cosa nostra. Your private togetherness. As if I don't know your style. I am the outcast when you guys get together Ingrid thought to herself.

They parted amicably. Ingrid hid her resentment well. She wished Gracy had never accepted the brother's offer to move to America. *Now I have one more to contend with. As if that big egotistic Diego isn't enough to influence Daniele!*

Chapter Twenty Two

The Rainbow Ballroom on the twenty fifth floor was decorated royally. Diego had required that Ingrid provide only the best. "Ingrid you are in charge, but you know what I mean when I say the best. I'm expecting excellence."

"At your service, Mr. Attorney." As she curtsied to him, she hid her resentment. *All I need that spoiled brat on my path. Do I have a choice right now? I better execute and follow through.* She had promptly moved on to check and recheck the details. The 'to do' list she had found on her desk was clearly spelled out. Ingrid was a perfectionist. Daniele had offered her additional help. Mr. Fernandez was to be at her service. Everyone had been called to a meeting for instructions. "Guys, it's a big celebration for the Fraranos; no expense must be spared. The flowers have been ordered. Two music groups will be taking turns. In the kitchen, you master chefs will be fully in charge. The food must be the best in the city. Mr. Fernandez, you have provided a complimentary violinist as a gift. A friend of yours will play as the guests arrive. The guest list has been checked and re-checked. Everything is moving forward nicely. I don't need to worry about anything being left out. Right Mr. Fernandez?"

"Yes, everything seems to be in order Ingrid. You are an excellent coordinator."

"Thank you."

She walked away murmuring to herself. *'Don't forget Mr. Fernandez, I am not here just for good time, like you. It will cost the Frarano brothers plenty to have me.* However, in her arrogance, she did not fully comprehend Diego's intelligence and intuition. Diego had his doubts about Ingrid's integrity. At times, when disturbing thoughts surfaced in his brain, he discarded them. After all, Daniele had chosen her as his sweetheart. He wanted to respect his brother's feelings for her and avoid any ill feelings that arose solely from his mistrust. He had to admit to himself that he wasn't easily impressed by the opposite gender; actually, he had been labelled a male chauvinist. Often, he related this in conversation with Uncle Anthony Taverna as he grew up. Their conversations focused on his father's escapades with the ladies of the night, the payoffs received without any consideration of their illicit liaisons and the injustice for the other person involved. *My poor mother.* Diego used to open his heart to Uncle Anthony or Cousin Fabiana because of his frustrations. Anthony Taverna supported Diego and his brother Daniele because he detested his brother- in- law's corrupt behaviour. Anthony knew he was a womanizer, a brute with no respect for his sister, a control freak who held his own rules above the law. He always told them "Thank God, you two boys have taken after your mother."

***

Saturday night had fast arrived. Ingrid had seen to it that all was in order. The violinist was at the entrance way welcoming every guest with classic melodies that brought pleasure and serenity. The room was festively decorated with an abundance of floral arrangements, especially roses in every color. The exquisite appetizers were being passed around. The elegant, stemmed champagne glasses were filled generously. Gracy walked in between her two brothers, elegant and distinguished. Her glittering silver and gold trim long dress with a split on the side accentuated her sexy body. The long brown hair pulled back in a chignon enhanced her cheek bones. She was the spitting image of Francesca, her mother reincarnated. Diego was speechless and Daniele in awe. The guests were introduced one at the time. When it all quieted down, Diego took Gracy on the stage and with the beat of the big band welcomed her to New York. She looked around at the room full of people; unbounded joy filled her heart. "Thank you, thank you everyone. I am nobody special, but you have all made me feel as if I am. I cannot believe you people are all here for me. I must confess that before arriving here I was living a lonely life. To find myself here tonight with all of you, it's an unbelievable dream. I thank the coordinator Ingrid Klein, my brothers, who I adore, but most of all you people for honoring me with your presence here tonight. You make me feel so special. Thank you so much. Have a great time and enjoy your evening." The clapping erupted long and strong. Gracy was not a practised speaker. The words came spontaneously from her overwhelmed heart.

Her brothers were soon at her side to rescue her since the paparazzi, looking for stories, were clamouring for her attention. The hotel was renowned for its popularity with celebrities, so the reporters were always seeking news. A lot of dignitaries and celebrities were among the guests to meet the English- Sicilian mystery girl with an Aussie accent. The guests were lining up for a chance to chat with her. Only one person stood aside leaning on the opposite wall and holding his admiring gaze on her. He was speechless over the beauty of the object of everyone's attention. How did one describe this astounding girl? What a combination she was! She speaks perfect English with rich and smooth tones that are music to my ears. He shook his head. *She said she was nobody special. If she isn't special, who am I? An immigrant with broken English, doing double duty to earn a living. She is both alluring and intimidating.* He didn't dare even look at the Frarano boys who were protecting their sister from any unpleasant encounters. He watched as many of the guests around them were trying to shake hands and connect with them. He detected other men's eyes fixated on the stunning young honoree.

Alvaro Fernandez walked away unnoticed and went to check the staff preparing specialty drinks at the bar. The kitchen was all in good order.

He bumped into Ingrid who, to his surprise, made a smart remark. "Eh! Mr. Alvaro Fernandez, have you had a chance to shake hands with the princess yet?"

"You mean Gracy Robertson, Miss Klein?"

"Who else would require all this fuss?" She grabbed his arm and said, "By the way, drop that Miss Klein call me Ingrid." She smirked.

"Okay, Miss Ingrid. As you wish. May I ask why you seem so resentful? Don't you like her?"

"What's there to like. She is spoiled rotten by her brothers."

"Ingrid, are you jealous? I thought you were part of their family?"

"No use talking to you Alvaro. You are naive."

"I am Spanish, a lover of music, people, and trying to get by the best that I can in life. I am more complex than you think. "

"For your information, I am German. When I do something, I do it well.

I expect to be valued and recognized. Don't you think it's only fair?"

"If you say so Miss Ingrid. I don't question things too much; I take life as it comes."

She walked away. "Suit yourself Alvaro. We are all entitled to our own opinions."

Alvaro Fernandez had recently joined the company. He considered himself fortunate to have been hired. He respected the Fraranos. He was going to do his utmost to honor their company. He hoped that with his best performance he would achieve impressive results for them. They did have a grand empire and, as he discovered this evening, a lovely sister. Even if he didn't know her yet he knew she was someone they could be proud of. He wasn't going to engage in any controversy or negative discussions with staff members, or Ingrid, against the Fraranos or Gracy Robertson.

The evening was stellar full of music, laughter and it continued to be a good time for all. Thanks to Ingrid everything went as planned and spectacularly well. Diego and Daniele were grateful to her and praised her immensely. Gracy, with sincere affection, hugged and kissed her on each cheek showing her gratitude. With tears of joy, Gracy kept hugging her brothers.

As the evening affair dwindled, Gracy glanced at her watch. "Oh my! The time- it was way too late to call Sicily. She promised herself to update Fabiana, Uncle Anthony and Joseph on her activities as she missed them immensely. She was wishing they could have been there. She met so many people that it was hard to remember all their names. A lot of them had invited her for lunch or over coffee and visits. She was pleased. This big city of New York was promising to be glorious. From her observations, it wasn't difficult to make friends.

Her mind wandered back home. She thought of what she had left behind- *her teaching, her patients at the hospital, her students- Gianni, Romero and poor Leonello Dante. The boys were victims of corruption living without guidance and living in misery. She understood their distress. The bad incidents replayed in her mind. Leonello could have wasted his life in jail if she have pressed charges. Instead, she had chosen to discover the goodness in him; that brought some peace to her soul.* She had promised him and herself to keep in touch and she would phone in the morning.

130

Chapter Twenty Three

Eight months had passed. Life had been good in this action- packed city but she needed more. Lately, Gracy's mind was churning, especially at night and her anxiety made her restless. Her luxurious surroundings and social schedule did nothing to settle her mind. Once more she arose after a restless night, dressed and got ready to meet her brother's friends for fruitless chit chat and luncheons that didn't amount to anything. In the end she picked up the phone and cancelled whatever was on the agenda for what would be another unaccomplished day. After that she dialed Diego's number and then Daniele's. I need to see them both and arrange a meeting at Diego's office. *This is necessary business and I will regard it as such.*

They were both there ready to listen. "Gracy I will not sit at my desk; I don't want to come across as your lawyer and you the client. This is a family discussion. Let's sit together around our coffee table here." Diego suggested. Once they were comfortably arranged, Diego proceeded "Gracy you sounded anxious. Whatever you want to discuss is an urgent matter. We are listening."

She started to cry.

"What is the matter?" Both brothers were alarmed. "What has happened? Don't tell me you want to go back home? Gracy! You seemed so happy!"

"I am happy. Don't get me wrong."

"Then what? Speak up?"

"Diego, Daniele, I am grateful to have you both and for all your attentiveness. Shopping, lunches, coffee meetings, they are fun for a while but not forever. I need a purpose in life. I want to work. I feel I am wasting my life. I feel like a parasite"

"Gracy, my dear Gracy I understand" Diego replied. "Too much work isn't good. Too much leisure isn't good either. We all must have a purpose in life."

Daniele spoke "Gracy, what would you like to do? You are clever in languages. Do you want to teach? Do you want work in one of our hotels in reservations in administration or in hospitality? Do you want to volunteer at the hospital? What is your preference?"

Diego put a sympathetic arm around her. "Dear sister, we admire you for wanting to live a meaningful life. You know Mom suffered so much because our dad forbid her to work."

"Yes, poor Mom. She was so gifted but forbidden to put her creativity into action. Gracy, whatever you choose, we will support you." Diego's promise was seconded by Daniele.

She hugged them both and wiped away her tears. "Thanks for understanding.

You guys are special to me."

"Gracy, you make the choice my dearest. Whatever makes you happy will make us happy. You could even pick something new for you to learn. Something that is a real change of experience compared to dealing with students.

You think about it and make a choice." Diego bent over to kiss her gently on her forehead. "We don't like to see your beautiful eyes ruined with tears. Gracy, it's such an easy problem to solve. I bet many girls wish they had your problems."

Gracy let out a big sigh of relief for their understanding. "Thanks, I need a purpose in life. Work gratifies me, especially when it helps others." She departed their company with a renewed purpose.

***

Later when she returned to her suite, her thoughts shifted to Leonello and his friends Romero and Gianni. She compared herself to them. They were victims of unfairness. They had suffered the misery of poverty and dysfunctional families. Yes, their growing up years had been bleak. Now, still in their teens, their lives could have been almost destroyed if she hadn't reconsidered her options. Thanks to her father, mother and the loving people in her life, she was a fortunate girl. Although she longed for her mom while she was growing up, her dad had been her life's salvation. He had motivated her from every direction. The miracle of finding her brothers had been another big gift. She went to bed in a different frame of mind, glad that her brothers were in agreement with her and had given her many choices. Gracy looked forward to tomorrow. With career choices in mind, she vowed to help the less fortunate, especially her former students. "I must call Leonello sometime soon."

***

Gracy had no way of knowing that while she had been living it up in New York her former student and friend Leonello had hit bottom. His state of mind in Agrigento had been despondent since his beautiful former teacher had left. The void she had left in his heart was more than he could cope with. As much as he tried, his irresponsive body wouldn't cooperate. The messages transmitted from his brain showed him a world of emptiness. Life felt purposeless. He had quit school entirely. His depression had gained control over him. His spirit was dead. His mom, between her sober spells, worried immensely. The teachers, Matteo Dario, his devoted friend Romero were concerned. Even Gianni had resurfaced worrying about Leonello's mental collapse. Their encouragement of and requests to help Leonello were totally ignored. As the days passed he slipped deeper into sadness. The melancholy had started shortly after the English teacher's departure. The days and nights passed monotonously. His was stricken also by guilt. He had hurt many people- Miss Robertson, Gianni, Professor Rondelli and others, many others. At times, alone, he cried.

Mrs. Dante, when she was rational, had summoned Gianni and Romero. She begged them to come to the house to visit her son hoping they would lift his mood. At first he wouldn't respond however, after his mom's insistence, he came out of hiding to see his old buddies. When he noticed Gianni was still fearful, he surprised his friend by asking forgiveness. "Gianni, I am so sorry for the rotten treatment, the beatings, and the criminal actions I forced on you. I wasn't myself. My God! I was totally out of my mind. I don't want to think about it."

Gianni, surprised, responded "It's okay Leonello. We are lucky we didn't end up in jail. Thanks to Miss Robertson."

"Yes! Thanks to Miss Robertson. We learned a lot from her. Now she is gone." His spirit lifted at the mention of her name but he remained disheartened.

Romero promptly agreed "She gave us her time, her kindness and guidance."

Gianni continued positively. "She meant well for all of us." He put an arm around Leonello. "I am glad you have had a change of heart. I hated it when you were ordering us to hurt people, especially Miss Robertson."

Romero hesitated but then interrupted. "Gianni! Don't rehash those actions. You didn't understand. Leonello was passing on to us what his brother was doing to him. He was destroying Leonello with drugs and whatever substances he was forcing him to take. Now he is behind bars. I hope he stays there along with his horrible father."

Their visit was over. On his way home Romero continued to relate to Gianni who listened wide eyed. "Gianni, our buddy has changed. But who knows, maybe it's the withdrawal or whatever. He doesn't give orders anymore. He is almost pitiful. You have nothing to fear from him.

He looks sad. The big bully cries a lot now. I cannot figure him out. All I know is that he is finished with drugs and he has become a lamb. Please help me and Marmellata can help also. We must convince him to return to school."

On the following Monday morning, the three of them – Romero, Gianni and Marmellata-detoured from school to Leonello's. Marmellata had never been there before. No one was home. The door was unlocked. Romero asked them to wait downstairs. He knew his way to the dingy attic. He climbed the step ladder easily and pushed the opening up. As he had figured out, there was his friend in darkness under a torn blanket. Romero stood there watching his despondent friend. He bent over to shake him, "Eh! Bro, come on; wake up. We came to get you. Gianni and Marmellata are downstairs waiting for us. Come on. We will be together again- the three of us. You must get back to school. Professor Rondelli and Mr. Dario are willing to help you."

"No, I can't. There is no hope for me."

"What are you talking about? Are you still dreaming? Wake up come on. It's early. You have time to get ready." He shook him. "Come on Leonello. We care about you." Leonello wouldn't cooperate. After a long wait, it was time to leave.

"I won't push you further this morning. We will return tomorrow and the next day. We are your friends and we won't give up on you."

"No, just leave me alone, go away. I just want to be left alone."

Romero, joined his friends down stairs disappointed. The trio decided to leave promising to return and see if they could get their friend motivated.

Leonello would lay awake at night tossing and turning with his heart and soul sinking deeper in despair. He was spending a lot of time cooped up in his attic. Going to school had become painful because it reminded him of Miss Robertson's absence.

Romero and Gianni, after many attempts, had stopped coming around. Leonello's constant refusal was discouraging. Romero had even suggested a good time with Marmellata to help with Leonello's depression. Enraged, he had refused. They were incredibly disappointed in him. Romero confided in Marmellata "Can you believe that the macho man gave us orders and now he has turned into mush? He won't come out of that hole. He has changed so much that I cannot figure him out."

Marmellata responded "Romero don't forget he was under the influence of drugs and alcohol! It wasn't him. Maybe his depression has to do with the withdrawal his body is going through."

"That could be. But I think it's a double whammy. He had the hots for Miss Robertson and now she is gone. I think his crush has crushed him."

"He's crazy! How could he dream of having a chance with her? As his friend, didn't you discourage him? He needs to get over her if that is the case."

"Marmellata sometimes you cannot help who you fall in love with. If you want to know the truth, I admired her myself and lots of other guys in our school did also. She is the real deal- knowledgeable, sexy, beautiful and kind. Who wouldn't like her? I wasn't going to chase an impossible dream but I think Leonello is cooked for her even if Miss Robertson doesn't even dream about him."

"Of course not, her family could never relate to his corrupted one. They are no match with nothing in common. She is gone abroad living the dream we all desire. She is educated, has everything going for her. What would she want with scum bag Leonello –a loser nineteen-year-old dropout? Romero, if he has a crush and you are his friend, you better convince him to get over his unrealistic dream. He cannot continue living in fantasy."

"Gianni, you should try to talk some sense into him."

"Me? He only wanted me around to be his patsy for dirty jobs. If I didn't execute them, he would beat me up. You know what he was capable of. I shouldn't even be here with you. I suffered immensely after our last episode. I am lucky to be alive."

Romero shook his head "I know. It was insane what he made us do-the plan he had for Miss. Robertson, the attack on our Professor Rondelli. He is not like that anymore. He wasn't himself. His mom is pitiful. She begged me to help since as much as she tries, he is beyond her reach. We must save our Lion, Gianni. We must get him well. He is changed. Don't you see he is punishing himself now?"

Marmellata jumped in and tried to advise "Guys. I have an idea. How about talking to Professor Rondelli. Maybe he can get in touch with Miss Robertson. Doesn't he live in her house? Maybe he can reach her and get her to talk to him on the phone at school. Then she can convince him to return to school."

"It's a good idea, Marmellata. She certainly cannot reach him at his place. They have no phone. If she calls him, Leonello might get motivated to get off his ass and come to school."

Gianni commented "Would Mr. Rondelli be willing to help him? You guys beat him up and threatened him."

"Yes, Leonello did most of the dirty work but word has gotten out about Leonello's change and Mr. Rondelli being a good man, might have forgiven him and me too. He might cooperate because he wants us to excel."

***

While all the planning in Agrigento was going on, in New York Gracy had awakened refreshed this morning. The meeting with Diego and Daniele last night had appeased her soul. She jumped out of bed and walked to open up her windows wide open to welcome in a new day. A gentle breeze softly caressed her warm cheeks. She admired the bustling city already in motion beneath her. She smiled joyfully and stretched her arms. A burst of energy zipped through her body, delivering both calm and exhilaration. The tension hovering over her recently was gone. She couldn't contain her excitement. *I will soon be working. My life will soon have a meaning- a blessing from the universe.*

She walked to the phone ready to pick it up. Hesitating her eyes glanced up at the clock to check the timing. *Perfect.* It was eight in the morning. She figured it would be two pm in Sicily. Before she could dial, the phone rang and startled her.

"Pronto."

"Si. Pronto, Professor Giacomo Rondelli here. Gracy, *Buon giorno, come state?"*

"Ah! Professor. *Bene, e tu?* I am well and you? I was just about to call you."

"Benissimo. Grazie. I am also very well, thanks"

*"Mi scusi. Noi qui ci credevamo che ti eri dimenticata di noi .*We thought you had forgotten us here."

"My apologies, they have kept me going here relentlessly. I would never forget Agrigento and all of you there. Please, tell me how is everyone doing? Update me please. How is everything going at the university? Your class? My old students, how are they? I am sure under your guidance they are behaving."

"Yes, I am pleased with my class. You know, it's such a pleasure when they are eager to learn. We educators feel rewarded."

"I know the feeling." She heard him release a sigh. Joyfully, she responded.

"I am happy for you and them too. I know how grateful you must feel."

However, he continued in a voice laden by concern. "Yes, Gracy, but I am sorry to report to you that one of your old students has totally fallen out of grace with me. He has dropped out of class after only a few weeks; and there is no way we can change his mind or convince him to return."

"I'm sorry to hear that. Who is he? Don't tell me it's Leonello Dante."

"You guessed right."

Immediately Gracy felt a sharp pain at her core. It took few moments to regain her stability. "I am so sorry. Why has he dropped out?"

"Actually, his mother came to the school in a pitiful state. She begged us to talk to him. Mr. Dario and I tried to comfort her. We promised to do all we can to help her with her son. The principal and I went and took the time to talk to him. We have not been successful. He has slipped into such a deep depression. It will take a skilled counsellor to bring him out of his present state."

"What has gone wrong to trigger his mental condition as such?"

"We suspect a nervous breakdown. The principal thinks we should raise some funds to provide him the care he needs. He won't listen to anybody. He dropped out of school but has not chosen to work or pursue other positive paths. I feel sorry for him and his poor mother. You know the father and brother are both in jail now. They were involved in drug dealing and crime of all sorts."

"What a shame. I suspected their abusiveness. This is why I ignored Leonello's bad behaviour. Deep down he is a good young man you know. He can be caring and kind."

"Yes, you and I know there is good in everyone. It's up to us to extract it. I hope he snaps out of it."

"That makes me sad. I thought he was well on his way when I left. When I set aside the unpleasantness, the good surfaced in him and he seemed to have a renewed life purpose."

Professor Rondelli continued. "I hope he snaps out of his condition with some help. Changing the subject Miss Robertson, the rest is all well. My family loves Agrigento. Thank you, for your home. It is a pleasure to go home."

"I am glad. Enjoy it to the fullest."

"You enjoy New York."

"I am. I will be happier when I start working."

"Will you be teaching?"

"Maybe not. I can always teach English part time to the new immigrants settling here in New York. I need a change in my life. I promised my brothers I would make a choice, so now I am entertaining the idea of hotel hospitality."

"I am sure you will excel regardless of what choice you make. You will make your brothers proud."

"Thanks for your confidence. Time will tell."

"Please, Professor Rondelli, we must try to help our young friend Leonello.

I care about the people I left behind. I will see what I can do from here. You and Mr. Dario don't give up on him; promise me."

After the phone went dead, she remained holding it. She was very disturbed by the news from Sicily. She loved people, guiding and helping them, providing for them and making them happy. It suited her personality. Observing the interesting guests arriving from every part of the globe at their spectacular hotels was fascinating. Now, after the phone call, a black cloud was hovering over her head as her thoughts turned to Leonello. She had been happy, thinking he had turned around. This news was disappointing. *What in heavens name had struck him? He seemed reasonably adjusted before she left.* The bad report from Professor Rondelli was unexpected and it bothered her immensely. *Why did he drop out of school?* Her dad had always stressed how important school and education was. She believed the same. *Something triggered this depression and moved Leonello's mind the wrong way. I must reach him to talk some sense into him. I must try.*

Chapter Twenty Four

Although nostalgic about home, deep in her heart, Gracy felt she had made the right decision to come to New York. Yes, every effort would be made on her part to empower and support her brothers in every way. She wasn't going to waste any more time brooding over her decision of which direction to follow. She got herself together and dialed Ingrid's number. Should she be available, Gracy wanted to have a short, private meeting with her. After all, she was Daniele's live-in partner. She loved her brother so she wanted to accept Ingrid in her heart as part of the Frarano family and as dear to her. She dialed Ingrid's office; her secretary promptly responded.

"Good morning, it's Gracy Robertson. Could I please speak to Miss Klein, if she is available?"

"Miss Robertson, Miss Klein is out of the office part of the morning. Is there anything I can help you with?"

"Oh! I wanted to request a short meeting with her today if possible."

"I will try to reach Miss. Klein and set a time for you. She is booked up until late afternoon. Nevertheless, I will pass on your request. I will get back to you Miss Robertson."

"Great! Thank you." She hung up the phone and sat idly for a while. *After all, what did I expect? This is the USA. People work hard here.*

To her surprise, Ingrid's secretary called promptly back. "Miss Robertson? Yes, Miss. Klein will be happy to see you around five o'clock, if that is fine with you."

She had hoped it would have been earlier. "Great, I will be there at five. Thanks." She would sit in the lobby and admire the people arriving, go to the library read up on hospitality or quiz the managers on duty if they had time for her. The lobbies of the hotels in New York were busy places. People back home were more lay back. *I will adapt to the American customs and fast paced lifestyle.*

When she arrived at the building, she made herself comfortable and analyzed her surroundings. The lobby was lively. People were arriving checking in while others were checking out. Many visitors nonchalantly wandered around. The ambiance was inviting. The crystal chandeliers were sparkling and luminous even in daylight. The plush furnishings were in blue velvet Barocco style. The silver and gold trim was reflected in the shimmery damask wall- paper adding depth and elegance to the lobby. The golden marble consoles topped in white Carrera marble were balanced by mirrors. The enormous, flowered arrangements infused a pleasant fragrance in the air. Gracy was mesmerized taking in her surroundings. She mentally noted the actions of the staff. A gentleman's voice interrupted her focus. "Miss Gracy Robertson! Hello!" She looked up and there he was- the handsome gentleman from her welcome party. "How are you?" A big smile was on his face. For a minute she juggled her memory for his name. "Ah! Mr. Alvaro Fernandez! Good and how are you?" Impeccable in attire and well-groomed, there he stood. His eyes captured hers. He gracefully extended his hand to greet her. "Nice to see you! Are you waiting for anyone?"

"No, not really. Actually, I was just sitting here admiring everything including the staff at the desk. I'm watching their work performance."

"I see. They are not even aware of being under your surveillance. Good for you."

She answered smiling "No, no, it's more for my benefit. It's not about them."

"Are you doing some research of sort or writing a book or a story on our hotel?"

She found him amiable and easy to talk to. "Mr. Fernandez, I plan to occupy myself in New York by working in hospitality, so I was analyzing and wondering if I would like this work?"

"There is no question that you would! There is never a dull moment. Good for you! I am glad. It's a personal choice but is rewarding. I think you will be great at this."

"Thanks for your confidence. How would you know? You don't even know me?"

"I can spot a candidate when I see one. Miss Robertson, your brothers speak highly of you."

She smiled gently at him. "Thank you. You mean my two protectors, of course! For them the only thing I was doing wrong was staying back in Agrigento."

His gaze was fixed on her lovely features and the wavy long hair adorning her face. "On second thought," he said "I am sure your brothers won't mind. Can I treat you to a cup of coffee or a drink? Whatever you would prefer?"

She hesitated for a moment, then considered that she did have time to kill. "I don't want to take you away from your work though."

"I was on my way to the west wing where Ingrid has done some major changes. She insisted I take a second look, before Diego and Daniele come in to give their stamp of approval. You know, we admire her work. She is a perfectionist. The best decorator in New York. But, another pair of eyes is always better."

"Yes, I am told she is a perfectionist. Actually, I am to meet her at five pm. I'm looking forward to seeing her."

"She is a busy girl. Would you like to join me on my inspection after our coffee?"

"Thank you, I would like that. I have nothing else to do. This is why I need to get busy before I go insane with too much leisure time."

"There is plenty of work here, especially with the Frarano brothers' empire."

"They must have told you that my dad was a Professor and I followed his path. I love people and I can dedicate myself to them by passing on the best of my knowledge."

"I am sure you will. Our guests and the rest of our staff will love having someone like you around."

"Mr. Fernandez, you are very encouraging."

Together they walked into the coffee shop; they sat chatting. Gracy, wasn't used to being alone in the company of an eligible male, but she felt comfortable. This nice Spanish fellow seemed sincere and genuine. She liked talking to him. Unexpectedly, he gently placed a hand over hers shocking her a little. There was an intense look in his eyes. Bending his head, he spoke.

"Miss Robertson, I know you come from Italy with its different customs. Here in America, we don't call a person by the last name for long. Please, I give you full permission to call me by my first name Alvaro. You are not used to that. You hardly know me and I am an employee; however, I wouldn't mind being your friend. If I can help you in any way, it would make me happy."

"Thank you" She smiled "Alvaro it will be." Her head nodded in affirmation. "Likewise, please feel free to call me, Gracy!"

His gaze held hers. He had been hypnotized by her beauty, her voice, her being. Time passed before they knew it. Mr. Fernandez glanced at the time. He stood up immediately excusing himself. "Gracy, I enjoyed your company immensely but I must get back to my duties before I get fired. I got pleasantly sidetracked. If you were serious about your new profession, you are welcome to join me on my tour. You might learn something for your new work."

She answered happily, "Álvaro! I would be delighted. Are you sure I won't slow you down or be a burden for you?"

"Gracy! Are you kidding me? I am honored to be in your company. Please!" He gestured with his extended arm. "After you."

Gracy, let out a big sigh of relief to his response. She felt so comfortable with this Mr. Alvaro Fernandez. He had brightened her day. This unexpected turn of events was going to be fruitful. Her life had been sedentary for too long for her. With an alert mind, she strode beside him, listening carefully and admiring the renovations. All the colours flowed harmoniously intermarrying perfection from the floor to the walls to the furnishings and to the touches of the accessories. "Wow. Seeing this is a treat for me."

"Ingrid' sure has talent. She knows what she is doing." He complimented the firm's designer.

"I see. Everything is coordinated to perfection."

Alvaro was well spoken. Gracy was totally captured by his explanations and his Spanish accent. Before she knew it, it was time to meet Ingrid. She hated to part ways. Her day had been splendid and fulfilled, so turning to her new friend she extended her hands to thank him.

Alvaro gently reached out to hold both her hands leaning his head. "Gracy, in Spain we part with our friends by kissing on the cheeks. Can we?" He reached out and kissed her on both sides of her cheeks. "Thank you for making my work much more interesting and fulfilling today."

While sitting in Ingrid's office waiting for her to arrive, Gracy couldn't stop considering the day's event. Alvaro's voice resonated like music to her ears. *He was helpful, cordial and most of all positively influential*. Now she was looking forward to relating it all to her brothers and to announcing her new career choice in hospitality.

The door opened and there was Ingrid furiously rushing in and looking at her watch. "Five o'clock sharp." She said "I didn't want to keep you waiting. The traffic here in New York is deadly."

"Ingrid, not to worry about me. These days I have all the time in the world with nothing else other than shopping and lunches with acquaintances or my brothers. I don't know which is better sometimes, leisure or overwhelming work."

Ingrid reached out and gave her a hug and sat beside her. "Tell me, what's on your mind?"

"Ingrid, I was at a loss this morning. I was resigned to spending another day in nothingness, Mr. Alvaro Fernandez spotted me sitting in the lobby and it turned out to be a marvelous day."

"Oh! What did you do?" Ingrid seemed very interested.

"We had a coffee and a bite to eat. When he was ready to get back to work he asked me if I was interested in going along on his inspection. I must compliment you on your work. I am impressed. Magnificent from every point of view. Mr. Fernandez had nothing but praise."

"Thank you. We need to create the utmost in convenience, comfort and beauty for our guests. It's my job to make sure everything is perfect. We get people from all over the world here, people with money. They only want the best. Mr. Fernandez has good taste but he hasn't been with us long. I am glad you had a good day with him."

"Ingrid, I have been at a loss for a while. I have been here eight months now. Diego wants me to be involved in clubs, foundations, charities, as well as enjoying shopping and leisure at his expense. I have no one else here other than my brothers. They mean well. But I need to work, to be productive. My life has to have meaning. Back home I was teaching. I had my students, my volunteer work at the hospital. I had a purpose. You read me? I love my brothers but if I don't have a career, my days feel empty and purposeless."

"What would you like to do? Have you given it some thought?"

"Yes, I have! I have been considering hospitality in the hotels, although I am inexperienced."

"Well! You sure will be busy. I don't want to discourage you. The demands, at times, can be endless and run you off your feet."

"I like to keep busy. My dad and I worked relentlessly. We only had each other; work was our salvation."

"Gracy, did you discuss your intentions with Diego and Daniele?"

"No. I haven't. I will tonight or tomorrow. This is why I wanted another woman's opinion, if you don't mind me burdening you."

"Oh! Not at all. I feel flattered you are valuing my opinion."

"Thank you. Today going around with Mr. Fernandez, watching him doing his rounds, I enjoyed it. It was an eye opener and it reinforced my decision."

Ingrid had been wondering, why a woman gifted in beauty and intelligence was not dating or committed with anyone of the opposite sex. She had never heard her brothers mention anybody interested in their sister. Maybe she is a lesbian, in the closet.

Without hesitation she asked. "I see. I don't mean to pry. Are you in a relationship with anyone? Do you have a boyfriend back home or are you seeing anybody here?"

"No, not at all."

"Have you ever been in love or considered marrying in the future? My apologies for asking all these questions because if you get into hospitality there are night shifts, which is fine if you are single and emotionally uninvolved. No marriage no children."

She laughed shyly "I understand; no one has struck me as the one yet." Then she placed her head down. *Yeah. Even those ridiculous kids at school with infantile crushes like the rest of the young men in Sicily were afraid to approach me, except for Leonello and his misguided declaration of love. Here they are more liberated and easier going. Other than admiring Alvaro, no one has touched my heart, but he could be just friend material.*

Ingrid poured out her thoughts. "There is a difference between us. You are anxious to work. I am tired of working. I want to get married, have more time to myself and be supported. Daniele doesn't want to commit to marriage. I get frustrated; we end up fighting all the time lately. I want a family. No, he likes things the way they are between us. I don't know what to make of him. Someday soon things will have to change, or I am out of here and goodbye Daniele." By now her voice was raised out of control. Her face was flushed, and her voice was angry. Gracy felt badly for her. If the cards had been reversed, how would she have felt?

There was no encouragement or advice from Miss Klein. They belonged to two different worlds. Gracy couldn't relate to Ingrid because marriage hadn't been on her mind. She had never been in love. No one had stolen her heart so far. The divorce factor in America was also another problem. The women back home tolerated more in marriage. She suspected that both of her brothers were afraid of a legal marriage, family and children and the possible negative consequences. She knew their thinking was skewed also. She almost sympathized with Ingrid if she honestly loved her brother. Her gut feeling gave her wrong signals. But, if she has other motives, God help both of them. *I can only offer her pity.*

A strong desire came over her to excuse herself and to exit as soon as she could. It had been a big mistake coming here. There was no selfishness in her heart and soul but Miss Klein's heart and soul seemed suspect. She stood up turned around placed a hand on Ingrid's shoulder sympathizing "Ingrid, I am sorry I bothered you with my indecision. You must be tired. It's probably been a long day for you. You need a rest. I hope you get what you are after and life works in your favor. Good night. I wish you a restful evening with my brother."

150

Chapter Twenty Five

While Gracy was trying hard to take in this new world of hers, back in Agrigento Leonello's body and soul had hit bottom. Totally out of breath, his elderly mom had just finished climbing the stepladder to reach her son's hiding spot. She slowly dragged her feet toward his cot. There he lay, mid-day, wrapped in a torn blanket. Mrs. Dante despaired. She reached out to him, trying to untangle his blanket. "Son of mine please do it for me. Come down. I have some warm milk and toast. Put some food in your stomach. Leonello, why are you doing this to yourself? You are the only hope I have left. Please *amore,* love, let me help you."

"Mom. No. Leave me alone. No one can help me. I have no desire to live." Leonello's refusal to leave the rat hole of an attic was adamant. He desired only darkness.

"Leonello, my dear, how long are you going to keep this up?" she asked while gently caressing his forehead and pushing back the unwashed hair covering his eyes. Leonello, didn't want sympathy. He rudely grabbed her hand and removed it. He preferred to abandon himself to solitary misery.

"Son, I went to the market. I ran into one of your professors. He asked me how you were doing. What could I tell him? I started to cry. He said he wants to come and see you."

"Mom, leave me alone. I don't want to see anybody."

"Why son?"

"Why? They don't care about me. Nobody does!"

"Why do you say that son? I certainly care for you."

"Yeah, only when you are sober, which isn't often."

"Leonello, please don't' criticize. I hurt also. People like your professor do care. He was a gentleman. He saw I didn't have enough money to pay for a ricotta cheese that I wanted to buy for you. He paid for it. I thought if you come down I will serve it to you for breakfast."

"Mom, you should have never allowed him to pay. I am sick of being a charity case. I hate life. Those professors think we are nothing more than peasants. That Miss Robertson was always preaching about doing good deeds. What did she do? She took off for the big life in America. As if she didn't have it made here. Mom they look down on us. They don't care about the miserable."

Mrs. Dante chose to ignore his comments. "Come on son. Get up. Wash up. Come to have something to eat."

"I am not hungry. You don't understand. I just want to be left alone."

"How long can you be left alone in this darkness? The sun is shining out there and there is a beautiful world waiting for you to live. Please, it is breaking my heart to see you wasting your youth into nothingness."

"Leave me alone Mom, will you. There is no beautiful world for me out there. I wish I was dead. There is no hope, no blue sky, no sunshine, just darkness in my world. I hate it."

His mom didn't know what to do anymore. Months had passed. He had slipped into this state that didn't make sense to her. She cried. *Who can I turn for help? So far no one has been able to alleviate him of his melancholy. His father has turned our lives into a nightmare, destroying myself and both of my sons.*

As more time passed, Leonello's body was getting weaker and powerless. Mrs. Dante didn't know where to turn for help. Her prayers hadn't worked so far. She was losing faith. There was no use talking to her criminal husband. He wouldn't be able to help his messed-up son. She had many sleepless nights. However, on this one morning, a light of hope flickered in her mind. She had a plan.

Mrs. Dante, ignoring her aching knees, walked a long way leaning on her cane to reach the university. She patiently sat like a beggar at the front steps of the entrance of the school. She kept watching the students mingling enthusiastically. That made her sadder Why can't my son be among them, living like a normal human being? She spotted his friends Romero and Gianni. "They must help me "she murmured to herself. Mrs. Dante knew Romero had shown some caring for her son. He had come a few times to the house to inquire about him, but lately he had given up. Her intuition was right. She quickly pulled her shawl over her head to further conceal her identity. She approached them pitifully. "Per carita, please, Romero, Gianni, can I talk to you."

"Oh, Mrs. Dante, how are you? Leonello, how is he?"

"Not good, my Leonello. I wish he was here with you."

"We wish he was also."

"Is he coming out of his depression Mrs. Dante?" asked Gianni

"My Leonello is so down that I don't know what to do with him anymore. He is wasting away into nothing; this is why I am here. Maybe you boys can help me talk some sense into him. I wish you would come and talk to him, please. I need someone to help me before I lose my mind." She broke down in tears. Both young men were moved. They knew Leonello always talked kindly about his mom so why was he now causing her so much grief. They couldn't understand. Gianni was the first to respond "Mrs. Dante, yes, sure, I will come."

Gianni still felt his role was less significant. Hesitantly, he said to Mrs. Dante "I cannot promise that he would listen to me. He considered me the third wheel. Romero might be more motivating."

Romero promptly intervened "Mrs. Dante. I have a better idea. We will talk to Professor Rondelli to see if he can help us. We have been discussing Leonello with him lately. It bothers us a lot what's happening to him. The professor is connected to Miss Robertson. He lives in her home. Maybe he can contact Miss Robertson for us. Something has to give; we cannot let our friend go much longer barred in that dark attic."

"Please, please, Jesus, somebody has to help that son of mine. My daughters don't want to have anything to do with him; my husband and his older brother are in jail with no parole in sight. People scorn us as bad people; they stay away from us. I have no one to turn to."

"Mrs. Dante, let me talk to Mr. Rondelli today. If he doesn't want to be involved directly, I will see if I can get him to give me Miss Robertson's address or phone number. I would have to go to the *piazza* at the pharmacy to use the phone because like you we don't have that luxury at home."

"Please, Romero, thank you. Somebody needs to reach my son in his misery. I will pray for both of your souls. I came to search for you out of desperation. You are giving me hope."

They parted and Carmela pulled out her rosary beads slipping them through her fingers in prayer as she walked home.

***

Romero missed his friend although he had resented him in the past for his bullying. Now he felt sorry for him. Their past corrupt actions, ordered by Leonello, had caused him panic in the past. They were fortunate that they weren't behind bars. Thankfully, their kind teacher had not pressed charges. Romero had reluctantly participated in some of the actions forced on him and Gianni by Leonello, but his friend Leonello was cooked for Miss Robertson. His hidden love had begun to reveal itself in different ways and many of them not good. Leonello was now punishing himself by destroying his life. He knew Miss Robertson's intentions were only to be a good teacher. Romero was a rational young man who understood that the difference in status between his friend and Miss. Robertson was huge. That was why he didn't encourage Leonello's infatuation for their teacher. When he noticed Leonello lost in his daydreams he chided him. "Eh! My friend you are chasing a wild rainbow. Snap out of it. She will leave soon."

Deep in his heart, he knew that even he could have become infatuated with Miss. Robertson, but, he knew better, and it was forbidden. She was stunning- physically fit, sweet, and she had a magnetic personality. He had noticed, especially close to her departure, that Leonello wasn't himself. The lion had become morbid and after she departed he had gone totally insane. Romero had warned him "You are getting emotionally sick my friend" The roles in their friendship had changed and he couldn't predict what was next for any of them.

156

Chapter Twenty Six

It was late morning in New York. Gracy woke up startled at the sound of the grandfather clock counting to ten. In disbelief she jumped out of bed, scolding herself. *Why did I allow myself to wake up this late?* As she moved forward her aching body reminded her of the restless night she had endured. The accidental encounter with Alvaro had been enlightening and pleasant. Afterwards, the conversation with Ingrid had revealed some worrisome details. The meeting with Ingrid had taken all her earlier enthusiasm away. As a result, she had tossed and turned all night long. Today her brothers wanted to meet her for lunch. She made up her mind to go ahead with her original intentions. No, Miss. Klein's shortcomings would not or could not disillusion her. Ignoring the unpleasant recollection, she jumped in the shower to get herself ready for a new brighter day.

She walked in, at la Rotonda on 27th Street to find Diego and Daniele waiting for her. After the affectionate embraces, she sat down feeling relieved in the company of her two protectors.

"Well Missy! You look fabulous as ever. We are so proud of you." complimented Diego.

"Thanks, you are always complimentary. I wonder if I really deserve all that admiration from you both." She smiled gracefully.

Daniele grabbed her hand and leaning gently toward her spoke. "So, let's get into business. The grapevine rumors are that we might have another entrepreneur joining us."

Gracy's face lit up. "Who are you referring to Daniele?"

"Come on Gracy who else! Mr. Fernandez, reported to me yesterday. He had the pleasure of doing the inspection with Miss Robertson. He has high hopes that you are serious about your new career. Then my Ingrid arrived home last night and related to me your new intention that you shared in a meeting with her."

"Yes Daniele, your information is correct. I would like to be in the hospitality industry. It would be new for me, challenging of course, but at the same time a break from teaching."

Diego reassured her. "Gracy, you will be good at whatever you choose, because you give all of yourself. There is no doubt that you will excel."

"You guys believe in me so much. God forbid should I fail your expectations."

"You've got our blood flowing through your veins. We are hard workers and we never give up until we achieve success."

"Thank you again for those words of encouragement. I guess the only thing left to say is when do I start and where do I start and who will be teaching me?"

Daniele, wide eyed, spoke. "Gracy, first and foremost, where would you like to start? You can pick and choose any one of our hotels. Las Vegas is new; they could use you badly there. The Regency here in Manhattan is always in need. The Plaza Hotel is another. You make the choice." Daniele had greater responsibility for the hotels. He could advise her better. Diego, with his involvement in the law firm, was better versed in legal matters for the corporation, his active law firm and the demands of his clients.

Gracy was nervous, and excited at the same time. This world was totally new to her. Teaching young people had its rewards. She had to admit that at times dealing with difficult teenagers had been nerve racking but, ultimately, it was fulfilling.

"When can I start?" She asked vibrantly

"I think for now, it will be better if you start in New York." suggested Diego. He was looking after her wellbeing by wanting her nearby.

"Diego, I know what my protectors hope for even if they say the choice is mine. I wouldn't consider taking off for Washington, Vegas, or Los Angeles. Yes! Without a question. I prefer New York for now. Who will be teaching me?" She looked at both of them but turned more toward Daniele.

Daniele was well informed as to the operations of all the hotels although he also was more committed to his architecture. Diego listened attentively as Daniele took the lead speaking wisely "Diego, Gracy is willing to work in New York. We want to keep her here don't we? That was the main reason for her to come- to be closer to us. So, with her approval I would say the Regency is a good place for her to start; don't you think?"

"I agree. Now Mr. Fernandez is back and forth. He supervises New York and Vegas. He can teach you plenty and be a good adviser for you Sis. The people on our staff are well trained. Gracy, you can learn a lot from all of them. Mr. Álvaro is one of our best CEOs; however, his demands are overwhelming at times. He might not be available for you at times. You can seek advice from our manager in Personnel, whenever you need it. Then there is Ingrid. You can reach out to her."

Gracy involuntarily shivered at the mention of her name. Ingrid Klein rubbed her the wrong way for some strange reason. She hoped not to need her advice in her learning processes. *God help me in this new career if I need her help.* She didn't dare say anything and kept her concerns to herself.

The next morning Gracy woke up early and invigorated. She was going to get ready for a new beginning in this amazing city. She pulled the curtains wide open. There a bright sky filled with gleaming sunrays seemed to be shining all in her favour. At nine o'clock sharp she reported to the Administration Office of the Hyatt Regency. Gracy didn't know who was going to be her tutor for this new day. When the door opened, Mr. Alvaro Fernandez, welcomed her in "Good morning, Miss. Robertson, please come in." He extended his hand "Allow me to congratulate you and welcome you to our group." He pulled a chair back inviting her to sit down.

Gracy's face lightened with her big smile. "Good morning! Thank you." Pleased to see her, he took a seat beside her. "I am truly honored that your brothers have entrusted you to me. Today is the beginning of your new adventure in this fantastic career in hospitality. I will do my best to show you the ropes of our operations."

As he continued speaking she surreptitiously studied him. He was impeccably dressed in his navy blue suit, crisp white silk shirt and a complementing paisley tie. His demeanour was sophisticated and his Spanish accent charming. He was courteous and well mannered. Gracy felt a great sense of relief. She had only heard praise for Mr. Alvaro Fernandez. While a warm rush zipped through her body, her cheeks blushed flaming red. She was excited at the prospect of working with him...of being with him. *Thanks to my brothers I am in good hands.*

Yes, Mr. Alvaro not only had a pleasant demeanour about him. He also manifested a positive aura that attracted others to his infectious personality. Before she spoke Mr. Fernandez, encouraged her, stating "Miss Robertson, I know you are determined to give all of yourself to learn and perform diligently. I have no doubt you will master the ins and outs of a hospitality career in no time."

"Thank you so much for your encouraging thoughts. I will work hard to measure up to your expectations." She took a deep breath. *No, I cannot afford to fail.* She pulled the note book out of her purse as well as her good luck pen gifted to her by her dad. "Mr. Alvaro, here I am with pen and paper in hand. I am ready to take notes."

He gently gestured to her indicating that they were on the way to start the day. "Well let's start our tour. After you. Miss Robertson."

"Mr. Fernandez, I thought we had agreed. Please call me Gracy."

"Thank you Gracy. I will brief you on the key needs in every department. You will master them one at the time. We will start from the bottom and move on to the top. As you have been advised, you will have others also teaching you. Your brother Daniele shifts me all over the place on short notice. We must make ourselves available where we are most needed. There are also some daily crises that occur unexpectedly. We must resolve all the issues by putting our guests first and foremost." Gracy was listening attentively, jotting down notes

"Let's start with housekeeping." He opened the door to a perfectly tidy room ready for occupancy. "It's very important when guests walk in that the rooms are well presented in perfect conditions- tidy, airy, lustrous, and all the toiletries and supplies in place." And so Gracy's lessons in hospitality began.

Chapter Twenty Seven

While Gracy was enthusiastically initiating her new adventure in search of success, back in Agrigento, the students she had so earnestly worked hard to save were on the verge of disaster. She had left hopeful that her good deed had paid off. Yes, she had given them her heart and soul. Now they could move on empowered. It would have never occurred to her that her students, especially the ringleader, Leonello, had seriously reached a point of no return.

As promised to Mrs. Dante, Romero had every intention to do his share. Lucky for him he had Professor Rondelli teaching his first class this morning. He grabbed Gianni by the arm, whispering to him "Look Bro, at the end of our class, we will approach the professor. You have to back me up. If we can convince Professor Rondelli to put us in touch with Miss Robertson, I am sure we can help our friend. You saw the state of his poor mother. We must try to alleviate her sorrow." Romero wasn't as gutsy now in Leonello's absence. Gianni had always been a compliant kid who Leonello had abused in the past. "Romero, I am with you, of course. I am ready to help if I can."

As planned Romero, with Gianni behind him, respectfully walked up to Mr. Rondelli after most of the other students had left. "Professor Rondelli can we talk to you please?" The professor was somewhat puzzled. He scrutinized them. After his bad experience with them, he wondered what they were about. He noticed the anxiety on their faces and Romero's shaky voice. He spoke in a clear-cut tone. "Yes. What's the problem guys?" His intuition anticipated trouble. The boys were looking at each other afraid they were about to be reprimanded for participating in that beating on that dark evening months ago.

"What can I do for you?"

"Professor Rondelli, you know Leonello has dropped out of school." Romero started off.

"Yes, I know. The president and I were discussing him the other day."

"If that isn't bad enough, he is so depressed and has no desire to live anymore." added Gianni.

"If we don't intervene, he is finished." continued Romero despondently.

"Professor, he won't leave that dark attic day or night." Gianni replied wide eyed.

"Professor, he won't take any more food. His mom came to talk to us before class begging us to help. She is heartbroken. We must help him somehow."

"Yes, the principal and I have discussed him a couple of times. It's a shame because we thought he had come around. As matter of fact, I mentioned him to Miss Robertson when I spoke to her recently."

At the mention of Miss. Robertson they jumped, encouraged. "That is why we came to talk to you." Both of them were racing to talk but Professor Rondelli spoke first.

"We are in touch with her every now and then. We do live in her home. I never thought the problem with Leonello was that serious. When you guys hung around together, he was a tyrant. I was warned when I first arrived here. What do you guys have in mind? Maybe the principal and I should pay him a visit. It's possible that we didn't try hard enough with him. I had had my encounter with him and it put me off. I suspected there were other hoodlums that acted with him. Maybe I should have reached out. The principal always encourages us to try to help regardless, when one of our students drops out." Professor Rondelli waited for their response.

Romero scratched his head. "We thought to get in touch with Miss Robertson, because she had helped him a lot. He had changed for the better. He respected her. I don't understand why he slipped into this awful mental state or why he quit school. He is not the Leonello we used to know anymore. He used to order us around, you know. If we didn't follow his orders, he would have his brother's goons beat us up." He thought it better to relate that version, hoping it would convince the professor.

"Fellows, sorry! I cannot get involved." He shook his head.

"Professor please, Miss Robertson would help."

"I would like to help sincerely but I cannot! Her private number and address are confidential and must be used sparingly. You are her former students. Dangerous ones if I might add."

"Professor, do you believe in saving a life?" asked young Gianni.

"The only thing I can do is relate what you told me to her and let you know what she says."

"Please Professor, I know she cared so much for our wellbeing."

"I understand. She is noted for her kindness but at this time I am not ready to hand you any information regarding Miss Robertson's address or private life."

Romero was disappointed. Gianni, after listening, decided to press again. "Professor, I respect your reluctance. If you promise to speak to Miss Robertson, tell her we just want to save him. He is in bad shape. His mom is pitiful to look at. We know he has been bad in the past; you understand me." He frowned without explaining further. "At the same time, she might be able to save him."

"I have a suggestion. You know his address? What if we ask Miss Robertson to get in touch with him?" suggested the professor.

Gianni answered "How can she call him? They have no phone. He doesn't get out."

"She can write to him. I am sure he will want to read a letter from his former teacher." He nudged him with his elbow. "Romero you know and I know he had the hots for her."

"What! You guys, you still want me to give you her address after hearing that?" He listened to them, puzzled. They just remained staring at him, both disappointed at his reaction.

"Professor, come on. Please." Romero responded.

"Not from me."

"Please we must do something, anything to help." They both begged.

"Wait a minute. Maybe Gianni is right. I will call Miss. Robertson, update her and suggest she write to him, only if she wants to. Okay fellows, I will not promise you anything." He glanced at his watch. "I must go now." Professor Giacomo Rondelli gathered his papers in his briefcase and ushered them out the door. Reflecting on the conversation that had taken place, he turned around and decided to knock on the door of the principal's office to discuss the matter further. *Call it fate or a change in my heart. I must admit to myself, it is admirable for those boys to help that friend of theirs even though he had been a menace in the past.* He walked into the principal's office. Matteo Dario was very accommodating and a good listener. "Matteo, with all due respect I want to relate to you what these two young men have brought to my attention."

"By all means, Professor, that is what I am here for. Hopefully I will be able to provide you with good advice."

"As you know I always want the right protocols in place. Deep down, I admire those two young men, wanting to help their friend. We are familiar with the situation of Leonello Dante, past and present. Now my question to you is, should you and I try further to help him or get

Miss Robertson involved should she be willing to work with a former student?"

He chose to ignore Gianni's revelations of Leonello's infatuation with Miss Robertson.

"I don't see any harm in asking Miss Robertson to help with the wellbeing of a former student. Yes, why not let her know of his mental state right now. I must say I feel badly for him and the poor mother. We know Leonello is a victim of abuse. My friend, do what you need to do. Maybe we can stabilize his mental health."

After the discussion with the principal, Mr. Rondelli felt better in moving forward. He promised he would call Miss Robertson. *I will suggest to her that she write a short note to the troubled former student. It could help save his life.*

Gianni and Romero, like the professor, had parted with deep hope rooted in their souls. They both anxiously waited for some uplifting news to turn the direction of Leonello's situation, especially for Leonello's sake.

168

Chapter Twenty Eight

Gracy's head was full these days. Once she entered her luxurious suite the routines of the past hadn't left her. She would pour herself a soft drink and step on the terrace. Here she would be admiring the amazing skyscrapers above and the traffic and fast pace of the people below. She compared it to the sights she left behind in Sicily. The quietness of her back home balcony and the view in Agrigento was peaceful. This new life in New York was invigorating. During the day she would be totally absorbed in learning something new. Once at home her brain wouldn't shut down. She recalled a lesson from her father. 'Gracy sit; focus on your thoughts and store the information in your memory. These recollections will serve you later.' She brought a hand to brush her hair back as if to clear her thoughts. *Yes, Dad I need to review the day's events.* Today, she was totally absorbed in the replay of the learning processes. Surprisingly, Mr. Alvaro Fernandez's voice resonated pleasurably in her head. *If only I could work more with him.* The staff were taking turns in teaching her the responsibilities of different departments. Every day was a new experience. Although the work was fascinating, she needed to open her mind to absorb it all. To her delight, that every night she couldn't wait for the next day to start anew.

The next morning for some strange reason Ingrid was waiting for her at the concierge. "Gracy, good morning." Ingrid greeted with a big smile.

"Good morning, Ingrid," she replied, surprised to find her there.

Ingrid turned to the staff at the desk and spoke with authority. "Rita, Frank, Miss Robertson will be working with me today."

Gracy was surprised "Oh! Not a bad idea. You will brief me on interior decorating?" She responded trying to sound upbeat. She smiled.

"Shall we go?" Ingrid walked away at a fast pace. Gracy marched alongside of her trying to keep up.

The two people at the desk looked at each other disappointed, because the day before they had been told that Gracy would be working there learning the booking part of Reception. Now that she was taken away, her absence meant that they would have to rearrange the day's activities. As much as they didn't agree with the change, they felt they couldn't protest. "That Miss Ingrid always walks in as if she owns the place." pouted Rita, to her colleague.

"Ingrid where are we going exactly?" asked Gracy once she saw they were at the front door of the hotel. The valet was bringing Ingrid's car around.

"You will be surprised. You have been working at the Hyatt for a while; a change will do you good. Let's do something different today."

"I am open." Gracy tried to erase any doubt from her mind.

Ingrid maneuvered the traffic well. Gracy admired her expertise while thinking *I need to acquire the same skills should I make New York my residence*. Ingrid pulled up in front of the Plaza Hotel. The doormen and valet promptly jumped up at her arrival. Ingrid knew everyone by first name. Gracy followed her like a little puppy. They approached the front desk. Ingrid stepped away to the Administrator's Office to get some keys. Gracy was admiring the spectacular lobby while she waited. The shimmery wallpaper complimented the marble floor lustrously and the enormous chandeliers were unique. The furnishings spectacularly enhanced the colour choices of the lobby's foyer.

She stood there spell bound. Her brothers had not brought her here yet. When Ingrid's voice jolted her. "Gracy! You seem hypnotized. What is it?"

"I must say this lobby is magnificent; did you put it together?"

"Yes I did. Don't tell me your brothers never brought you here?"

"It's not their fault. Every time I came to visit, my time was constrained. My classes and my students were my priority and so I was always rushing to get back. Also, my dad was my main concern then. You know I just lost my dad last year."

"Oh, yes I was told. Well, you are here now. We are going to work on the penthouse. The place needs to be revamped. We host most of the dignitaries from the Far East at this site. They only want the best and they have the money to get it. You will see." All the while, Ingrid's eyes were darting everywhere- checking people arriving, staff at work, or anyone she knew as part of the hotel operation. She must have spotted someone. She suddenly grabbed Gracy's arm to stop her from proceeding forward. "Excuse me Gracy, wait right here for a minute. I will be right back. I need to have few words with that gentleman there." Her high heels clicked as she quickly walked across the polished floor to talk to an attendant in uniform. Gracy, remained waiting, standing there keenly observing Ingrid in her calculated approach. *Ingrid's personality switched to meet her needs and the situation accordingly. I was brought up to be more reserved, more detached. Oh well to each her own.*

Now Ingrid was walking toward her with the fellow beside her. "Gracy, this is Walter, an old friend of mine from Washington."

He extended his hand "My pleasure to meet you, Miss Robertson."

"Likewise, Walter, nice meeting you."

"You are in good hands here. Ingrid is one of the best in her field."

"So, I am told. Looking forward to being enlightened by her today."

"Well, we must get going" Ingrid stated.

"Great meeting you Miss Robertson."

Then he turned to Ingrid, "See you around Ingrid. Have a good day." He walked away.

"By his uniform, he must be a security officer." said Gracy.

"Yes, he is employed by a private company. I helped him get the job. We went to school together. I tried to help him. He wanted badly to move to New York."

The door opened to the penthouse that they were going to refurbish. Here Mr. Alvaro Fernandez gracefully welcomed them. It was a total surprise for Gracy, since she had not seen him for several days. Her heart flipped. Gracy, couldn't understand why nervousness took over her body at the surprise appearance of this Spanish fellow. Her gaze fixated on him. She saw Ingrid falling all over him, embracing and holding him close. Ingrid's enthusiasm for him was overboard and disturbing.

It was Mr. Fernandez that broke the embrace. He turned to Gracy, half embarrassed. "Miss Robertson, you are in good hands to-day."

Ignoring her body's reactions, she smiled at him "I can't wait. Every day is something new. It is all interesting and good for the soul. I must admit it stimulates my brain"

Mr. Alvaro continued on in his usual pleasantness. "Well girls, I will leave you two as I must move on." He excused himself exiting the suite.

Ingrid picked up a paper on the desk to see what orders Mr. Alvaro Fernandez had jotted down. Although she was the best of the best, everything that was needed to be done required his stamp of approval. Ingrid with her conniving ways always worked her way into the process.

She turned to Gracy who was standing there admiring this spectacular place. Ingrid interrupted her by mentioning Mr. Fernandez "Gracy, what do you think of Alvaro? He is in high demand here; his expertise is highly sought from one hotel to the other."

"I am told he has come on board with a wealth of knowledge." she responded.

Ingrid had other motives for quizzing Gracy. She was no fool and had noticed how Gracy's sparkling eyes widened when seeing Alvaro. She asked. "You worked with him few days. What do you think of him? How would you rate him? Has he impressed you with his advice, gentility, and endearing manners?"

"He is a gentleman, a great mentor. It was pleasurable working with him. I learned a lot."

She envisioned him waiting for her on those first mornings. That gave her great pleasure. If only he could have been around more often to show her the ropes. She loved his advice, concern and, most of all, his accent. She wasn't going to confide her feelings and desires to Ingrid, because deep down the gut feeling about Ingrid didn't sit well with her.

Gracy Robertson had never been involved romantically. She had no expertise in the dating world. She only knew her father's love, the love her stepbrothers and hers for them. The rest was left to fate when the time was right. Godmother Fabiana had been her mentor throughout her adolescence. Modesty, humility and good behaviour had been encouraged. Integrity was always important to her. Diego had been such a protector since they relocated to Agrigento from the far land of Australia. They were not quite familiar with the Sicilian customs, but they lived in the best way they knew how. Now here in the USA, she had noticed the genders were more liberated from traditional roles. It was admirable in certain ways. Almost every night she dined with her brothers. Often their girlfriends joined them. Diego, smiling one evening after a drink of wine with his meal, had cheered "Eh Sis, should you fancy someone or your heart awaken to a New Yorker, it's okay. You are entitled."

"I totally agree." added Daniele. She blushed "You guys want to get rid of me?"

She had to admit deep down she felt like the fifth wheel. Ingrid was all over her brother making a nuisance of herself. Rosella, Diego's girlfriend seemed more modest and well behaved.

"I am not in any hurry fellows. For your information, I am perfectly fine until my heart desires otherwise."

Ingrid had often questioned her about dating. Ingrid was shocked at her reservations. At times Gracy had caught her rolling her eyes when they introduced her to other gentlemen. Gracy always behaved in a reserved manner that others might interpret as prim and proper. Ingrid didn't suspect that her future sister- in -law, disapproved, but Gracy didn't appreciate her brother's girlfriend falling all over other fellows and lingering with her arms around their necks. In fact, she silently disapproved of Ingrid's flirting especially when it was with Alvaro Fernandez.

The next day she was stationed at the lobby front desk again at the Plaza Hotel. Gracy, was in full view of the entire large lobby. The people were coming and going like bees buzzing around their hives. It was a busy morning. She spotted Ingrid, with an arm around the guy in uniform that she had casually introduced the day before. She was standing so close to his face that she was almost touching his lips. She was becoming more aware of her Daniele's girlfriend's inappropriate behaviour. She simply didn't like it. Every day there was an episode to observe. This morning Gracy was assigned to the Hyatt Regency working at Reception to receive and check in guests. She liked that as she didn't have to ride with Ingrid to the other hotel. To her surprise, Mr. Fernandez came to her station looking for her. Her heart flickered when she saw him. He was all smiles greeting her with a handshake. "Gracy, good morning. I have been waiting for you."

"Oh! Did you get a report on my performance?" She smiled and tried to be humorous.

"As a matter of fact, I was wondering if you have time for me today. We could meet for lunch. It is the only time I have and we can go over some notes on your progress."

"That sounds great. It's fine by me."

"Would you like to go to the bistro around the corner? The food is good and the place is casual. A change of scenery will do you good. How is I: 00 pm?"

Gracy couldn't care less if it wasn't the Ritz. She was looking forward to his company. "Fine, see you then."

"I will come for you; we will walk over together."

All morning Gracy kept glancing at her watch trying to control her anxiety. It was now 12:50. To her surprise, as she looked up, she spotted Ingrid, high heels clicking and coming toward her. As Ingrid approached the front desk she asked with an air of authority "Gracy have you had your lunch break yet?"

Why is she here now? I am surprised. Gracy hadn't heard from her all morning. Which wind had blown her over to this hotel when her duty today was to finish the crucial touch up for the arrival of the dignitary from Bali at the Plaza Hotel? Recomposing herself, she answered "No, Ingrid. I am going in few minutes. I have to meet Mr. Alvaro."

"Really, by yourself? Or is Diego joining you?" she asked, sarcasm dripping in her voice.

"I think it is just the two of us."

As she said that, Alvaro promptly arrived. Ingrid didn't waste time jumping all over him with her flirtatious behaviour. Gracy attempted to hide her distress. *She is so overboard her version of friendliness. It is embarrassing. Her flirtation is hard to take but who am I to judge? Maybe this is the custom here.*

Alvaro slowly took Ingrid's arms down from his neck to free himself; he was somewhat annoyed. "Are you ready to go Gracy?" They proceeded to walk away. Ingrid stood aside disappointed. She was angry and insulted to be discarded by Mr. Fernandez. *It's because of me, he has this job:* by highly recommending him for the CEO position. Ingrid stood there venomously staring at them as they walked away. "You will be sorry Mr. Fernandez. You too bitch, for disrespecting me." She stomped away in fury.

Chapter Twenty Nine

Smiling to herself Gracy happily approached her suite at the penthouse. "Another beautiful day in paradise." she quietly acknowledged. She was jiggling the keys at her door when she heard the phone ringing relentlessly. She tried to hurry; she wasn't fast enough. *Oh, well, whoever it was will call again.* Having had lunch with Alvaro Fernandez, her energy had been reinvigorated. Tonight she felt like having a Margherita to celebrate the end of a meaningful day. She poured herself the spiced drink and sat there reminiscing. *I must admit his presence creates such a pleasurable effect in me. I have never experienced that before. It's soothing and exciting at the same time. Is my attraction to him and my resentment of Ingrid touching and flirting with him jealousy? The butterflies in my chest when I see him, his pleasant voice, God help me, are they the signs of love? Am I falling in love with Mr. Alvaro? What do I really know of love? I have been sheltered all my life. I must share this with Godmother Fabiana.* She looked up at her clock on the wall. It was shortly after six in New York. *Too late. I will call first thing in the morning.*

Early the next morning the phone beside her bed rang, disturbing her earlier than usual. Half asleep, she reached out to answer. When she heard an Italian voice greeting, her ears perked up. *"Pronto?* Ready? She sat erect on the bed to listen attentively. *"Oh! Pronto! Buon giorno!"* she recognized the voice of Giacomo Rondelli.

"Gracy, it's Giacomo here. Sorry for waking you up this early. How are you? "

"No problem! How are you?"

"Fine, everything is good at the house. My family is well. I cannot thank you enough for your generosity."

"Don't mention it. It has worked out great for both of us."

"Gracy I apologize for burdening you. I thought to call from the office here at the university. The principal is with me. He will talk to you also. It's regarding one of your previous students, Leonello Dante."

Gracy held her breath, "Yes, what's wrong?"

"As I mentioned to you awhile back, he had dropped out of his classes. Apparently, I am told, he is in a bad mental state. His two friends, Gianni and Romero, tell us that he won't eat or won't leave the dark dingy attic he has closed himself in. He is diminishing physically and emotionally day by day. His mother is devastated and so are those two young fellows that cannot talk sense into him. The principal and I tried. We cannot reach him. We wondered if you could help."

Gracy' listened hard. She thought Leonello had completely come around.

"I'll let you speak, to our principal here."

"Miss Robertson, Mr. Dario here. Sorry to bother you. As Professor Rondelli explained to you,

If you could help this young man, it would mean a lot to all of us. We know he was a ruffian. He had come around. We were all happy. Unfortunately, he has had such a relapse. It is sad. You should try to talk to him. Or write to him, see if you can reach him somehow."

"Mr. Dario, I am so sorry to hear that, because he was doing fine before I left. What has happened to him? I don't understand"

"Will you please try to write to him? "

"Yes, of course. If it's necessary, I will try to fly back for few days even. I worked hard to ignore the shenanigans he initiated. After all that effort, we cannot allow him to waste himself away."

"Thank you, thank you, Miss Robertson. I knew you would cooperate."

They hung up the phone; the principal and the professor felt encouraged. As for Gracy, she felt worried and remorseful. *I have been selfish. I have abandoned my students. I gave up my volunteer work at the hospital and abandoned those lonely souls that looked forward to my visits. I left to chase my own gratification. I did make my brothers happy but I may have hurt others by not staying.* She felt torn between obligation and personal pursuits.

She got out of bed with a dark cloud hanging over her head. She wished to talk to Leonello, but how? Phones were a luxury in the village that only a few could afford. She dialed Diego's number to get his fatherly advice. Diego, as much as he sympathized with her and admired her devotion, wasn't too pleased with her idea of taking a trip back right now, just as she was making much needed changes in her own life. "Gracy, try writing to him first. Maybe he will snap out of his misery. You are not a psychiatrist; that's what he needs."

Gracy tried to cheer herself up. The news had ruined her morning. She was preoccupied all day. Diego and Daniele took her out for dinner but her mind was still troubled. The elation of the day before had totally left her. The brothers sympathized with her concern. Diego scratched his head, choosing his words wisely to talk some sense into her. "Gracy, your somber mood makes me unhappy. I swear that in you I see my mother as she was in my younger years worrying herself sick about us being in America. And she, herself, was a prisoner kept in Palermo without her boys. We were her sons! Your students left behind are what they are, students among many others. That one particular student shouldn't affect you as much."

"You are right. That is the way it should be. I should not be so emotionally involved but I cannot help it. This young fellow had such an abusive upbringing. It breaks my heart.

That's what made me tolerate his bad behaviour. What bothers me the most, I thought he was fine after our summer of tutoring was completed."

Daniele spoke up. "Sis, sometimes people come into our lives to test and challenge us. We have to learn when to let go." She bristled a little at the advice. It was strange that Daniele of all people should say that to her. Ingrid Klein should not be in his life. She couldn't understand why she was and why her brother couldn't see that. *I have been in the US a short time and I strongly feel that Ingrid Klein shouldn't be in my sweet brother's life. My sympathy for Leonello is out of compassion. Daniele is supposedly in love with Ingrid but did he really know her and should he consider letting go of her challenges. It's better not to say anything.* She decided to keep her suspicions to herself.

The next morning, her alarm clock woke her up earlier than usual. Determined, she sat at her desk with a pen and paper in hand. Her brain switched easily to her teaching mode.

Dear Leonello,

I left Agrigento happy and smiling. Yes, I was sad to leave my surroundings, my home, my students and my dear people at the hospital. I was rejoicing because my three troubled students had successfully turned from hoodlums wasting space at our renowned university to brilliant students. They had earned well-deserved marks, especially you Leonello. You gave me hope; you gave me faith. I felt your gratitude. You have no idea how wonderful it feels for a teacher to be part of a student's accomplishment. Because I cared for your wellbeing, I was proud of the great future ahead of you. The path in your life had been set up for you to share and pass on the good to others.

You want to throw it all away! Why? The way I understand it, you are being selfish. Are you feeling good wrapping yourself in self-pity? Leonello, consider your mom and how you can help her. Your dad is behind bars as well as your brother. You need to rise above them. Don't you want others to look up to you? The only way you can shine light on those who need you will be by moving forward, empowered with knowledge, good deeds.

Leonello, you are a lucky young man. You have an abundance of love- yes, your mom's. You have no idea how sad it can be growing up without a mom. I know; I endured the misery. Stop feeling sorry for yourself and regain what you have thrown away. I am saddened for you but I am not disappointed in you. You can make us all proud by choosing to fight for success. Were all our efforts futile? My heart bleeds for you. Leonello, I will not relent writing to you until you promise me that you will start living again.

Professor Rondelli called me with your news. I promised him, should it be necessary, I will fly home, for a short time, just for you. Please help us help you. We are your caring friends. You cannot let us down. Let me hear from you. In the meantime, I will pray for you. Please stay focused on the goodness in the road ahead of you.

Looking forward to your response in good news.

Warm regards with full support.

Your teacher,

Gracy Robertson.

182

Chapter Thirty

Leonello continued to be a prisoner of his own confinement, ignoring his mother's begging and shutting the cruel world out. That is what his mind was telling him. Of course with barely any nutrition and hydration, his brain could hardly reason. One day rolled into another with no recognition between daylight and the darkness he was in. Since he hadn't been mobile, his legs could hardly hold him up. Empty days and nights were passing by in agony as he waited to let go of his life. A couple weeks later the postman, jolted Mrs. Dante from her prayer. "Mrs. Dante, *Buon giorno!* I have a letter for your son. Here it is, post marked from far away."

The poor woman's face immediately lit up, "*Per piacere*, please, tell me who is sending this letter to my son. I cannot read."

"No problem. The sender is a Miss Gracy Robertson, addressed from New York."

"God bless. *Grazie molto*. Thank you." With her hands shaking, she brought the letter to her chest. Looking up, she couldn't wait to climb that step ladder to surprise her son. She whispered to herself, 'Thank you God. Thank you Jesus.'

Out of breath she made her way to Leonello's bed. "Son, please get up. I got a surprise for you, look." She held the letter up. But there was no interest, no response, no movement and no life. After a while she threw the envelope on the floor and descended the dangerous steep ladder with her head spinning. She sat by the table, dejected as tears ran freely down her cheeks. Leonello despised everyone these days. He had been sympathetic toward his mom at one time. Since his depression had set in, he was resentful for being placed on this earth, especially with that brutal father of his. All his love for his mother had turned into resentment. In his confusion, he was wrong about his mother and his life. Mrs. Dante, his mother, adored him. He occupied a special place in her heart. Like a broken saint she walked around fixed on Leonello. He seemed to be the only soul she had left in her life. Now, she had lost him too. Her misery drove her further into the stolen alcohol.

Leonello's body was slowly losing his vitality. He could hardly stand up anymore. His back was full of sores. Struggling with himself he fell on the floor. There he lay on top of Gracy's letter, making matters worse. He managed to extract it from his back, but with a blurred vision he could hardly distinguish the post mark. It was dark; he needed more light. "Mom, Mom," he strained in a weak voice trying to be heard. No response. *Why would I bother opening and reading this letter?* "I don't want to know about her life in New York. If she cared for me she would have stayed here. She never did realize how I felt about her. I was only her student to boost her achievement so that she could be admired by the principal and other teachers." The letter was left unread.

***

In New York Gracy was anxiously waiting every day to hear from the professor, the principal, or to receive a reply to her letter. No word or phone call, no mail. She was going around these days with her head in the clouds. Her brothers were out of town; she missed them. Whenever she encountered Ingrid Klein, the woman was flamboyant and too forward with any of the men she met. That bothered her. Daniele had flown to Bali, attending to business, and was on his way home. When he was around Ingrid could easily charm him with her artifice. Her brother, overwhelmed by his busy life, was blind to it. Tonight, she was going to have dinner with him and, maybe, in a delicate way offer some good advice for his protection from Ingrid. She had not seen Mr. Alvaro Fernandez much lately. He was in negotiations for a new hotel in

Chicago. Daniele and the CEO needed to be briefed on this new one after they completed the study. Ingrid would be assigned the interior design. Gracy's mood hadn't been the best these days as everything seemed to be a struggle lately.

She was a hard worker but her challenges had been minimal lately. Diego and Daniele were waiting for her at their favorite restaurant, La Scala, were the trio saw each other often when in town. In their private booth, they could be secluded from the demands of other clients or business ventures. Gracy, was promptly escorted there when she arrived. Seeing them she was energized. "Here are my protectors, lucky me." She affectionately hugged them both.

"Gracy, we missed seeing you. Sorry, Sis. What can I say? Business is business."

"I will say that I was starting to feel abandoned here. Well, Daniele, I am glad you are back. I missed you immensely. How is Mr. Fernandez? He is the best adviser and teacher for my new job you know. He hasn't been around either. I was starting to feel deserted."

"Are you sure that's the only reason you missed him?" asked Diego kiddingly.

"What are you insinuating? He is just a nice fellow."

"I second that." responded Daniele.

"Tell us all about what you have been doing, and what you have learned." he continued.

"Not much has been happening lately. I got a disturbing phone call from one of the professors from the university, telling me that this student I worked so hard to rehabilitate has gone into a deep depression and dropped out of school since I left. That has made me sad."

"Sis, you cannot save the whole world with your good intentions."

"I can try. As matter of fact, I am concerned for both of you. Do we need to conquer the world with these new hotel deals? Do we really need them?"

Diego responded "Sis, we are not going after these deals. They come to us. When the ball starts rolling, it just continues so you have to take advantage until it stops."

"Okay but you can refuse some so we can be together more. Work and business have taken over our souls."

Diego jumped in feeling more tired than usual. "Daniele, she is right. We have neglected our young sister lately. Give more responsibility to Alvaro or hire more help. Let's be real. We have been going hard these past couple of months." Diego was serious.

Gracy wasn't thinking about herself; she was more concerned about them, especially Daniele who was off here and there out of town and who was only a part-time partner for Ingrid. Maybe this is why Ingrid behaved the way she did. She needed more love and attention. They were living together, and she was owed a full-time partner. Once more, she held back any comment as she felt the time wasn't right to say anything. Anyway, would Daniele listen to his younger sister's advice concerning the truth that his business drive came first?

Over the next few days, time moved slowly; Gracy had been waiting but there was still no word from Agrigento. It was Saturday morning. She picked up the phone, dialed her home number. *No answer, at home. It's the weekend. Maybe the Rondellis have left for Bari. I will try again on Monday.*

In the village, Mrs. Dante languished as nothing had changed with her son. When a familiar voice called out from her opened door. "Mrs. Dante, *Buon giorno.*" She let go of her rosary beads that were always in her hands.

There was Romero leaning in her entrance way. "*Buon giorno,* Romero, come in, please come in. Which wind has blown you here? I am so glad to see you."

"I know I should have come before now. I have been helping Professor Rondelli doing chores around his place. I have been wanting to check on Leonello; how is he doing?"

She broke down crying as usual, "How is he doing. He is wasting away waiting to die."

"I cannot believe he went from a powerful devil to a powerless nothing."

"He has destroyed his life and mine. He was my hope, my reason for living. Even God has abandoned me with him."

"Can I see him? Professor Rondelli called our old teacher. She was going to write to him. Has he received anything?"

"Yes but he wasn't interested and threw the letter on the floor. I cannot read because I am *inalfabete*, illiterate."

"Let's go up and see him. "

"Yes please. "

Romero quickly scaled the stepladder. Once he stepped on the uneven floor he gingerly stepped to the cot that Leonello's body lay on. He couldn't believe what he was witnessing. "Dear Jesus! He is skin and bones; his eyes, cheeks- caved in. He needs to be taken to the hospital."

Mrs. Dante, breathless, finally reached the attic. "He won't eat any more; he won't drink. He is just waiting to die."

"I will get help. We must save him."

Mrs. Dante saw the letter still on the floor unopened. She picked it up and handed it to Romero. "Romero, here is the letter. Read it to Leonello; by the look of him, he wouldn't be able to understand anything." Mrs. Dante was anxious to know what the teacher had to say to her son. Romero was more interested in getting immediate help for Leonello and taking him to the hospital.

"Mrs. Dante It's evident he won't make it on his own. The letter can wait. I must get someone else to help me here." Gracy's letter was put aside. Romero left to go fetch Gianni and Professor Rondelli. With their help, an ambulance was called. Leonello was taken to the hospital where he could receive professional help. The hard efforts of rehabilitation were to begin. Dr. Attilio, a specialist in internal medicine was brought in. After a physical examination, he called in his specialized colleagues for consultation. Leonello needed to revitalize his entire body, including his mental state. Dr. Attilio was made aware of the patient's background and history of abuse from every direction. Romero and Gianni, kindly stood by offering their help in every way, including lending a hand to Mrs. Dante.

Professor Rondelli, admired the affection his two young students had for their friend. His conscience was touched and so he decided to help Leonello the best he could, even though Leonello had harmed him at the time of his arrival to the city and university. *Forgive and forget.*

While these fellows were hard at work trying to help Leonello, Gracy in New York was relentlessly trying to get in touch with Mr. Rondelli. All her calls had been unanswered. There was no response in the mail. She was in the dark, wondering. The silence was distracting her from her learning these days. Ingrid had been working at the Plaza Hotel lately. Mr. Fernandez had to be at her service since an intense upgrading was going on. The situation was intense as a lot of expenditures were at stake. Daniele had given Ingrid a budget which was difficult to stick to. Mr. Fernandez served in consultation and to supervise the whole process. Once more Gracy realized how the people worked hard here. If America was admired world-wide it was because they earned it. Y*es, we are more laid back across the Atlantic.*

The next morning, she dialed her number back home. Finally, *"Pronto,"*

"Mr. Rondelli, *Buon Giorno*. Gracy here. How are things? I haven't heard from any of you there. I have been left in the dark. What's happening? How is Leonello?"

"My apologies Gracy, you are right. I have been so taken with everything going on. I have been negligent. Often when I wanted to call, the timing wasn't right. As for Leonello, we got him in the hospital which is a good thing. If we hadn't intervened, he would have been done in. Gracy, he is pitiful; the doctors are shaking their heads. They are working hard to save him."

"He is that bad. What's gotten into him?"

"He is lucky Romero pulled him out of that dungeon he was in. If he hadn't gone to his rescue, Leonello would be finished."

"Professor, you mean it is that serious?"

"Yes. I am afraid he is too far gone."

"Romero is an honorable friend. Those two young guys are good fellows. Out of admiration for them, I got involved. Now I understand how you dedicated yourself to them. You were right to believe in them."

"Yes I did. That is why Leonello's situation is disappointing for me."

"Apparently something snapped in Leonello for him to have slipped into such a deep depression."

"I am sorry to hear that. Please let me know how he is coming along. As I said, I will fly home for few days if it is needed to help improve his situation."

"His mom has asked me to be with her to talk to the doctor. I will get back to you once I talk to him."

"Please Professor. I hate to think that all my efforts and his hard work didn't mean anything to Leonello."

"Let's hope for his physical health to improve. Then, we will move forward to his mental health."

They closed the conversation with a promise. Gracy paced the floor. She shook her head not knowing what to do. *I cannot abandon him now that he is so sick. Did my father ever give up on me when I gave him a hard time?*

She picked up the phone and got her brother on the line. "Diego. Hi, how are you? How was your day?"

"Never mind me. Sis, what's up? You sound anxious. Is anything wrong? How are you? How are you making out? I haven't seen you for a couple of days."

"I know. You and Daniele have both been so busy. I miss you guys. How about dinner tonight?"

"Would I refuse my favorite and only sister? Of course, meet you at seven, our favorite restaurant."

Gracy, was looking forward to tonight.' I will talk to my brother.' She mumbled to herself. At work she presented herself to the supervisor; he handed her a list of work to complete. She moved along quickly, assuring him it would all be taken care of. But her troubled mind wouldn't relent this morning. Mr. Rondelli's news replayed in her head, disturbing her immensely. She moved around in a daze. The tasks were taking her to several locations. She was back down on the main floor turning the corner hoping to catch the next elevator. There she saw the security guard that Ingrid was flirting with days ago. He stepped right beside her trying to keep her pace. He was the last person she expected to converse with today.

Her morale was down and her mind was overrun by her concerns. She was on a mission to get her assignments done. She couldn't even remember the security guard's name. She reminded herself that she had spotted him and Ingrid inappropriately close to each other; a dislike for both of them had manifested in her being. He was all smiles- friendly and cheerful. Gracy scolded herself. She tried to hide her ill feelings.

"Hello, Miss. Robertson, nice to see you again. How are you making out in your new career?"

"Great, love it! Every day is something new,"

He put a hand on her arm trying to stop her from walking further "I want to point out something to you." He looked her straight in the eyes and said smiling "Did you realize we have the same last name?" Gracy wasn't finding him funny or pleasant. Don't be rude, she thought.

"Oh really! What is that?"

"Robertson. Isn't your last name Robertson?" Gracy tried to loosen his grip on her arm, wanting to excuse herself and walk away.

He was standing right in front of her now, continuing his banter. "Who knows? We could be related."

"Robertson is a popular name." She forced a half smile, wishing him away. He wanted further chit chat.

"Sorry. I must go now. I am expected at housekeeping. I have special guest checking in tonight. I need to go do my inspection. See you around." She walked away quickly to get into the elevator to regain her lost time.

Walter Robertson didn't like the cold shoulder or being brushed off. He would find out more about her. He always had Ingrid as a source; they often exchanged information and favours. *The Italian signorina will someday bow at my feet.* He walked to the valet and picked up the phone to dial Ingrid at the other hotel. "Hello," she answered.

He quipped. "Eh! Sexy, how are you doing?"

"Oh! It's you Walter. I am fine, working away, trying to get things finished here,"

"How long it's going to take you? I miss you around here."

"I would be finished if I had more help. They have to get me someone soon, before I explode."

"You need to speak to that guy you choose to sleep with Sexy. I told you that you shortchange yourself. When can I see you? Your beau is out of town still, isn't he?"

"Walter, sorry I'll have to let you know. I must go now, lots to do here."

"Ingrid, lately you have neglected me. I need to see you. No excuse."

"Fine, I will see what I can do,"

"Ingrid, I need to talk to you, before your rich boy comes back. Don't give me excuses."

"Walter, if you don't hang up the work won't get done. I won't be able to meet you for sure as I will be stuck here."

"Wait a minute. Why don't I meet you there tonight? I am off duty. I started early this morning."

"I will call you later. Depends how far I get."

Walter Robertson hung up the phone, laughing under his mustache. He was going to change into his best suit and go to the luxurious Plaza Hotel, and pretend to be Mr. Bigshot Businessman. '*She needs me more than I need her. It's not my fault that she sticks around that wasp of hers waiting to become Mrs. So and So. That will never happen from the looks of it.*

***

Gracy, had completed her work and was ready to leave when from the corner of her eye she saw Alvaro Fernandez leaning on by the front desk. A tour from California had just arrived. The lobby was crowded. She needed to get out of there and go meet Diego for dinner.

With butterflies in her chest, she spontaneously walked toward him. "Gracy! Nice to see you! How are you?" He looked at his watch "You are still here! Past your time?"

192

Gracy, didn't want to move; she was so delighted to see him. She was hypnotized by his voice and big brown eyes.

"Nice to see you too. I am going to meet Diego. I plan to go straight from work."

"I see. I am out of luck. Had you been without plans we could have had a bite together.

I would love to hear about your progress. Sorry I haven't been much help lately. I have been in Chicago with that brother of yours."

"Yes, I know Daniele has been absent a while now. He is doing a great job in redesigning the whole place, especially the lobby. He is creating perfection." Gracy answered.

"He is gifted. I am proud of him."

"Well, Miss Gracy, I don't want to keep you from your brother. Give him my regards.

Promise me you will have dinner with me. I shall be in New York for the rest of this week."

Gracy, thought she was going to faint. As she was trying to leave, she almost stumbled into someone approaching the front desk. She was so mesmerized by Alvaro Fernandez. *Am I going crazy? Why this effect when I see him or hear his voice, that accent of his is provoking.*

Diego was waiting for her at the restaurant. She hugged him excusing herself, as she was half hour late.

"Sis, did you have a good day? This morning you didn't sound too upbeat."

"Oh! Diego, I had an eventful day. I even ran into Alvaro Fernandez as I was leaving."

"Nice fellow. We are lucky to have him."

"I think so too. He cares about your business. He strikes me as an honest fellow, loyal to his job and patrons. We have Ingrid to thank for him; she recruited him and some others from Washington. "

"I must tell you I had another encounter today with another fellow. A security guard on the first floor. I must admit he rubs me the wrong way. I had no time to chat. I wanted to carry on with my work. I think I gave him the cold shoulder. I believe that he is also someone Ingrid recommended."

"Gracy! Do you have any idea how many employees we have? I don't know this fellow or many others."

"Diego, I have been upset, since Mr. Rondelli called me. I never thought the situation was that serious! Yes, it's about my student. When you are a teacher you thrive on your student's success. Now I hear my troublemaker, Leonello, who I worked so hard to rehabilitate, is in such a bad shape that he is near death. I think I must take a trip back to Agrigento."

He looked at her keenly "Are you serious?"

"Diego, I have too; otherwise I'll never forgive myself. Do you want to go with me?"

"Gracy! I am swamped. Daniele is away. The hotels, the firm, and my clients- they all need my attention. I can't just pick up and leave."

"Diego. I am talking about saving a life- a young one. Think about it. Besides we will always be busy. We haven't seen our family now for a long time. It's time we pay a visit. Think about it Diego, I want your company."

"Let me see if I can make it happen."

Then, Alvaro came to her mind. He wanted to have dinner with her. She couldn't wait for it to happen. She knew the special way she felt when seeing him. She questioned herself. *I am attracted to him. Is it love? I want to talk to my Fabiana. Who can I confide in? Certainly not*

Ingrid Klein? My brothers are men. They wouldn't understand. Whatever it is- nervousness or physical attraction- I like him. I don't want to miss the opportunity should he ask me out.

"Diego, let me know as soon as you can so I can rearrange my schedule. I am a working girl you know." She went home with mixed feelings. Her heart was paining for Leonello. Why was this happening now in the middle of her training?

***

Back in Agrigento, Leonello had been admitted in intensive care. The doctor in charge and the nurses were vigilant in doing all they could to improve his deteriorated physical state. He was hooked up to intravenous and respiratory machines, as his lungs were hardly functioning. His heartbeat was weak. Mr. Rondelli and Matteo Dario, the principal continued to help as well. Romero and Gianni, with Mrs. Dante concerned also and supportive. They couldn't understand why Leonello himself wasn't fighting for his life. How could they motivate him to respond? Romero kept thinking that only one person could boost his willingness- Miss Robertson. She was way across the ocean. Maybe she felt that those students that she once worked so hard for were in her past. Romero was wrong. The kind soul of Gracy, wouldn't let her ignore them. Gracy was lying awake in bed reminiscing on her dad's words. "My sweet Gracy, if you want peace with yourself, always try to help those that need you the most."

She turned the light on to check the time. Sicily would be six hours ahead. It was nine o'clock in the morning. She placed a call to the university where she could reach the principal and the professor. The secretary connected her to Matteo Dario.

"Buon giorno, Signorina Robertson. So glad to hear from you!"

"All is good here, thank you. Signor Dario, sorry to bother you. I was wondering if it's possible to talk to Professor Rondelli. I hate to disturb him in class right now. I have been troubled about our student

Leonello, since the professor called me. I wanted to know how he is doing."

"I can page him for you. I must tell you, there is reason to be concerned. We have all been involved. As you must know we have him hospitalized now. His condition is touch and go, in bad shape."

In the meantime, he buzzed his secretary to page Professor Rondelli. In no time he was there.

He handed him the phone. *"Pronto!* Oh Gracy, it's you! I am so glad you called."

"Tell me, I hear things are not good with our student."

"No, Gracy, you mentioned coming home. I wish you would. Leonello has lost all stamina, who knows. . . Romero seems to think you are the only one who could motivate him. He is unresponsive. It is heartbreaking."

"Professor, yes, I am making arrangements to come. I am waiting for my brother to give me the time and to book my flight."

"The boys were hoping you would. You are our last hope for him. His mom is devastated; he doesn't respond. It's such a shame. We have all worked hard for him and to see him leave us it's so sad."

"Professor, say no more. I couldn't sleep. It is three in the morning here. This is why I called. I will try to speed up our plan. I need to give notice at work and I will be there as soon as I can."

"Great! Romero, Gianni will be happy to see you. I will give them the good news."

He hung up the phone elated to give the boys the news. The principal was delighted also.

"Professor, you didn't have a chance to meet her dad. I can tell you that he was the best of the best in education. His daughter had a good teacher. She is no different than him."

Gracy, placed a call to Diego first thing in the morning. "Good morning"

Clearing his groggy voice Diego picked up. "Gracy, it's early. Can't you sleep?"

"No, Diego I can't. Please ask your secretary to book our flight to Rome or the closest airport to Sicily. I must get to Agrigento. My student is dying."

"You are kidding me."

"No. I am not; whether you come with me or not, I must go."

"When did you get all this news?"

"During the night while you were sleeping."

"Your job, don't you need to give notice or ask for permission?"

"Diego, this is an emergency. Besides, doesn't being your sister mean anything?"

He realized there was no use arguing with her. *She is stubborn as my mother used to be at times.* He decided it was better to call his secretary and book a flight as soon as possible for both of them. As for his clients, he would call Rosella to take care of things while he was away. As Gracy stated, it was urgent.

A couple of days later, Gracy, accompanied by Diego who was holding her, walked through the entrance of the hospital to check on Leonello. Diego commented "Sis, no wonder they love you here. You interrupted your own plans and travelled this far to benefit this young fellow."

"He was my prodigy lost in the fog. My soul would not allow me to ignore him. I must try once more to encourage him- if it's not too late." After inquiring where Leonello's room was, a nurse accompanied them to his room. When she entered, the vision of his lifeless body lying there hooked up to tubes and monitors was overpowering. The patient was hardly recognizable. She walked over slowly, afraid to disturb him. Her inner fear wanted to scream. Wide eyed she whispered to the nurse and Diego. "My vivacious student who was once so irresistible, instigating other students, irritating the teachers and restless, how can he lay here so helplessly?" She moved over to him, carefully took his hand, leaned over and kissed him on his forehead, caressing his hair gently. A motherly instinct came over her like he was her lost child. She looked at him intensely, wishing some of her life force to be transmitted to him. He looked vulnerable and defenceless. Gracy's warm tears filled her eyes. Diego moved over to her and put an arm around her shoulders. "Sis, have hope. He is young. He will pull out of this. You will see."

But Leonello was in a total catatonic state. Gracy frantically called out to him. "Leonello, it's me here, your Miss Robertson, your teacher. Have you forgotten me? I traveled back just to see you. This is my brother Diego." There was no sign of acknowledgement or response. His empty eyes stared up into nothingness. The nurse had stepped out. "I want to talk to the doctor, Diego, to see what the diagnosis is. Has he lost his speech? Why doesn't he respond? Can he hear? Does he recognize me? I don't think so."

"Gracy, we will talk to the doctor to see what he has to say; don't upset yourself."

"Diego, you wouldn't believe the nineteen-year-old young fellow I knew and the one I am looking at now. It is shocking."

"Gracy, you are here trying to help. I am with you. We will get the best medical care for him. Do not jump to conclusions and get discouraged. You must be encouraging him and yourself. I know it is hard try to be uplifting around him."

"Diego, I am so glad you are with me. God help me, I don't I know what to make of his sickness! I am so confused because I didn't expect him to be this bad."

They stepped out to go to the nursing station, to request the doctor. The head nurse was busy and asked them if they could wait. "Dr. Mancini is in consultation at the moment. I will try to get in touch with him later."

Gracy wasn't going to leave until they talked to him, hoping to hear something encouraging.

"Yes, we will wait for him" she told the nurse.

While waiting for the doctor to be paged and to see them. Diego suggested "Sis, let's go in the waiting room." He was puzzled by the fact that no one else was there to care for Leonello.

"I don't understand, where is his family? You told me the father is in jail, the brother is also in jail. What about his mother? Any other family members?"

"Diego, he has no one except a couple of friends, the principal, teachers at the university. His mother is a good woman. Unfortunately, she drowns herself in alcohol. Two older sisters are out of the country. They have alienated themselves from the family because of the criminality of the father and brother."

"What has the father been convicted of?"

"A long list of crimes that I really didn't want to know. I think Leonello, being the youngest, was forced to be submissive. The poor fellow was left to hold the fort of their derelict household." Gracy continued "This is why I was taken with him- out of sympathy. It wasn't easy. He caused me many heart racing moments, but I thought I had him on the right path." She shook her head in disbelief. "He was good before I left. I never expected this relapse from him. I must have deluded myself."

Dr. Mancini, an intelligent, middle-aged young man, appeared at the door. They both jumped up, eager to speak to him.

"Dr. Mancini, I am Gracy Robertson. This is my brother Diego. I am Leonello Dante's former teacher and friend. We are much concerned. What is the prognosis?"

He seemed to hesitate. Then reluctantly he responded in an apologetic voice. "Miss Robertson, *mi scusi*, I am sorry, I am not sure I am at liberty to discuss the condition of my patient, without permission from his family."

"Oh, Doctor I am sure you can trust us with the personal Information. I travelled a long way to check on his wellbeing. As you must know, he has no stable family to care for him. This is why we are here."

"I understand, but I have to follow our regulations. I still need a signed medical consent form to discuss my patient's health condition."

She turned to Diego "I could try and get permission from Mrs. Dante should I be able to find her in a sober state. My colleagues at the university could help." Leonello, in his condition, couldn't help in any way since he was unresponsive and still considered a minor. His mother seemed to be the only choice. After going through all the red tape, finally, Dr. Mancini sat with them.

"I apologize for the inconvenience. My patients are entitled to the privacy of their privileged health information." As nice as it was to hear Dr. Mancini speak with his eloquent Italian, Gracy was getting impatient to get to the information and the root of the problem. Where was Leonello headed from here on?

"Miss Robertson, when Leonello was brought in, he was in a delirious state, feverish and dehydrated. He had an alarmingly low blood count. Our team intervened trying our best to stabilize him. We are pleased his blood count is improving nicely. We need to be patient. His neurotransmission is at a standstill along with his speech. I am confident that once his physical body heals we can coordinate work on his mental capability. He is young. We have many approaches to motivate him.

Looking at him now, it's disheartening; however, we have some clever psychiatrists here in Sicily. I will consult and call in some of our experts from the Psychology Department from the mainland. He has the advantage of youth. It's to our goal to save him."

Diego's interest was piqued. He spoke up "Dr. Mancini, we appreciate your assistant and interest. As I understand this young fellow is in dire financial need. Should you need monetary funds, my sister and I are willing to contribute to any expenses that are incurred."

"Thank you. I appreciate your offer. We will try our utmost to bring him out of this trauma that has almost paralyzed his brain. Leave it with us." He got up, signalling to leave.

Gracy's eyes were imploring. "Dr. Mancini, tell me. Is there anything more my brother and I can do to help him?"

"Be supportive. Keep coming, to see him."

"He doesn't even blink an eye. I get the impression, he doesn't know we are there."

"No, that's part of his malady. His brain doesn't allow him. Let's give him time; eventually he will come through." He was being paged. He quickly excused himself, shook hands with them and walked out the door hurriedly.

Gracy and Diego looked at each other not knowing which direction to go. Diego knew in his heart that his sister wanted to go check on her precious student once more before leaving the hospital. Before he spoke, Gracy, with pleading eyes, asked in a low voice said "Diego, do you mind if we go see Leonello once more? It would make me feel better."

"Sis, of course! You want to follow up on what Dr. Mancini suggested."

She smiled at him. He was so dear. "How did you know?"

They walked the long corridor toward Leonello's room. Romero, and Gianni were just sitting there like two disheartened souls. They jumped up seeing Miss Robertson. Romero nudged Gianni's shoulder. "I told you she would come."

"How could I not? I would never abandon you guys. Here, I want you to meet my brother, Diego Frarano, from New York."

The young men were both courteous in greeting Diego with their best manners taught to them by none other than Miss Gracy. They turned to stare at Leonello laying there under his tubes. Romero, with a sad voice whispered "Miss Robertson, what are we going to do about our friend?" Gianni seconded *"Yes, Professoressa.* There must be something we can do for him."

She focussed on the Doctor's conversation. "We must be optimistic. It will take some time. We will get him back, you will see."

"You think so," Gianni placed his hands together in prayer wanting to believe her. Romero continued sadly. "Miss Robertson, I am not sure if he hears us. Does he understand what I am saying or even know we are here? After you left he got sadder and sadder. He told me that you left a hole in his heart."

"Really! He seemed fine with me leaving. I never imagined my leaving would have such a powerful effect on him."

"Slowly, slowly, as days passed, he wasn't the same Leonello anymore. I think he felt abandoned. We didn't count much anymore, Gianni and I tried, to no avail."

Gianni, innocently added. "Romero even got Marmellata trying to play her tricks on him.

He was furious with her, chasing her away. He called her a dirty slut."

Gracy and Diego listened. For Diego with his worldly expertise it didn't take long to figure out, that poor young man immobilized there had deep attachment to his sister. It was most probably a young crush, easy to catch once kindness and attention were shown and even if it was not reciprocal.

While Diego was weighing the situation, Gracy turned toward Leonello, hoping for a reaction but there was no sign what's so ever. "Dear God, what a big change in him. Guys, we won't give up. He has us and together we must bring him to his old self again."

As they were getting ready to leave, Mrs. Dante walked in. When she saw, Miss Robertson, she cried hysterically. She looked pitiful, but she was holding her beads "God bless you Miss. I hope you can help my son. My poor boy, there he is all that I had; now I've lost him too."

"Mrs. Dante, no, don't say that. He will be fine. We talked to the doctor. There is hope.

You are a religious woman I see; pray for him." The woman, put her hand in her ragged pocket, struggling to retrieve something there. She held out, Gracy's letter. "This came in the mail. The postman told me it was from America. Leonello didn't read it. He had no interest. Myself, I cannot read. You must give it to him. I saved it for him. It was on the floor in his attic."

Once Gracy glanced at it, she immediately recognized her letter. To think she had been waiting in vain for a reply. Leonello hadn't even opened it or read it. She was disappointed but she put an arm around the pitiful woman and guided her toward her son. "Mrs. Dante, don't despair. He will eventually come around. You will see."

The time was overdue for them to leave. Diego, asked "Mrs. Dante how did you get here? Can we give you a lift home?"

"It's a long walk. I had to come and see my son." She responded bent over.

Gracy, suggested. "Diego we are all hungry. Why don't we take Mrs. Dante and the boys with us to our favorite restaurant? We will treat them."

"Good Idea. Ask them."

Mrs. Dante, wiping her tears, said "Thank you, your signorina. Grazie, God bless you. I am not decent to go anywhere. I will just sit here and pray for my son. I will stay longer. The boys can go with you. They are good kids. They love my Leonello."

Gracy put an arm around her shoulders affectionately. She turned to Gianni and Romero and nodded in agreement. "Let's go for a good meal. You need the strength to support our friend." She had totally erased the mischief they had sometimes caused her from her heart and mind. It was all in the past and forgiven.

Chapter Thirty One

Time passed slowly in Agrigento. Diego insisted that they take a drive to Palermo.

"Sis, we don't want to be disrespectful to our family there. We must go pay them a visit especially our Fabiana. We cannot forget mom's grave"

"Oh! Yes, we mustn't. What about your dad's?"

"As for his grave, visiting it is questionable. Gracy, I know you're such a forgiving soul. I hope someday this pain deep in my heart goes away. My brother and I cannot forgive him for what he did to our mom." He put an arm around her waist. "This is why we love you so much. You are the image of our mom reincarnated."

She smiled at him "You and Daniele, are the most precious gifts I inherited from mom."

"Too bad you never got to meet the woman that gave you your life"

"Not to worry now. I gave my dad such a hard time about that from my early childhood.

I had tantrums because other children had mommies and I didn't."

"You poor child."

"Dad kept saying that the good Lord needed my mommy in heaven. The more he said that, the louder I screamed. Why didn't he need my friends' mommy instead of mine? I moped a lot, especially at night. I was jealous of my neighbours' moms."

Once again, they arrived in Palermo and the Tavernas were waiting outside for them. All the family gathered as usual. The joyful hugs lingered with everyone, especially Fabiana, her surrogate mother. "You must have a lot to tell me. I want to hear all about New York. You and I have to have a heart-to-heart Missy."

"Godmother, I never hide anything from you. You know you are my confidante."

"Oh, I am not so sure about that. I was expecting some promising news but nada." She flipped her hand from her chin, the Italian gesture of nothingness.

"Godmother, I do have a lot to tell you. My new career is opening a new world for me- new learning every day, new faces, people from every race. It's interesting.

I love it. "

"Gracy, that part is fine. I want to hear about your love life. Don't tell me that your beauty and vitality hasn't struck some handsome young American during a full moon."

"Godmother, you know I have two Sicilian brothers. According to your custom, the poor guys might feel intimidated about asking me out. Then they would have to pass the brother test."

"Nobody, and I mean nobody, will take advantage of our young beautiful sister. They would have to deal with us first." answered Diego.

"You hear that Godmother!"

"Diego, don't be so overprotective, scaring people away. We don't want Gracy to end up a zitella, a spinster. You live in America. Forget the old-fashioned customs of Sicily."

"Fabiana, I am kidding. We only want her happiness, but we do worry for her. We would never want someone to take advantage of her or mistreat her, like our poor mom."

Gracy reproached them both. "You two are funny. You talk as if I wasn't here. It is my life, my future. Let nature take its course. I am not desperate. Right now, my goal is to master my new and invigorating adventure in hospitality. Anthony Taverna appeared "Everyone, step in the dining room. Lunch is ready to be served. Our aperitifs are poured. Let's go."

Afterwards Diego suggested they go to their paternal home. Gracy, didn't feel comfortable in that large home where her mom had spent many unhappy days and nights in solitude. Aunt Lori, Fabiana's mother, had recounted many episodes of her sister-in- law's past.

Gracy excused herself. Her intention was to spend some private time with Fabiana in girl talk.

The climate was mostly pleasant in Palermo. The serene blue sky brought peace to her body and soul. The rest of the family had gone inside the house to indulge in their afternoon naps. Fabiana suggested they go sit in the shade under the large fig tree full of green thick leaves. They sat on the cushiony striped chairs. Once they were settled they had their heart to heart talk. Fabiana had a strong affection for Gracy. She had been at her side from the day of her birth. Likewise, Gracy loved and felt loved by her cousin who, at her baptism, had also assumed the role of Godmother. Gracy stretched herself comfortably, fighting the relaxation- the effect of the red wine and aperitif. Fabiana was waiting anxiously for Gracy to relate to her life's events in New York.

"Everything is good. You are familiar with my accommodations at the penthouse in the Hyatt. I have privileges any time of day or night on that VIP floor. I am spoiled. What did I do to deserve all this abundance in my life?"

"You were lucky to be born in a good and prosperous family."

"My brothers detested their father."

"Do you blame them? He ordered their mother and you to be killed, for heaven's sake. Please, let's not go there. Tell me some good things. Have you met anybody that you fancy?"

"As matter of fact, yes I have. A fellow new with the company has caught my eye. He is qualified in the hospitality industry, not like me who is just learning. I like him a lot," Then she giggled. "Fabiana, I must confess. He has an effect on me that I never felt before and I don't understand. He gives me the shivers when he nears me."

"Oh! Oh, you are attracted to him. It's a good sign of being in love. Is he eligible? Does he have the credentials to pass inspection with those two guys of yours? You know how protective they are."

"Oh, Godmother, he hasn't given me any inclination of interest other than work related. I am falling in love with him but I don't know if he returns it."

"If you really like him, pursue it. I am told the girls In America are open and nothing like here. God forbid." she slapped her hand down.

"Fabiana, it's really nothing. I shouldn't even mention him because there is nothing there on his part suggesting any romantic ideas."

"Never mind Gracy. Don't underestimate yourself. Anybody interested in you is a lucky fellow. You are the real thing in every way."

"We will see where it goes. Every day I am longing to see him."

Fabiana was all smiles. "I wish you all the happiness my darling. You certainly deserve it."

"Never mind me. Fabiana, I must confide in you something that is troubling me. I hate to burden you with these negative thoughts of mine."

"Gracy, we all need someone whom we can trust. You can unload on me."

"Talking about girls being more open in America. I am worried about our Daniele and this girlfriend he lives with. I have a strong feeling, that she isn't sincere or faithful to him."

"Gracy, that's a big burden on your conscience. What makes you suspect that?"

"I hope I am wrong. The way she acts, the way she is all over some fellows. She flirts with them embarrassingly."

"Gracy, being friendly or innocent flirting is not a crime. However, if you are truly concerned, remember that you people there have everything going for you. Diego being a lawyer has private investigators, undercover agents, cameras in the hotel lobbies, hallways. Put them to use. Don't wrack your brain worrying. It's her loss if she spoils what she has. Daniele is a priceless young man."

"I know! He is pulled here and there. He is away a lot. They are both workaholics, especially Daniele. When he is back from work he looks done in. She bamboozles him with her charm and sex."

"Did you mention anything to Diego?"

"No, I haven't. Diego knows she pressures Daniele to tie the knot. They fight often, about that. The good part is Daniele keeps resisting by telling her that they are fine the way they are."

"Well, he has a lot to lose. Diego should advise him on a prenuptial agreement."

"They shouldn't be living together to start with."

"Ingrid, I believe, would find her way in anything she puts her mind to. . ."

Gracy didn't trust Ingrid with Alvaro Fernandez, either. She would bet anything that any guy would fall for Ingrid's tricks. Suddenly she was restless to be back in New York, but she had to be here. She felt wretched about Leonello's situation. If he only would respond or give some sign of cooperation, there would be hope in moving forward.

She returned to the hospital the next day where they consulted with a couple of top doctors brought in from Bari- Professor Rondelli's connections. They reassured Gracy, Diego and Professor Rondelli that they would take charge in assisting with the internist. Both consulting doctors would take turns giving Leonello their devoted attention.

Two weeks passed. When she walked into the hospital, the nurse at the desk saw her and smiled. "Miss Robertson, I will walk with you to Leonello's room. You will be pleased." Gracy, encouraged, walked beside her. Maybe Mrs. Dante's prayers had come through. The sun was shining through the window and the room had been transformed from grey and stark to warm and welcoming. Holding her breath, Gracy approached Leonello's bed. For the first time he looked at her, his quizzing eyes were fixed on her face.

"Leonello! How are you?" she asked caressing his forehead. To her surprise, a weak voice responded. Yes, it came right from Leonello's lips. "Miss Robertson, are you really here or am I dreaming?"

"Oh! My dear God. Leonello! My dear one, yes I am here, right beside you."

"You came back?"

"Yes, I did, just for you."

"Life wasn't the same after you left. I didn't care to live anymore."

"Why not, my dearest? What a shame."

"Miss Robertson, you don't understand. I have nothing to live for. You were the only one that seemed to care. But you chose to leave."

"How wrong you are. You have your mom, Romero, Gianni, Professor Rondelli and the principal at our university. They all care for you. I came back from New York just to check on your well- being. You have scared us all."

"Miss Robertson, my mom is drunk most of the time. As for Romero and Gianni, they are only a source of amusement for me. I beat Gianni;

we beat up the professor. We threatened him one night you know. As for you, when you scolded us, I wanted to burn down your house. You drove me out of my mind sometimes because I thought you looked down on me."

"Leonello, how wrong you are. Remove all those bad thoughts out of your mind. It's time to get a hold of yourself. You have a great future in front of you."

"Yeah! What is that- rotting in that dumpy place of mine? There are no jobs here. My brother might get out of jail. He beats me up to do his dirty work. I am doomed Miss Robertson. I don't care to live this miserable life anymore."

"I refuse to hear you talk like that. I have plans for you."

"What plans? You abandoned me."

"Listen to me Leonello, I didn't abandon anybody. I did what I had to do move on in life.

My brother and I consulted the best physicians from the city of Bari. We want you to get well."

"Why would you care for me?"

"You were one of my students. I had to help you find the correct path, right along with Romero. Gianni is a good kid, different from you two." She tried to talk his language to reach him. "Leonello, please I beg you get yourself in shape physically and mentally. I promise to help you. Enough for today. I don't want you to get tired. I am so pleased that you are talking. I will see you tomorrow. We will talk some more."

As she said that Mrs. Dante walked in. Gracy kissed him goodbye on his forehead. After greeting his mom, she said. "Mrs. Dante there is hope." Gracy left elated.

Diego was starting to get restless. As much as he liked Agrigento and Palermo and the excursions to the beach, it was time for him to get back. He was talking to Rosella, the CEO and Daniele, every day. Their affairs were under control. He felt they must head home. He hated to leave Gracy behind. He preferred for them to fly back together. To his surprise, when Gracy bounced back in, she hugged him affectionately, thanking him. "Diego, the miracle I have been wishing for has happened. Leonello, talked today. He opened his heart to me- his family situation, the nothingness in his life drove him to the deep end. I was thinking, we should send Mrs. Dante to rehab. She is all he's got. We can afford private consultation for her."

"Sis, if we can, go ahead. Our accountant has a yearly percentage aside for charity.

All we have to do is direct it to him. I will talk to my secretary and give her instructions. Gracy, I must get back. You are leaving with me please."

"You are right, just give me few more days. I want to make sure my patient moves forward. God forbid that Leonello should feel abandoned again as he put it."

"Sis, he is such a handsome young man. He should be chasing girls at this time in his life."

"I agree Diego. His mentality is not in gear, therefore he doesn't reason properly. You should know that. Didn't you study Psychology in law school?"

"At his age, Daniele and I could have gone insane under our dad's tyranny."

"But the scars are still there. Why do you choose the single life? Daniele doesn't want to commit in marriage either?"

"Gracy, that applies to yourself also. You haven't been looking for love either. I am fine with Rosella. We have a mutual agreement. As for Daniele, he will work out his problems with Ingrid or find a way out."

"Diego, now that we are on Daniele's relationship. Do you trust Ingrid Klein?"

"Why you ask? Do you have doubts?"

"Diego we are dear to each other the three of us. I just don't want any of us hurt."

"What do you mean Sis?"

"Nothing, just over concerned."

"Ok! Mother hen. We are so lucky to have you." He put his arm around her shoulders affectionately pulling her toward him in support.

A week later after many recommendations from the doctors and everyone concerned, Gracy and Diego were bound back for New York. The next morning, regardless of the jet leg and the sleep schedule, Gracy was at work earlier than usual. In good spirits she took the elevator to the Administration Office. Alvaro Fernandez was there placing an assignment in her mail slot. The clicking of her high heels made him turn to find himself face to face with Gracy. "Miss Gracy! So glad you are back. We missed you around here."

"Glad to be back. Good morning Alvaro. How are you?"

"Now that you are here, much better. Thank you?"

Gracy's heart fluttered. She gave him a pleasant smile.

"You know it's always crazy around here. I will let you regain your bearings for a couple of days. There is something I would like to discuss with you."

"Oh, I am fine, whenever you are ready."

"Great! I shall call- maybe tomorrow or the next day?" He stepped back for a minute gazing at her, but then, hesitantly he moved on. Gracy thought: *It is puzzling. With all the expertise in his field, I detect some insecurity in him in a strange way.* She could never imagine that Alvaro's insecurities were stimulated by fear of her rejection.

Alvaro walked away, mesmerized by her beauty. Shaking his head, he was worrying about this attraction of his since had first laid eyes on

Gracy. It was futile. He came from a poor Spanish family who immigrated to America from Madrid. Alvaro being the youngest of the three children had come along with them. Two of their siblings had remained behind with his grandparents. Later, the way the situation presented itself, they couldn't come as the older parents' health was declining. Alvaro's parents were scrambling to make a living. His mom and dad each held two jobs. They hardly spoke English. They needed to support the old parents and the son and daughter left behind. They lived in a rented two-bedroom home in a suburb of Washington. Alvaro himself went with them to clean homes and do yard work to earn extra money to pay for his education. He had been a good student excelling not only in English but in all his subjects. He had gone to university and graduated with honors in the Hospitality program. After holding few positions in the industry in the state of Virginia, he had gained some practical experience. One day he had run into Ingrid, an old schoolmate. She had eventually recommended him highly for the job in New York. Mr. Fernandez was introduced to Daniele Frarano. Here he was now, the CEO of the Frarano's empire. In his humility, he didn't feel worthy of the admirable sister of his employer.

Gracy returned to her office to find her desk piled up with assignments from every department. She wondered how she was going to do it all. The thought of having Alvaro work in the same hotel today energized her. As matter of fact, she bumped into him on some of her excursions. Her heart continued flipping as his big brown eyes had followed her. She scolded herself. What is getting into me? She forced her footsteps to move on, giving him a short wave and a smile. Her mind kept replaying their morning encounter. *I mustn't let him distract me and interfere with my work performance.* Still her silly heart kept racing. She couldn't wait to hear from him regardless of the subject matter.

The next day her phone rang. It was ten in the morning. "Hello Gracy! It's Alvaro here."

As if she wouldn't know his melodic accent. How could he not be recognized?

"Yes, Alvaro how are you?"

"Great and you?"

"Good, thank you."

"Gracy, I am needed at the Plaza today. I will miss seeing you around."

Gracy tried to be in control of her excitement. "Supervising me you mean?"

"No, no. I love watching you in action especially with our European guests. You have what it takes."

"Thank you, it's encouraging"

She was waiting but he was quiet. "Sorry Gracy, can you hold on. There is a knock at my door."

"No problem."

While waiting on the line she could hear the charming voice of Ingrid. Alvaro sounded low key, trying to excuse himself to return to the phone and then it was quiet again. She wondered what was going on. *I wouldn't be surprised if she has her arms around his neck smothering him- her usual way of greeting man.* After what seemed an eternity to Gracy, she heard a click of the door finally closing following Ingrid's sweet words of goodbye. He picked up the phone. "Sorry about that. Ingrid dropped off a report I need to go over." He sounded disturbed.

"You don't need to explain, its fine." She was covering up her annoyance. She didn't trust that Ingrid.

"Gracy, as I mentioned yesterday, can we meet for lunch tomorrow? I should be working there all day."

"That should be fine. It's a business lunch right. I presume."

"Gracy, for me is business and pleasure. I love seeing you. I will come and call for you at your office. We will walk together to Vincenzo's, the Italian bistro."

"Thank you. I will take that as a compliment. I'm looking forward to tomorrow." Her mood was improving.

Maybe Ingrid's approach with males, which was not a saint's, was the approach she needed to take. Especially if her heart did summersaults when seeing someone she was attracted to. Modesty worked in Sicily but not here in America. This Spanish fellow influenced her without a doubt. Gracy went through the day in a daze. She couldn't wait until tomorrow, but her tiredness seemed to be kicking in from the long flight. She went home earlier than usual and early to bed.

The next morning her energy was replenished. She took a deep breath and opened the window to let in some fresh air. A bright sunshine day presented itself out there and there was not a cloud in the sky. She stretched her body and meditated in order to make herself calm and collected, ready for the day's challenges.

She dressed professionally, conservatively in a light blue suit complimented by a crispy white blouse. Her long brown hair was pinned back over her shoulders. She applied make up which she hadn't been accustomed to. Her eyes sparkled with light blue eye shadow. Her cheek bones were highlighted with rose' blush that accentuated her oval face. She was ready for the challenges of the day.

As she stepped out of the elevator, heads were turning to admire her. She spotted the annoying security guy on duty today at the door. He was a friend of Ingrid's; she hoped he would be off duty by noon when she was supposed to walk out with Alvaro. Her gut feeling about him was worrisome. She didn't know why. Maybe because he was also overfriendly, especially with Ingrid.

When Alvaro arrived to call for her, he was dumfounded "Gracy! You are beautiful."

He was being sincere and for few minutes he stared at her speechlessly.

"Thank you. Since I am going for lunch with my supervisor, I thought to take a little extra time putting myself together."

"Gracy, you sure know how to make a humble fellow like me feel good. I am honoured to be with you. I maybe your supervisor but you are actually my boss, part owner of this conglomerate."

"Alvaro, I am not your boss. I am simply the professor's daughter. That is who I am. My brothers are my earthly gift from my beloved mother whose love and affection I missed."

"You know Gracy, from the day I laid eyes on you, I got this message in my being that you are special."

"Let's go before our lunch hour is over." She was pleased to walk beside him.

He was a total gentleman, well-mannered and respectful as he seated her. Vincenzo's was nothing fancy, but Gracy felt in heaven being with Alvaro.

"So, tell me. You have made me curious, business first, then we will move on to pleasure as you said." Gracy started the conversation as she extended her hand amicably encouraging him. He gladly took both her hands caressing them spontaneously without reservations.

"Gracy! I must tell you, having you on board with the company is a bonus. I couldn't be happier. Please tell me you are enjoying this new adventure also."

"Alvaro, I can't wait to get to work every day. I love it. It has nothing to do with the money.

It's the people who make me happy, their appreciation. The well-appointed premises, the upbeat atmosphere, our foods, and the aroma of our coffee shops- everything that comes with it makes me proud. The pianist in the main lobby, the soothing vocalist singing at happy hour and even the daily crises, which we promptly solve with our well-trained service people- it's all good."

Her face radiated as she spoke. Alvaro knew she was more than the right candidate for the new assignment he would be suggesting to her.

"Gracy, I read you well. You express yourself with joyful enthusiasm. I have something in mind for you. It will add to your workload. I have no doubt, you will do a great job for us."

She perked up. "What would that be Alvaro? I am listening." He reached for her hand again stroking it. "I would very much like for you to be my assistant. Would you be willing to expand your labour of love to some of our other hotels? It takes some travelling, Chicago, Los Angeles, Vegas- wherever the company is extended. Those brothers of yours are relentless. Once we take over new locations, supervision is needed to train the staff and to oversee all aspects of a new place."

She was listening, as her heart was flipping. "Alvaro, thank you for the confidence you have in me. It's encouraging. I am honored that you would consider me capable of assisting you. The travel wouldn't bother me. I am kind of new as an hotelier so I am not sure that I am what you need."

"Trust me. I know you will do an excellent job. There is no one else I would prefer if you were willing to accept my offer." He waited for her response.

At that moment her cheeks blushed like red flames. Gracy wanted jump out of her seat to grab him and lock him in a big hug. Slowly her raised blood simmered. She calmly responded. "I am more than willing Alvaro, Thank you. If you don't mind, out of respect, I need to relate it to my older brother Diego. He is my protector." She smiled jokingly.

"I understand. I respect your relationship. I must confess, before talking to you I discussed it with Daniele. He was in full agreement."

"Glad to know that but Diego is my older brother, in the old Italian style, respect. . ."

"Tell me about yourself, your family." She asked Alvaro, keenly interested in his answer.

"We came here from Madrid, poor immigrants, couldn't speak English. My parents and I have always worked hard. We had a few mouths to feed and support back home too. I managed to put myself through school. Once I graduated, I immersed myself in this industry which I always found fascinating. One evening, at one of our convention halls, I discovered this girl standing across from me totally oblivious to my observations. I stood there magnified by her beauty. Then later, I discover, that here she was gifted to me in this industry I love passionately. Therefore, I am choosing you because I saw the same passion in you. Together we will make a good team. I have responsibilities for my family, myself, most of all my employers. The opportunities they have given me require that I honour them and their company. With you joining in, my hard work will be pleasurable."

"Wow! How can I refuse?" She reached out to grab his hands. Alvaro gently brought them to his lips and kissed them tenderly.

They walked back like two best friends. Gracy felt so comfortable beside him, as if she had known him forever. They stepped exuberantly into the Hyatt's lobby. Alvaro was highly regarded by everyone they encountered. The staff detected the pleasurable gleam in both of their eyes. Gracy's footsteps suddenly came to a halt. She spotted two familiar people huddled in a half hidden corner. There they were, Ingrid and the security guy, in a compromising position. Her mood turned quickly from joy to turbulence. She didn't mention anything to her friend, quietly thinking to herself. *Why are those two secluded of there? They both give me an uneasy feeling.*

At the end of her shift, she returned to her lovely suite. Yes, housekeeping had been there, lucky for her. She could sit down to rest her tired feet. The high heels she had been wearing all day had enhanced her appearance but certainly were not kind to her feet. She had just put her feet up when the phone rang, "Hello Gracy! How are you?"

"Oh, Diego, it's you. "

"Who did you expect? "

She wished it would be Alvaro. His voice alone could awaken her senses. She didn't dare mention anything of sort to her brother. "Fantastic, Diego. I just feel tired. The backlog on my desk was overwhelming; however, I managed to cover everything."

"Are you interested in meeting for a bite to eat?"

"Diego, you must have had a demanding day also. Why don't we skip tonight and plan a short lunch tomorrow? I had lunch with Mr. Fernandez today. He made a proposal to me. I would like to discuss it and go by your approval."

"Gracy, we have faith in this fellow. He has good intentions for our company."

"That's very encouraging. We will discuss it tomorrow. I better get a good night's rest and be fresh as a daisy in the morning for another day's work."

"See you tomorrow same place same time. If Daniele is in town he might join us but I won't promise." As soon as Daniele's name came up, Ingrid's image with the security guy popped back in her vision. What was she doing in that secluded corner with him? Why was she tormented by this woman? Was her exasperation with Ingrid a response to protect Daniele, herself or the company? She was determined to find out.

Chapter Thirty Two

From the time that her father had died, Diego had become her protector and confidante. They met for lunch and she was glad to discuss the offer received from Alvaro Fernandez with him. Although she was excited to work with him, her brother's opinion mattered to her.

"Diego, I like what Mr. Alvaro has presented to me. It will expand my horizons, in many ways. I must confess he is a delightful person to work with."

"Yes. He is a good man. Daniele and I admired him for discussing his intentions with us before presenting the new position to you. We both agreed. It's a great opportunity for you my dear sister. As you know you are our closest family member. What's ours is yours. We couldn't ask for a better mentor to teach you." Gracy was immediately excited by his response. She attentively listened with pleasure as her admirable half-brother continued.

"Gracy, with your intelligence, there would be no boundaries."

"Thank you for your confidence in me Diego."

Her brothers' support was important but she was somewhat concerned about Aunt Lori's old stories about the risks of mixing family and business. Many families in Sicily had been destroyed because of conflicts that arose from money and inheritance. She confided her concerns to him and clarified her feelings. "Diego, my dear brother, I must confide in you, that wealth or monetary accumulation is not my goal in life. Happiness, family unity, love and affection in good relationships is what I seek."

"Gracy, I understand. Thank God you don't know how miserable it is to be broke and poor. Neither do we. Daniele and I have never experienced the misery because we came from a rich family. You, my dear, inherited mom's wealth as well as her generosity of spirit. She took care of you in her death even if she couldn't in her life. My father was the worst person anyone could have for a father-a tyrant, a womanizer, a corrupted man. His motto in life was to conquer. He provided well for us, but it was torture living under his discipline. Yet here we are now with this empire we continue to expand. We can enjoy the benefits with all our hard work and one of those benefits is sharing with you."

"Diego, I am questioning your reluctance to settle down. What will happen when you decide to marry and have a family? Daniele is a concern as well! Ingrid's relationship with him is disturbing me."

"Sis, I am fine the way with I am, nobody to account to, except you my dearest. My intentions have always been not to marry. As for Daniele, why are you concerned? Once he decides to tie the knot, we will create a pre- nuptial agreement that no court can undo."

"Aside from the pre- nuptial agreement, what about her behaviour with other men? It doesn't sit well with me. This feeling churning inside me when I see her or talk to her is disturbing. I hate myself for it. I cannot pinpoint why, other than not trusting her."

"Gracy, relax. The girls here are free and open. You cannot compare them to the reserved ones in Sicily. This is America, the land of freedom. The women are gutsy. I admire them for their determination and forcefulness, in every way."

"Okay! Maybe I am wrong. What do I know? I was overprotected by my dad. Sorry, I shouldn't have deviated to this subject or said anything."

He stretched his arm reaching out with care for her hand. "Our mom was like you. There is nothing wrong with caring too much. You are playing mother hen, especially to Daniele."

She smiled back at him, rather pleased. She didn't like her disturbing thoughts. "Diego, I want to like and love everybody here."

"You will; just give yourself time. You just need to get used to this new way of life. This is America. Live it up."

Gracy hugged and kissed her brother on the cheek, thanking him and apologizing for her apprehensions, especially those about Ingrid.

The next morning as she walked into Alvaro Fernandez's office, any apprehensions fled from her mind. Here she was with a smiling face that came naturally to her. Once she heard his voice, her heart soared. He welcomed her in. "Miss Gracy, I am dying to hear the good news."

After Diego's advice, Gracy, decided to change her tune, playfully.

Inclining her head, she teased him. "You guess Mr. Alvarez. What do you think? " She added a Spanish finale to his name.

"Please, please God Almighty, let Miss Gracy work beside me.

I need her badly."

Her lips parted with a flirting smile "How could I ever refuse one of the cleverest gentlemen I know and from whom I am dying to learn? It will be my pleasure to assist you, Mr. Alvarez. At your command!"

"Thank you. We can start by going to see what's going on at the Marquis today."

"I am ready for whatever comes our way!"

They walked out to valet to get the car. Alvaro was taking Gracy for her first tour at the Marquis Hotel in Manhattan and she was eager and motivated to meet the day.

***

She entered the lobby of the Marquis. She was breathless, taken by the Renaissance architecture, the ambiance, and the selected furnishings. The enormous glittering chandeliers created a romantic atmosphere. Then Alvaro guided her toward the spa that offered services beyond anyone's imagination. The luxuries one could indulge were mind boggling. She placed a hand on her chest. She mentally patted herself on the back for having decided to come to New York. She was grateful for the opportunity offered to her. To top it all, this wonderful young man was her teacher and mentor.

As she was digesting all the amenities, she looked at her watch to check the time. It would be four in the afternoon in Agrigento. Leonello came to her mind, "Why now?" she wondered. "Is he in need? Of course, I should have checked on him before now." she muttered to herself. She wondered if all this abundance in front of her produced guilt for the miserable condition and life of her student. With all the excitement since she had returned here and catching the American bug of business, she had neglected her duties in Sicily.

After they left Sicily Diego and Gracy had hired two of the best counsellors from Bari. They were scheduled to start their sessions with Leonello. *Shame on me. My mind has been sidetracked for a while in this land of opportunities. I must focus and faith to help those students of mine, especially Leonello who has lost all his hope in life. How can he ever imagine the availability of life's luxuries when he has only known abuse and misery? Much had been given to her, so much was expected of her. She would pay it forward with her former students.*

She got up early the next morning to place a call to Dr.Ferrari, the senior psychiatrist and chief counsellor they had hired. He couldn't be paged as there had been a crisis at the hospital during the night. He wasn't going to be in until late afternoon. That worried her. She didn't want to dwell on it. Her head pounded wondering why suddenly Leonello had come to her mind. Was it remorse for abandoning her students? Was her conscience playing tricks on her for leaving the lonely souls at the hospital where she used to volunteer? Again, as those thoughts were going through her mind a bout of guilt struck her. She asked to talk to the nurse in charge. The response was "Miss Robertson, the patient is resting comfortably now. It would be best for you to talk to Dr. Ferrari."

"Can you tell me about the best time for me to get hold of him? With our time difference, it's hard to know when it is a good time to call."

"I will tell him that you called. Maybe he can return your call."

"Thanks, it might be hard for him to reach me. I will try again in the morning."

She hung up the phone in a somber mood. There was a convention going on tomorrow at the hotel. There was a special request for the Moonlight Room. Special guests from several European countries had been arriving all day. A welcoming party was planned for tonight. Alvaro had asked her to oversee the organization. Flowers had been ordered. The chefs had been busy all day preparing exquisite appetizers and the bartenders creating luscious drinks. They had carefully selected musicians for the evening's entertainment. Three violinists in formal attire were to play classical music throughout the event. The limitless budget meant there had been no shortchanging in any part of the evening.

Alvaro Fernandez had been selected to handle the convention details. He chose Gracy to head up the on-site organization, feeling confident. He knew in his heart that Miss Robertson would dedicate herself fully to make the evening a professional affair. Indeed, Gracy, placed aside all her concerns for Agrigento, made the sign of the cross and moved ahead with her tasks. One day at the time. *This day was important. Tomorrow she would deal with Dr. Ferrari, and Leonello.*

At the end of the evening Alvaro, complimented her on a job well done. "Miss Gracy! I must inform you that the president of the company has left a hefty tip for us and our staff."

This was all new to Gracy. She couldn't believe the generosity of these people. In Italy and most European countries, including Australia where she had lived, tipping was not expected or accepted. "Oh my! This is all bonus. I feel badly taking it."

"You can always donate it to charity." he commented and thinking *what a difference.* When he had hosted conferences with other staff members, they couldn't wait for the end of the evening. Their big interest was in how much tip there was to add to their salary. They were perturbed if it wasn't an acceptable percentage. Ingrid had been one of them, bitching to no end because of mediocre tipping. As for him, the honor and good reviews from his clients were more important. Yes, his future endeavours depended on it. He admired Gracy's attitude, but still he considered her a young woman with the advantage of a family of means. Little he could imagine the pain and suffering caused by the loss of the mother she never had the opportunity to know. Although all this wealth impressed her, the happiness in her heart was for the dear ones close to her.

Chapter Thirty Three

Gracy had set her alarm clock earlier than usual. She was determined to get in touch with Dr. Ferrari or to speak with Leonello. If she heard his voice, she would be able to tell if his situation was promising. When she rang the hospital, to her surprise, the nurse answered "Miss Robertson, Dr. Ferrari is right here. Hold on. I will ask him to take your call."

"Pronto, Dr. Ferrari here."

"Buon giorno, Dr. Ferrari, how are you? I am so glad we connected."

"Ma si! L'infermiere didn't want me to go far. She told me you would call this morning."

"Grazie molto. Tell me doctor, how is my student doing? I have had some anxious moments. I regretted leaving. . ."

"Miss Robertson, he is in good hands. As I explained to you and your brother, I have done an intensive physical examination on him. I wanted to make sure there wasn't any chemical imbalance in his blood affecting his physical body. As you know, he had been starving himself. We are rehabilitating him and working on providing the necessary nourishment to improve his health. Then we can proceed to work with his mental health. Looking at his history, it wasn't difficult to reach a diagnosis. The violence he has been exposed to, the lack of maternal nurturing, family neglect, abuse and the squalor all contributed to his deterioration."

"Dr. Ferrari, he had come a long way. He had applied himself and studied diligently. He passed the exams. I was pleased."

"Yes, Miss Robertson. I understand what you are saying. In his weakened mind your leaving was another loss. His self-esteem plummeted. He looked to you as his saviour, someone that cared. Then you left and he felt abandoned once more. The emptiness in his life set in. His depression progressed in full force, even propelling him towards death."

"What a shame!"

"Miss Robertson, human beings crave love and care. Leonello is no different. Once that affection is lost or taken away, a feeling of worthlessness sets in, followed by depression. When its sets into the core, it's hard to eradicate. In my studies and practice I have yet to come across individuals that don't seek gratification and care.

"I understand. I shouldn't have left."

"No, you have your own life to live."

"Dependency is not good especially for a young man. Dr. Ferrari. Where do we go from here with him?"

"It will take some time. We will help him. Don't worry. In a couple of weeks, we will start psychotherapy along with antidepressants. We might include his mother in some sessions. Her drinking problem also contributes to her son's catastrophic emotions.

Afterwards, my colleague will try Cognitive Behavioral Therapy.

It will help change his mood. Eventually, his feeling of worthlessness should disappear."

"I hope so Doctor. Please keep us informed. Can I call you again, next week? Or would you like to call me at your convenience. I can be reached anytime, during the day or evening." She gave him her phone numbers. Gracy didn't want to be too demanding. After all he was a busy man who was in high demand. Hopefully next time, if she could talk to Leonello and hear his voice, she would automatically feel more assured.

The grandfather clock chimed eight times. It was time for her to get herself groomed and in her business suit. Alvaro would be waiting for her with new instructions. She was to meet him in his office this morning. He told her last night, there would be some unfinished business to investigate at the Hyatt.

She was promptly at his door by nine o'clock. She knocked and, without thinking, grabbed the doorknob ready to turn it. Something jolted her chest and stopped her in her tracks. At the slight opening of the door, a pair of high heels and legs hit her eyes. She hesitated with the door ajar.

"Come in," Alvaro's voice called. Her hand moved slowly to continue opening the door. As she reluctantly stepped in, her eyes glanced upon a short skirt and then Ingrid turned to face her. "Good morning Gracy!"

"Good morning,"

"What's the matter? You look puzzled, as if you have seen a ghost?"

"Sorry, just surprised. I didn't expect you here."

"You are liable to find me everywhere." She stepped aside to put her arms around Alvaro pulling him toward her. "Eh! Alvaro," and then looking at Gracy with a grin on her face she exclaimed "These fellows cannot function without my input."

Gracy forced a cold smile. *My morning wasn't meant to start with Ingrid Klein's sarcasm. I wish she would let go of the Spanish fellow's neck and disappear.*

Ingrid continued blabbering away about working on the third floor today. She had brought in a carpenter from Washington. She turned to Alvaro inviting him to stop in sometime during the day. She planted a kiss on his cheek and suggestively swinging her hips, she finally left.

Gracy, remained taciturn for few minutes. Alvaro's voice broke her silence. "Well, Miss Gracy here we are again. It is another splendid day at work at the fantastic Hyatt Regency. Different from yesterday, I can assure you but as alluring in different respects."

Gracy, didn't seem too enthusiastic. Alvaro noticed her lack of response. He looked her straight in the eyes "Is anything wrong? You prefer to work at the Marquis?"

"No, not at all. I think it's interesting, everyday something new. It's great. I am ready. What's on the agenda today?" She was trying to respond in an uplifted tone.

"Miss Gracy, I am glad. You had me worried there for a minute."

"It has nothing to do with my work. I had a long discussion, early morning, with my student's counsellor back home. I am a bit concerned. That is all. I shouldn't let that interfere with my work here." She grabbed her notebook and pen. "Here I am ready at your service."

She wasn't going to tell him that Ingrid's presence had disturbed her. The way she was dressed, the way she behaved and her flirtation with him were disconcerting.

She asked herself *Am I jealous of her? Yes and no. She rubs me the wrong way.* Alvaro was looking at his notes for the day. Clare, the receptionist, had handed him a list as he had arrived in the morning. Ingrid had barged in and now he was behind schedule. He quickly finished highlighting the priorities. "Okay, Gracy here we are. I need to place someone in charge of final hiring for new staff. Would you be interested?"

"It's new to me. I can apply depending on the requirements."

"You are an educator; it shouldn't take long for you to learn the requisites."

"You really do have confidence in me. How can I refuse?"

"I suggest you do research and update your knowledge of labour laws. The rest is easy- intuition, characters, experience, gut feeling. You will be required for final approval only. We will have Margie in Personnel to do most of the paperwork."

"I will need to learn so much in this new career of mine and will never run out of work it seems."

"There is more. All the boutiques in our lobbies are individually run. They need to be inspected weekly. We have to make sure they run following the proper rules and regulations, acceptable by our company code."

"Alvaro is there anymore? Please don't overload me. I have my brothers to look after also. I need to make time for them." she half-teased as she smiled.

"Miss Gracy, time for me too. I would love you to have some time for me outside of work for dinner, dancing and walking under the moonlight on some Saturday night."

Gracy swallowed hard. "Wow! Where did that come from? Doesn't that break a rule? One shouldn't never get intimately involved with a co-worker?"

"You already studied the rules I gather, Miss Gracy? When there is an attraction between two people, the heart knows no rules." With pleasure she responded "We are breaking the rules right now. We should be productive instead of being sidetracked."

She got up to get started on her busy day. Her mixed up brain was playing havoc with her heart. *Is Alvaro trying to tell me that he is attracted to me?* She noticed that he had made that comment without reservations. She walked in a daze for the rest of the day, revisiting his words. He had left assignments for her to execute. Gracy wouldn't disappoint him. Alvaro's demands were plenty. It was nearly lunch time, when she spotted him moving swiftly in the lobby with a couple of security fellows on each side of him. She was reluctant to stop him.

When he got closer, he quickly excused himself and called out to her. "Gracy, I am on my way out. I must get to our hotel by the airport. I hate to tell you, but this is bad news." His sweet voice sounded pained.

"What has happened? Can I help?"

"No. I won't expose you to such danger. An armed robbery and a shooting has taken place. A few of our guests have been injured. The whole place is in chaos. I must get there at once."

"Alvaro, never mind the danger. Take me with you."

"Sorry, Gracy, I am in a hurry. I must go."

He hurried out with the security guards before she could insist. She had never allowed herself to think about crime. To date she had only seen the glamor, the beauty, the happiness of the hotels. She had only considered the worry free stays, the amenities and the extraordinary service the hotels brought to their guests. The possible ugliness had never occurred to Gracy. Unfortunately, it happened everywhere. New York City with millions of people, especially, had its share of daily mishaps. Their five-star hotels were not spared even with cameras or tight security measures. They didn't prevent the bad guys from doing bad things.

A cloud of worry hung over her head. The word soon spread like wildfire to the rest of the staff. The news media was relentless. She stopped work a few times to listen to the news from the lobby's televisions. The broadcasters and reporters mentioned the injured who had been taken to City Memorial Hospital. No names were released.

Gracy tried to call Diego. He could not be reached. Daniele, as far as she knew, was in Las Vegas. She needed to hear their voices for reassurance. Her nerves were getting the best of her. She made the sign of the cross begging. "Please God, I hope no one is seriously hurt." The televisions kept blaring away with updates. "Four people have now succumbed to their injuries from this morning's gunfire at the Hilton Hotel. Three more are in critical condition. No names can be released until next of kin have been notified." *Oh my God! I must try again. I need to talk to my brothers.* She ran back to her office where she could collect herself. She had just grabbed the phone when it rang in her hand. "Hello"

"Gracy!"

"Yes! "She held her breath, recognizing Ingrid's voice.

"Oh! Ingrid it's you."

"Yes. Are you still working?" Ingrid sounded tense, even shaky.

"Yes, I am trying to Ingrid. What has happened?" Her own voice was shaky. "Do you happen to know where my brothers are? I haven't been able to reach either of them. I know Daniele had an early flight to Vegas." Ingrid didn't answer for a second.

"Gracy, get to the City Memorial Hospital; your brother has been hurt in crossfire. He is asking for you."

"My brother! Which one?" She placed a hand on her chest to hold her rapidly beating heart.

"It's Daniele." Gracy's phone dropped out of her hand. Her legs buckled and she fell on the floor.

"Gracy, Gracy! Are you still there?"

There was no answer.

234

Chapter Thirty Four

Gracy's lack of response exasperated Ingrid. 'Great, what has happened to her now? Mumbling to herself about Gracy making the situation worse, she reacted quickly. Diego couldn't be reached. She paged Walter Robertson. He had returned to his duty at the Hyatt. "Walter, you need to go check on Gracy'. She was in her office. I think she might have passed out once I gave her the news of her brother being injured. Attend to her needs first. She needs to get here; her brother is calling for her. I am trying to find Diego." Ingrid had been trying to move Daniele's flight to a later one. The change in flights was all emergency work related in her mind. Then she would have seen him off at the airport but the unexpected happened. Daniele's departure never took place.

Alvaro's day also had been disrupted. He was being pulled from every direction. The police interrogation, the cordoning of the lobby, the elevators, and the corridors. In some of the rooms the disarray needed immediate attention. The new guests who were arriving were confused, disappointed and demanding. They needed to be relocated. Some of them were not too pleased. Their choice of hotel was based on being close to the airport; they found the other locations inconvenient for them.

Diego had been detained since early morning on discovery in a case all day. When he was tied up in court, in pretrial or discovery, he would leave strict orders not to be disturbed. A serious client was being wrongfully sued for multimillions. He was totally oblivious to what was happening on the news or television. His focus was on settling the case out of court. He was highly sought after as a lawyer because he was so dedicated to the success of his clients.

***

Walter Robertson walked into Gracy's office to find her on the floor. She was white as a ghost and not responding. He could barely detect her pulse. He immediately called 911 and radioed for assistance. By the time an ambulance arrived, Gracy, confused, had come to. She was looking around her wondering what had happened. The paramedics were checking her pulse, her heartbeat and asking questions. She recollected the bad news. Gracy kept mumbling "I must go see my brother. Please let me go." She felt lightheaded as she tried to get up. She insisted on going to the Memorial Hospital to see Daniele. Walter who had been informed of the events by Ingrid, offered to take her as soon as she was cleared by the paramedics.

By then another security guard had arrived so she chose to go with him. Once they finally reached the hospital, she spotted Diego at the nurses' station. Gracy took a big breath of relief. *My Saviour,* she threw her arms around Diego's neck, crying incessantly.

"Gracy, get a hold of yourself, please. We need to be strong. You must let go of your emotions. We don't want to alarm Daniele. We need to be optimistic."

"I know, I can't help it. I got so frightened."

"Sis, Daniele will be fine."

"I must toughen up. I will feel better once I see Daniele and know he is okay."

A group of trauma surgeons and Dr. Bernardino, an intensive care specialist had been summoned. They had removed two bullets from his abdomen trying to save his life. Daniele was in Intensive Care being monitored by two nurses and vigilant GSW physicians to monitor any developments. He was hooked into all the medical apparatus needed to continually monitor his responses.

As they approached his room, Ingrid greeted them in the corridor. They were only allowed access to the waiting room. The nurse advised that they could only go in one at the time to see the patient. One of the nurses warned them, "Your brother is heavily sedated in order to alleviate the pain. He may not respond to your presence."

"I want to talk to the doctor. I need to know his condition." Diego insisted. Gracy clutched his arm. Both were desperate for answers to their many questions.

"Mr. Frarano, Dr. Bernardino has been in surgery all day. I am not sure if he could be paged. He looked exhausted; they were in surgery a long time."

"Regardless I need to know."

Ingrid was fast to add "He woke up from the anesthetic. His first words were calling for you two. Then they gave him a needle for pain and then he went out like lightning.

Gracy, was shaking, afraid to faint again. She continued to hold on to Diego's arm tightly like a frightened kitten.

"Of all days I was tied up in court out of state!"

"We couldn't get a hold of you, Diego. He was bleeding profusely. Thank God they were able to stop the bleeding. The doctors had no time to waste in getting him to surgery," responded Ingrid.

The nurse interrupted and asked Gracy and Diego "Who wants to go first?"

"Can we please go together? We won't stay long, and we'll try not to disturb him." Diego knew Gracy needed him beside her. In her past, especially with her father's death, grief had overwhelmed her. The nurse reluctantly allowed them in the room together even though she had initially instructed that they could visit only one at a time. Together they entered Daniele's room. By some miracle Daniele opened his eyes and gazed at them both.

"Bro, you surprised us. What are you doing here? You were supposed to be in Vegas."

He forced a smile, but, as his lips moved he only managed a whisper.

Gracy bent over and kissed him on his forehead, trying to find space between the multiple tubes. She tried hard to cover up her stirred emotions. "You will be fine Daniele. Yes, you will." Caressing him, she was trying to reassure herself.

"I'm sorry but time is up." said the nurse.

Daniele's condition was more serious than anticipated. The recovery would be uncertain.

Gracy's days were dragging slowly. Her primary interest was the wellbeing of her brother. Daniele wasn't responding to the medication as well as he should have. Dr. Bernardino, at Gracy's and Diego's insistence, called in other internists for consultation. Originally the doctor had given them encouragement saying "He is young and fit and should bounce back soon. Let's give him some time. I predict a recovery." They felt encouraged. Unfortunately, as time passed, Daniele's condition worsened. Diego and Gracy kept pressing for answers. "We don't understand. There have to be more injuries internally than meets the eye."

The doctor kept saying. "It's the trauma. For some it takes longer than others" They continued with MRIs, ultrasounds, research and consultations. As much as they wanted to be optimistic, things didn't look promising. The siblings were troubled.

As Daniele's situation worsened, Gracy lost her enthusiasm for work. Alvaro Fernandez had been complimentary regardless of her achievements. Her interest in all things had declined. She knew in her heart her only interest was to see her brother recover. It hadn't happened. Winter had settled in New York to make matters worse. The days were darker and shorter. The cold penetrated deep in her bones. The snowstorms had been relentless. She lived in the penthouse high in the sky and the furious winds from the North Atlantic battered away each night keeping her awake. Awake, discontent, tossing and turning she prayed. 'Dear God heal my brother.' Then to add to her worry, Leonello would surface in her mind. *I must call and check on his progress, my poor abandoned young man. She was awake anyway and with the time difference she thought she could reach him. I could call and find out how things are going at the other side of the ocean. At least she would get something accomplished while she couldn't sleep.*

She switched the light on and dialed the number. The operator promptly responded. In no time she was connected to the hospital's reception desk. "*Pronto*, hello, can you connect me to Leonello Dante please?" The phone kept ringing as she gave out a big sigh, feeling defeated. A faint voice answered on the fifth ring. "*Pronto...*" the voice was low and barely recognizable.

"*Pronto!* Leonello! Is it you?"

"Yes, it's me."

"Leonello, how are you? It's Miss Gracy here."

"Miss Gracy! Is it really you?" She detected his pleasure.

"Leonello, how are you doing? Tell me, how are your sessions going? I have been praying for you."

"You have! I thought you didn't care for me."

"Why you say that Leonello? Of course, I care."

"You left again. You forgot all about me. My mom prays also; what good does it do?"

"Leonello, don't talk like that. You have so much to live for."

"I don't think so. My life is empty. I have no reason to want to live."

"I want to talk to your doctor and see what he thinks. Leonello you need to cooperate and practice what he tells you."

"Miss Gracy, if you had any feelings for my wellbeing, you wouldn't have chosen to move to New York leaving me in misery."

"Stop that nonsense again. Leonello, I see you are better already because you are argumentative again. So, fight for your mental wellbeing. You have the world at your feet. It's your choice Leonello. I can help you if you will allow me."

He didn't respond, she hoped he was reflecting on her words. When the quietness lingered "Leonello, are you still there?" She could hear shuffling. "Leonello, I will call the doctor tomorrow. Be good for your own sake. I must go now. You take care of yourself if you want to make me happy."

She ended the phone call somewhat encouraged. *At least he talked; that alone should be a good sign.* It was five in the morning in New York. She tried to get some sleep, but her body was completely awake. She got up and brewed some camomile tea instead of coffee, trying to calm her nerves.

Lately the stars were not aligning; they had been moving the wrong way. The joy filling her heart since she had arrived at this glamorous city had vanished. She continued reflecting on the challenges that life was throwing their way until the nebulous night transitioned into daylight. The sunrays pushing through the clouds were promising a bright morning. She tried to put a smile on her face and presented herself at Alvaro's office. He got up from his desk lighting up as he saw her. *"Buenos dias mi amor! Come stas?"*

"Alvaro, I need your warm Spanish greeting badly this morning?

Life has been so hard lately." Driven by her need, she put her arms around his neck and just rested her face on his chest. Both of their bodies felt electrified. She let go of herself in total abandon. Gracy realized that she had been too forward; she apologized.

"Alvaro, sorry. I didn't mean to misbehave. Maybe I shouldn't have since you are my boss."

"Hush! Hush, stop being so modest. Didn't you feel my heartbeat? I certainly felt yours. I wished our embrace could have lasted here for an eternity."

"Alvaro, you always know the right words to say." she answered modestly.

Deep down Alvaro's revelation had ignited a spark in her heart. She was embarrassed and somewhat shook up. She tried to hide her gratification. How she needed that hug. All the upheaval lately was too much for her fragile emotions. She let out a big sigh. "Where am I assigned today? I better get to work."

In his gentle manner he put an arm around her shoulders "Gracy, I must go to the Marquis. Another big group is arriving from Germany today-a big convention. I was going to ask Ingrid in case I needed her to translate for me. You know she is fluent in German." He hesitated for a moment, his eyes on her. "How about you go with me instead? I am sure we will manage. It'll be good for you; it will keep your mind off your troubles. You need a change of atmosphere."

Gracy felt flattered that he wanted her. Her spirit lifted somewhat. "Alvaro! I would love to spend a day there working with you. Besides I find the place uplifting."

"The place? I thought working with me was uplifting for you."

She liked his playful mood. "Of course, I do. As long as I don't get into trouble with Ingrid." With some boldness she adjusted his tie affectionately. Her dad had always reminded her that she had her mother's blood in her veins; Italian affection was easily shown. He believed that while the British cared they were less likely to show it. She felt happy showing her emotions.

Alvaro and Gracy, chatting and smiling, got in the car and were ready to leave the Hyatt. A knock on Gracy's window startled her. She rolled down the window. It was Ingrid.

"Gracy, where are you going?"

"To work at the Marquis."

"I thought you were working here today. I wanted to show you a couple of rooms. Later I am going to run to the hospital to see your brother."

Alvaro intervened "I need Gracy to assist me today. We have a big convention." Ingrid furled her brow. Without responding she snappily walked away.

"Sorry Ingrid." His apology trailed after her.

From the corner of her eye, she watched them drive away, muttering to herself "That bitch is privileged not only by her brothers, but she also has a spell on our CEO and our staff." She decided to go talk to her buddy Walter Robertson if he was on duty. There was no sign of him this morning. She left word at the front desk for him to get in touch with her as soon as he reported to work. She needed to vent her anger; Walter would sympathize with her and right now she needed a sympathetic friend to help her with this Gracy situation.

Chapter Thirty Five

Gracy and Alvaro were madly in love. They couldn't deny their attraction for one another. The Spanish CEO was glorying in the fact that Gracy was beside him. He preferred Gracy, above all others, to assist him. They managed to control their longing for one another during their workday, but no one could limit their love once their duties were over. Their thirsty bodies feverishly indulged in all the affection they both craved. "Gracy my love, you are irresistible. I will love you eternally."

"Likewise, my darling." Her lips met his in total abandon.

***

Gracy's concern for her brother Daniele clouded her happiness, often leaving her shaken. Two months had passed, and his full recovery was still questionable. He was having problems walking. The many consultations with the doctors and specialists had been not satisfactory. Diego was hurting also but he tried to cover up his feelings for her sake. His sister knew that deep down he was trying to protect her from worry. When Gracy pressed for answers, they were evasive. The fear inside her relentlessly churned. Alvaro had come in her life at such a crucial time. She needed his affection, love, and sincere support. He had become her lover and best friend. He always uplifted her spirit.

The word had been spread that the two were madly in love. That raised eyebrows with some of the staff. The corporate policy discouraged intimate relationships between coworkers. Unfortunately, Alvaro and

Gracy could not control their hearts. Workplace resentment was manifesting itself, mostly in Ingrid Klein.

Ingrid was plotting with her friend Walter to destroy the passionate love affair. "Since she arrived all our people bow at her feet. We must stop it somehow. You owe me Walter. Let's put a plan in place." Ingrid put her arms around his neck, pulling him to her. She pinned her breasts on his chest and smothered him with wet kisses leaving him breathless. If she wanted something badly she was willing to use any means possible to con her prey. After the kiss, he asked "What do you want me to do?"

"Didn't you tell me that your brother Morris, wanted to move here?"

"Why are we looking for my brother Morris?"

"You told me he is an influential financial adviser involved with powerful people. I could use him."

"That was just talk. I don't really know who he influences."

She slapped him on the shoulder. "Are you playing dumb with me?"

"Who do you mean? He hangs around with a lot of guys I don't really know."

Ingrid pushed continued probing. "I'm talking about the guys he hires when he needs something private done. I don't remember their names but you must"

"Roy Gagnon and Mark Diez, those two. Ingrid do me a favour, concentrate on your boyfriend's wellbeing. That's your best bet to get what you want. He is still at the hospital? Focus on him and don't bother me with your shenanigans."

She grabbed him by his shoulders. "Walter, if you know what's good for you, you will do as I say. Who got you this job? Who encouraged Daniele to talk to the accountant into raising your salary? Furthermore, if you don't help, you can forget about any future promotions I might support on your behalf. Do you understand me? So, my friend, suit yourself. You will always be stuck in security working shifts."

She let go of him after giving him a good shake and she walked away. He was ready to throw that fancy uniform away and walk out but the pay was good and the benefits incomparable. Life was expensive in the big city. He needed his job but resented her demands. "I am sick of her demands. I wish she would leave me alone." He swallowed hard, put his head down and returned to his duty. His beeper went off. "I expect you to have a meeting with your brother and have him call me." Ingrid ordered.

She is relentless. God help me. Why did I ever get involved with her? He had wanted a taste of the sex with her that the other boys used to talk about in high school. Her talents in the bedroom always promised a night to remember.

246

Chapter Thirty Six

Regardless of the situation that Gracy was in, she concentrated on performing the best that she could for the sake of the guests and the company itself. Gracy and Alvaro's work partnership was admirable. They were such a synchronized team. Hotel profits soared because of their ideas and actions. Should one of their hotels be full, Alvaro with his diplomatic ways always managed to talk their guests into another of their locations. Gracy, would follow up with the details of complimentary packages to honor their clients. Full occupancy was their goal for her brothers. Gracy wasn't concentrating much on the dollar signs; however, to her wonder, their efforts had stimulated great success. Their loving relationship kept them going every day and it spilled over in the work.

That didn't stop the hidden pain for her brother Daniele that always resurfaced. Neither had she not forgotten Leonello, especially at night when she was alone. She would drop in to see her brother at the end of the day. She would find Diego sitting beside him either by the bed or in a chair in Daniele's private room. They would be all smiles at her arrival. "Here is our *fatiatore*. Our hard worker." Diego would say. "I second that." added Daniele. She would hug them both tenderly "You guys give me strength."

"Are you sure it's us guys? I think it's more that CEO of ours, the Spanish stallion. Looks like he keeps you on cloud nine with his charm."

Her face lit up at the mention of Alvaro. "I will not deny it.

Alvaro is marvelous. I love working with him."

"Never mind working with him. You are madly in love Gracy! Good thing we approve of the fellow. Aren't you glad you joined us in New York?"

"Yes, that part is all good. I will not deny it. I have fallen madly in love with Alvaro. He makes me feel special. My work is not work. It's a joy to share responsibilities with him and it is rewarding to be a part of your company."

Daniele contradicted her last words. "Never mind our company. You are part of us. Us includes you Sis- the three of us only always!"

"Daniele, you have Ingrid. You are living together. You are going to marry her one day and you will have children."

"Sis don't include Ingrid yet. It's us three that count. We are blood. Never forget that."

"Daniele, my main concern is for you to get completely well. I am happy with work and having Alvaro at this trying time. The thorn in my heart is you. I want to see you up and functioning. It's time!"

"She is right Bro. I want to have another consultation with the doctor. The recovery is slower than we anticipated."

"It will happen eventually. It's my back more than my abdomen that won't hold me up."

"This back problem of yours needs to be investigated further. We must arrange for a new consultation, Daniele. I am tired of living on promises. Tomorrow I will make few phone calls." Diego stated seriously. Then he turned to Gracy. Diego asked, "What do you hear from Agrigento, Sis? How is the other concern going?"

"I didn't want to bring it up. We have enough to deal with here. During the day I am so busy which is good, but I must confess, when I go home at night, my mind is tormented. I wonder about Leonello. I pray he pulls thorough his depression. I feel responsible. He is fixed on the fact that I abandoned him."

"Sis, he is young. Sometimes these young pups get infatuated with their teachers, especially with the kind of life he's had. He looked up to you. It's good that you got away. He had to face reality eventually."

"I know. I still feel sorry about his state of mind."

"He will grow up one day."

"He should, providing he snaps out of his depressed state."

While Gracy paced Daniele spoke.

"Time will tell about him and me. Anything can happen. Look at me sitting in this wheelchair. I never expected to get shot. Why didn't I go straight to the airport that day? The whole incident was so freaky- the wrong place at the wrong time."

The therapist arrived to interrupt their discussion. "Mr. Frarano, it's time for your work out. Are you ready?"

"No, I am not. Do I have a choice?" He answered with a sorrowful smile.

"You don't have a choice! You must if you want to get better." The therapist cautioned him with a serious look. He tried struggling to get on his feet by himself. He couldn't.

The therapist offered her aid. "Not to worry we will try something else for today" and she proceeded wheeling him away. His siblings shared their concern.

"We must do something Diego."

"Don't I know it? That this is heart breaking. Let's walk to the nursing station right now. If they can page the doctor, I'd like to talk to him immediately."

"It is late and he has probably finished for the day. I don't think you will find him still on duty."

"I can leave word for him to get in touch with me first thing tomorrow. Sorry, I am not buying his promises anymore." Diego added. He was very disturbed.

"There has to be something more seriously wrong with Daniele that prevents his mobility."

As suspected the doctor had signed off for the night. Diego left instructions to be called the next day. Even better, he would be there the next morning. To them both, Daniele was more important than anything else. Gracy excused herself from work the next morning. She would report to the hotel later. Diego picked her up. Together they went to check on Daniele first. He was groggy because he was doped with pain killers. They were alarmed, wondering what on earth had taken place after he had been taken for his exercise. After their inquiries, the nurse said "Mr. Frarano was restless all night and in severe pain. The doctor ordered some pain killers to alleviate his suffering so he could rest."

Diego struggled with this new information. "I don't understand. He seemed better a couple of days ago. We need to talk to the doctor; this is why we are here."

"Yes, we have already notified the doctor. He will talk to you as soon as he comes in."

Diego was restless, impatiently walking the hallway, while Gracy quietly sat beside Daniele stroking his hand. He was sleeping deeply. Finally, Dr. Bernardino arrived. He invited them to a room where they could talk privately. Diego and Gracy were ready to bombard him with questions and were expecting answers. He very calmly, explained. "Mr. Frarano, Miss Robertson, your brother was hurt badly. He is lucky to be alive. We have detected a strange blood disorder that needs to be investigated. I have called in two top hematologists, for consultation. We will run all kinds of tests on him. Once the results are in, we will share the findings so that we can develop a strategic plan that will assure his progress."

"Doctor how long is this going to take?"

"He is scheduled, as of today, for x-rays, CT scan and ultrasound.

Once we analyze the findings, I will have more answers for you."

The doctor was paged once more. He left them without any real answers and new questions. Diego let out a big sigh. He tried to put on a happy face so as not to worry Gracy. He placed an arm around her shoulder "Sis, let's return to Daniele's room. I want to check on him once more before we leave." He hoped to convince himself that his brother would be soon his old self. Once they got there they found that Daniele was still sleeping peacefully. They had no choice other than to walk away and wait for the doctor to get in touch with them.

***

The next morning Gracy was up bright an early due to another restless night. She decided to call Sicily, thinking that she might as well be brought up to date on what was happening there. She called the hospital, asking to be connected to Leonello. She was hoping for a good report. It was 1:00 pm there, a good time to talk. "Pronto!" Leonello answered quickly,

"*Pronto*. It's Miss Robertson Leonello. How are you?"

"As well as I can be. Life would be much better if you were here Miss Robertson. One day drags into another. I miss seeing you. My heart will not stop wishing that you will come back."

"Leonello, please, you know I have obligations here with my brothers. Especially now, they need me badly. You cannot be selfish. I will tell you what; promise me you will try your utmost to cooperate with the counsellor and to remove your negative thoughts. Go back to school; concentrate on studying English as your second language. Once you graduate, a new life is all yours to enjoy. If you say you care, can you do that for me, will you?"

He was listening. The music therapy ordered by the counsellor to soothe his mood swings was playing softly in the background. Gracy wasn't sure if he was still there. He wasn't responding. "Leonello are you there? Did you hear what I said? Will you follow up on my advice?"

Finally in his low voice said "Yeah, I heard you. Easy for you to say. Hard for me to execute."

"Leonello you must try. Promise me you will. There is a great future in front of you, one step at the time. I will help you along the way in any way I can but for now it must be from here. I need your cooperation even if it is long distance."

"I cannot promise anything. I will relate what you said to the psychiatrist."

"Bye for now. I'll call you again. Concentrate on my advice."

She hung up the phone, hoping good results for Leonello.

Her concern switched to Daniele. What had gone wrong with him since his relapse? Alvaro had missed her immensely as she became more preoccupied with her brother's situation. He knew how devoted she was to her family, so he didn't want to press her with work demands. A few times he had to resort to using Ingrid in her place.

Gracy was anguished and overwhelmed at this time, running to the hospital every chance she had. Diego found support having Gracy at his side. They shared the same pain and concern. Two days had passed with no word from the doctors. The worry was escalating. It didn't look good. Diego's and Gracy's fear were off the chart.

On this day, the sky was dark and gloomy today. The sun had been hiding behind the heavy clouds threatening a downpour. They stood there watching Daniele move in and out of consciousness. Ingrid walked in and asked in a strangely cheerful manner, "How is my fellow?" She made her way over to Daniele, planted a kiss on his cheek and turned to Diego. "Diego, has the doctor given you any results yet?" She totally ignored Gracy. "Yesterday, when I called him, I was told he was in consultation with the hematologist and oncologist, and we would have an answer today. This is why I am here this morning."

"I was told the same thing." Diego responded tersely, somewhat disturbed by Ingrid's cheerfulness.

As they were speaking the doctor walked in. They all rose, eager to see him. Dr. Bernardino approached Diego. The look on his face was serious and he seemed hesitant. Gracy grabbed Diego's hand for support. "Mr. Frarano, Miss Robertson, would you mind stepping in our private conference room. I will go over our findings." He hadn't addressed, Ingrid so she asked. "Doctor, I live with him. I am entitled to know as well!"

"Sorry, please join us."

They squeezed into the small room. Diego couldn't wait for the doctor to speak. He finally did.

"Intensive tests have been done. We have the results. As you know we had detected a blood disorder in his lymph nodes and vessels. Apparently, his body is not able to fight these infections. His body is out of balance. When this happens, other organs get damaged. A Para spinal abscess has formed in the lower back. This is from the original injury caused by the bullet. The prolonged illness is causing a walking issue. As I mentioned to you, we had our top hematologist, an internist and an oncologist with us as we went over the tests. These are the results."

"What can we do about it? Can he be cured? Will he improve?"

"We will wait and see. In the meantime, we are trying everything we can. Let's hope for the best. I am sorry I don't have better news for you. " He got up.

Diego asked. "Can we take him home?"

"I suggest he be kept here for a while longer. Once home, he will require medical assistance."

Gracy, was in tears. Diego, tried to be strong but he was shaken.

Ingrid tried to lift their spirits. "We have to be optimistic here. Daniele is young. Whatever has come over him, he will fight." Ingrid's positivity was good but could not help. Unfortunately, Diego's heart was aching for his brother. He detested the prognosis. Gracy was no better emotionally.

They had every right to be worried. They didn't know that Dr. Bernardino didn't have the heart to reveal the totality of Daniele's fate at this meeting. There was still the possibility for things to change and so he had provided the most important information. He had told his colleagues. "This is the worst part. I detest having to tell the family bad news. These people have endured enough trauma from the shooting incident. I wished to tell them that everything would be fine with this remarkable young man." Doctor Bernardino was terribly disturbed himself. He had heard of the nobility of the Frarano boys. They were an asset not only to the city of New York but to all of the country. He had faith in their strength and resources to ensure the best for his patient.

Chapter Thirty Seven

Gracy's heart was broken for her beloved brother. Every day she found comfort only when being with Alvaro. He would encourage her with promises he hoped could be kept. "*Mi amour!* Don't despair. We will search the globe to help your brother. Daniele will be his old self again." He would encourage.

"Alvaro, yes, I need to believe we can. He is such a good soul and so gifted in his abilities. No one and nothing can take that away from him."

"You see my dearest! Even if he cannot walk, it's not the end for him." he remarked.

Time passed; spring was approaching. As the season of renewal promised, some good was happening. She was sorting out her mail. A letter post marked from Italy was misplaced in her junk mail. She recognized the writing. With her hands shaking couldn't wait to open it.

My dearest Miss Robertson,

I finally have the courage to put these words on paper. As you know, my resentment of your departure was immeasurable. You were the only person in my life that I admired. It was my understanding that you cared for me. When you abandoned me, the devastation set in so deep that it carved into my heart more and more each day and night. I couldn't see my beautiful teacher whom I adored and loved any more. My world had fallen apart, getting darker each and every day. I had no reason to live anymore. Thanks to your intervention and the aid of my counsellors hired by my caring teacher, Miss Gracy Robertson, I have been improving. They have helped me see the light. You will be glad to also know that I have resumed my studies with the help of Professor Giacomo Rondelli and Mr. Matteo Dario. Every now and then some darkness slides over my brain but I remind myself of your kind praises and the encouragement you gave me. The promise of a significant future ahead of me helps me to erase those unfavorable thoughts. It also gives me courage to move forward. I felt obliged to let you know, as my soul tells me my wellbeing will make my teacher happy.

I want to wish you well.

Affectionately,

Leonello Dante

Gracy read the letter over and over, bringing it close to her chest. *This is the best news I have received lately.* She glanced at her watch, again, the timing for a call wasn't right. She promised herself to place a call the next day and thank the people that had made it happen. She dialed Diego's number to share the uplifting news from Leonello. "You see Sis, there is always hope. Let's think positively for our Daniele too. Miracles do happen."

The next morning Gracy couldn't wait to see her much loved Alvaro. She arrived smartly dressed and animated. "Mi amor, que pasa?"

He reached for her, pulled her in his arms and held her tight without speaking while her head relaxed on his chest. When she pulled away smiling, she stated. "There is a spark of happiness in me since last night. Leonello, my lost student, is back in school."

"What excellent news. I am happy for you. I know how worried you were for him."

"*Now mi amor*, if only Daniele could make some progress, my world would be complete."

"*Mi amor*, it will happen. We will consult with every specialist on the globe to get him well. You have the means to do so."

"What about Boston, Spain or Madrid? Rome or Bologna, they have the best research centres." Gracy was getting excited. Alvaro was encouraging, getting her hopes up. He planted a vigorous kiss on her lips, rendering her breathless. Gracy wished she could remain in the protection of his arms all day. Alvaro hated to let go but his grip relented and he looked straight in her eyes. "Now *mi amor*, we must get to work. We need to check with the kitchen staff to see if they received all the supplies. There is a large wedding reception here tonight. The couple has made considerable requests. Our head chef was suffering from palpitations last night. There was a problem with some of the deliveries."

"Give me that list and I will follow through with everything."

"There you go, my dearest. I know I can count on you."

Gracy, grabbed the order sheet and was ready to move swiftly.

"Not to worry *mi amor*; everything will be in order. Leave it to me." Whatever obstacles they encountered at work, Gracy had a way of solving them successfully.

She wished her brother's problem could be resolved with the same efforts. To her disbelief Daniele was still hospitalized. She faithfully visited him every single night after work. She knew that Daniele's days rolled monotonously one after the other. As much as his optimistic willpower urged him on, his body would not comply. There were some encouraging days with less pain in therapy. Then, on other days, he was hardly able to move. When he required strong medication to control his pain, sleep would dominate. The company was suffering from his absence; but Daniele's wellbeing was their priority.

A board meeting was called to make key decisions on a temporary replacement for Daniele. Diego and Gracy, agreed it was time to hire a new expert architect. The chain of hotels, were in daily need of solutions one way or another. Since Daniele's injury, new projects were placed on hold. It wasn't easy to recruit a new qualified individual as gifted as their brother. Finally, with everyone's approval, a new fellow was hired. His credentials topped everyone else's that had been interviewed.

Martino Guerrier from California was the successful candidate. He was a clean-cut, young man in his mid- thirties and of medium stature. He had jet black hair that sported an army cut, a pleasant smile and sparkling deep blue eyes. He would be a strong team player and Daniele, on his good days, would be able to coach him and advise him. Ingrid would have to abide by his recommendations for any projects of remodelling and upgrading. Mr. Guerrier assumed his position and was welcomed on board as assistant to Daniele, the principals of the company and the staff at large. Since he was of such likeable nature, his new position, looked favorable.

Diego and Gracy, had been hard at work convincing the doctors at the hospital to discharge him. They would provide medical assistance for him at home. Daniele could only make it to the wheelchair with the help of an aide. He needed high dose of pain killers to make his days liveable. Gracy and Diego had no choice than to be resigned to his fate and to be thankful they still had him.

The harsh winter passed. Spring had turned into summer. It was a scorching summer day at the end of June. Alvaro and Gracy had been spending less time together lately. Diego needed his sister beside him when it came to the well-being of Daniele. Business had become secondary. She arrived at work later than usual. Alvaro kept himself occupied in his office waiting for her to check in. The door opened *"Good morning mi amor! Come stas?"* It was the greeting he preferred. "Finally, *mi amor*! I have been waiting for you."

"Here I am my darling. All yours." Gracy had come out of her shell. Her modest behaviour had changed to that of a woman in love who was not afraid to manifest her feelings. She walked over to him and pressed her lips on his with all her affection. "There, I missed you too. *Mi amor.*"

"I have a surprise for you." He held her by her arms not letting her go.

"What do you say if we both sign off today? It's kind of quiet and everything seems in good order. I want to take you to the beach. Just the two of us. We owe some time to ourselves. Darling please."

Gracy liked the idea. *Was it possible? Both of them gone for the day?*

"Alvaro I would love to but who will replace us?"

"Leave it to me. We are entitled to some free time together."

"Alvaro, are you sure of what you are doing?"

"*Mi amor,* get your beach attire. Meet me by the valet at the front lobby. The day is ours."

"You are crazy. You are also the CEO. If you say so. I will follow your orders."

Alvaro had ordered the kitchen staff to prepare a picnic basket with soft drinks and a bottle of champagne. He was ready to go.

He had met with Ingrid earlier and asked her to respond to any major crisis should anything arise. He would be off for the day. She had agreed without any question, happy he had chosen her. He did not mention the beach or being with Gracy.

Ingrid always had Walter Robertson at her command. She wasn't too anxious to get home anytime soon. Daniele as an invalid and nurses were with him around the clock. The turn of events in her life at this time meant that she spent more time at work and less at home.

Alvaro and Gracy, stepped on the sandy beach of the Hamptons with their specially prepared food for the day. The sky was a serene blue, and the ocean was calm like a sheet of glass. An umbrella and lounge chairs were already reserved for them. Alvaro couldn't wait to get his loving actions in motion. Gracy, observing Alvaro's exuberance, had managed to discard all her worries. *He was such a darling* she thought. He took her hand and asked her to go for a walk. They dragged their feet in the wet sand like two youngsters. Afterwards he pulled her in for a swim, playfully rolling along with the gentle waves.

The ocean and the blue sky were in unity. The couple hugged and kissed; their bodies craved their own unity. They were both in their glory for having found each other. Alvaro considered himself so lucky. How could this beautiful creature be in love with him? Gracy, likewise couldn't believe her good fortune at having found Alvaro. It was the first time she had ever been in love.

"*Mi amor*, it's time for lunch. The swimming, the air, this ocean have boosted my appetite." He helped her out and they ran toward the umbrella. They ate; they drank sparkling water. Alvaro pulled something out of his bag and ordered her to close her eyes. "Alvaro, mi amor, you are being silly." she giggled.

"Do as I say, *mi amor*!"

"Yes sir, my superior!"

He knelt down, with his hands together. "Open your eyes now."

There he was, a box in hand. He presented it to her.

"My darling, I have been waiting for this day all my life. Will you marry this Spanish guy who has loved and adored you since the day he laid eyes on you?" Gracy', wide eyed, remained speechless.

"*Mi amor!* What did I do to deserve you? You are my heaven on this earth. Yes, yes of course." she cried out with joy.

He placed the diamond ring on her finger. He kissed her passionately leaving her gasping for air. "Darling, I have been waiting for all the calamity and heartbreak to calm down, but I couldn't wait any more. We have to make our happiness. I want us to get married. I want you to be my wife."

"Oh, darling you are so dear to me. I desire nothing better than to be your wife."

"Let's open this bottle of champagne and celebrate."

"I wish my brothers were here and my dad. He would be so happy for me."

"Darling we will go to your brothers. Your dad, I am sure he knows. We need to be happy ourselves *mi amor.*"

"My darling, I couldn't be happier."

They got back at dusk. Gracy couldn't wait to go tell her brothers in person. She placed an excited call to Diego. "Diego, meet Alvaro and I at Daniele's. I have some good news to share with you."

"Tell me, what is it?"

"No, I want to see the reaction on your face Diego. See you at seven."

"Daniele is walking?" he asked.

"No, that will come too. Don't worry. See you later." Diego checked his watch. He couldn't wait to meet his young sister to discover what news had generated this child like joy. *Thank God we have her.*

Daniele had a pretty good day. His nurse Gilda, who catered to his every need, was pleased. Gracy arrived with Alvaro holding on to his treasured hand like it was the most precious object she had ever held in her life besides her Dad's hand as a child. Happy greetings were exchanged. Ingrid wasn't home yet. Shortly after Diego arrived, he gave his greetings to everyone. He questioned Alvaro. "Your night off from I gather?"

"Yes."

Daniele asked them to sit down. The nurse retreated to the kitchen to brew some tea.

Gracy, spoke first. "Alvaro and I have an announcement to make." She got up and went to sit by Diego, putting one arm around his shoulder. Then she joyfully extended her arm and spread her hand up to show her jewel. "We are going to get married and we would like your blessings."

Diego and Daniele, stared at each other, smiling. Diego spoke. "What do you say Bro?" The gleam in his eyes told him everything. "Gracy, Alvaro, it's the best news we have had for a while. When is the big day? Congratulations!" He hugged and kissed his sister affectionately.

Daniele, followed, "You're going to have to come to me Sis. I wish you all the happiness you deserve my dearest."

"Alvaro, you got yourself a good girl. You, Gracy, likewise, Alvaro is a fine fellow."

Daniele felt a boost of energy in his spine. He was so happy for his sister. "I hope you will be blessed with a beautiful family. Gracy you must promise me; your first child will be named Daniele. After all I recruited Alvaro for our company."

Diego interrupted. "Wait a minute here. I am the older brother!

Where do I come in?"

"Now, now you guys are jumping too far ahead."

They were laughing when the door sprang open. Ingrid had returned home. "Oh! I didn't know we were having a party?"

Daniele promptly responded, "Darling, it's no party. This is family sharing good news for change. Gracy and Alvaro, have something special to tell you."

She looked at them frowning. Gracy put her hand up immediately.

"Ingrid, Alvaro and I are engaged and planning to get married."

Ingrid looked disturbed. "When did all this happen? When is this wedding taking place?"

Daniele was quick to respond. "Ingrid dear, congratulate them; reserve your questions for later. Be happy for them."

How could she be happy? *Since Gracy had appeared the entire world seemed to revolve around this bitch.* A cold congratulation took place on her part but in her heart she wished the plan would fall apart.

"Have you set the date?" she asked.

Gracy felt the lack of enthusiasm. She responded with some caution.

"Yes, Alvaro and I have agreed on a mid-September wedding."

Ingrid quickly calculated. Four months to work on Alvaro to sway him from his absurd infatuation with the overrated ragdoll who had a hold on him and her brothers.

264

Chapter Thirty Eight

Back in Sicily, Leonello was adjusting well in his new environment. Professor Rondelli and his family had taken him in. Their polished manners and the family atmosphere made him feel special. Life was looking up for him. His grades had improved immensely. To Romero's and Gianni's surprise, he had become their good advisor now. They followed him in a good way. He was practising his English with them, feeling proud. He would kid them. "Should we win the lottery someday, we'll surprise Miss Gracy by taking a trip to New York. Wouldn't that be something?"

"Keep dreaming Leonello. It would sure be nice. Gianni and I can hardly afford buying our food. Helping on weekends at the open market, we get few miserable liras." retorted Romero.

"If you ask me you have it pretty good with Professor Rondelli and his family. You even get a bonus at the month's end. Plus free tutoring-nice environment. Our friend here is lucky." Gianni slapped him on his shoulder.

"I know I am. I can't wait to graduate and get a real job. My mother needs to be taken care of. The time in rehabilitation has improved her wellbeing. She still lives in that dark dump. My heart pains when I go see her." added Leonello.

Gianni responded. "Eh! Leonello. We are in the same boat. My mom is no different except she doesn't drink. The church is her refuge. We are dirt poor."

Romero suggested "Okay you guys, let's change subject here. How about meeting Marmellata tonight for our treat. It's time, especially for you Leonello. It would do you good." Ever since Leonello had softened out, Romero had taken over the lead in the friendship.

"No, not for me. You guys go ahead. I have work to do at the house. Plus, we play *scopa*, cards, after supper with the family."

Leonello couldn't wait to get home. The sun was descending toward the horizon and the air was calm. The soothing breeze in the garden looking down the valley was refreshing. His hard work in the garden had turned into a labour of love. The shrubberies and flowers were admirable. They had just finished supper and the phone rang. The professor answered as he usually did. Leonello and the children were clearing the table, looking forward to their game.

"Pronto. Si, Miss Gracy, *ciao. Come sta? Bene, bene, grazie."*

The usual greetings took place. Gracy, still in her euphoric state from the day's event couldn't wait to share her good news.

"Professor, I want to let you know, that I am getting married."

"Congratulations! I am happy for you. Who is the lucky fellow?"

"I mentioned him to you from time to time, our CEO. The Spanish fellow. We have set the date for the middle of September.

I will keep you informed with more details later on."

"Great news. I will pass it on. We just had supper. All is well here. Leonello is maintaining the grounds spectacularly. You would be proud. We are just getting ready for our ritual game of cards. Would you like to say hello to Leonello? I am sure it will make him happy."

"Yes! I would love to hear his voice. How is he doing?"

"Fantastic, we are very pleased with him. Let me get him for you."

"Leonello, surprise. Miss Gracy is on the line. She wants to say hello to you."

Leonello ran to the phone tripping over chairs on his way. "Miss Robertson! How are you?"

"Great! How about you?"

"I am fine. I love it here, thanks to you."

"I am delighted to hear that Leonello."

"Are you planning on coming back sometime soon?"

"I might surprise you, later this summer. We might plan our honeymoon, in Sicily."

"What! Your honey moon? When and with whom?"

"Leonello, I am getting married. I have fallen in love with a lovely Spanish fellow, Alvaro Fernandez."

The phone fell out of his hands. Leonello dragged himself to the solitude in the living room. He crouched in a corner, put his head down between his legs, brought his arms up and held his head down hoping the world would go away. Gracy's voice could be heard from the kitchen, "Leonello, hello, are you there?" She was getting no response until Mr. Rondelli picked up the phone. "Miss Gracy, what happened?"

"You tell me Professor. I am not sure. Where is Leonello?

He is all right?" By now she was upset. *What on earth could have hit Leonello?* She wondered. . . *Don't tell me he is still! hung up on his illusion of us. The counsellor told me he was fine! He had come to terms with his delusions.*

"Miss Gracy, hold on. I will go check on him."

The professor kept calling Leonello but there was no response. "Leonello please, where are you?" The children spotted him in the corner behind the piano. He was crying like a child who was hurting deeply. "Leonello, what got into you? What has happened? You left Miss Gracy hanging on the phone. Don't you want to say goodbye to her?" No response or motion whatsoever. Mr. Rondelli, now also upset, ended the phone call with Gracy. He and his wife called the counsellor. It was evident Leonello was having a relapse.

Gracy's joyful day at the other side of the world had suddenly turned sorrowful. There were two people not pleased with their news. Ingrid's reaction had not been pleasant. Now Leonello's relapse was totally unexpected. The heaviness suddenly sitting on her head was like a heavy rock weighing down her thoughts. She didn't know who to call first- Alvaro or Diego. She couldn't burden Daniele for sure. God forbid Ingrid would answer the phone. There would be no sympathy from her.

"Diego, sorry to bother you. Something has happened."

"Sis, you never bother me. You are my life. I promised your father to look after you through thick and thin. Never forget that."

"I made a call to Italy, announcing my news of marriage. I think Leonello had a relapse. I talked to his doctor last week. He assured me that he was doing well. They were all so pleased with him. Now I feel my news has caused him to regress."

"Gracy, Gracy, my dearest. It's not your fault. You did enough for him. He needs to work out his own issues. He was never loved. You are the only person that cared for him. He is terrified that you will divert your love to someone else. Once he is reassured, he will be fine."

"I hope the psychiatrist makes him understand?"

"Gracy, work on your wedding plans, promise. Daniele and I thrive on your happiness. We want you and Alvaro to have the best life together. You've got yourself a good mate. Now, go rest and don't worry about a thing. God willing, I will always be here for you" Gracy's morale was lifted somewhat. She went to bed trying to get a good night's sleep.

The next morning Ingrid got up earlier than usual. She was determined to get to Alvaro's office before little Miss Sicilian arrived. She liked every man to be under her spell. It made her feel proud. If their interest was captured by another woman, she had to dissolve that interest. Ever since Alvaro had laid eyes on this Gracy, he had lost his head. She wasn't pleased with him, therefore she had to act. *Who had advised Daniele to hire him and that Walter guy too? I need to press the right buttons to place him back on track. Walter was easier to control. Alvaro thought he was above her now, marrying into the fortune of the Fraranos.*

Ingrid judged everyone by her standards. Her number one interest in life was wealth. She had been a gold digger since her childhood. She felt deeply humiliated when others taunted her, saying that she was beneath them. She educated herself so she would be empowered and to show them who was the best. Her plan was to be in a big city where her knowledge would be rewarded. Her knowledge would reward her, but her narcissistic love would help her to soar above the rest.

270

Chapter Thirty Nine

While the news of the wedding plans was joyfully received by the Frarano brothers, Alvaro couldn't wait to announce and celebrate with his family. The engagement and wedding news spread out quickly at work. Everyone congratulated the happy couple. On the American side of the world the news of the upcoming marriage was well accepted with the exception of one person.

Across the ocean another person was disappointed. 'Leonello,' had been placed in seclusion for intensive therapy. He had become taciturn once more, however, the doctor was optimistic. He promised Mr. and Mrs. Rondelli that the emotional imbalance with the young fellow would be only temporary. His body and his brain were strong. "My sessions are set in place. He will benefit from this renewed therapy. He will come to fully understand that it's his fear losing love that is driving this minor setback." They listened carefully. Mrs. Rondelli had accepted Leonello willingly since day one and had treated him well.

The doctor couldn't stress enough the importance of their support. "You see, this young man has grown up enmeshed in trauma all his life. It has left such a scar on his wellbeing. When a threat arises, the loss of security already established in his mind retriggers. Immediately the emotional wound reappears. We will treat it again. All he needs is loving care, affection, security and a promise of stability. Deep down, we all do. Miss Robertson is probably the first person that had shown interest in him. He is frightened to death of losing her. She is older than him so his need for her can be connected to the lack of consistent motherly nurturing. He relied on her for security. To him, she was everything he never had as a child growing up, his saviour. He is young, only twenty. He is also resilient. He will be fine. I will send the report to Miss Robertson."

***

On the same day the Rondellis met with the doctor in Agrigento, in New York, Ingrid stormed into Alvaro's office, dressed to the nines. He got up to greet her. She shocked him as she put her arms around his neck, pulling him to her furiously. She tried to press her lips on his mouth to kiss him. He forcefully untangled her arms to free himself. "Ingrid! What's gotten into you? You know I am committed! Please let go of me. What are you trying to achieve with these advances?"

"That is exactly what I want to talk to you about. How can you plan to marry that Miss Priss from Italy? I thought you and I understood each other. We are only here for the ride. I am in love with you Alvaro. Why do you think I advised Daniele to hire you?"

Alvaro was beside himself. "Ingrid! Please what are you talking about? You are with Daniele. You have been living with him for years."

"Alvaro, you are so naive. He's my security blanket but you are the man I love. My life is so empty with him. He is obsessed with his companies. Now, to make a bad situation worse, he is an invalid. I was pressing for commitment. He ignored my requests in the past. Now I don't want it. I don't bother him anymore. I am with him for the money I'm entitled to and the convenience until I get it, nothing else. Now you throw your matrimonial plans with Miss Priss in my face. Please Alvaro, don't break my heart."

"Look here Ingrid. I don't care what you have in mind or what your plans are with Daniele. I am madly in love with Gracy. I don't care about her money or her estates. I love her for herself only. I am fortunate that she loves me too."

272

"Alvaro, your weakness disgusts me. I got you this job because you appealed to me and despite your naiveté I still do. I won't give up on you but remember, I do not take anyone's refusal kindly, and especially someone who owes me. You will pay for this. You better think and think hard. You were drawn to me before she appeared and, mark my words, you will be again." Holding back angry tears, she left the room slamming the door behind her.

Gracy was approaching from down the hall, making her way to Alvaro's office. It was her duty to check in and pick up her daily list of orders. When she got closer, she noticed Ingrid, in her perturbed state. Without saying anything Ingrid gave her a raw grin, turned her back and went the opposite way. It wasn't the first time Ingrid had given her the cold shoulder. Gracy, decided to ignore her and walk forward to see her beloved Alvaro.

"Hola mi amor! Como estas?"

"Delighted to see you, *mi amor*." With his open arms he encircled her and kissed her passionately- almost to assure himself that nothing in this world could take this precious girl from him. Alvaro held her longer than usual, afraid to let go. Deep down he was troubled. He wasn't sure what Ingrid's menacing words promised but he knew it would be nothing he wanted. Why did she want to spoil their happiness?

All day he searched his soul wondering if she had misinterpreted his kindness for love. He respected Ingrid, admired her work. He did find her behaviour forward. Yes, it was embarrassing at times, but he never considered her more than a friend and co-worker. She was Daniele's girlfriend. Why would she want to mess around with him? She had definitely succeeded in spoiling his first day of joy over his engagement. He wasn't going to allow her to interfere with the upcoming plans for his wedding. She should erase him from her mind. Alvaro felt that he and Gracy were meant for each other. Their love was sincere.

While he had become aware of Ingrid's misplaced affection, he was not aware that another, across the ocean, was pining for Gracy's love and condemning their union. Both of Gracy and Alvaro, for different reasons, secretly had their pain sealed at the bottom of their hearts. Gracy was worried about Leonello's negative reaction and Alvaro about Ingrid's shocking revelation. She consoled herself with the fact that Leonello was young and infatuated. He consoled himself by admiring his sweet Gracy. He couldn't wait to share the news with his own humble family.

Mr. and Mrs. Fernandez were happy to speak with their son. He had called his mom but his father picked up on the other line also. "*Hola Mom, Dad.* Can we meet tonight at our favorite restaurant, The Clarkson House in Manhattan?"

"Son, that sounds wonderful. We would love to see you! Will your Gracy be with you?"

"Yes, mom, Gracy and I can't wait to see you both. See you around seven."

The Fernandezes were down to earth people without false pretenses. They were loving and genuine. Alvaro adored his parents. He had no doubt Gracy would too. Likewise, his mom and dad with their good nature would be kind to Gracy. Mrs. Fernandez had always said, "Alvaro, we want you to be happy. Whatever makes you happy in life makes us happy." She had never dictated to him or imposed her wishes. They were so proud of their son, in every way. They showered him with love and affection. He had inherited his parents' genial nature, work ethic and sense of honor and respect.

The meeting was glorious as expected. After the cheerful greetings, the maître di proceeded with the orders placed by Alvaro earlier. He had ordered Spanish cuisine- tapas, tortilla Espanola, Machen- goat cheese, chicken paella, and leche frita adorned with a selection of rich fruits. As for drinks, he had ordered the best sangria ever tasted, mixed with fresh fruit and brandy. They poured the sangria in stem glasses.

Alvaro, holding Gracy's hand up with the glittering diamond said "Mom, Dad, we have a big announcement to make. Gracy, and I are engaged and planning to get married. It wouldn't be perfect without your blessing." In their melodic Spanish accents, his parents blissfully offered the couple their blessings. Mrs. Fernandez hugged Gracy with all her best wishes, saying over and over, "You are so special my dear. I wish you and my Alvaro the best that love can bring." Gracy was overjoyed with Mrs. Fernandez's motherly love. She needed it badly having never experienced it. She responded with tears of joy.

"I am so lucky to have found your son. He has opened a new world for me. We shall be happy together, no matter what life presents to us. Thank you both for sharing him with me." She got up and gave them both an ardent and appreciative hug.

Chapter Forty

The time was racing along faster than anticipated. The preparations for the festivities were well in place. The wedding reception was going to be held at the Marquis, Alvaro's and Gracy's place of choice.

Diego and Daniele insisted on having a coordinator from their hotel handle everything even though Gracy had insisted on doing it herself. "No, Sis," they had both stressed. "We only want you to give your approval on the choices; let them handle it. This is why we offer wedding for hire. Our staff is well trained."

"I am well aware of it; but they are not for me. They are for paying clients."

"No, buts. We want you stress free. Just worry about the guest list and your personal preparations. You will be the most beautiful bride of our century."

"Oh yes, our guest list. I definitely would like to have all my family from Sicily and my dear friends from Agrigento."

"What about London? You never mentioned your relatives from your dad's side of the family. Do you have any? Do they exist?" asked Diego.

"Funny you should ask me that. I was reminiscing the other night. Growing up I had asked my dad many questions about his family. He was always evasive. He didn't want to talk about his side of the family."

"That is strange. Why not? How can anyone live without seeing his family?"

"I pressed him many times. He kept telling me to consider myself fortunate. I had the Tavernas and they were my only real family."

Daniele exclaimed. "Eh! What about us?"

"Daniele, don't forget we came in afterwards. Gracy lived a secret existence hiding in jolly down under."

"Our lonely sister, hidden in no man's land- this is why we need to make it up to you."

"Let's not change the subject here. We still would like to know the English side of the family. Are there any?" Diego persisted.

"Okay, let me tell you. When you guys appeared on my horizon Dad said "Now my angel you got it made. You have two brothers to love and protect you. Should I pass on, you are in good hands."

"One night, I sat on his lap and told him. " Even though I am very happy with mom's side of the family Dad, I will never stop wondering about yours. You must tell me." She remembered her insistence.

Finally, against his will, Andrew opened up a little. "Gracy, there isn't much to tell. Your grandparents were two poor souls, hard-working people. They had two boys, my younger brother and me. I liked school and my brother detested it. That caused my parents a lot of heartache. He was always in trouble one way or another. He grew up resenting me. Then he disappeared. He would be in touch only if he needed money. When your grandparents passed, he didn't even show up to their funeral. He contested the will. I inherited that dumpy place we lived in while I was looking after our parents. He never cared for them. He is in the United States somewhere with a wife and four kids. We are not on speaking terms. You don't need to know them. They're bad news." This is all I know. I took Daddy's advice and never bothered looking for them."

"I see. It's a closed case then. Gracy, you are all ours. We have a beautiful Sicilian girl all to ourselves."

"I am honored to be, my dearest brothers."

***

September' 15th soon arrived. The invited guests from out of the country- Italy and Spain- were arriving in advance. The Marquis' fourth floor was all reserved for the guests. Her favorite, Godmother Fabiana, had arrived with all her family. Her uncle and cousin Joseph Taverna from Palermo followed. Gracy, Alvaro and Diego greeted them at the airport. The number of musical instruments they brought were endless. Gracy laughed at the sight. "Uncle Anthony what is all this? You guys came loaded?"

"Gracy! We couldn't let you get married without our *organetto* and *Maran -Zana*, the mandolin. We will play and sing the Sicilian *tarantella* for you!" She had missed their festive celebrations after she had left but now here they were all equipped to make sure that the celebration would be complete with all the traditions.

The Agrigento friends were next to arrive. She was pleased that Professor Rondelli with his entire family and Matteo Dario, from the university could attend. Matteo had called Gracy to advise her that his wife had a fall so she couldn't attend. He, however, wouldn't miss the opportunity. He was looking forward to her wedding and to seeing New York for the first time. So, he had decided to accompany Gracy's three favorite students. Gracy had offered to pay for all their expenses. It had taken some cooperation to get Leonello on his feet. With help from the counsellor and everyone else involved, he had come along. Gracy was ecstatic at seeing all her dear relatives and beloved friends together once again. Her euphoria was immeasurable. She hugged everyone with total abandon. Once she got to Leonello, she grabbed his hand and placed it on her heart. "My dear friend. If you feel the rhythm that beats in my heart, know that it is the joy you have brought me, seeing you all here- especially you Leonello. I recited a special prayer daily for your needs and here you are my dearest." Álvaro stood behind her admiring her kindness. Gracy turned around, took his arm and introduced him to Leonello and the rest of the clan.

Well, the party was on its way. After a favourable meeting with the Italians, Alvaro wondered if his Spanish relatives could compete with these Sicilian mariacheros. Their uplifted spirits and their authentic love was admirable. They gave him a new experience to be learned.

There was only one person that didn't share their enthusiasm- the German girl, Ingrid Klein. After Alvaro's rejection, the humiliation had rendered her more vindictive. She had confided in her friend Walter. He had to sympathize with her; otherwise, she would turn her nastiness on him. His life would take a turn for the worse. She wanted to get in contact with his brother Morris. It bothered Walter greatly. Morris wasn't one eager to engage in meaningless relationships. He would bother only with certain people of his choice. Walter's brotherly neglect was the reason he had submitted himself to Ingrid's unpredictable behaviour. She had promised him a job in New York and Walter wanted to distance himself from Morris because his brother made him feel worthless. Morris preferred his rich shyster friends to his only brother. Ingrid's tireless requests and threats meant that he could no longer avoid contacting his brother. If he didn't do it there would be hell to pay.

Chapter Forty One

Gracy and Alvaro were united in matrimony with all the blessings of the Catholic Church. The wedding was celebrated with all the bounty life could offer. The families on both sides were joyous for the happy couple. Diego and Daniele felt relieved. Their beloved sister was in good hands with her new husband Alvaro. The honeymoon was postponed to a later date. After most of the out-of-town guests eventually had taken their leave from New York, Gracy, had to take care of her other important mission-Leonello and his two other friends. She had taken them and their problems to heart so a meeting with her brothers was called. Diego was well aware of Leonello's situation. He didn't need much convincing. Daniele, because of his generous nature, wanted to please his sister. Alvaro was asked to participate in the meeting. Deep down felt his wife's involvement was a bit much. He thought. After all they were only her students. *Why is she so concerned, especially with this Leonello guy that has shown so much dependency on her?* He kept his opinion to himself since Diego and Daniele wanted to appease their sister's wants. After all they did have a monthly charity fund for the less fortunate. After the wedding, Alvaro instructed Ingrid to oversee some of his obligations. On the surface she seemed happy to oblige. Swallowing hard at his instructions she thought: *You still need me. You will owe me Mr. Big Shot CEO.*

The meeting was taking place at Daniele's residence since he wasn't too mobile these days. Both Diego and Daniele admired their sister's determination and kind spirit. "We have to give you credit Sis, and you too Alvaro. You have put your honeymoon on hold to look after somebody else's affair."

"Don't hold me to that. It's my wife's idea! Of course, what my wife wants, my wife gets."

"*Mi amor!* I thought you were in full compliance. You wait until we get to Cefalu'. You will not want to come back to New York. My dear a real treat awaits us." Ironically, she was unaware that Cefalu' was the place, where her mom and dad had given in to the heightened emotional longing and consummated their forbidden desire.

Her dad had always advised her, "Gracy if you get married you must spend your honeymoon in Cefalu'." He went on to describe the spectacular setting - the sky, the mountains and the Mediterranean Sea. *'Incantevole*- magic.' He had never told Gracy the real reason he loved the place so much even when she asked "Dad, why is it so magical? Did you have a romantic interlude there?" Andrew would close himself in his private thoughts without responding, fighting the tears that overwhelmed him.

Diego spoke up. "Let's focus back on our meeting here. What is your request my dear?" She looked at them, including her husband. "We have so much work here. We are employing so many people. I want you, Diego, to make all the necessary arrangements to sponsor Leonello, Romero, and Gianni. It's hard to find good jobs in Europe. I am sure we can accommodate them in our companies, somewhere for them to get a sense of achievement from honest work. This thought has been on my mind since I got here. I know how desperate these young people have been. Leonello had it the worst of them all. I know we have the means to help them."

They looked at each other quietly assessing the request. Diego and Daniele didn't seem to have a problem. It was a matter of getting the papers in place. Alvaro wasn't convinced. "Diego, I gather this Leonello young man was attached, putting it lightly, if not infatuated with my wife. I am reluctant to have him come here."

"*Mi amor!* He lacked nurturing. He was a desperate young teen without any family love. It's not the kind of love we share my darling!"

Alvaro didn't know what to make of it. He wasn't comfortable with which ever kind of love it was. Maybe he was jealous. After all, Leonello was a handsome young man which became clearer when he had been meticulously groomed to attend the wedding celebrations.

Daniele, responded. "Sis are they willing to emigrate?"

"Oh! Yes, I communicate with Leonello's counsellor regularly. Leonello is the one that needs help the most. He has never had anyone to show him affection or care. The other two are poor but not as badly off.

I would like them to come here together. They will support one another."

"I see. Your intentions are good Sis. Well, our attorney here can expedite the papers and Alvaro can be in charge of the placement." Daniele said.

"I need to meet with them and analyze their personalities, wants, and needs." Alvaro indicated.

"I couldn't stress enough the importance of taking English as a second language. They speak with a strong accent but you will be able to communicate with them." said Gracy.

Diego brought the discussion of the boys' futures to a close. "Great! We can move forward. Alvaro, you do the interviewing; get in touch with them and fill me in."

Alvaro, turned to Gracy. "*Mi amor.* After this matter is looked after, we are off to our honeymoon. You must promise me, we will detour to Madrid after Cefalu."

"Darling, once we get away, I am all yours. You are the CEO with so many demands on your time. I suggest you get a subordinate to carry on with your orders and obligations"

"Mi amor, you promise me your undivided attention. I will make sure my obligations here are well covered."

Alvaro carried on his duties, not only with the young Sicilian fellows, but also with who to leave in charge while he was away on his much delayed honeymoon. He couldn't wait to have his precious Gracy to himself so that he could shower her with love and affection. He had never been to Sicily which most people enthusiastically described as the land of inspiration. *'Ciele, mare e terra.'* 'Sky, Sea, and earth'. It was a land where a splendid sun hovered over nature's bounty.

***

Leonello was elated. His confused feelings were mostly positive. At least Gracy was here within reach. He could see her if nothing else. His secret love would be buried deep in a corner of his heart. She gave him a sense of protection and security. One day he confessed to his buddies. "Romero, Gianni, I don't know if you understand me. I am okay with Mr. Fernandez. I don't resent him as long as he is good to Gracy. I am happy for myself that I am able to reach out to Miss Gracy."

"We are glad you think that way. She is our protector. Look, hasn't she gone out of her way to help us? We could never afford to be here enjoying New York without her help and the generosity of the Fraranos. This is a lifetime experience for us." said Romero.

"If we get to emigrate here, guys we will have it made!" exclaimed Leonello, extending his arms around both of his friends and pulling them to him.

"I am prepared to work hard no matter what jobs they assign me. I need to earn some money. My mom needs help badly." Gianni added.

"My crazy father always said America was the land of opportunity for whoever was lucky enough to get there. He could never emigrate because of his criminal records." Leonello stated, remembering with sadness his father and the family's broken dreams.

284

"Eh! Leonello, I hope his records will not reflect on you." Romero replied.

"Don't you worry we will vouch for you. Besides, we got Miss Gracy's brother. He seems influential." reassured Gianni.

The trio were treated royally, as special guests and they never had it so good. They hoped their good fortune would come to fruition with

Gracy's brother Diego looking after their affairs.

Alvaro had absolutely no problem interviewing them. They were good candidates- eager workers for the company. Youth was in their favor. These were great qualities for employment. When it came to experience, he always preferred to train his own people. They performed well, distinguishing themselves from other candidates. "We need to be comprehensive and unique in our service to others," he always preached to his trainees.

As much as he had a good gut feeling about them, his nagging insecurity about Leonello bothered him. He was a handsome young devil- tall and slim, with great features including the teasing eyes women seemed to love. Could he be a temptation to his lovely Gracy? He suspected the young lad had a crush on her. Could Leonello jeopardize his marriage? He wouldn't dare mention his doubts to anyone because his insecurities felt foolish.

The New York journey and holiday was over for the Sicilian boys. It was time to return home until they were called to the consulate. Alvaro's and Gracy's honeymoon began. They embarked on their luxurious cruise liner from New York and headed across the ocean to the Mediterranean coast. They were to disembark in Messina. Alvaro had never been to this splendid part of the world. With Gracy by his side holding his hand, he was walking the avenues of Taormina in amazement and marvelling admiring the base of Mount Etna. The oleander trees were in bloom and mesmerizing. The distant view of the horizon extending to the intensive blue water of the mare Ionio was incomparable.

"Alvaro. Let's go to the baya of the Sirene. Isola Bella in its rock formations is a sight to behold. The palm and cypress are glorified by the mist of the seas."

"Gracy *mi amor.* How could you leave this paradise to come to New York?"

"My brothers, don't forget, are my life."

He pulled her close to him with loving arms. "My darling. I am so happy! If you hadn't come to New York we probably would have never met."

"Alvaro. I believe our path in life is designated for us. Yes, from heaven above. We were meant to be together. I never want to lose you my darling. We must cherish every moment we have together."

The tour continued from one spectacular place to another. They didn't leave one place untouched. After the historic valle dei Tempio, they ended their tour in Cefalu'-the place of Andrew's loved memories. In her youth, Gracy, sometimes, had been annoyed listening to her father tell the same story over and over. However, with her husband at her side she had a deeper understanding of her father's fascination with this beautiful place.

Cefalu' was another admirable place with lots of fun and plenty ice cream to indulge in. It's beautiful beach lined the bottom of the rocky elevation, along the coast of the north Mediterranean Sea. Each evening, their love making expressed the beauty of their magical unity. They spent six fantastic weeks. It was time to return to New York for serious business.

Before leaving Gracy felt it her duty to visit her mom's grave in Palermo. For the first time, she agreed to stay in her mom's empty home in Palermo. She had Alvaro there as her strength and support. She wanted to eradicate her childhood emotional fears. She would feel better accepting what was left of her mom's memories.

***

While his sister and her husband honeymooned in Sicily, Diego, had earnestly worked hard. The preparations for sponsoring the Sicilian boys was going well. With everything in order, within six months at the latest, the young men would be able to emigrate. Gracy was so happy to receive Diego's information. She was sure the young fellows would cooperate accordingly. Leonello's doctor had assured her he was well adjusted. His depression was being managed admirably these days.

Gracy' wanted to check on her brother Daniele, wishing for more good news. She arrived at his place and found Ingrid bickering and infuriated. Immediately she felt uncomfortable. At the same time, her heart was pained seeing her brother struggling in his wheelchair. He was trying to pacify Ingrid. "What is going on here?" Gracy asked' Ingrid responded, livid with anger. "I asked him last week to put money in my bank account. He didn't do it! I had to suffer the humiliation of my debit card being rejected and my credit card denied. Me, Ingrid Klein, without money. Am I supposed to be his partner without benefits?"

"Ingrid, calm down. You will not accomplish anything in this rage of yours."

"You, Miss Priss, are not going to tell me what to do. Why don't you mind your own beeswax and go back where you came from?"

Gracy didn't know what to do. She couldn't leave her brother with this lunatic. She stood her ground. "Ingrid, you have a job. You get paid. Don't you have your own money? You depend on my brother-why?"

"What do you think? I am his live- in just for a good time? He won't make a commitment and he doesn't give me any money. Now he is an invalid. Who wants him?"

Gracy was appalled. *My poor brother* "If you don't like your situation, why don't you leave? Furthermore, I forbid you to call my brother an invalid." By now her blood was boiling "How dare you?"

"Look bitch, things were much better before you got here. Since you arrived, he has been less committed to our union. I don't like it. I have invested years of my life with him. I need to be rewarded."

Daniele was in excruciating pain. He wheeled himself out, left the room and locked himself in the bedroom. He plugged his ears to avoid Ingrid's menacing words. He felt sick to his stomach and embarrassed for Gracy to be in the middle of this tantrum. Ingrid had too many outbursts since he had instructed his accountant to reduce her expense account. Ingrid's demand for money was endless and her money problems were a sign of more problems to come.

Chapter Forty Two

As time rolled along Alvaro and Gracy grew more blissfully in love.

They continued to work together. Gracy would accompany him on his out-of-town excursions where his expertise was required.

A year had gone by. Diego finally delivered the good news. "Gracy, our three young immigrants got the green light. All their visas and papers are in order. We need to decide where we will put them up. You, Alvaro, must determine their work placements."

Gracy was delighted with the news. "Diego, great! We will be regaining some of our old compatriots. Yes, we must find them accommodation."

Alvaro, afraid she would offer to take them in, immediately responded. "Mi Amor, I'll find an apartment not far from work. That will be ideal."

She agreed. Alvaro was relieved "Then, let's wait until I decide where they will be placed. We will go from there."

Diego responded "I will leave that to you two. Daniele, will book their trip. We are sponsoring them so we will have to pay for them in advance, the trip, accommodations as well. We can deduct the cost from their weekly pay."

"Daniele oversees the financial statements. He runs a strict financial plan. He will make sure his accountant keeps the records well in order." Alvaro stated.

"He has to; otherwise, we would be out of business fast." responded Diego.

Gracy joked "I am glad I have you fellows to worry about all that. I would rather engage in the arts and literature."

"Gracy you never need to worry. You always have our protection. My dear sister don't forget you inherited us and a legacy to live worry free." Diego reminded her of her many blessings.

***

The young Sicilians stepped on American soil in the spring. They couldn't have been happier. Leonello, with so much to look forward to, did not let depression invade his being. He and his friends were ready to experience prime tourist season in first-class hotels. They shifted from bell boys to any job that required their help. They were eager to work. They were being paid. They couldn't believe the tips. The guests were generous; something they never had experienced before. Their obligations to work always came first and foremost, but they would meet often with Gracy, for a short lunch or dinner.

Alvaro was so pleased with them. They had not been coddled like some of the employees that took their positions for granted. One worry marred Alvaro's peace of mind. At times, he noticed Leonello's gaze on Gracy. He would shake it off but, deep down it bothered him. He loved her immensely from the sincerity of his heart. He didn't want anyone to threaten the unity of their souls. He truly believed that he and Gracy were meant for each other. He had diverted Ingrid's advances successfully.

He had dispatched Ingrid to Las Vegas for extensive work. It was mainly to get her out of his way. She had persisted in hanging off his neck anytime she could, despite his efforts to curtail her efforts. Many times he pulled her arms away to free himself, reminding her over and over, "Look here Ingrid. I am a married man now. Please, I don't appreciate your advances."

"Alvaro, you are nothing more than a poor sucker consuming yourself working for the Frarano's enterprises. I was good for you before Missy arrived. Since she appeared you have been moonstruck. Remember, the storm always comes. One day you will be destroyed by lightning and you will be looking for me."

"Look Ingrid. I don't care what you think. I love my wife and I choose to be in this love for as long as it lasts."

She laughed in his face. "I can wait."

"Ingrid, don't you think you should focus on Daniele? Does he deserve your betrayal and the escapades with other men?"

"It's none of your business. Daniele gets what he deserves.

He has no intention of legally making me Mrs. Frarano. He has cut down my expense account. He is wheelchair bound and is useless to me, especially in the bedroom. He used me to make him look good and now I'll use him."

"Ingrid, he is my brother-in-law and my boss. It bothers me that you mistreat and malign the unfortunate fellow. If you don't like your situation, leave."

"It's easy for you to say. What about my work?"

"So, it's beneficial to be his live-in girlfriend when it suits your needs. Be loyal, and decent toward him. Conduct yourself with dignity and appreciate the gifts you have in life."

She didn't want to hear those admonitions. She left and slammed the door on her way out. Alvaro was grateful. He wanted her as far away from him as possible

Gracy, had gone home earlier than usual. She had prepared a special supper for Alvaro. It was cooked with tender loving care. A table was set with all the trimmings for a celebration.

"*Mi amor!* Coming home to you is a nightly celebration! I have placed you in my heart and plan to keep you there and never let you go." Alvaro picked her up and twirled her around. "Tell me. Tell me. What is the surprise?"

"I love you so."

He sealed her lips with an extended kiss.

"Sit down, it's not time yet. After dinner my love; be patient."

She proceeded to serve the lavish meal of *pasta rigata* with red and pesto salsa, arancini, followed by Spanish paella and roasted rabbit with fresh tomatoes, stuffed creamed cannoli with fruit to end the meal. A bottle of champagne was opened and each glass was topped with a drop of limoncello. Alvaro poured the champagne into stem glasses. "Now *mi Amor!* Will you please tell me! I am dying from the suspense?"

"*Mi amor,* I am the happiest girl alive at this moment. We are going to have a baby. We will be parents Alvaro!" She raised her glass in a toast but did not drink.

Alvaro was speechless for a moment but then he went over to his wife hugging and kissing her to no end. "*Mi amor!* Are you for real? Is this really happening to us?"

"Yes my love." She responded ecstatically.

"I have more to tell you. You know I have been looking around with an agent for a home for us. With the baby coming we need a bigger home with property so that our child will be able to play freely. Well, if you approve, I think I found the perfect place for us to raise a family."

"*Mi amor!* Whatever makes you happy?"

"We both need to be happy. I want you to see it. I will not move forward with the purchase without your approval."

They purchased a stunning two-story home on a quiet dead end street in Greenwich. The fine European style home was a dream come true for Alvaro. The new home had plenty of outdoor space in both the front and back. It was gated for safety. Gracy could picture her children playing outdoors. It warmed her heart to envision the children having a loving relationship with their daddy just like she used to have with Andrew. "Darling, this is such a special time in our lives."

"*Mi amor,* I am overjoyed can't wait for us to be parents."

Diego and Daniele were joyous over their sister's announcement. They all couldn't wait for the addition to their family. Gracy's heart was only pained, when she thought about her brother Daniele. His blood disorder was a problem. Ingrid's nastiness troubled her immensely. Lately, Gracy hadn't seen her around much and that was a relief. The rest seemed to be all good. Her husband's reports about her three ex-students was encouraging. They were deeply immersed in their work and already on their way to advancement.

Their employment in the hotels was allowing Gracy to work less these days. She needed to keep up with doctors' appointments, the nutritionist, and prenatal courses. She was also working on the interior décor of their new home. She was a busy girl and not as available as before.

One of the advantages in this new stage of her life was that Ingrid had been sent away to work out of town. Gracy was unaware of Ingrid's forward behaviour with Alvaro. If she had known, she would have been even more grateful that Ingrid was in Vegas. Daniele was well taken care of by his daily nurse. Gracy had contemplated having a serious talk with Alvaro about letting Ingrid go with a generous severance package.

She would have a good heart to heart talk with her brother Daniele. He needed to free himself from his toxic relationship. It was bad for his health. That was her plan, and she was ready to act upon it; however, the course of her pregnancy sidetracked her good intentions.

Chapter Forty Three

Gracy's morning sickness was more than she could bear. Often she couldn't get to work until much later than her usual start time. Alvaro and her brothers were concerned. They encouraged her to take time off as much as she could. But Gracy was trying hard to keep up with her schedule; some days were harder than others. Today she had an appointment with Doctor Huntly. Alvaro insisted that she take the day off after a restless night.

The doctor had suspicions but he didn't want to say anything unless he was sure of his diagnosis. Her blood was low and her complaints of fatigue were concerning. She was more exhausted as the days progressed. The doctor wanted to run more tests to discover the source of the problem. Today he was going to do an ultrasound. Gracy's happiness about the pregnancy was starting to fade away as her body was falling apart.

Dr. Huntly always greeted her in good humer. Gracy tried to keep her discomfort to herself. "Let's check your tummy, and listen to the heartbeat," he said. Puzzled, she watched his concerned facial expression. The doctor's voice was low as he told her "I am not sure. I want you to have an ultrasound." Alarmed, Gracy asked "Doctor is anything wrong? Please tell me."

"There is no need to be alarmed. We just want to verify certain symptoms and their implications for your health and the baby's."

Sure, enough the ultrasound revealed the doctor's suspicion. "Congratulations, Mrs. Fernandez. You are carrying twins."

"Oh my God! Twins, how can that be?"

"You are a lucky girl. Just imagine you will be going through this pregnancy receiving a double bonus. It will be a bit hard, nothing we cannot take care of. You will be well rewarded. I will give you a prescription for iron pills that will boost your energy. So knowing this, we can move you forward in optimum health until the big day."

Gracy experienced a wide range of emotions from happiness to confusion to distraction and to some degree of melancholy. She wished her mom could be here to share the news with her. The women who had been mother figures for her could not be here with her. Aunt Lora was now dead. Godmother Fabiana was so far away. *Yes, Godmother Fabiana had been good to her, unfortunately she had always been too far to reach on a daily basis.* As much as she loved her brothers and her husband, she felt the need for a female companion.

She went home, threw her body on the sofa and gave in to her emotions until they faded away. She lay there and didn't even call Alvaro. His phone calls weren't answered. He was worried. He checked out early and went home. When he opened the door, he saw her resting on the sofa. *Mi amor!* I have been calling you all day. How are you? I was going crazy! Why didn't you call me? What did the doctor say?" He could see her eyes were red and swollen. "Gracy, what has happened? Please tell me?"

"I feel foolish to be so sad when we have such good news. We are to have twins, Alvaro."

Alvaro was both relieved and overcome. When Gracy's news finally hit home, he exploded with joy. "This is such great news Gracy. Why are you so sad?"

"I just wanted my mom. I wished to share the news with her.

I haven't been able to do that all my life. Alvaro! You don't understand."

"Gracy, you have me? I am your husband. I love you. Just imagine we will have two babies at once."

"I know that. I am ashamed. I cannot understand what came over me. I fell into self-pity, just like I used to do in my childhood."

"My poor adorable Gracy. I love your honesty so much."

Gracy continued. "I was hoping that at least Ingrid would be my friend and if she was I could use her support as a woman. I know now I was wrong. If nothing else she detests me."

Alvaro, didn't respond. He couldn't tell his wife that Ingrid plagued him with her unwanted attention. So he changed the subject. "Darling, my mom- what about my mom? She would love you to get close to her."

"*Mi amor!* You forget she doesn't speak English. How am I going to converse with her?"

"How about you learning Spanish. My mom is a kind woman. She immigrated here at her older age. She told me many times that she would have loved to speak better English. As much as she tries to learn it won't enter *la cabeza,* her head." That comment brought a smile to her face. The few times she and Alvaro's mother had been together they had to rely on Alvaro's translation.

"I should consider learning Spanish, now with two babies on the way. I was told grandparents are an asset for them."

"I can vouch for that."

"I would never know. I had no living grandparents on either side of the family. No family on the English side that I have ever known. That is why I get sad sometimes. Today it's been one of them."

"*Mi amor!* You have me, and your brothers. Your Sicilian friends and your family in Palermo. Now we are going to be blessed with our own family. You have reason to be happy."

"Yes. You are right. It must have been a moment of weakness. Maybe I'm fearing that I can't take care of two babies."

"We will hire the best trained nanny available, from England, to help you."

"Oh, no. I will take care of my own children. Although I have no experience. I am taking classes and will follow my instinct."

"Gracy. You will need help. Don't forget you have a husband also, that needs to be loved. We better start looking for a nanny." He hugged her tenderly close to his heart.

She had indulged in a moment of self-pity but in the end the joy of her twins easily outweighed the longing for a mother figure who was close by. Over the next few months she reflected on her life. Even though she had been well loved and nurtured by her dad and even though she had the support of strong men, these episodes of loneliness for a strong female mentor arose occasionally. How she wished she had a mother to talk too, to share her love and advice, but she counted the blessings she did have.

The new home they purchased was well exposed to the sun, rendering every room bright and airy. Since, Dr. Huntly revealed that she was carrying a boy and a girl, she had assigned the selected rooms to the new babies. It was time to decorate the nurseries. She hired a decorator from California. Once Ingrid got wind of the news. It infuriated her even more. On a return trip from the Vegas hotel, she stormed into Alvaro's office. "It is an offence to my professional integrity that she has chosen an unknown decorator over me. Ingrid Klein is regarded as the top interior designer of the Eastern seaboard. Here my future sister-in-law slaps me in the face by replacing me."

"Ingrid! Calm down. Gracy is very considerate. It is not what you are thinking at all. She knows how busy you are and she knows Daniele needs you at home more. You are handling big jobs. She didn't want to burden you with the nursery and rooms for our babies."

Ingrid's tantrum continued once she got home to Daniele. One more strike against Gracy. One of these days, she would make Gracy pay for all her wrong doings. Again, she called her buddy Walter asking if he had arranged a meeting with his brother Morris. "No Ingrid I have not. He is busy these days. He has not returned my calls."

"Keep trying! Let me know?" She slammed the phone down, knowing Walter could be pushed around.

Gracy was hardly working these days. Her pregnancy was progressing fairly well. Since she was anemic she tried hard to maintain the proper diet. Her energy level was still poor. Since Daniele was still recuperating at home, she chose to visit him more and more during the afternoon. Some days were worse than others for his pains. Daniele's well- being was worrisome.

Diego was concerned also. They had consulted with all the best doctors around. All of them had given the same results. Disseminated septic emboli Septic thrombosis of the vena cava and the common iliac and renal vein and retroperitoneal abscess secondary to pyogenic spondylitis of the lumbar spine. It was a heartbreaking diagnosis, and His recovery was questionable. He hadn't been travelling since his incident, so Alvaro had assumed most of his schedule.

With Gracy's encouragement, Alvaro was taking Leonello along on the out-of-town excursions and teaching him. It suited Alvaro fine, because he was young and eager to learn. Besides, it kept Leonello busy and away from his wife. Leonello was pleased with the new opportunities opened to him. He had a new interest in life. Gracy had encouraged the boys to take night classes to perfect their English and further their education. Leonello was excited about his new learning. He felt empowered and it gave him an assurance never felt before. His admiration for his ex-teacher was even more profound.

Chapter Forty Four

Diego, as usual, was hard at work in his office concentrating on a very intriguing court case. He was questioning whether to accept it or pass it on to one of his colleagues. It had to do with the drug cartel. He was cutting down his workload. At his stage in life, he could pick and choose the cases to pursue. He preferred simpler cases that were not too time consuming because he wanted to spend more time with his brother whom he had in his heart more than ever lately. There was also Gracy who would be soon giving birth. *Yeah! I need to spend more quality time with my family.* Diego didn't realize how right he was. His phone rang. It was his secretary who had been given strict orders not to disturb him because of the case he was evaluating. He picked up. "Yes, Clare?"

"Sorry, Mr. Frarano, I have your sister on the phone. She insists on talking to you."

"Clare, please put her through. I didn't mean for you to restrict my family's calls."

"Diego, it's me Gracy." He sensed her troubled voice.

"Gracy! What's up? Are you ready for delivery?"

"No, Diego. It's our Daniele. I am at the emergency at Bellevue Hospital. Come as soon as you can."

"I will be right there."

Diego didn't ask any more questions. He flew out the door.

Daniele had developed a blood clot which spread throughout his body via his bloodstream. He became delirious as the infection spread and then it was too late. Despite the doctor's efforts, their beloved Daniele was gone. Diego, and Gracy held each other, crumbling in despair. Gracy's legs buckled. She was not able to hold herself up. "No, our dear, dear, Daniele is gone for ever." screamed Gracy. "How can it be? From that shoot out no one could even begin to anticipate. He wasn't even supposed to be there." The pain was just more than she could bear. Shivering she fainted in Diego's arms. The nurses ran in and Dr. Huntly was paged. The trauma was more than Gracy's body could take and her condition escalated to emergency status. They had to perform a caesarian. The two babies were taken away from her womb just as she had been extracted from her mother's womb on her deathbed.

Sorrow and happiness were happening at the same time.

Gracy's morale was down. She felt ever so cheated. "Almighty God. I am grateful for my babies. Why couldn't I keep my brother longer? He didn't even have a chance to see my new born babies." She kept repeating the conversation with God constantly. Alvaro arrived stunned by the shocking occurrences. Diego also couldn't register the impact of the turn of events. He had been contemplating spending more time with his brother and family. Why now, when they were to celebrate the new life with their new born, did this happen? Diego summoned Ingrid to impart the tragic news.

She wasn't pleased with the turn of events. The first thing that popped in her mind was- *now that Daniele was gone, what would happen to her position and her allowance? Where would she live in New York? Housing was expensive.* She was troubled immensely, concerned only for her own wellbeing and not with any pain or loss for her lover who had passed too soon. Even coming out of her operation and still under the influence of her meds, Gracy could read Ingrid's coldness and she knew that she hadn't be wrong in suspecting Ingrid's selfish intentions.

Diego organized the funeral arrangements for his dear brother. Through the course of their lives there had been periods when they were both totally disheartened by what life had thrown their way. They had relied on each other every step of the long road to success. He wondered how the two of them had found strength to go on. Connecting with Gracy after their father's demise had given them hope and had reconnected them with their mother. Now, when they were at their happiest with the miracle of birth to come, Daniele's loss was too hard to take.

Gracy's weakened state didn't allow her to attend the funeral. The doctor reassured Alvaro that she would be fine in a couple weeks or so. The twins were progressing well, a perfect baby boy and a beautiful baby girl. Alvaro and Gracy rejoiced on the blessing of the twins despite the pain of losing Daniele. Alvaro and Diego walked into Gracy's hospital room after Daniele's funeral. She was holding her babies on each of her arms. Alvaro bent over and encircled the three of them in his arms. *"Mi amor!* I will love you eternally. Let's find courage to be happy going on. We have been blessed with a son and daughter. Daniele, up in heaven, is smiling at us." Diego stood there watching them, wiping his tears. Yes, he agreed they had been blessed, nevertheless it was hard for him to accept a life without his brother. They had shared their souls in togetherness.

The nurse marched in cheerfully and broke the spell. "Sorry, it's time to get these babies for their nap." She gathered them gently and scooted away. Alvaro hugged his wife tenderly, hoping to comfort her between the joy and the pain.

Time is a great healer although nothing on earth could ever totally mitigate their loss. Diego worked less in order to spend more time with Gracy, Alvaro and the newborn babies. He regretted not having made the decision earlier to spend more quality time with his Daniele. He never suspected his brother would leave them. He must have been suffering more than he let on. Some time ago Daniele had requested to have his will revised. Diego had joked with him, "Bro, you have lots of time to revise your will. What are you worrying about? Wait until you marry or have a family."

"Diego, do as I say. I don't feel my affairs are in order. You should know better than to counsel me to wait. You are a lawyer."

"Eh! If you insist. I will revise it."

He had brought the papers over. They had gone over the details carefully. Daniele specified. "Diego I want you to be the executor. All my assets and holdings are to be passed on to my sister Gracy Robertson. My shares of our company's future growth and development are also to be inherited by my sister only. As for contributions to the charities and medical research, leave it the way it stands- a certain percentage calculated at year end. Our accountant knows what to do."

Diego asked, Daniele, "What about your live-in friend? Where does she come in? I think these decisions may be premature in light of your implied commitment."

"Diego never mind about my live- in."

"What if you get married? Have children? The situation will be different."

"Diego! Do as I say now. Later, time will tell."

"Whatever you say. It's your will."

"My decision, my will. You certainly don't need any of my assets. You have more than you can ever use. You don't plan to marry.

You should make certain your wishes are in place as well."

"I hate to think of or to discuss wills. They spell a death sentence."

"That's absurd coming from a lawyer."

"Okay Daniele. I will do whatever you say. How do you want me to pacify Ingrid? God forbid she is excluded from your empire."

"Bro, I will leave her whatever cash I have in the bank and some investments. That should be good enough for her."

"Daniele, sometimes a fortune is a curse when we are dealing with who gets a share of it."

"You are telling me. I kept quiet but with Ingrid it was never enough. I think she is an opportunist. Besides, she has been cheating on me. I was suspicious and was watching her closely when I could get around more. She uses any man that could serve her. Why you think I stalled the marriage? I have been telling her to leave; she doesn't.

She puts on a fake show with love and tears. Diego, I am no fool. She doesn't want to lose her prestige and comfort. She can claim herself my live-in partner. I have it recorded and documented how many times I have asked her to leave. She is pitiful. I should have her thrown-out."

"Daniele I am sorry to hear that. I must confess both Gracy and I thought your relationship with Ingrid was questionable."

"Here are the videos and my handwritten notes. I will make a copy for your records."

Diego replayed the conversation in his mind. '*Why did my brother call me and confide in me. Did he have a notion that he was going to die?*'

Regardless of the unanswered questions, it was time to move forward. He needed to call a meeting with Gracy, Alvaro and Ingrid Klein and the accountant William Spark. The meeting was scheduled for the following week.

The only one anxious to attend the meeting was Ingrid. She couldn't wait to hear of her inherited fortune. Maybe she wouldn't have to work as much anymore. Before Daniele died, she had tried to control her outbursts and forced herself to be sweet. She kept company with her friend Walter who helped her to boost her patience with the billionaire Fraranos, and that sister of theirs.

Gracy attended the meeting with her head in a fog. Nothing on this earth could replace her brother. The reading of the will only brought her sorrow. Alvaro, noticing his wife's discomfort, kept squeezing her hand for support. Gracy didn't care about gaining more wealth. The inheritance from her mother was more than she needed. Francesca, her mom, had paid for her inheritance by sacrificing her life, Aunt Lora used to say.

As the meeting wore on and the wealth was being distributed to others, Ingrid was getting angrier. She turned blue in the face. "Diego, he must have left another paper for me. A deed to some hotel or property, assigned to me?"

"Sorry. This is it. My brother's wishes were executed shortly before his death. I hated to do it. I had no choice but to abide by his wishes."

"I have been with him almost ten years working tirelessly in the hotels which to the best of my knowledge are worth much more than the paltry amount I have received."

"Ingrid, don't forget you got paid for your work. The benefits, an expense account- you lived in luxury. William is here. He has all records of your expenditures. You have been our most rewarded employee."

"I wasn't just an employee. I was also his live-in."

Diego didn't say more. He thought, *Yeah! For how long? Until you started sleeping around deceiving my brother.* He wouldn't show her the videos his brother had insisted on giving him. No wonder Daniele didn't commit to her. Their father used to say "Don't mix business with pleasure. You boys don't get involved with any of the staff that work for us. *Capisci e basta.* Do you understand what I mean by enough?" He was hard on them but some of his advice had been wise. Daniele must have remembered his father's words. He realized he was in a situation involving business and pleasure and that pleasure had gone sour as time passed. His change of heart had come with the two bullets in his abdomen.

Ingrid vowed that she wasn't going to settle. She would contest the will. If looks could kill, she would have. She turned to Gracy with a defiant angry stare and spewed venom. "You will all pay for this injustice, especially you Miss Priss." She pointed at threatening finger at her. "Since your arrival in New York, you have influenced my Daniele. I promise, you will pay for it."

Gracy, in her pain, was shocked. Alvaro was mortified. He knew Ingrid had made passes at him and she was hurt by his refusal. God help him. He had had few escapades with her in the far past but from the time he met Gracy, he didn't want anything to do with her. Would she expose his past with her and hurt his wife? What did she have in mind?

Diego tried to pacify her. "Ingrid, look here. You are upset now without reason. I think my brother looked after you well. He left you a fair amount of money here. You should be happy. You blame innocent people, especially Gracy. You need to come to terms with yourself. I am not sure what you expected."

"You will find out Mr. Big Shot. I will get my own lawyer but not one from New York who you can influence. I have my own connections. I come from Washington. You forgot?"

She stormed out with her papers. At work she didn't have to sign in or out, after all she hadn't been an ordinary employee. She dialed Walter's number; he wasn't picking up. *Okay,* she thought. *I will call his brother myself.* She looked at her watch. It was five o'clock. That big fat Walter was probably stuffing his face somewhere out to dinner at some early bird restaurant to save money. He would never amount to any good in life. I better get on to his brother. Driven by her anger from the afternoon, she didn't want to lose time. She went home and dialed Morris's number.

"Hello, Morris, how are you. It's Ingrid Klein from New York."

"Ingrid what a surprise. Nice to hear from you. How have you been?"

"I have been fairly good until today. I was waiting for you to get in touch with me. Did Walter call you?"

"No, sorry. He didn't tell me anything. As matter of fact, I haven't heard from him for a while. What's up?"

"Leave it to Walter to mess up. You know, one cannot count on him. His main interest in life lately is eating and drinking."

"That's Walter for you. He is lucky to have a job, thanks to you."

"Does he show up for work every-day?"

"He has to otherwise he won't be able to eat."

"That's for sure. He cannot loaf off my parents anymore since they died. Enough about Walter, tell me about yourself. What's going on with you?"

"I was doing fine but not now. You know my boyfriend Daniele died."

"Oh! Sorry to hear that. No, I didn't know."

"He was at the wrong place at the wrong time. There was a robbery at one of the hotels and he got hit by two stray bullets. His health went from bad to worse. He died."

"My sympathies. I know you were planning to get married."

"I was. He kept stalling and then the shooting happened. It changed everything. I had been with him for ten years."

"Again, my apologies, my brother never mentioned anything. Although I must say I don't talk to him often."

"The reason I am calling you is his will. He hardly left me anything. I want to contest the will. I would like the best lawyer from Washington. As you know, big shot Frarano is influential in New York, but there are other issues. We will talk about that another time."

"Ingrid, I feel badly for you. I need to know all the details before I can advise you one way or another."

"When can we meet? Can you come to New York or should I come to Washington?" she asked. When he didn't answer immediately, she became more aggressive. "Morris! Let's set a date. I will come to you so we won't raise any questions here."

"Good. Bring all your information and we will go over it carefully."

The following week, Ingrid left for Washington to meet Morris Robertson. She would do anything necessary to get him on her side- anything! He would do summersaults for her. They had gone to school together; she knew Morris well. He was a shyster just like her. Advancement at any cost was his motto.

He was tall and charming. He was always well groomed and dressed in exquisitely tailored suits. His inquisitive eyes and instincts helped him pick the right people. He had advanced in life by rubbing shoulders and doing business with the elite. He made sure to have memberships at the best social clubs. In his swift, smooth way, he was accepted in their crowd. He had been divorced twice. He was on his third relationship, with a widow. He wasn't seriously interested in her but the financial holdings were lucrative. He was a financial broker, therefore his interest was money and people with big assets to invest. They were his main targets. He had no trouble, especially with the women of Washington. There was a lot of old money in the area. He professed that he wanted to help them and himself. He knew his work and knew it well.

Ingrid had dreamed she would be in a good position marrying Daniele. He had never mentioned prenuptial agreements. She was grateful for that. The marriage had never taken place and she never understood why he kept stalling. Then the shooting stalled her plan further. She couldn't believe his fortune was left to his half-sister. How could Daniele leave her out in the cold like that? In the first few years of their relationship, he was insanely in love with her. At times he had commented on her flirtatious behaviour; however he seemed deliriously happy in her company. Yes, right up until his sister had arrived. Ingrid resented and blamed Gracy for everything.

Walter the security guy, as simple as she thought he was he, also disliked her flirtatious behaviour. He had warned her about it. He had watched her walk out of special guest's room, many times, especially when Daniele was out of town. She would threaten him or have him fired. God forbid, if he dared say anything. The next evening, she would be all over Daniele smothering him with fake love.

***

While Ingrid was putting in her plans in motion, Gracy was missing her adored brother. She would have sacrificed anything to save him. The only time a smile would come to her lips was when she watched her two beautiful babies. Their first smiles were amazing. When they started crawling, she couldn't believe their accomplishments. They progressed daily in growth and intelligence. The three of them, Alvaro, Diego, and Gracy shared in the happiness.

Often, they would invite their Sicilian paesanos- Leonello, Romero, and Gianni- to show the twins off. They had hired a nanny to help out, but Gracy possessed a strong sense of motherly protection.

She had given up working mainly to dedicate herself fully to the children. They had named the baby girl Francesca, after her mother. The boy was Andrew. It was the Sicilian custom to name the first born after their grandparents. She apologized to Alvaro. "Mi amor! Don't feel bad. I like a big family. We will have other children; we will name them after your side of the family. It's lonely to be an only child you know. I cried a lot in my childhood, growing up only with my dad. When my brothers found me, it was the biggest gift of my life."

The memory of her brother Daniele overwhelmed her and she ran in the other room for a good cry. Lately, she had been having a hard time coping with his loss.

310

Chapter Forty Five

Ingrid, still feeling entitled as Daniele's girlfriend, went ahead with her plan to meet Morris Robertson in Washington. Alvaro was her boss, but she considered herself above him. Taking time off for her own affairs didn't bother her even if Alvaro did mind. He was hesitant on approaching her to moderate her sense of superiority. She would be rebellious, reminding him of who got him where he was. Lately her actions had been bolder than ever. Something needed to be done. He thought it would be better to let the storm go for now. He would deal with the matter in due course.

Ingrid had bought herself a new navy-blue power suit. She had paired it with a stunning white blouse, added classic jewelry and stunning stilettos. She hired a make-up artist and hairdresser to come to her in the morning. The make-up artist created a picture perfect effect for any man to admire. That was her goal- admiration and head turning. Her meeting with Morris was scheduled at twelve noon over lunch, at his business club. She made sure she was ten minutes late so her entrance would be perfect. Morris was waiting in a secluded booth. When she made her entrance, he remarked "Well! Well, if it isn't my admirable girl, stunning as ever." He got up greeting her gallantly. "How are you? You look fantastic!"

"Seeing you I feel better already. You always brightened my day, Morris." She hugged and kissed him, enticing and managing him at the same time. She complimented him; after all she needed him. "I had such a mad crush on you in our high school days. I recall competing with all the girls in high school for your attention."

"Yes, they were fun days weren't they? My dear girl, Washington wasn't good enough for you. You wanted the glamor and billionaires of New York City. We little guys here were forgotten for the city that never sleeps."

"Morris, an opportunity was presented to me, and I took it. I lived well and did well. Now I feel disillusioned. I had plans and everything has fallen apart. You know the results."

"Ingrid knowing you, you will find someone else. I am sure."

"Morris, I invested ten years of my life in that relationship. I have worked hard, contributed to their financial gain. Now what bothers me is that this Sicilian girl has robbed me of my inheritance."

"Let me see the papers and what they indicate-what you have been left and what you are entitled to. We are experienced in these issues. I can give you some advice. We will consult a qualified lawyer on the subject matter." He glanced over the papers.

"Where does this Sicilian come in?" Morris was confused.

"She is supposedly a half-sister. Ever since she stepped foot in New York, the sun and the moon and their lives revolve around her."

"What do you mean them?"

"The two brothers."

"The brother has nothing to do with Daniele's ownership. It is specified that his share would go only to this sister of theirs. I have been left a measly sum of cash. I was to be his wife. I lived with him for ten years."

"Any mention of you in his will?"

"Yes, I only got ten million in cash. My salary is guaranteed, going up accordingly. I have secured employment which has nothing to do with the inheritance. I have an expense account. The bulldog of an accountant has been restricting me. I must explain and present every bill of purchase."

"I gather that before this you had free reign."

"I hate all these restrictions. It all began when Miss Priss arrived."

"Why you think that? Is she an expert in finances or business administration?"

"I don't think so. Daniele seemed to change his tune when she came. He changed."

There was no way she was going to reveal all of the facts. She did not mention her illicit escapades in a continued attempt to manage the information and him.

"We can meet with a lawyer friend of mine. Ingrid, to be honest, I think you did very well by the will. I can invest your money for a good return. You are young. Find yourself another man and move on."

"Morris, Daniele, was worth a fortune. She took it and what was mine. She will pay for influencing her brother against me. I swear it."

Morris Robertson was a wily fox. He wondered if Ingrid had changed her old habits. She was wrong not to acknowledge her own behaviour. *Ingrid considers herself above it all. With her impressive appearance and her calculated charm, she could conquer the world. As for the opposite sex, yes, they bow to her. Her manipulations had been effective since she had reached puberty. They had gotten more effective as she matured. Her manipulations were almost an uncontrollable sickness. It was as if she didn't realize the wrong that she was doing to innocent people. It would backfire on her later in life.*

Ingrid was driven by her greed. Now she needed Morris Robertson. I will work on him. *He is well connected and well matched to my purposes.* Morris was her kind. Before they parted he asked her "Ingrid do you have plans for tonight?"

"Why do you ask?" she positioned herself offering her lips as temptation.

"If you are free we could have dinner and spend some more time for old time sake. We can relive our high school days."

"Morris, I would love to but..." She grabbed him by his tie, teasing him, "Aren't you working on your new relationship?"

"Don't worry about that. I can easily excuse myself. Besides isn't our meeting business and pleasure?"

She brought her hand to his cheek to caress him tenderly "I have no problem. You are the one with commitments."

"A phone call will take care of any commitment I have. When it comes to business, she will understand."

"I am game my old friend. Where and what time?"

"I will book a room at a place you will love. We'll order room service."

"I like the Jefferson, the Willard, and Shoreham. I admire their lobbies and architecture so any one of them will do. After all, you are in the company of a top interior designer, don't forget." She teased him.

"My apologies. I forgot your exclusive taste!"

"What time and where? Call me later!" She gave him her number. After a lingering and provocative kiss to arouse him, she pulled herself away. "See you later."

***

While Ingrid was plotting and planning, in New York Gracy was having a wonderful evening with the twins. The Sicilians guys were visiting. Francesca had taken her first wobbling steps. The adults including Diego, were celebrating the accomplishment with a sumptuous supper and after dinner drinks in the living room. They were watching Francesca do her thing and she was encouraged by their animation.

Andrew, crawling behind her, sought his own attention. There was lots of laughter and hand clapping to Francesca's astonishment. She was encouraged and Andrew kept trying harder.

Gracy' was in her mid-thirties. She wanted more children. Alvaro was working harder these days. The demands on him were incessant. Often their out-of-town hotels needed his advice. Gracy, was no longer working in the company. Alvaro missed her input. She was smart and cared for their progress. Now her interest had shifted totally to her family. He understood and admired her priorities. Their lives had changed. Her devotion to the family was important for Gracy. As a teacher she had worked with many children who lacked nutrition and affection. They were victims of neglect. It wasn't going to happen to her two-year-old children.

Six months later Gracy got the good news once more; she was expecting again. This time one heartbeat was detected. The doctor said. "Mrs. Fernandez, no bonus this time. Congratulations, you are expecting again. Everything is perfectly fine." Gracy, was happy. She would announce the news to Alvaro. Her heart was beaming; she couldn't wait. This time she was hoping for a normal delivery. She had plenty of help at home. There was absolutely no problem. Gloria, the nanny, was fabulous and attentive. She had been hired with all the necessary credentials. Gracy made sure she was always within reach.

Lately she had become concerned for her husband. Alvaro was coming home later and tired. The out-of-town demands were relentless. He was missing out on the children's development. She kept encouraging him to hire more help. Often, he would delegate Ingrid to deal with the increasing responsibilities. It pained Gracy to watch him stressed out.

After dinner while Gloria was attending to the children, she poured a calming tea for both. "*Mi amor,* we like you home more for the sake of the children. We miss you terribly. I have a suggestion. It might solve our problem. Would you consider hiring Leonello as your assistant? You could also assign Romero more responsibilities. Place Gianni in charge of bookings and reservations. You can trust those young men; the staff and guests like them. They are hard workers and sincere."

Alvaro didn't respond. Tucked away, at the back of Alvaro's mind, a churning jealousy flickered. *Leonello was maturing and becoming such an attractive fellow. Could it be that Leonello was still passionate about his wife?* He had erased the concern away, but it would resurface occasionally. He didn't dare confide his ridiculous feelings to his wife because she would definitely scold him. *It wasn't their fault they had suffered in poverty for most of their lives. Those unfortunate young fellows thanks to Gracy's noble soul, proved to be respectful, hard workers who were grateful for the opportunity they had been given.*

Gracy was right to help them in every way. They deserved everything life offered. Now they were repaying them back honorably. They never refused to work overtime. Diego, often commented on their availability in comparison to others.

Once again, tonight when Alvaro got home, Gracy greeted him in high spirits. As he walked in, the aroma of a special dinner filled the room. There was a celebration of sorts in the air. The dining room table was set for them including a bouquet of red roses and candles. Gracy loved roses so he knew something was up. After they sat, she poured the champagne in his stem glass and placed sparkling water in hers. "Gracy, please I cannot stand this suspense. Tell me!"

"*Mi amor*! We are expecting another child, another miracle of our love."

Alvaro, reacted enthusiastically. "*Mi, amor!* Cheers, we are blessed with another child." He hugged her tenderly and kissed her longingly. "Darling. I want to enjoy them with you. You are right. I need to slow down. I will have to get an assistant." He offered a toast. "Let's drink to that too, my love."

"Our twins bring so much joy. I don't want you to miss it. You work so hard. I feel guilty for not being able to help you. I'm needed here at home, my darling. Now with a third, I will be a busy mommy."

"Mi amor! I am happy for the new baby." He placed a hand on his chest. "I need you too, my darling. We have a nanny, don't forget."

"You poor soul. I would never neglect you mi amor and, yes, the nanny is great but don't forget our children belong to me."

"Darling, you are so dedicated. I admire your devotion; however, we need some time to ourselves." Alvaro loved his children. At the same time he badly desired private time with Gracy as well. His universe had changed but Gracy was still its center.

"Mi amor don't forget. I grew up without a mommy. A part of me was lost. I felt it when I saw other children with their mommies. My babies will have a much different experience."

The next day Alvaro went to the office. He summoned Leonello, Romero, and Gianni. Diego was needed also for his approval. A very serious meeting took place. The decision was made. Leonello was going to alleviate his workload. Romero was going to assist. Gianni would be in charge of registrations. Diego agreed. Alvaro needed some relief. He needed to spend more time with his growing family. Gracy wasn't a complainer, but he knew that many times dinners with her husband weren't shared because of an unexpected crisis at work. So, Leonello would become the official assistant to the man in charge. Hopefully these changes would help everyone concerned.

Chapter Forty Six

Leonello, Romero and Gianni took their promotions seriously. They vowed to honor Alvaro and their benefactors through their hard work and loyalty. All three of them knew Gracy had played a role behind the scenes on their behalf. The new arrangements irritated Ingrid immensely. She had been corresponding with Morris lately. It was easy to confide in him because he sympathized with her. His brother Walter, instead, was not cooperating. Ingrid knew that he would never amount to anything other than a low level security officer. His ambitions in life were nil. His brother Morris shined. He could help her better; he had given her his private number. She could reach him anytime. She dialed his number promptly. He picked up. "Hello! How is my favorite girl?"

"Lousy at the moment. How are you?"

"I could be much better in your company *mein schatz.*"

"Me too! Why don't you come over tonight? We will have dinner.

We will spend the evening together."

"There is a good possibility I can make that happen. I have a meeting in New York this afternoon. I could meet you afterwards at your place."

Morris looked forward to meeting Ingrid. She always gave him a good time. He had his own premeditated intentions for their alliance. She could open many doors for him.

Once more, Ingrid put aside her sour mood. When she returned home, she dressed and ordered in for two. She would serve a tantalizing meal for her friend. Champagne was chilling beside a romantic table setting. Her charm and soft music were turned on. Morris arrived on time holding a vase of white orchids in full bloom.

"Morris, leave it to you to know the way to a girl's heart. Thank you! They are splendid."

"Like you my dear. Look at this place! You have never invited me here before. I have missed out."

"Daniele and I really never entertained. Now that I'm alone I can do what I want."

After dinner, they sat in the living room. Ingrid was anxious to spill her concerns to Morris. After all, she hardly had any friends in New York since Daniele's death. The Sicilians weren't coming over anymore.

She didn't really care for them anyway. With the changes in the will, her resentment was growing in leaps and bounds.

She sat close to Morris. He put an arm around her shoulders and his hand was busy finding its way up her legs. "Morris, I need a real man's affection. I have felt so lonely and unloved for a long time."

"Tell me; has this place been left to you or you are renting?"

"Yes, I am privileged to live here or so I was told by the attorney."

"Ingrid you lived with your fellow for ten years. You earned the right to live in this apartment. You are entitled to the ten million in cash and whatever is in your bank account. If you continue working with the company, you can continue to build on these assets."

"Yes, but don't forget I was supposed to be Mrs. Frarano. The Fraranos are worth billions so I am entitled to much more than an apartment and a meager sum of money."

"Ingrid, he never married you. You have no children. If you ask me you did pretty well so why are you pushing the envelope?"

"Morris, everything has changed since the bitch sister got here. She got three Sicilians guys to emigrate. Guess what? They have climbed up the corporate ladder in position and status. So, the Fraranos have no problem taking care of strangers but not someone who was in essence family. They owe me and I will get my due. "

"Ingrid, you need to explain to me carefully in what way and why they turned against you."

"You want to know more. Here it is. She first influenced her brothers. Then she shone her attention on the CEO, whom I found for them. He got the job because of me. Unlike your brother he was top notch-a hard worker, excellent for the company. He consulted with me often. She arrived and I became second fiddle. He kept me at a distance and now the Sicilian guys have been promoted to major positions of responsibility while she shuns me and steals my influence."

"Ingrid, I like you. Don't get me wrong. Might this be a simple case of jealousy with this Gracy girl?"

"I hate her for the humiliation she has caused me. She married Alvaro Fernandez who was hypnotized by her for some incomprehensible reason. I don't need to tell you how she melted her brothers' hearts and displaced me from her brother's affection."

"Ingrid, maybe I can help you. I would like to meet her under the pretense that she might need a financial adviser. How about introducing me to her?"

"She quit working. She has two children and is expecting a third and has no financial issues. She has the support of the Frarano empire. Do you really think you can convince her that she needs you?"

"Give me more information. I will check her out on my own."

"I resented her before but now, she is my enemy."

Even though he promised to help Ingrid, Morris had his own interests with this Gracy girl. "Does she speak English?" he asked.

"She does but the newcomers don't speak as well as she does. She was an English teacher and spent time in Australia so her command of both Italian and English is exemplary. She is a *professoressa* with impressive skills." Ingrid's words seemed complimentary, but her tone was mocking.

"Good for her! She sounds very interesting. I would love to meet her. More than anything, I would like to check her out and see how I can use her to meet our needs."

"You won't meet her through me. I am not on speaking terms with her."

"Ingrid, don't underestimate me. I have other sources. Why do you think I have been successful? I will dig out everything about her. I have my ways."

"Morris, you always intrigued me. What a difference between you and your brother. He is a laid back eight-hour man with no advancement in his life. You, on the other hand, are relentless and so am I."

"You don't worry about anything. I have an associate who works under the radar. He will dig out everything I want to know about Mrs. Fernandez. The fortune that she is worth might be benefit us as well."

After spending the night under the spell of Ingrid's bliss, he couldn't wait for the morning to get back to his office in Washington. He called his buddy Marc Diez. "Good morning my friend! How are you?"

Marc Diez had been up all-night investigating for other clients. Half asleep he growled "Eh! Morris what's up? Why call me so early? You know I am a night owl. If it's not critical, call me back around noon?"

"Marc, you know me better than that. When I have something under my skin, the sooner I satisfy my curiosity the better."

"Go to hell will you. Let me sleep."

"Marc, don't I pay you well? I can go to someone else if you don't want my money."

Marc Diez knew Morris was used to having his way. He rubbed his eyes with the back of his hand, cleared his throat and said "I am listening."

"Remember Ingrid Klein?"

"Who doesn't remember Ingrid Klein? Her bedroom tricks could put you in orbit."

"Well, she is still pretty good at it. I just spent the night with her and let me tell you it was ecstasy."

"Morris, did you call me at seven in the morning to tell me about your party with that slut Ingrid Klein?"

"Marc, you underestimate me. You are supposed to be the undercover detective, but I have to find the information and bring it under your nose. I need you to check this dame out, Mrs. Gracy Fernandez. She married the CEO of the Frarano's empire. You've heard of them, right?"

"Who hasn't heard of them Morris? Continue."

"I want you to find out everything about her. She is supposedly their sister. She came from Sicily. A former teacher, well-read but now she is a stay at home mother."

"What's your interest in her?"

"Her inheritance jackass! You're supposed to be smart. Why do I have explain everything?" He was frustrated with Diez.

"You want to get hold of her money and invest it for her? Right?"

"Right. I like to be informed. Then I decide if it is worthwhile pursuing or abandoning the idea."

Morris looked after number one first. As for Ingrid, he thought, *she doesn't deserve more. She profited greatly from the misfortune of Daniele Frarano.*

Marc Diez was a sharp and meticulous investigator. He knew Morris was shrewd and demanding. Morris paid him well so he couldn't afford to ignore his demands. Marc decided he better get on with Morris' demands and provide him as much as he could find out about this Mrs. Gracy Fernandez.

It didn't take him long to find out she had come from Agrigento, Sicily. She had taught literature at the university. She had rave reviews from everyone that knew her. Her maiden name was Robertson, English. "Like Morris! Strange coincidence." He furrowed his eyebrows. Everyone informally referred to her as the Professor's daughter. The puzzle of Gracy Robertson- Fernandez would eventually unravel itself because Marc Diez was good at untangling puzzles. He wasn't going to report anything to Morris, until his investigation was thoroughly completed. The answers to the many questions about this woman were waiting to be discovered.

Chapter Forty Seven

Ingrid Klein was obsessed. She was convinced Gracy Robertson was the culprit at the center of her troubling situation. She believed Morris would help her contest the will. She didn't trust the lawyers in New York because everyone knew the highly regarded Diego Frarano would not be beaten. After many phone calls from Ingrid pestering Morris, he finally got back to her. "Ingrid, I have explained your situation to my colleagues. They all feel that you have not been shortchanged. I myself believe you have done pretty well for yourself."

A hot flash of blood, raced to Ingrid's head fogging her brain. "I should have known better. You guys are all the same. You are after one thing, especially you Morris. You are a narcissist. Forget it, I will pursue it myself. Maybe your brother can help me better than you have." She hung up the phone infuriated and went to look for Walter.

She stormed into the lobby of the Hyatt Regency. Walter was nowhere to be found. Instead, she ran into Alvaro accompanied by Leonello.

She immediately changed her mood and put on a happy face. "Hello! I see you guys are still here. Especially you Alvaro, I am surprised. Shouldn't you be home with the family?"

"Hello, Ingrid how are you these days? We haven't seen you much. I know you are busier than I am with work. Excuse me, you've met Leonello Dante before I presume." Leonello smiled at her pleasantly.

"Yes of course a while back. We originally met at the wedding." She sized him up and down. "You look more mature and americanized."

"Yes, well time has flown since we arrived, so change is natural."

"As you know, these boys are hard workers. They can take the long hours, and pressure. Leonello is stepping into my position. My Gracy is expecting again. I need to be spending more time with my family."

"Yes, you should Mr. Alvaro. I agree." She sounded convincing. Leonello was impressed. He stood there admiring her and listening.

"Alvaro. I was looking for our security guy Walter. I don't see him around the lobby or at the front entrance. Is he off tonight?"

Leonello responded. "We had to put him on duty in our parking garage over the last few evenings."

"Why is that? I thought valet boys made the rounds in that department."

"We needed someone with more security experience. Some vandalism has been occurring late in the evenings. The security department has been assigned to look after that area. Walter has been positioned there until they get more help."

"I see. I haven't been here for a while. I see some changes have taken place."

"Yes, change is always on the agenda."

Alvaro and Leonello, had no idea of her motives or her interest in the security guy. She wanted to keep it that way. *Their ignorance is an advantage for what I need to do. I have to work on Walter to stimulate his brain. With manipulation, maybe he can serve me better than that pompous brother of his. Morris thinks the rest of us should bow at his feet. I'll show him who really needs to bow at whose feet.*

Ingrid in her high heels and tight skirt wasn't going to the parking garage looking for Walter. She went out the front lobby and ordered the shuttle to take her back to her apartment. She preferred spending the evening scheming on how to reclaim the stolen inheritance she truly believed rightly belonged to her.

Now lonely as ever, she vowed that was not going to give into sorrow. Right now there seemed to be no more claim or hope. The possibility of becoming Mrs. Frarano had been alluring. Instead of marriage, she was left only with a miserable ten million to live in New York. She was going to fight this all the way even if the only one she had to help her was Walter Robertson.

***

In Washington, Morris was busy these days also. He had met with Marc Diez and given him instructions and received feedback. It wasn't much. He counted on Mr. Diez to provide him all he could regarding this mysterious Miss Gracy Frarano who had married Fernandez. According to Ingrid, she was considered the salt of the earth by everyone she knew, especially the young Sicilians. Morris was only interested in her fortune not her achievements, personal or otherwise. If he was being honest with himself, he did have to admit that Ingrid had built up his curiosity about this person.

Marc Diez was his preferred investigator. They had exchanged favours in the past. He warned him "Marc don't get back to me unless you have a complete report that has useful results for me. My friend seems to have directed her anger at Gracy Fernandez out of envy or imagination or both."

"Morris, did you at least consult a qualified lawyer about your friend's inheritance situation?"

"Don't insult my intelligence. My friend did pretty well. She lived with that fellow ten years. He left her ten million cash in the bank. If I know Ingrid, she screwed around on the poor fellow. He was a businessman who travelled often. If you ask me, he was kind to her."

Marc was shrewd and had the observational skills to determine if people lied. Right now he didn't have the time to determine if Ingrid or Morris were telling the truth. He needed to focus on the subject of everyone's interest "Our main interest here is this Mrs. Fernandez. Enough about Ingrid Klein. What if I have to take a trip to Sicily? Will you cover my expenses?"

"If you make it worth my while."

"My job is to deliver you correct information about her. I cannot promise you that you will get a hold of her billions for your gain. That is your department."

"Marc, I trust you will be conscientious. Do what you have to do. You know me better than that. Once I have the information, I will find a way to her."

They shook hands and parted. Marc Diez wasn't the kind of person to stall on his assignments. He got back to his office and immediately went into action. He had connections not only in USA but abroad. With luck he could make contact with some of his sources in Italy. Despite their broken English, he had gotten used to their methods and understood them. His own broken dialect learned on the street from his school buddies didn't help much.

As soon as he landed in Sicily, he got busy. His research proved interesting not only the background of old Mr. Frarano, the patriarch, but also with his corrupt reputation. When it got to the sons, the reputation changed from murky to impressive. Everyone praised the Frarano brothers. There were stumbling blocks with the girl. He was puzzled. *She was a half-sister. Her last name was Robertson, very English.* That motivated his interest even more. Questions raced through his mind.

He got a hold of his old friend who had retired on the island. He instructed him to find out as much as he could about this famous *professoressa* who had taught at the university in Agrigento. He needed to know everything about her. People weren't too cooperative or willing to share. Some really didn't know. It was taking longer than anticipated. Morris was pounding Marc Diez for answers but so far there was nothing concrete really to report.

She was the daughter of an English professor, relocated to Agrigento.

Both were admired and well educated. They had come from out of country. They limited the number of their friends. They lived in an imposing mansion in the suburb of the Valley of the Temples. The people at the university had only praises for them. He asked his source. "How are they related to the Fraranos? Are they just friends? How can she be their sister? The bond between them is incredible I am told."

His friend suggested a more hands on approach for Marc. "The Fraranos are from Palermo. Maybe, you should be digging for information in Palermo."

"I might have no choice other than to get there myself."

"I think you should my friend. I came here to baste in the sun and swim in the sea. Sorry buddy. My brain isn't into that anymore." responded Mr. Romano, his former associate.

Marc was intrigued. How was it possible that the Robertsons had surfaced on earth from nowhere? He arrived in Palermo. He began at the city hall but there were no registration or birth certificates. There was no trace of any documents he could get his hands on. Finally, an employee at the Registry Office told him something that might help. "The Tavernas were friendly with them. Maybe they could enlighten you."

It wasn't easy. Fabiana was a journalist herself who had studied in England. She spoke a perfect English. She wasn't going to give out information about her dearest goddaughter or the horrible fate of her aunt. The alienation, fear and misery the professor and Gracy had undergone had been immeasurable. It was a sacrilege. It would never be revealed to anyone by Fabiana or any of the Tavernas.

Marc scratched his head. *My Lord what an entangled mystery am I cut into! Where do I go from here?* He thought it was time to put his hands in his pockets and find someone to bribe. He started to frequent the coffee shops and the piazza. Men gathered there to pass time. Maybe some of the older fellows knew something from years back. He needed anything as long as he could move forward with this case he shouldn't have never taken.

The grandparents, mother and father of the Frarano boys were all dead and buried in the mausoleum. He had some suspicions, but he needed proof. Sicilian women were much more reserved and expected to follow a strict moral code. Could something have happened with one of the Frarano women? *Could there have been a liaison? Now there was yet another missing piece of the puzzle that needed to be found.*

He got a phone call from Morris. "Marc! Hello! How are you doing? I bet you are enjoying that stupendous island and have forgotten all about me here waiting for some news."

"Morris, I am regretting taking this assignment. In Palermo no one knows anything about your Mrs. Fernandez. The only relatives I know and approached have tight lips. In Agrigento, the professor and other staff have only rave reviews. Their residence is an eye opener."

"Marc, you should know better. Dig out someone on the wrong side of the law to help you. It's the only way you will find out something."

"I didn't want to resort to that, but I guess I have too."

"Now you are talking. Good luck."

It wasn't as easy as Morris suggested. These folks were serious, afraid of their own shadow or giving out information about other people.

One Sunday morning he went to the coffee shop that old Mr. Frarano frequented on his return visits to indulge in his espresso. Two old guys sitting with cappuccinos waved him over. "*Eh! Paesan!* Are you visiting here?" They waved him over. That was all he wanted. Smiling, he joined them.

The place was empty except for those two old guys who were bored and looking for any stimulation. Luckily for Marc Diez it was Fausto Tarantano. Now old and frail, he had survived two strokes with only some speech impediment. They got acquainted over coffee. The other old man was a retired policeman named Vincent who was hard of hearing. Marc scratched his head. *I got myself two crazies here. No wonder they waved me over. No one else wants to put up with them.*

Patiently he conversed with them the best he could. He asked some questions and to his surprise Fausto Tarantano, despite his speech impediment, started talking without fear. He provided some interesting information. Marc's ears perked up. Tarantano related the story he had brought to Anthony Taverna. They had saved the professor and his daughter from the clutches of Francesca's husband. So many years had passed. Tarantano had had near death experiences, but he was no longer fearful of those mobsters. A lot of them had died. He still felt proud of himself having secretly warned Anthony Taverna of his corrupt brother-in-law. Yes, he had refused the take part in Frarano's dirty work. Too bad Taverna hadn't been able to save his sister, Francesca.

Marc, couldn't believe this stroke of luck. He got the entire background story from those two old guys. The old, retired policeman, deaf as he was, knew enough to finish the story. Marc felt good, but there was more work to do. He decided a stop over to London to research more. Investigation there was much easier because there was no language barrier.

He got history on Andrew Robertson but not much of his daughter. They confirmed he had a daughter; her biological mother was Francesca Taverna who had been previously married to Frarano. She had been killed in a tragic accident. He quickly wrapped up his information and headed back to New York on the first flight. As soon as he got in, he dialed Morris Robertson's number. "Hello my friend."

"Marc, about time. What information have you got?"

"I got all the information you need. Can we meet tomorrow night?"

"I have an engagement, but I can get out of it."

"See you at seven, at the Matador on 28th St." He ended the call. He couldn't wait to relate his information to Morris. Now he needed a good sleep. His brain had to be at his best to relate all the findings.

Chapter Forty Eight

As anxious as Marc was to relate, Morris was even more to hear. A strange feeling had come over him. It had made him uneasy all day. He was sitting at a secluded corner table waiting for Marc Diez when he finally spotted him. The maître'd was leading Marc in his direction.

"Well, how is the guy who travelled the world at my expense?"

"You know I had to detour to London to get all the information you needed. That detour payed off."

"I heard you had gone to England. Your secretary mentioned it when I called to check on what was going on with you."

"You wouldn't believe it. At first, I was disheartened chasing dead ends. Those Sicilians don't talk. They are tight lipped about anybody else's business."

"Didn't you say you found out more than you bargained for?"

"Luckily I did. That's why I detoured to London England."

"Interesting! Tell me."

"Let's order a drink first. We need all night. It's a shocking story but your Gracy Fernandez does comes from good stock."

"Okay! Move on. Is she worth a lot of money like Ingrid thinks?"

"Forget the money. Morris, can you change your focus sometimes?" Marc was annoyed. "I am more interested in the stories, the happenings, and the discoveries. There is so much more than just money."

"Okay, have it your way but share your findings quickly." Morris didn't want to express what he was really thinking. *Yeah! Detour to England on my expense.*

"It wasn't easy I will tell you, but it paid off. These two old guys in Palermo, almost on their last breaths filled me in. One of them was actually involved."

"Marc, get to the point."

"You are not going to believe this. Your subject is the fruit of a love affair. Her mother was a mobster's wife who fell in love with this English professor. I don't have to tell you her fate. She got killed and a price was put on the Englishman's head by her husband. Apparently he survived to look after their child. The bad guys are all dead now. One is still in jail. When the coast was clear, the professor and daughter returned to Sicily. She had been left a fortune by her mother. The Frarano boys, the mother's children from the marriage, embraced her lovingly. Apparently, the senior Frarano was a tyrant who had ordered their mother killed. The old Frarano had dominated the family and his corruption almost ruined them. There you have it."

Morris was astonished. Something told him there was more to the story that Marc still didn't understand fully.

"Marc, where in England did the professor live?"

"I was told he lived in London. He taught at the university. He was a brilliant literary scholar."

Morris wasn't sure if he should say something or keep it to himself.

He listened hard to what Marc had to report. He asked him to put everything in writing and drop it at his office the next day. "Marc you must be tired and so am I. Let's talk further once I review your findings. We both had a busy day."

They parted for the evening. Morris couldn't wait to be alone to put his thoughts together. They had the same last name. A flashback to his youth with his father replayed in his memory. They were always short of money. The mother and father bickered about their financial misery. Ian, their father, used his brother as an excuse. "I can't help it. That son of a bitch brother of mine has taken my portion of the inheritance from my parents." He resented his brother immensely. He hated his parents also. The older brother, Andrew, was their favorite. They punished Ian often.

Could Andrew be his uncle who was so hated by his father? Could it be possible that this Gracy Fernandez was his uncle's daughter? All these questions were going through his mind. His father, Ian Robertson, never accomplished anything. He left London and came to America where he continued without really finding the American dream. He had always said that his parents and his brother were his enemies. He hadn't even gone to their funerals. His father, obsessed with hatred, couldn't even recognize that his parents and his brother were not the culprits.

Morris had visited them once in his childhood. He barely remembered his grandparents. They were humble folks who worked earnestly for their meager salaries. Morris remembered his father coming home drunk on pay day. He was an alcoholic. Most of his wages were spent at the bars or in liquor stores. Their mother had no money for groceries or to pay the bills. His life had been one hell of a mess until Morris was old enough to find jobs to support himself. That is when he strove to ensure that he never lacked what life offered. As for his brother, he didn't have the same drive. It was his prerogative.

He would look deeper into this revelation. *Life's surprises are amazing sometimes. Could it be that this Gracy woman was an estranged relative?*

He got in touch with Ingrid the next day. "Hello Ingrid, how are you these days?"

"How do you expect me to be? I haven't heard from you. Since

I couldn't count on any help from you, I decided to keep company with your brother. He might be more helpful."

"Ingrid, don't pout. How about lunch today? My treat."

"No thanks, I have a previous commitment."

"Ok! How about dinner? Our usual place."

"That's possible. What time? Seven usually works for me."

"Let's meet at Lizard's. A treat for us both. Italian food."

It was a stellar evening. The moon was shining splendidly in the brightness of many stars. The air was calm. Morris thought that if he was lucky Ingrid would invite him over to spend the night. She had been perturbed with him lately. He needed to be careful and choose his words. He could find out some more about Mrs. Fernandez from Ingrid. She must have known something more that hadn't been told. Maybe the shared name was just coincidence.

A secluded section of the restaurant was reserved. Ingrid arrived stunning as usual with a lovely V-neck black dress that showed her cleavage. A delicate gold chain with matching earrings enhanced her look. She was never one to overdo with jewelry. She always felt it would take away from her own beauty. Morris, gallant as usual ordered Merlot with Ingrid's agreement. "I have a craving for osso buco and fresh home-made pasta with tomato salsa. I feel like going Italian tonight, Morris. What do you say?"

"Perfect!" He was going to use this time over dinner to quiz her on her Italians associates.

The server poured the wine. Morris lifted his glass and cheered, "To our Italian friends Ingrid. They know how to create delicious meals."

"I can agree to that. I have been missing it more and more, since Daniele is gone."

"Ingrid forgive me for inquiring. I don't mean to invade. You never told me much about the relationship with Gracy Fernandez and the Frarano boys."

"Relationship? Are you serious? Daniele and Diego adored her. Diego values his sister more than his life. Now that she has those two children, don't even mention it. She is pregnant again, I am told. If I'm looking for Diego, guess where he spends most of his free time- at his sister's, adoring those children."

"It sounds like a wonderful family. Is she an adopted sister?" He kept encouraging her to drink and talk more.

"The brothers were a little evasive about her. They never wanted to answer me straight. I dug up some information here and there, listening in sometimes. She is their half-sister."

"How is that?"

"Morris are you pretending to be dumb?" She took another sip of red wine.

"They were born by the same mother and a different father"

"Really! How did that come about?"

"You guess."

"How can I guess? I've heard that single southern Italian girls don't engage in liaisons. It's a strict society, so I would assume married women have to follow the same rules, even more so."

"Apparently it happened. There is more to the story that I wasn't told. She is well educated in English. I am told her father was an English professor." Morris scratched his head.

"Her maiden name is Robertson like yours, you know."

"So, I am hearing."

"I mentioned it to your brother. He shook it off saying Robertson is a common name"

"Yes, so I am told. It is intriguing. I would like to know more about her. How can I find out?"

"I cannot help you with that. She isn't my favorite person. Besides you certainly didn't help me with contesting the will."

"Ingrid all the lawyers I talked to laughed at me. Asking them to review your situation was an embarrassment professionally."

"Morris, I will find my own way. Now should you want to know more about your Mrs. Fernandez, you have to look elsewhere. I suggest you try Mr. Alvaro Fernandez."

"I would love to meet them."

"You have to find your own way." Ingrid's short fuse was escalating. Morris grabbed her hand caressing it.

"Let's change the subject. Why don't we spend the night together?"

"No, we can't. I have an early morning commitment. I need a good night rest."

They parted somewhat amicably. Morris was disappointed. He knew Ingrid was playing games. His intuition bugged him more and more. He wasn't going to give up. Ingrid's lack of cooperation wasn't going to stop him. He would meet Mrs. Fernandez, one way or another.

The next morning, he instructed his secretary to place a call to Diego Frarano's office. An appointment was set up. Morris Robertson was going to inquire about legal advice regarding his own affairs. At the same time, it would open contact with the people of interest. Luck was on his side. Diego received him respectfully. Diego asked. "Now that we are on the subject of financial investments, I would like to open an education fund for my niece and nephew. My sister is expecting a third and in good time I shall take care of that child also."

"Mr. Frarano, I would be more than happy to take care of that for you. There are some good programs available. I can get back to you with the information. You might also want to have your sister present since it's for her children." Morris' opportunities were opening up. He wasn't going to miss the chance.

"Thank-you Mr. Robertson, I will check with my sister. We could meet next week sometime." Morris was all smiles on his way out.

***

These days Gracy's body wasn't responding well. Her pregnancy had rendered her restless and tired because of the sleepless nights. During the day her legs were swelling. Lately, she had stopped taking the children to the park. Gloria, the nanny, had taken over the responsibility for their afternoon walk and the trips to the playground they enjoyed so much. Gloria knew how to pacify them if they were misbehaving or ill tempered. Gracy needed some quietness and rest. Alvaro had been getting home later more and more these days. It was high season and the hotels were fully booked up. Even with Leonello taking most of the responsibilities, Alvaro's demands seemed endless, so he was telling his pregnant wife.

Gracy was totally absorbed with her two adorable children and the baby's arrival. She was in another world these days. This second pregnancy had been more difficult.

Alvaro loved his children. At the same time some resentment was brooding in him. He felt neglected by his wife sometimes. Many times, he had attended functions on his own. Gracy was so possessive of her babies that relying on the nanny wasn't her idea of being a good mother. Often, they argued about that and other matters. He wanted her at his side. Gracy was getting tired of their social life. Home with her beloved children was preferable so almost all the socializing had been curtailed. Alvaro, often resentful, had been giving her the silent treatment. Their loving relationship was changing dramatically.

Diego stopped by every day to amuse himself with the children.

This evening he had come by as usual. "Sis, I would like you to come to my office next week. I need to open up an education fund for the children. I want you to meet this fellow who I'm thinking of hiring to take care of it. We will decide together what is best for them."

"I don't feel like going anywhere these days. I find in the last stage of my pregnancy that the heat and humidity make me feel uncomfortable. However, if it's important for the children, I will make an effort."

"Should I ask Alvaro to attend?" Diego asked

"It's your money Diego. I don't think it's necessary." Gracy responded.

Diego had noticed some coldness lately between them. He hadn't wanted to interfere or ask questions. It bothered him though.

"Gracy, are you guys getting along? I want you to pay attention to your husband. He doesn't seem as happy as he used to be."

"Diego, I am content with my family, our children. I love him dearly. He should be as happy as I am."

Diego shrugged his shoulders. He was no authority on marriage.

He gave her a hug and kissed her on the cheek. "See you in my office on Monday."

Chapter Forty Nine

Gracy hated to leave her adorable Francesca and Andrew. They usually pulled on each side of her skirt when she was ready to leave. Tears were spilled easily; Francesca wouldn't let go and soon Andrew would join in. This was the scenario every time they parted. This is why she preferred to stay home with them. Her heart easily gave in.

Gloria was good. She would entice them with toys, games and reading story books. Gracy, in her love for their children, may have been too soft-hearted. This morning was no different than any other time when she was required to attend functions or affairs of any sort. Alvaro had been supportive at first; lately, he was often annoyed. He felt there had to be limitations on Gracy's part to coddling the children. He had pointed this out to her more than once. "Gracy! I love the children as much as you do. Gloria is here to help and take over when she is needed. You also have obligations toward me. I need you with me elsewhere."

Gracy didn't understand. Any other obligations weren't as important as her two precious children. She was pregnant and feeling very big, so she was already sensitive to criticism. Alvaro should understand. A turbulent cloud continued to hover over their relationship. Alvaro wasn't as attentive as he should be. Slowly he was turning to drinking to calm his anxieties. It soothed him for a short time. He had been fighting to find the calmness needed to reason with his wife. Lately he wasn't looking forward going home.

***

Monday morning, as promised, Gracy walked into Diego's office to meet Mr. Morris Robertson the financial broker. Diego introduced him. They shook hands, pleasantly. "It's great meeting you Mrs. Fernandez."

"Likewise. How do you do Mr. Robertson?"

Gracy hesitated. "I must say we have something in common! My maiden name is Robertson."

He looked at her for a split second before he continued. "Is that right? Where are you from originally?"

"England, my dad was English from London. I was born in London."

There it was. All the questions answered. "Oh! How nice, so was my dad. He came from England. London also, as a matter of fact. He emigrated in his early twenties. You never know. We could be related."

They both laughed. Gracy echoed his thought. "Yes, you never know. Anything was possible in those days."

Diego interrupted "You two should sort that out sometime. For now, let's see what we can do today to set up something appropriate for the twins and the new baby as well."

"We open an account in each of the children's name with the contributor in trust. It would be also advisable to add the mother's name, as the beneficiary for distribution. We can secure the funds on a long-term investment for a better return. As for the monthly contribution, we can automatically withdraw from your personal checking account or whatever account you might prefer Mr. Frarano."

"We have an account set up for distribution to charities, medical research and other foundations. I will discuss it with our accountant of course and he will advise accordingly."

"This account should be set up exclusively as an education saving plan.

You, Mr. Frarano, would be the subscriber appointed beneficiary for the children. The subscriber can be appointed in the will. The investment options vary from ultra conservative to very aggressive.

The decision is up to the subscriber. Generally, the funds are paid out for the expenses related to the post-secondary education of the beneficiary."

"That sounds like it will suit the needs of the children." Diego and Gracy were pleased with the potential plan.

"What about Mr. Fernandez? Would you like me to add his name to the accounts for security provision in case of Mrs. Fernandez's incapability or demise?"

Diego's gaze was fixed on Gracy for her response.

"Let me think about it. My brother would be my first choice. I will bring it up with my husband and let you know."

Diego knew how much his sister totally trusted and relied on him.

He was also disappointed with Gracy's hesitation at the mention of her husband. Perturbing questions ran through his brain. *What was happening with Gracy lately? Was her relationship with Alvaro, dwindling away, turning sour? Was her marriage in trouble and what would happen with the children?* Diego had grown up through a turbulent marriage. It had left such a scar on his soul. He didn't trust the promises of eternal love in lasting relationships. He had been highly desired by female companions but he was glad to remain uncommitted. Despite his own feelings for himself, he knew Alvaro and Gracy were perfect for each other; where were they now going wrong?

Morris broke his spell. "I will set up the papers Mr. Frarano. You let me know the opening amount and the monthly contribution. Mrs. Fernandez, please get back to me regarding your husband. We must meet again. We will finalize the signatures and it will all be taken care of."

Morris Robertson, wanted to meet them as frequently as possible.

A relationship with these people was important to him. "Mr. Frarano, if I can assist you in any other investments, I would be glad to." He turned smiling to Gracy. "You also Mrs. Fernandez. If you have any questions, you can reach me anytime. I promise you to look into our ancestry should we be by chance related." They laughed at the mention of the coincidence and left.

Diego wanted to question his sister about her marriage. He wasn't sure.

Instead, he decided to pay an unexpected visit to Alvaro at the office.

On his arrival at the Hyatt, the secretary was obliging. "Good morning Clare, I would like to see Alvaro if he is available." Reluctantly she answered. "He is Mr. Frarano. He has someone with him right now. I am not sure if I can." Before she could continue, he walked forward toward the door. "Not to worry. He will be happy to see me."

Diego knocked and opened the door at the same time. There was Ingrid sitting on his lap and kissing him. Diego collected himself from his shock and slowly closed the door, pulling it and himself quietly away. He turned to Clare. "I changed my mind. I will be back later don't bother telling him I was here or anything."

The two in their passionate embrace didn't even hear the door or any other disturbance. Diego walked through the lobby gravely perturbed. He didn't know what action to take or which direction to go. His mind raced with disquieting thoughts. *Ingrid's wicked machinations were relentless and far reaching. His brother had been a victim of her maneuvers. Now Alvaro was her prey, at the expense of both Gracy and the children's. He needed to protect his sister and her children. Having seen the Ingrid and Alvaro together, the big question was what should he do next?*

Chapter Fifty

Gracy was aware that her husband had been distancing himself from her more and more. His cold behaviour and resentment of her was evident. When she shared her problems, he seemed totally removed, offering no sympathy. At this time, she was in the late stage of her pregnancy. The misty, humid air of July had rendered her powerless and tired. Her body didn't allow her to function as well as she should have. Francesca and Andrew were two vivacious children. Her undivided attention to them meant that at the end of the day she was exhausted.

She expected Alvaro to come home at a decent time and assume his role with the children. Gracy, as kind as she was, begrudged her husband's change of personality. She had attributed his work stress to her absence from the workplace. Now he had the help he needed with Leonello and the boys. He had no excuse for his lack of sympathy. He had no excuse for not spending more quality time with the children. To her disbelief, their love had turned into turbulent arguments and bickering. Tonight, once more, Alvaro arrived home late and in a resentful mood. Gracy tried to ignore his coldness with a cheerful greeting. "*Mi amor, que pasa?*" She lifted herself up on her feet and reached up to kiss him on his lips. He brushed her away. She had not been able to attend few functions that had taken place lately. Gracy figured that he was still brooding over that and resenting her.

***

As time passed, with no doubt, Alvaro's tender feelings toward Gracy were changing. He wasn't looking forward to coming home as he used too. He didn't like the way his marriage was turning out. In some lucid moments he reasoned with himself about his fault in creating the situation and other times he was totally unreasonable and saw her as the sole source of the conflict. *I understand her dedication to the children. She is admirable as a devoted mother. But what about her duty as a wife? I need her also. Our relationship has lost its passion. It isn't what it used to be anymore.* He was selfish and confused. Ingrid's scheming was affecting him. Her manipulation of his physical desires and his feelings of being neglected had him making foolish choices. What could he do? Ingrid made him feel so good when his wife wouldn't. He wasn't the only one who was failing the marriage.

Ingrid, of course, was smiling over her progress in using Alvaro's low morale to her advantage. She had not given up on her vengeful vendetta. Morris' refusal to help her had reinforced her resolve. "That Sicilian girl is going to pay one way or another. She told her confidante Walter "I will get back whatever belongs to me."

"Ingrid, how do you intend to do that? The law is involved. You need a lawyer?"

"I have other plans. You are going to help me Walter, my boy." She pulled him to her and pressed her lips on his. He liked her attention since he wasn't too popular with women. As simple as he was and as much as he craved her attention, he hoped he wouldn't have to pay her back by being involved in her vendetta.

Ingrid had gotten into the habit of dropping in on Alvaro every morning with two cups of coffee in her hand and her charm turned on. Her smooth talk was primed to praise him. "Alvaro, I know you are a busy man. I feel so encouraged when I show you my plans. Your stamp of approval means so much to me. It's my tonic for the day and only then I can perform to the best of my ability."

Her compliments boosted Alvaro's morale. "I feel honored," smiling he would put an arm on her shoulder. Both egos were boosted. Ingrid smiled to herself. *It's working in my favour.* She would continue rubbing Alvaro's back. "Alvaro, I always admired you, and your professionalism."

"Likewise Ingrid. You are clever at what you do."

"Oh my dear friend, your compliments give me energy especially in the morning." She utilized every opportunity to praise Alvaro. She was like a bird of prey. She had been secretly checking his schedule and watching his every move for months. When Alvaro looked troubled or morally down it was a chance to caress him. Her soothing hands would be all over him, changing his gloom and uplifting more than his spirits. At first he reminded her. "Ingrid, I am a married man don't forget."

She would ignore his protest. She was on a mission to turn the course of her life in a direction that could only go to the top. Since that princess' arrival, her life had turned downward in both popularity and financially. Now with Daniele gone, even her future had been compromised through the meager inheritance. However, her plan looked encouraging, Alvaro had been responding lately to her affection. She had treated him to a few peaceful and romantic evenings at her place. He had been in no hurry to leave to return to his pregnant wife and children.

This morning after leaving Alvaro she detoured to Walter. Now she needed to sweet talk to him. Although she found him repulsive, her pretense would fool him also. "Walter, good morning!" She reached to kiss him caringly.

"How are things going with you?"

"It's been pretty quiet. No, complaints, how about you?"

"I could use some company. How about dinner tonight? How is my place after work?"

"I could use a good dinner. Love to, what time?"

"Seven thirty or so. All set, see you then. I must go now." She gave him a big hug even though she found his big belly revolting. Ingrid knew he loved his food more than anything, otherwise he wouldn't be so overweight.

"I'll bring the wine." He shouted as she hurried away.

Leonello, who was supervising that morning, observed that the staff in all different directions were hard at work resolving issues. He noticed Ingrid fluttering like a lost butterfly. He didn't like it. He questioned himself. *Should I discuss her lateness with Mr. Fernandez, or mention it to Diego Frarano?* He beeped Romero instead. "Romero, do me a favour, keep an eye open on this Ingrid Klein. Her activities seem suspicious."

"Consider it done my friend."

***

At home Mrs. Gracy Fernandez's emotions had reached the boiling point. Alvaro had gotten into the habit of showing up home later and later. His emotional support for her and the children had changed immensely. She had been having sleepless nights since Alvaro was returning at all hours of the night. She had resorted to making excuses and apologies to Gloria. Lately, she hadn't been accompanying her to the park. The late afternoon outings with the rambunctious. Francesca and Andrew were challenging. Andrew was a wanderer, always wanting to explore anew. Their energy level was immeasurable. One person alone couldn't keep up. Gloria, as clever as she was with recurring problems, had not completely managed Andrew's misbehaviour.

The nanny had been instructed by Mr. Fernandez to have the children wait for him before putting them to bed. After many nights of long waits, she would excuse herself. "Mrs. Fernandez, I'm sorry. I cannot keep the children awake any longer waiting for their daddy. They must go to sleep."

"Yes of course Gloria, they must. You have done your duty. Go take a rest. I will say the evening prayer with them."

Afterwards she would retreat to her room and have a good cry.

This evening her labour pains were relentless and it seemed the baby would be arriving sooner than expected. Alvaro wasn't home, Gracy and Gloria's attempts to find him were futile. Diego was called to their rescue. Gloria remained at home looking after the children.

Their third baby Sabrina was lifted in her mom's arms with Diego sharing her tears of sorrow and joy. She didn't want to relate her suffering lately to Diego. She did not want to upset him. "Alvaro must be somewhere unavoidably detained. We couldn't get in touch with him. This baby was in such a hurry that she picked her own due date."

He hugged lovingly. "Sis, let's be grateful that everything went well. We have another beautiful healthy baby girl. Congratulations."

"We have named her after Alvaro's mom. Sabrina Fabiana Fernandez."

"It sounds great Sis."

They both knew Gracy was making excuses for her husband although neither said it. That's why they were both grateful for the distraction of the healthy baby the nurse brought to them.

***

Gracy was not aware that Diego was on the same emotional wavelength that she was. He also had been having sleepless nights since discovering his brother-in-law in a compromising position with a woman who was not his wife. *I don't want to upset my sister. I need to handle this matter man to man and stop this insanity that has taken over Alvaro.* The next morning Diego Frarano, much preoccupied, was sitting at his desk undecided on what action to take. He couldn't remove the vision of Alvaro and Ingrid from his mind. Their liaison had taken away all trust and admiration he had for his brother-in-law. It needed to be addressed one way or another, regardless of the consequences for Mr. Fernandez.

Gina Iafrate

Chapter Fifty One

While Diego was despairing of the confrontation that needed to take place in New York, Morris Robertson in Washington was sitting in his glamorous office hard at work. The puzzle of Gracy Robertson from London was not yet solved. This morning he was on the phone talking to Marc Diez.

"Good morning Morris. I got good news for you."

"I am listening."

"Yes, Gracy Robertson is the daughter of Andrew Roberson. Her mother, Francesca Taverna was married to Frarano. She is Gracy's biological mother. You are definitely related."

"Is that so? I had that strange feeling that something tied us together somehow."

"I have all the details in writing. I will deliver it to you with my invoice."

Morris hung up the phone. This verification of his suspicions was a game changer. *How will I approach this matter from here on?*

***

Ingrid's distorted mind had fuelled her desperate plans. Over time, she had taken total control of Alvaro by spiking his drinks that she prepared for him during their clandestine evenings. He spent the intimate evenings with her totally under her spell. It was satisfying for Ingrid to make love to the man belonging to the woman she resented. She was smiling these days. Walter also jumped to her service. All she had to do was cook a good homemade meal and serve a few drinks; he could be manipulated as she desired. The only stumbling block was those lousy Sicilian guys Gracy had brought around. *That Leonello Dante stares me up and down. He doesn't like me. I don't like him or his two buddies. They are that bitch's prodigies, and they are trouble. I wish I still had the power to have them all fired.*

She had tried turning Alvaro against them. He had simply responded. "Leonello Dante, Romero Placido, Gianni Cecco are untouchable according to my wife and my brother- in law. They have a long history together. They are her former students you know, from Agrigento and both Diego and Gracy feel they are the most precious human beings on this earth."

"Big deal! You Alvaro, what do you think of them? It doesn't mean they are superior to you my dearest?"

"Ingrid, Diego and my wife consider them family because they are paesani from the same place. They are at our home for dinner and for every family celebration. My wife didn't allow any one from my side of the family to be godparents to the children. Leonello was nominated for that role. As the godfather he plays a significant role. Should anything happen to us or should Andrew ever be in need, Leonello will act as a surrogate father. That tells you how untouchable he and his friends are."

"God help me." Ingrid rolled her eyes in frustration.

Now I have to worry about those guys impeding my vendetta against Gracy. "So those guys are totally on her side, supporting her every wish."

"Ingrid, I don't have to tell you. They adore my wife and my children. I must admit that at first I thought it was because they all had eyes for my wife, especially Leonello. He got over it though as he matured."

"Are you so sure Alvaro? Maybe she is having a fling with him."

"Absolutely not! My wife is the most honest and loyal person you could ever meet. She is older than he is and she would never be unfaithful with anyone, let alone a former student. She's not like us"

Despite the effects of the spiked drink, Alvaro was still capable of speaking the truth about his admirable wife. Ingrid refilled his glass of merlot. Alvaro Fernandez didn't know that while he was violating the sacred bonds of his marriage in a drugged haze, his devoted Gracy was delivering his third child without his support.

***

Walter anxiously glanced at his watch all day. He was looking forward to spending an evening with Ingrid. His brother Morris was anxious as well; he had requested a meeting with Mrs. Gracy Fernandez. It was some months since her third child had been born, so he used the education fund as an excuse to see her. She had agreed to meet him for lunch. Gracy, thinking it was simply regarding the education fund for the children, asked "Mr. Robertson have you checked with my brother if he is available?"

"No! I haven't. We can consult with him later. I would like to see you to discuss another matter. See you at noon at La Rotonda."

Morris didn't want to go in details on the phone. His main interest was Gracy herself. Besides the news of family ties, he was eager to become her broker. He hoped that, with the announcement of being related, she would trust him more in investing her fortune.

356

Chapter Fifty Two

As much as Gracy, didn't mind meeting Morris Robertson, she wished Diego could be there also. It would have given her a greater sense of security since he was one of the most highly sought after lawyers in New York. After all, they were dealing with a fair amount of money and his experience with the law and finances would help in decision making.

Morris with his best manners greeted her courteously. "Hello, Mrs. Fernandez. How are you?"

"Wonderful! Thank you. Sorry I am a bit late. It's always a chore leaving my children."

"Please, no apologies. I understand. I must say I am delighted you could meet me on such a short notice."

"Mr. Robertson, I never asked before. Do you have children?"

"Please call me Morris. As to your question, unfortunately or fortunately- no I do not. My marriages didn't last long. Who knows what the future brings?"

"I am sure when the right time comes, everything will work out in your favour."

"Thank you for your kind wishes. I am sure you have a lovely family."

"Yes, I must say we are blessed with three beautiful healthy children. They are my life."

"Talking about family. I know we have limited time here today. I will try to be brief. You will not believe what I have discovered."

Gracy's curiosity sparked. "We kidded about our last names being a common one. Well, after all this time, I have finally found traces of my side of the family. You are my cousin."

Gracy's blood jolted through her body. "What! Morris are you sure?"

"As sure as I am sitting here looking at a blood related member of my family from London England."

"You aren't joking with me, are you?"

"No, I am not. I have all the official proof here in writing!"

He pulled out a large white legal envelope. "It is all here."

Gracy gave a quick glance at the papers. There it was in black and white. "How did you get all this information?"

"It wasn't easy and it has cost me. I must say it's been worth it."

"My dear God! I don't believe this revelation. Morris, I begged my dad many times to tell me about his side of the family. He would never talk about them. All I was told of my grandparents was that they died when he was younger. I never met them. He mentioned a brother with some family in America only once. He told me I didn't need to know or want to know them. He said I was the luckiest girl with my Italian family and to stick with them only. All my life I have wondered about his family. My dad and I lived alone for years. I was always told about the Palermo family. We never lost touch with my Sicilian family. Later, my brothers came into my world. They have given love and support to my life." She broke down in tears when Daniele surfaced in her heart. Morris took her hands rubbing them gently.

"Gracy, you don't mind if I call you Gracy? I can tell you about our side of the family here. I think my dad was estranged from his family. I hardly remember my grandparents. We rarely visited. I do remember that Dad resented his brother. They never communicated. Then when he got a letter that his parents died, he burned it into the fireplace. He never attended their funeral. When he was drunk, he bitched about his brother inheriting his money and the parents flat in London. Yet, after all the secrets, the resentment, the separation and the lost time, here you are. It's fate that we should meet."

"I don't know what to say. All I have known is my dad. He loved me immensely and took care of me. As you probably found out, I was taken from my mother's womb. She died at my birth and I have never known my mother. Because of the threats on our lives, my father kept us cloistered and on the move. One of those moves brought us to safety and my Italian family. Now this move to America has brought me to you. As you say, here we are. I don't know what my father would have made of this reunion but I say welcome to my world cousin." They hugged each other as blood relatives.

She encouraged him to tell her more about his family. Morris seemed reluctant. "I am not too proud of my family. My mother was Irish, a humble woman. My dad wasn't a good provider. They had four children to feed and not enough money to go around. They argued a lot. Dad, I guess, blamed everyone else except himself. As for us children growing up, it wasn't pleasant. I managed to put myself through school. I am proud of that. Here I am today with a degree in Finance, no thanks to my father. It was hard for all of us. My brother Walter is lucky to be employed right now in one of your companies. He had a hard time holding on to jobs before because his absenteeism, but he has been holding on to this job for some time."

"You don't mean our security fellow. I have met him briefly. He is usually on duty at the lobby of the Hyatt Regency. Dear Lord! It is a small world." She shook her head in disbelief. "He is a friend of Ingrid Klein I was told."

"Yes, she got him the job. We went to high school with Ingrid "

Morris continued "One older sister is married out of town. The other is divorced, struggling with two or three jobs to feed her children. I am ashamed to admit but we are not a close family."

Morris' feelings, influenced by Gracy's gentle sincerity and joy, were transforming. He felt tender and more loving. What had begun as a meeting to manipulate on his part had become a celebration on both their parts. Both of them were so overcome with their discovery that they forgot to eat. Morris really liked Gracy. She was an admirable human being. He was mortified about pursuing her only for his gain. Before they parted Gracy said. "You should join us for dinner at my home sometime. Yes, we will make a date for you to come and meet my husband and my children. Maybe, someday, I will be able to meet the rest of the Robertson family."

"That would be nice. I would love to join you." They hugged and parted like family.

Gracy couldn't wait to get home. Alvaro had promised to be home tonight. Diego had called Gracy that morning to say he would come by also. She was elated on her return home. She couldn't wait to relate her new discovery to them.

Gracy did not know how troubled Diego was. His solemn duty was to straighten up his brother-in-law. He wasn't going to tolerate the nonsense that Alvaro had been engaging in lately. He needed to put an end to it immediately. His absence at the birth of his new baby was unacceptable. *Where in hell had he been?* Diego had his suspicions. His sister was too precious and self-sacrificing to deserve any mistreatment, infidelity or deceit. His attempts to set a meeting with Alvaro hadn't materialized yet. He needed the right opportunity.

The evening at the Fernandez home was glorious. Gracy loved having her favorite people around her supper table. The children were well behaved with daddy sharing their meal tonight. Gracy had promised them a bedtime story. The twins could choose between the two adults. Mommy would help the nanny with the baby. Afterwards, Gracy would encourage Gloria to go rest. The three of them could retreat into the living room for an after-dinner drink and dessert.

Alvaro was in agreement and cooperative with young Andrew pulling on his arm. Diego turned to Francesca. "Are you ready Missy? It's you and me." The children uplifted his spirits always. He loved them dearly. Finally, all had quieted down. Alvaro and Diego were sitting comfortably waiting for Gracy to return. She was cheerful tonight because she had her dearest close to her. She came into the room carrying a tray of goodies in her hands. Alvaro jumped up to her aid. Diego watched and wondered. *Should I spoil this night for my sister or take the matter with my brother-in-law to him only, man to man.* He took a deep breath and took a sip of the brandy that Gracy handed him.

"Diego hold on. We have something to cheer here tonight." She lifted her glass. "I have an announcement to make."

"*Mi amor,* you are keeping us in suspense! Come on. You are not pregnant again?"

"Alvaro, you haven't referred to me as 'mi amor' for a long time.

It is good to hear it now. It is also good to have you home on time for a change. No! I am not pregnant again. We will discuss that privately. Diego isn't interested in our intimate life. I have other surprising news."

"Gracy, you are behaving exactly like mom used to. Come on what it is?" Diego asked.

"I had a meeting with that Morris Robertson today. He asked me to lunch. I was surprised when he said it was not necessary for you, Diego, to be there. At first, I questioned it but after our conversation I understood why he wanted privacy. He brought official papers but not for the education fund. They were birth, immigration and citizenship documents that prove we are related! His family are the lost relatives in

America that my dad never talked about. He ignored my pleas over the years telling me that I didn't need to know them and now here they are. I have four cousins. One works for us. He is that security guy walking the lobby at the Hyatt Hotel. Can you believe it?"

"Gracy, are you sure? How did it all come about?"

"It's a long story but all the research has been verified. He hired an undercover investigator. He is a clever fellow that Morris Robertson."

"I am told he is a clever man- a hard worker, successful and cautious at the same time. My clients vouch for him and his financial magic with their excellent returns. This is why we chose him for the education fund we set up." Diego commented.

"So there Alvaro, mi amor. It's great to finally discover I do have some family on my dad's side. I questioned it all my growing years.

My dad denied it. After talking to Morris, I understand."

They had been listening attentively. Diego didn't want to spoil Gracy's happiness with a discussion about or with Alvaro. He decided to keep his mouth shut. *I will handle it my way later.* When it was time for him to leave, he asked Alvaro "I would like to meet with you tomorrow. Are you in town?"

"I should be, unless something unexpected happens, or my secretary has booked me without my knowledge. I can always pass any work on to Leonello. What time would you like to meet?"

"I will be in court in the morning. By 1:00 pm. I should be fine."

"Great, we will meet for lunch at our country club."

"Fine, see you tomorrow."

Diego tried to contain his feelings. He hoped to remain calm and handle the matter tomorrow in a gentlemanly manner.

It was hard. Anyone who hurt Diego's family, even if they were family like Alvaro, had lost his respect and would not be in good stead with him.

364

Chapter Fifty Three

Ingrid had also been hard at work on her mission of vengeance. She had been feeling victorious with Alvaro under her spell. He had been spending a lot of time with her. She smiled to herself. *Eat your heart out Miss Priss from Sicily*. Now she needed Walter to take action for her. The only way to him these days was through his stomach. Tonight, they were at her place and Ingrid had ordered a luscious meal. Walter was all smiles. The aroma of the roast warming in the oven was mouth-watering. All through his life, he had never been too popular. Friends were few and far between. That was why any invitation from Ingrid meant so much to him.

Ingrid made sure he was well fed. The bottle of merlot was almost empty. She needed him relaxed to drill her message into his brain. After dinner she grabbed his hand and pulled him away from the table. "Let's relax on the sofa, Walter. Yes, put your feet up. The evening is ours."

Walter was in heaven. He hoped the evening would last forever. Then Ingrid started with her requests. "Walter, I need you to help me."

"Ingrid, you are on top of the world how can I help you."

"You are the only one. You know I have been cheated of my inheritance. I lived with Daniele ten years. The Sicilian arrived and took over everyone including Daniele's fortune. I slaved all these years creating beauty for them. Here I am left to live in New York with only the leftovers."

"What can I do for you? How can I help you with that part? You don't need me. You need a lawyer I told you."

"No, no lawyer. I am going to handle it my way. I need you."

"I don't understand."

"You will once I instruct you. I thought your big shot brother could help but he is only after his own gain. But you Walter are kinder; this is why I love you. I will tell you what I need from you." Walter was listening while she was rubbing his back.

"You told me your brother had connections. I would like you to get in touch with whoever they are. You need to make the arrangements and if you do, I will share the gain with you."

"Ingrid, I don't know what your plan is. I am just a poor security guy. I don't know what connections you think I have."

"Walter, you can help me. My plan is for you to get in touch with those guys and I know you know who I mean when I say those guys. Mrs. Fernandez is going to be sorry for what she did to me. I am told by her own husband that those precious children of hers are her life. My plan is shockingly simple. We will kidnap one or two of them, for ransom of course. I am told she is so dedicated to them that she won't even trust the nanny to do her duties. Her husband tells me that lately she has relented a little to attend her third born. The nanny goes to the park with them every afternoon alone. I am told the boy is a wanderer. It should be easy to snatch him away. These guys you hire will know what to do. We will not hurt the boy. Once we got the ransom, I will share some with you. But you need to handle the situation carefully my dearest."

"Ingrid, I have never done such thing before. That is a big job." He protested.

"Walter, you don't have to do anything. Just find someone to carry it out."

Walter was torn between refusing and pleasing her. Ingrid was not going to relent. "Promise me you will do this. You will be highly rewarded and not just with money. I keep my promises, don't I?"

Walter didn't like the idea, but he had to admit that of all people Ingrid had helped him along his lean years. His own brother always criticized him. His sisters were lost causes. He had suffered bullying at school and in the neighbourhood. The ridicule of his weight had sent him deeper into the abyss of solitude. Yes, Ingrid as self -gratifying as she was, had rescued him a few times from his misery.

He contacted Roy Gagnon, met with him and instructed him to act upon Ingrid's orders.

Walter had underestimated him. The first thing Roy Gagnon asked for, was money. "Oh! Buddy. Are you joking?"

"I don't start taking action without money in advance. Who's your boss? He or she needs to put out some *moolah* here and plenty! This matter is serious! Lots actions to take, heavy involvement- so I need lots of cash."

"How much do you need? I will relay it to my party."

"Half a million to start with. The other half on delivery." He pointed a finger at him. "I don't take care of children. It will be your responsibility. You will have to take care of them in the interval between the ransom and the return. You understand me"

"What about the pickup of the ransom money?"

"A big risk. I can do that for you or whoever for another, say, two hundred and fifty thousand. Let me know when you are ready." He walked away.

Walter was overwhelmed. He needed to consult Ingrid. He had been meeting with her often since they set the plan in motion. He felt almost like a normal human being having someone wait for him after work and share a meal. "Ingrid where are we going to keep the boy in hiding? How are we going to release him?"

"Walter, this is why we are hiring this fellow. It's up to him. You are to assist. We certainly don't want to harm the boy. This is only to get money that belongs to me."

"I need the deposit for him, otherwise he won't move."

"Do what you have to do, teddy bear, as long as you don't mention my name or involve me." She continued rubbing his shoulder.

Ingrid hated to part with the money left to her in her bank account; however, she needed to use it to complete her revenge. She felt it was rightly hers and it had been taken away. The time and place would be set up and action to be taken as soon as the opportunity presented itself without compromise. Roy Gagnon waited for his retainer. He would only then go to work studying the best time and the easiest way.

***

While all this was going on, Diego was meeting Alvaro to give him a piece of his mind. Diego sat waiting for his brother-in-law. As he waited he recalled the two cheating culprits together. His nerves were raw. Alvaro soon appeared, walking toward him. He greeted him cordially. Alvaro was handsome as ever, well dressed and smooth talking with his Spanish accent. Diego thought *any woman would go for him. Ingrid is a hunter. Too bad he has fallen into her trap. Now he has to deal with me.*

"Hello Diego!" He was polite and shook hands. Diego also stood up, reciprocating his greeting.

"Should we order a drink? What will you have?"

"I am fine. I prefer not to drink as I'm still on duty for the day. How did things go in court for you this morning?"

"Good! We wrapped up the case in no time. Both parties were in agreement and the problem was solved in fair terms. Right now I am looking after another problem that has arisen."

368

"Oh! What is that if I might ask?"

"Alvaro, I hate sitting here and needing to ask you what has come over you lately."

"What do you mean Diego?"

"Alvaro don't play innocent with me. What have you been up too this past while? I will get to the point. You have been unfaithful to my sister."

"No, I haven't "

"Alvaro, we are at our country club. I don't want to lose my composure. You are talking to your brother-in-law here, Sicilian blood. We are not fools. My sister doesn't deserve infidelity. She is purity and heart. Do you understand? I saw you with my own eyes with Ingrid. My sister has not been happy lately. You have three children. Where have you been spending your nights? Don't even try to lie Alvaro. I hired someone to watch you. Our most sacred duty is to protect our family and you have failed in that. I won't. You have disappointed me and disgraced us."

"I am so sorry. Please forgive me. I have had my reasons."

"You had no reason. My sister is priceless. She has given you three beautiful children to go home too. You chose to deceive her with a no good tramp like Ingrid. Do you want to see the videos Daniele left me?

She will go after any man that meets her fancy. You fool, you have been one of them."

Alvaro was mortified. "Does Gracy know?"

"I am not sure. I came over last night to talk. When I saw her so happy I decided to keep my mouth shut and talk it out with you first."

Alvaro, embarrassed, fought to compose himself. "Diego, I love Gracy. I must confess that since she has become a mother, the children have become an obsession for her. I don't exist. When she was pregnant many times, my advances were not appreciated. She made every excuse to refuse me; not to go with me to functions. We hired a nanny. She doesn't even trust the nanny to look after them. Gracy feels she has to be there with them. I felt abandoned most of the time. I lost her devotion. Ingrid was always there tempting me. I fell in with her but I still adore my wife."

"Alvaro, I am not sure if Gracy suspects anything or not. Or if she would ever forgive you. The way I see it Gracy never had our mom; she suffered from that loss as child. This is why she is so attached to her children. That is no excuse for you, a married man, to get involved with anyone, especially Ingrid. You should be at home with your wife and children. Did you see how happy she was last night?"

"I know, I am torn. What if she finds out and never forgives me?"

"My friend, you deserve what you get. My father was a womanizer.

I hate to tell you what it got him! My poor mother. This is why I prefer being single. Your children and Gracy are the most precious possessions in my life. They should be in yours as well."

"God help me. What have I gotten myself into? Diego, I am so sorry. Do you think I should confess to Gracy?"

"I am not advising you what to do in your marriage that you have put in jeopardy. I will tell you that the first thing you should do is fire Ingrid."

"How can I fire Ingrid? Her work in our hotels is unique. She has a way of bringing luster to our properties, lobbies, our rooms, our board rooms. She does it all on budget. Ingrid saves us a lot of money."

"Alvaro, integrity is the most important characteristic of any human being. Ingrid's lack of integrity doesn't sit well with me. You should expect the more admirable qualities of anyone, but especially our staff."

Alvaro was deep in thought as Diego spoke. Leonello has often made critical remarks about our interior designer. She did make a fool of me and I let her. Diego noticed Alvaro was preoccupied. He spoke up to break his spell. "Well Alvaro, the ball is in your court. I will leave it with you to decide how it will be done."

They both left in a somber mood. Alvaro's worst fear was losing Gracy. He was deeply troubled to the core. As for Ingrid, firing the top decorator was another troublesome matter, but that was necessary if he had any chance to appease Gracy and satisfy Diego. He was going to have a meeting with Leonello Dante. He would have to handle this crucial task with finesse. No one liked firing an employee, especially one like Ingrid. It wasn't going to be easy. Alvaro sensed big trouble brewing.

The Professor's Daughter

372

Chapter Fifty Four

At the Fernandez's home life was full of vitality as ever. The children were running after each other laughing, crying, and bickering with each other as usual. Gracy was ever so pleased indulging in their wants and wishes. Strict discipline was not needed today. As Alvaro walked in through the door, the two older children ran to him wrapping themselves around his legs. The baby reached out to him, her arms in a gesture that asked he pick her up. Gracy was all smiles as she admired them together. "*Mi amor!* You are home early tonight." She reached up to plant a kiss on his cheek. Gloria was getting supper together in the kitchen. The shouts of joy from the kids made her peek at the hallway. "Oh! Mr. Fernandez you are home early. It will be nice. I will set a plate for you at the table."

"Thanks Gloria." A pang of guilt hit his heart.

After dinner he turned to the children. "Which one of you, would like daddy to read a bedtime story tonight?" Francesca and Andrew shouted "Me, me, me Daddy" as the one-year-old baby Sabrina crawled around after them. Andrew was the loudest.

"Now, now, one of you has to go with Mommy. We can't leave your mommy out."

"We will take turns. How about Francesca and Sabrina go with Mommy. We let Daddy and Andrew be together." Gracy interjected.

"It's not fair, I want to be with Daddy too." Francesca started to cry.

Alvaro tried to calm her down. "Gracy, it will be fine. I will read to them all and we can carry Francesca to her bed afterwards."

"You see *mi amor.* It's a treat for them to have you home. They are starving for your attention." Gracy added.

Alvaro knew deep down, she was right. He hated himself. How could he have allowed himself to go astray? He asked himself if Gracy could ever forgive him. They went to bed. He tenderly took his wife into his arms. His heart ached in deep pain; but, his wife's tender performance in comparison had lost its sparkle.

The next morning, he arrived at his office earlier than usual. His first call was to Leonello. In no time he was sitting in his office. "Alvaro, how are you? I sensed the urgency in your voice. Here I am."

"Thanks for your promptness Leonello. We have a big problem on our hands."

Leonello perceived that Alvaro was disturbed. "We do? What is it that we cannot resolve? How can we help?"

"I hope you can. Diego has ordered me to fire Ingrid Klein." His voice trembled saying her name

"Ingrid the designer?"

"Yes."

"It's about time."

"Why would you say that? Do you know of a problem that I don't?"

"If you consider getting kickbacks for jobs she does for our companies a problem, then maybe I do know something you don't. Romero and I discovered it soon after we were appointed- that and the fact that she manipulates every man she can."

Alvaro was immediately uneasy. "How do you know that?"

"Alvaro, we don't sleep on the job. We have been hired to be supervisors. We supervise."

"Are you guys sure she does that?"

"As sure as I am standing here. I can also tell you that she doesn't like us much, both my friends and I. Maybe it's because we are newcomers. Most likely it's because she knows we have great respect for Gracy."

"Well, I am asking you to handle her dismissal. Offer her severance. The accountant can help you out how much she deserves."

"I am sure she will give us a hard time and fight back. Meaning no disrespect, I have noticed her being pretty sweet on you at times. Maybe she would take the news better from you."

"I am a married man with three beautiful children. Why would she be sweet on me?"

"You know Alvaro, that lady gives me a bad impression. The only person that matters to her is Ingrid Klein. She strikes me the wrong way every time I see her." Leonello replied, shaking his head.

"Well, she is all yours to handle. I prefer to stay out of it."

Leonello returned to his office and got all his paperwork ready. He rushed to the accountant. Shortly afterwards he called his buddy Romero. "Guess who we get to fire, Ingrid Klein."

"Really? When did the decision come about and by whom?"

"It's not important. You and I have to handle it. I will deliver the news to her. You, my friend, will be the watch dog. She doesn't strike me as one to take it calmly."

"Leonello, I've got your back."

"Thanks, my friend. Should you need Gianni, inform him. He can always find someone to cover his bookings. Keep me posted."

He didn't waste any time setting the process in motion. His receptionist was already on the phone calling Ingrid Klein. "Hello Ingrid, how are you? It's Lorna Doyle here. I am calling for Mr. Dante. He needs to talk to you. Can you come to the office this morning?"

"No I can't. I am very busy. Sorry, I have a job to finish."

"How is after one pm?"

"I can try." *That punk ignoramus. Who does he think he is to order me to see him in the morning on short notice?* Despite her annoyance, at one pm, against her will, Ingrid stepped into the door to Leonello's office.

"Good afternoon, come in Ingrid." He got up and greeted her like a gentleman should.

"Good afternoon Leonello. Your girl said it was urgent. What's so important that you took me from critical work?" She assessed his response to see if she had intimidated him. She had to admit that New York must agree with him because he looked handsomely mature.

"Ingrid, I have been instructed to terminate your service at the Frarano's corporations. I have all your necessary papers and your severance pay. You are to clean your desk and leave immediately."

Ingrid was shocked. She felt faint. She took a deep breath to steady herself. "Are you serious? Is this a joke? Who ordered it?" Her voice was getting louder and angrier.

"It doesn't matter who ordered it. I have been appointed to execute it. You can leave now Ingrid."

"You are going to be sorry. You and your bitch princess. All of you are going to pay dearly. Nobody gets rid of Ingrid Klein just like that." She walked out slamming the door.

Her brain was fuming. 'Which direction will I go first?' She was talking to herself. Without hesitation, she went directly down the hall to confront her beloved friend Alvaro. The secretary's pleas to stop her going forward were totally ignored. To Ingrid's dismay he wasn't there.

She went to search for Walter. He wasn't on duty until late afternoon she was told. *Has everyone disappeared today?* In the meantime, she dialed Diego's private number. He didn't respond. She wasn't going to clean her desk has ordered until she checked with Alvaro or Diego. She wasn't going to take orders from that Sicilian puppy. She was getting desperate. She kept calling Alvaro- no answer. She had a feeling he was the number one reason for her dismissal. *His wife must have ordered him to do it. The last few nights he had refused to meet with her.* She didn't like it. She thought of calling Morris Robertson. He was useless. He would never side with her. His aim was to get on good terms with the Sicilian princess. She would have lots of money for him to invest. Distracted, she walked around lost until late afternoon.

Finally, she found out Alvaro's whereabouts. She cornered him. "You have been avoiding me the past few days?" Pinning him to the wall she asked "Can you explain me why I was served with these papers today and by of all people that Sicilian twit?"

"Ingrid, it wasn't my idea. I am afraid this time I cannot help you."

"You better tell me this is a joke otherwise, lover boy, I will go straight to your wife and tell her how you spent the late nights with me when she believed her husband was slaving away."

"Ingrid. You will do no such thing. I love my wife and my children."

"You do? Well, you should have thought about that before you were enjoying your uncontrollable sex urges between my sheets. You loved it didn't you?"

"Ingrid, please I don't know what possessed me. I must have been temporarily insane. How can I make this easier? Maybe I can help you find another job."

"Mr. Fernandez do you forget who found you this job? Who introduced you to the Fraranos? Do you forget that I lived with one of them for ten years? I was to marry Daniele if he hadn't died."

Alvaro didn't respond. He couldn't tell her that Daniele knew she was not trustworthy. But, then shame on him also. He had fallen into her trap and enjoyed moments of physical ecstasy. His consternation over being discovered was overbearing. He couldn't lose Gracy or his beautiful children. He knew Ingrid wouldn't stop. Big trouble was ahead for him.

Chapter Fifty Five

Refusing to clean her station, Ingrid walked away from the hotel. Walter called her with a message from the hotel management team. "One of the maids has gathered your belongings, Ingrid. They are ready to be picked up." Things were falling apart quickly for Ingrid. She had been given one month's notice to vacate the penthouse she occupied at the hotel.

Diego had refused to talk to her. He had no respect for home breakers, especially when it affected his sister and her children. He had lost respect and admiration for his brother- in -law. For the sake of the children, he was going to keep his thoughts to himself, so he let actions speak louder than any words could.

Ingrid wasn't going to be stopped. The only ally she had was Walter. She resented Alvaro immensely. She got into her car and decided to pay a surprise visit to Mrs. Gracy Fernandez. It was payback time. Time for Gracy Fernandez to have her beloved husband's activities exposed. She pulled into the driveway of the Fernandez home and walked to the front door. The impressive stature of the home spoke to luxury that would never be hers. Gracy had never invited her to visit her home which made this unscheduled visit even more satisfying for Ingrid. Gloria greeted her at the door. "Hello, can I help you?"

"I was wondering if I could see Gracy."

"Is she expecting you? Please wait while I check with her."

Gracy heard the conversation from the family room. She walked to the door.

"Ingrid! What a surprise! Come in please."

"Hello Gracy, it's been a long time. The children must keep you really busy."

"Yes, they are a handful for now. They grow so fast. I will return to work later when they need me less."

"You have a very nice place here."

"Thank you, it's accommodating, mostly for the children."

"Yes, I see a park close by; schools are not far. It's ideal for raising a family."

"I must admit we made a good choice moving into this neighbourhood. We are happy here. It's a little out of the way for Alvaro's commute but he manages it."

"Speaking of Alvaro how is he these days?" asked Ingrid.

"He is a hard worker. We are lucky he is so dedicated." She called Gloria over. "Gloria maybe our guest would like some tea or coffee. Would you mind serving some? Ingrid what would you like?"

"Nothing for me thanks."

"Tell me, what brings you in our neighbourhood? Other than Diego and our Sicilian fellows, I really don't see anyone else from the hotels."

"Gracy, you haven't heard the news apparently? I have been fired from the Frarano's corporations. I no longer work there."

"I am sorry to hear that! Why? I am surprised!" She was sincere in her sympathy for Ingrid's situation.

"I was shocked myself. I think Alvaro had something to do with it"

"What makes you say that? He never mentioned anything."

"I can see why."

Ingrid continued as Gracy, disquieted, listened. This was the perfect time for her to drop the bombshell that would destroy Gracy Fernandez's world. Ingrid spoke with what could only be seen as elation. "Gracy, all the late nights when your husband told you he was working late, he was with me at my place. He lied to you."

Gracy couldn't believe what Ingrid was saying. "What do you mean? Was it related to work?" She had some doubts. She wasn't going to admit to herself that her sweet Alvaro could be deceiving her.

"No, it wasn't related to work. It was for his own pleasure. In fact, it was for much needed relief from work and, especially, you and the children. That's what sex does. It relieves you."

In distress, Gracy jumped up screaming at Ingrid. "Get out of my house. Now! Don't you ever step foot in here again. You, Ingrid Klein, how dare you accuse my husband of such unfaithfulness?"

Ingrid had never seen Gracy so angry. She was delighted to have stimulated the strong reaction. Alvaro would be in deep trouble with his loving wife from here on.

Gloria was outside playing with the children. She heard the shouting and came running hearing. Gracy was fuming. Ingrid flew outside and the door slammed shut behind her.

"What's going on? For a minute I thought you were going to kill someone." Gloria was alarmed by Gracy's intense emotion.

"Believe me I could have. I will have many questions for tonight when my husband gets home." Gracy, having heard the shocking revelation, had hours to figure out what she would ask and what she would do.

As Ingrid left the home, she was more than satisfied. The reaction she had gotten from Gracy was perfect. Big trouble for Alvaro

Fernandez was imminent. She smiled. *It's exactly what he deserves for discarding me.*

Gracy, on the other hand, was upset all day. She couldn't wait for Alvaro to get home. She had known his behaviour had been unpredictable and their relationship was growing more distant of late. She had avoided confronting him, hoping it was just a phase. She couldn't believe the love and respect they had for one another would be shattered in extramarital affair. Gracy had been keenly aware of Ingrid's behaviour with men but she would never have believed that she would sway her husband. Her much trusted Alvaro was genuine in his heart. He would never betray her.

Alvaro got home. After supper she asked him. "*Mi amor*, can we have a private discussion in the library? Gloria can take care of the children tonight." Alvaro's sensed something terrible was going to happen. "You make it sound so secretive *mi amor*. What's is it?"

"It is nice to hear you call me *mi amor*. I have missed it for a while."

Gracy tried keeping her composure and smiled but her heart and her soul were tormented. "My dear, I had a visitor today."

"Let me guess, Morris Robertson the broker?"

"No, Ingrid Klein." It felt like a knife had cut through Alvaro.

"She came here?"

"For good reason or so she thought."

"She has never come before, even after the children were born."

"Alvaro, Ingrid is not the kind of person to care about your children. She came here to inform me about your liaison. When you were supposed to be working late and staying away from your wife and children. She says you were with her intimately. All I want to know from you is it true? Yes or no?"

He wanted to die right there and then. He looked at her without responding. She stared at him. "I am waiting for your answer?"

With his hesitation she knew. "It's true."

"*Mi amor*, forgive me. I must have been insane. I never stopped loving you and never will."

Gracy's sad smile spoke volumes. "Mr. Fernandez, I will allow you to sleep in the guest room for tonight, only by the grace of my children's love for you. You have the choice to leave this house right now or leave in the morning, but in the morning you will take only what you need for now. You shall provide me your new address. The rest of your belongings will be delivered to you. You will be contacted by the family lawyer."

"Gracy! *Mi amor,* you cannot be serious. I love you and always will."

"Don't call me that anymore. I am not your *amor*! You have destroyed everything Alvaro. It's finished between us. I cannot ever trust you again. It's over." She turned her back to him and walked out. He was left there dumfounded. His beautiful world had collapsed, destroyed by his weakness.

384

Chapter Fifty Six

Gracy's love had turned into bitter pain. Alvaro had been her first true love. They had created three beautiful children. She would cherish that gift from him for the rest of her life, but they were the only real goodness he had left for her. The rest had been a lie. She was now in her late thirties. Alvaro's many attempts at reconciliation were all denied. Her heart had been broken. The unhealed bruises would remain there the rest of her life.

Time passed; Diego was her constant support. He kept encouraging his sister to have a life for herself beside the children. "You are such a good mother." He kept telling her. "Gracy my dearest. I know how dedicated you are to your children. *Tesoro,* my treasure, eventually they will have a life of their own. I am getting on. You are still young now. I will feel better if you find yourself a companion."

"Diego, my life is full. I have no desire to get involved with anyone."

"Sis, I am looking after your wellbeing. I won't be here forever. Your lovely children will have loves and lives of their own. You need to make a life of your own."

"My dear brother, my decision should make you happy. I have decided to get back to work, only part time for now. I still have my dedicated Gloria here. The children are in school all day. They don't need my attention as much so, I have decided to get back to my old job. That will help fulfill any gaps that I have in my life."

"Good idea. I am glad. You will work with Leonello. He is in full charge of our New York area hotels. He is a tireless worker who never complains."

"Yes, I was told. Leonello, Romero and Gianni are valuable assets for our companies."

"The profits are definitely speaking for themselves." Diego replied.

"Yes, I know!"

True to her word, Gracy resumed work at the hotel. It was almost like she had never left. She fell easily into the routine and took pleasure in working with Leonello, Romero and Gianni again.

"Over the years you've turned into a real business lady as well as an excellent *professoressa*." Her brother complimented her.

"Well, now I have my children to protect. It's their future."

"Gracy! You are our mother reincarnated."

"I could only hope to be. Back to business Diego. I instructed our accountant to provide me a monthly statement. I have keenly been analyzing the expenditures. Our Sicilian boys have presented me with three quotes for each new contract involving the hotels. We analyzed the pros and cons and prepared the statements for the Board's review."

"Well! I am impressed. Good for you Sis! Leonello must have related to you what was going on with our former interior designer."

"She was there to take us all in every way she could."

"I heard she shacked up with some guy that used to work at our firm. Her survival instincts are indisputable."

"I hope he was available to shack up with, not that would make any difference to her. Single, divorced or married, she targets anyone that could serve her purpose."

As a single mother Gracy had been working things out discretely.

Morris Robertson had been appointed as her financial adviser. Her investments were showing good returns. The children's education funds were growing in partially reserved and partially aggressive investments. Alvaro had been transferred out of country to work at the Hotel Franciosi. He wasn't around as much. She wanted to erase him from her life but she couldn't because he was the father of her children. She didn't want them to suffer the loss of a father as she had suffered the loss of a mother. It was hard, however, having to communicate with him regarding the children.

Andrew didn't suffer from losing his male role model because Diego was happy to assume that role. The boy and the girls respected him immensely. Life continued in the household as it usually did. The Sicilian fellows were always invited to celebrate at any festivities. Leonello as Andrew's godfather was available for all the children, especially for Andrew. He was sincere in his duty. Life went on even after the blow they had been dealt by the betrayal.

***

When Gracy had returned to her old job at the Hyatt, it felt strange at first. Alvaro's office was now occupied by Leonello. It brought back some sentimental memories. In her innocence, her heart had believed her love for Alvaro would be forever. She relived the heart palpitations she felt seeing him in those days. He had sent shivers through her body. The thought of him making love to Ingrid had destroyed her trust in men. The bitterness would resurface occasionally but she made every effort to move beyond it. After all, she knew many admirable men, Diego, Leonello, Romero and Gianni. They restored her trust in men but she doubted that any man could ever capture her heart and soul again. After losing her beloved father, Alvaro had sparked strong emotions and had created the connection she needed to move on with her life. That connection had brought motherhood with it and she was eternally grateful for that. However, she just couldn't fully get over the way in which he had broken the connection. They were now divorced. Perhaps she had some fault- a little less attention to the children and a little more to Alvaro might have changed things but it would have never stopped the infidelity. It would only put it off. A cheater was always going to cheat and so she blamed him for the greater fault in destroying their marriage.

Diego was her emotional saviour, but he continued to encourage her to put the past behind her and continued to advocate for a life with someone new.

"Diego, what do you want me to do? I have you my children and our Sicilian boys. I am fine. Don't worry about me."

Her decision to return to work was good for her soul. She would arrive home glad to hug her children. Although her physical body was tired, it resulted in a good night sleep. She was getting more and more involved in her work. The children were growing like weeds. Leonello had Andrew involved in different sports. Often all of them would go and watch his games. Hockey was one of his favorites. They would be there cheering for him and afterwards they would go out as a family. Gracy had enrolled the girls in tap dancing, judo, swimming, and music lessons. Francesca played the piano. Sabrina insisted on playing the accordion. Andrew, motivated by his sisters, tried different instruments. He had chosen the drums. The racket in the house was enormous but the adults were there being entertained. The time passed faster than Gracy realized.

She was getting closer to middle age. The business was thriving; but her heart felt empty. She often experienced moments of disappointment. One morning she had gotten to work with no energy to carry on. She sat there behind her brown walnut desk. She placed her head down in her hands, warm tears rolled down her cheeks. A knock on her door forced her to move on from her moment of despair. She quickly wiped the tears away to conceal her sadness. "Come in."

Leonello opened the door, papers in his hand. He stared at his boss for a moment. "Gracy, have I come in at a bad time?"

She continued to wipe her eyes and face "No, no, sorry. It's just me. I get carried away sometimes. It's just one of those blue days I guess. I must have gotten up on the wrong side of the bed this morning." Leonello, wasn't sure how to respond. He had been watching her lately. Gracy was losing her enthusiasm for life.

"Gracy, is there anything I can do to help?" He stared at her with sorrowful eyes. He truly cared about her wellbeing.

"Thanks Leonello. I will be fine." She tried to turn to hide her face.

"What have you got there?"

Leonello hesitated. What he had received was the last thing Gracy needed this morning. He wasn't sure if he should show it to her or handle it on his own. It was impossible to know which approach was best, but she needed to know what was in the papers.

"This summon was delivered this morning. We are being sued."

"We are? By whom now?"

"I hate to tell you. It is Ingrid Klein."

Her anger escalated. "She is evil. Hasn't she caused enough harm to my family?"

Leonello placed an arm around her shoulder. "Gracy calm down. I will take care of it. Don't forget, I have Romero and Gianni with me. If we have to use other means to make her back off, we will."

"Leonello, please, I am grateful. We don't want to put ourselves on her level. Pass it on to Diego's firm. Let them handle it."

"Gracy, I will never forget what you have done for us. I will always be around to protect you no matter the situation. You must allow me."

She just smiled at him gracefully. Leonello was now in his thirties and he had matured into manhood admirably. However, on some level, Gracy still considered him her student He was handsome and intelligent.

He was always impeccably dressed. His position in the company proved his many undeniable merits.

Even though she was eight years his senior, Leonello's love for her had not diminished. Why couldn't she get past the age difference and see him as the man he had become? He had never given up hope. He had been dating girls from every nationality in New York. Every relationship would end up in cold interest. He confided with Romero one night. "You and Gianni are fortunate. You enjoy your freedom. I am content to pass the evening watching the Fernandez children play and Gracy sitting around them."

"Leonello, I suspect you still have the hots for your old teacher. Get over it? It will never happen. Gracy's standards are high. We are her employees."

"Romero what are you saying is absurd. Don't you think I know that? I cannot help it if this heart of mine will not warm up to anyone."

All three of them were still single. They preferred their freedom.

Leonello deep down in his heart knew what he wanted. He hoped her heart would change. Until then, he would be near his beautiful teacher that was better than nothing.

Chapter Fifty Seven

Ingrid's torment grew with each passing day. Her many attempts to get Alvaro back had failed. He resented her and blamed her for destroying his marriage. Now he was paying the price with remorse, missing his children and most of all his wife. All his attempts of reconciliation with Gracy had been in vain. Ingrid had become his worst nightmare. His rejection made her more determined to get even with all of them. She believed strongly that their wrongdoings had shortchanged her from every direction. The lawsuit she had launched, had been just a scare tactic. Most of the lawyers she had consulted with had advised her against her claims. The countersuit was another disappointment. No lawyer wanted to take her case. Should she ever end up in court, she would be her own defence. It was too discouraging; she aborted her claim.

Her blood was poisoned against them all. Failure was not an option. In denial of reality, she still pushed for revenge. The only person she could talk too was lonely Walter Robertson. His obesity had worsened; food had become his only pleasure and so the attention Ingrid paid him was welcome. This evening they were meeting once more.

"Walter, I need you to help me. Remember the plan I confided in you long ago. I was going to abandon it. I tried other avenues. They didn't work. I am afraid we have no other choice than to go ahead with it."

"Ingrid please, that is too dangerous."

"If you give your guy the right instructions, it can be simple. I will look after you Walter!" She rubbed his back knowing the physical contact weakened him.

"Ingrid, it feels so good. Don't stop." A woman's touch felt heavenly for him.

"Walter, I can give you more pleasure and more. Just carry out what I have been asking of you."

"The guy will want money in advance. Have you got the money for him?"

Much of her money had run out because of lawyer's fees and court time. "Walter try to have him reduce his advance. Tell him we will pay him when the job is done."

"I can try. He is a pretty shrewd fellow. You should talk to him?"

"Walter, I can't. Don't even mention my name. It's between you and him. As for your reward, I told you before, I will share a portion of our payoff with you."

Walter, as simple as he was, had his doubts about doing what Ingrid asked. He went ahead and called Roy Gagnon again. He got a recording. 'Leave your number I will call you back.' Roy Gagnon wasn't one to answer the phone. His jobs were shady so he always screened his calls. He dialed the number back. Walter promptly responded. "Roy, its Walter here. Remember I talked to you about this friend of mine. She wanted to hire you?"

"Yes, I remember you. I told you money talks. Do you have money up front?"

"She can only get her hands on one hundred in advance. The rest will come on completion of the job."

"Listen here, tell your friend to go fly a kite. High-risk jobs involving children are high cost. A quarter of a million or Roy doesn't move his ass." He responded loudly and seriously.

"Alright. Don't shoot the messenger. I am only doing her a favour. I'll tell her."

"Have this woman call me. I will straighten her out. Who does she think she is to bargain with me? Does she have any idea of the risk involved here?"

"I'll pass on your message."

Walter hated to get involved in such messy work by even just talking to characters like Roy Gagnon. He was totally removed from Gracy Robertson Fernandez-what her family represented, who she was where she came from, how many children she had. He hardly knew her. Maybe he thought *I should confide in my brother Morris. Ingrid is too much for me to handle.* He didn't follow through on that hunch. He reasoned more clearly when he was away from her, especially when he was sober. However, the wine Ingrid kept pouring in his glass rendered him foolish and powerless. Ingrid Klein knew how to control her men by exploiting their weaknesses and Walter had many.

Roy Gagnon was no fool and wouldn't bend for any dame. After some agreement was reached, Walter delivered the money and instructions. He didn't even read them. He was only the delivery boy. He met Roy hours after his shift at the hotel. He had seen Gracy there and felt guilty but followed through with Ingrid's plan.

Roy Gagnon was a big man, husky, broad shoulders. His square face was characterized by a long nose and inquisitive black eyes. One look at him and no one would want to cross him.

He took the money and the envelope with the information. "Buddy! If the amount is correct, you will hear from me when the time is right. I'll put my plan into play." Gagnon was an expert who knew his stuff. Before leaving he pointed his finger at Walter. "Listen here, I am a man of few words. I don't want to be bothered with phone calls from here on. I'll notify you when it is completed." He walked away. It suited Walter fine. Roy Gagnon was intimidating. *The less contact with him the better,* thought Walter.

Chapter Fifty Eight

Gracy had given over some control with the children lately. She had to. She was not feeling well. After a full day's work her body was tired. Gloria had assumed more responsibility. They had hired a tutor also to help with schoolwork. The girls were obedient. The nanny had no problem with them. Andrew, being the energetic boy that he was, challenged her at times. Leonello did encourage him and support him in sports activities, but, for Andrew, the activities were never enough. His restlessness would often get him into trouble. Francesca and Sabrina had nicknamed him the wanderer. Gloria was patient and accepted his disobedience with kindness. Lately he had been complaining, "I don't want to be picked up after school. I want to walk home on my own or with my friends." She would let Gracy know when she returned from work. Gloria obliged Andrew, thinking that his friends must have been teasing him. He wanted to feel grown up. Against her better judgement, she obliged.

This afternoon, time had lapsed with no Andrew arriving home. The girls were doing homework with the tutor. With no sign still of Andrew showing up, Gloria was getting worried as more time passed. She questioned the girls. They had seen him after school. He had strayed to the park to play ball with a couple of friends. It was getting dark and there was still no sign of Andrew. Gloria's skin was starting to crawl. She felt something was very wrong. Hours passed, still no Andrew. Gracy had called earlier "Gloria, sorry, I will be home late tonight. They are short staffed at the front desk. They need me here. A load of guests are arriving from Europe."

"No problem Mrs. Fernandez. You do what you need to do. I will make sure the children are fed and looked after."

Of all nights, why were things turning chaotic. Gloria was panicking. Andrew had never resorted to such grave disobedience before. They called the two boys he had been seen with. They both stated he had remained behind kicking the ball around when it was time for them to leave. He was so taken with sport. The passion pulled him in like a magnet. Gloria's fear was out of control. She called Gracy and then she called Diego. They arrived home immediately, alarmed and ready to take action.

Diego called the authorities while Gracy, in a panic, called Leonello. "I will drop everything and be right there." He instructed one of the girls to summon Romero and Gianni. In no time they were at the Fernandez house to get more details and to get going on the hunt for Andrew. Leonello tried his best to reassure Gracy "Don't worry, we will find him."

They began their search with what little information they had been provided. The fear was unbearable. Gracy's mind was playing havoc with her. The word and the news got out. In no time people joined in on the search. The family doctor had to be called for Gracy to give her a sedative. Her body was totally out of control. Uncontrollable shivers had taken over her body.

The three Sicilian fellows were persistent in their search of the surrounding area. The police were still questioning the two boys who had been with Andrew. Detective Gordon Santoro asked "Did you spot anyone around watching you while you played- a man or a woman? Were there other young people around?" At the question, the older boy who had been worriedly gazing at the ground suddenly remembered someone. "Yes, there was a man. He was sitting sideways on a bench. He was glancing at us now and then. His head was down and he had a hood over his head."

"Was there anybody else around? This fellow was he young or old?"

"I couldn't tell. His face was partially covered."

"Was he a big guy? How would you describe him?"

"I think he was a bigger man."

Then the other boy added. "Yes, now that I think about it. I noticed him too. I didn't really pay attention though. I was too busy concentrating on dribbling the ball."

"When you both left was he still there?"

"I am not sure." said the younger boy.

"What about you? Did you notice when he left?" The policeman asked the other boy.

"No. When I turned around at the end, as we were leaving the park, he had gotten up but he was walking slowly, like he was kind of hanging around."

"Andrew was still around moving around with his ball."

"Yeah. I shouted at him to go home. He ignored me. He waved his hand without even turning around."

Detective Santoro turned to his assistant and the other policeman roaming around searching for clues. The only clue was the soccer ball abandoned on the grass. The boys were telling the truth.

"We need to find this guy. I wish we had a better description." There were no cameras in the park around and no other leads. *The unknown man could be the answer. Who was he? Had anyone else spotted him?* These were all unanswered questions that were making their search difficult.

Walter was watching the news report about the missing boy on the screen in the hotel lobby. He was agitated and starting to panic. *What has Roy Gagnon done with him? He wasn't supposed to hurt him. This whole kidnapping thing was only supposed to be for the money.*

A couple of days had passed with no news of the boy. Gagnon had had no trouble grabbing Andrew under his one arm. He had used a spray to blur the boy's vision and muffled his mouth with the flat thick and double tape he had purchased and prepared. It all happened so fast. Andrew in total shock had struggled, kicking and swinging his arms to free himself. His captor's effortless, strong hold kept Andrew secured tightly under his arm. He was thrown like a bag of garbage in the back of the car. The doors were securely locked. Roy Gagnon knew the game plan well. The car was totally isolated and hidden behind overgrown bushes. The windows were tinted dark. He left the car with Andrew in it where it couldn't be seen and went on his way. He left a crying Andrew confused, terrified and breathless. Totally paralyzed, he tried to understand what had hit him.

The next day Roy moved the boy to the abandoned, musty wood barn from long ago. He was the only one that could stand the mould invading the place. He had used the place before, hiding drugs and other illicit loot. His prisoner was going to be fine for few days. As long as his parents delivered, he would be free to go. He had no intention of messing up. Like the client that had ordered this job, it was only about money for him. He disguised his voice like a woman and placed a mask on his face, whenever he spoke to Andrew. "Look buddy, all they want is the sum of money typed on this paper. You are going to call your parents and have them deliver a suitcase with what they are asking for. You will be free to go home after that. Until then, I will bring you food and drinks. You can sleep on that pile of dead leaves there on the floor. The door is bolted. There are no windows here. You can't escape, so don't try anything."

Andrew stood in a corner cold, petrified, shaking like a kitten. He whispered "What about mommy? She won't be able to find me." He cried profusely. "Mommy, mommy, I want my mommy." He felt sorry that he had not gone straight home. He wanted to tell his mother and Gloria that.

At home the fear was escalating with every minute that passed without knowing Andrew's whereabouts. Gracy was in total anguish. Diego needed to notify Alvaro. He felt it was his duty to let him know of his son's disappearance. He was in France. Diego made the phone call and after a tense conversation Alvaro promised to fly home with the first possible flight. Gracy in her devastation was asking for him. She knew that he would be in as much pain as she was. They needed to be together.

Sadly, alcohol had become Alvaro's companion since he had lost his family. The few relationships he had were short lived. He knew he had lost an irreplaceable wife and mother, his beautiful children and a warm extended family. He had to sober up before he got to Gracy's.

Roy Gagnon in his disguised voice had placed the call. The command was severe. The request was firm. "You know if you want to see your son again, follow my instructions. He is fine for now. If you try anything he won't be. You will deliver twenty million dollars in a box unmarked bundles at the cemetery behind the southwest gate at midnight. No police and when I get the money, I will notify with your son's location."

Gracy felt faint too weak to handle the call. She passed the phone to Diego. He had taken over trying to prolong the conversation in order for the police to trace the call. The phone went dead. At home, panic and tears were abundant. Alvaro had arrived home late the previou day. He appeared distracted, aged and pitiful. He stood there motionless and overwhelmed by what was going on.

The three Sicilians were hard at work with the police and volunteers searching every lead but nothing was working out. Leonello encouraged his buddies "Come on guys, let's see what we can do with our own expertise. I remember my crazy father and brother and the hiding places they used to stash their stuff. They would search for abandoned pagliera where no one dared to look." So they kept on searching, looking for abandoned sheds or barns further into the rural area just outside Gracy's neighbourhood. Leonello was carrying some miscellaneous tools and all three of them were equipped with makeshift weapons of some sort. A few hours into the search, Romero spotted a barn like structure. "Guys look there" The sun was hiding behind the clouds. A fine rain was coming down. Most of the other searchers had gone the opposite way. Leonello didn't mind. He preferred to be on their own. They followed the direction Romero had indicated. The three of them agreed it was a good hideaway and quietly approached it.

It was covered with long branches, dried straw and rough shrubbery. It was in an isolated extension of rocky land that was hard to get to. "Look. There's a huge drop right beside it. We can climb down." said Romero.

"It looks scary." added Gianni.

Leonello was determined. "I want to see what it's inside this shack."

He started to strip the branches away like a mad man. The rotten wood underneath started to fall apart. Andrew who had given into his exhaustion, had fallen asleep. The banging woke him up. He got up disoriented and crying calling his mommy. He started shouting from inside even though he was terrified. Hearing the noise, Leonello was more determined to look inside. "Romero and Gianni come, help me pull this door apart. It's half rotten."

"It's not coming loose."

Gianni commented "No windows, maybe we can get through a break in the wall?"

"Gianni yes, let's push through it. I have never seen a pagliera with a window?"

"Here, I almost have it. Grab at these two boards. Pull down. Romero, good!" Down come two wooden boards leaving a narrow opening.

Andrew, wide eyed, stood there speechless. Leonello was the first. He squeezed himself in, followed by Romero, and Gianni. "Thank God Andrew! We found you?" He swept him in his arms. Romero took his jacket off and covered him. Gianni was consoling him." Andrew feared that his captor might return but he knew he was in good hands now. With Andrew in his arms and his faithful friends by his side, Leonello raced home. He walked in with Andrew's arms clutched around his neck. Gracy had been given another sedative.

The minute Leonello appeared with her son, Gracy forced herself past her grogginess. Her elation swiftly carried her toward him. After embracing and smothering Andrew, she hugged Leonello, for the longest time. Tears of joy streaming down her face. "Leonello my dearest friend. I know now why the universe itself never allowed me to abandon you."

She turned to the others. "Romero, Gianni -thank you, thank you for being in my life also." The rest of the family joined her happiness. Alvaro looked on, taking it all in with remorse for something that was lost to him forever.

Once all the investigations were complete, Ingrid ended up behind bars as well as her friend Walter who was charged with being her accomplice. With Roy Gagnon's criminal record, it didn't take long to track him down. He ended up back in jail where he belonged.

When it was all over, a contented Diego counted his blessings of the last several years. He still had his companionship with Rosella. He had lost a beloved brother but he had regained a much loved nephew. He had lost a key employee but had gained three who were more like family. His businesses continued to thrive and grow, as his family had. He had lost a brother-in-law but soon he would gain another. His treasured sister was finally completely happy.

Later when life had returned to normal, Gracy finally, after many months of reflection, realized that Leonello had always admired and loved her. He had matured into an extraordinary man. She shouldn't think of him as her young ex-student. Age was only a number. Months later, they were united in matrimony. With the devotion that Leonello possessed for her and her children, there was no question that Leonello was the soul mate Gracy had long sought. Life and love had come full circle for the English professor's daughter. She had a love as strong as her parents and that would stand the test of time. The road had been long and bumpy, but her heart was finally home.

9 781777 074951